KU-752-158

THE

Ghost Tree

THE
Ghost Tree

SARA BAIN

urbanepublications.com

First published in Great Britain in 2015
by Urbane Publications Ltd
Suite 3, Brown Europe House, 33/34 Gleamingwood Drive, Chatham, Kent ME5 8RZ

Copyright © Sara Bain, 2015
The moral right of Sara Bain to be identified as the author of this work has been
asserted in accordance with the Copyright, Designs and Patents Act of 1988.

All rights reserved. No part of this publication may be reproduced, stored in a retrieval
system, or transmitted in any form or by any means, electronic, mechanical,
photocopying, recording or otherwise, without the prior permission of both the copyright
owner and the above publisher of this book.
All characters in this book are fictitious, and any resemblance to actual persons living or
dead is purely coincidental.
A CIP catalogue record for this book is available from the British Library.

ISBN 978-1-910692-24-0
EPUB 978-1-910692-25-7
MOBI 978-1-910692-26-4

Design and Typeset by Julie Martin
Cover by the Invisible Man

Printed and bound by CPI Group (UK) Ltd, Croydon, CR0 4YY

urbanepublications.com

The publisher supports the Forest Stewardship Council® (FSC®), the leading international forest-certification organisation.
This book is made from acid-free paper from an FSC®-certified provider. FSC is the only
forest-certification scheme supported by the leading environmental organisations, including Greenpeace.

To Skye, Aidan, Hayley and Sasha, my life's greatest work.

Contents

Foreword

I first met the Ghost Tree when researching stories for a running feature on local hauntings for the Dumfries and Galloway Standard.

The chilling tale of the 'Mackie' or 'Rerrick Parish Poltergeist' has haunted me for over a decade and is one of the only officially documented accounts of 'true' poltergeist activity in the world. The event allegedly took place in the Parish of Rerrick, Auchencairn, Dumfries and Galloway, Scotland, in 1695.

The old gnarled tree in the picture on the cover is all that remains of the haunted plantation where stonemason and farmer Andrew Mackie contended with a violent noisy spirit that pestered his family for a few months at the turn of the 17th century.

Reverend Alexander Telfair (1654 to 1732), the minister who performed the two-week-long exorcism, published his experiences in December of the year the event took place, giving it a rather lengthy title. This is the abridged and more contemporary version: *'A True Relation of an Apparition, Expressions, and Actings of a Spirit, which infested the House of Andrew Mackie, in the Parish of Rerrick, Scotland, in the year 1695.'* Telfair's account was validated by the signatures of fourteen independent witnesses, all either men of the cloth or upstanding members of the community, and who had all personally witnessed the events.

There were three trees in living memory. The locals call them 'the Ghost Trees'. The two beeches died some time ago but this enduring oak was more resilient to the sweeping winds of the Solway hills and has survived both the ravages of time and, if Telfair's account is to be believed, a very noisy ghost.

Local legend has it, when the last of the Ghost Trees dies, the Rerrick Parish Poltergeist will return.

I always wondered what would happen if the ghost tree died and Mackie's violent poltergeist did return today. Research has taken me to the realms of the fantastical, through religion and to quantum physics, but the answers to the existence of a paranormal dimension remain elusive.

This is a work of contemporary fiction: a paranormal romance with the Mackie poltergeist at its heart. The house in the book and the characters are purely fictitious, apart from Andrew Mackie, his poltergeist and, of course, the Ghost Tree which, so I understand, is still very much alive and well. Any resemblance to actual people – living, dead or in spirit form – is purely conceived by coincidence and an over-active imagination.

Sara Bain
October 2015

THE 1695 TROUBLE

Andrew Mackie hurtled through the door and almost fell on the loosened stone at the threshold. His children screamed. A stone hit his back and another scuffed his cheek as he rushed through the house, the panic welling in his chest. A clod of burning peat just missed him as he reached the children's room. It smashed against the wooden door and exploded into a shower of bright sparks before snuffing out, thumping against the floor and coughing out weak plumes of smoke.

He threw open the door. His children sat huddled together in the cot; a small fire burned on the boards in a corner. The youngsters wailed when they saw him. Mackie pulled off his coat and slammed it against the flames, using his anger and terror to beat at the fire until the charred boards no longer glowed.

A series of loud bangs caused the whimpering children to look up, the horror of their ordeal frozen on their tear-stained faces. They shrieked again as the ceiling tore and a wooden staff ripped through the gaping rent above their heads, showering them with sharp splinters.

Mackie could only watch in horror as the wooden stick hovered above the children's heads and juddered there in mid-air as if held by a furiously shaking hand. Pulling his reserves together, he leaped at the staff. It resisted his grasp.

'Out, children. Run!' he yelled as he wrestled with the

unseen wielder.

Another ball of burning peat flew at him, scuffing his shoulder before it fell smouldering on the wooden chest. A stone clipped his ear before the entity let go of the staff and Mackie fell to the floor with a cry and a heavy thump.

'Lord, illumine me in this darkness,' he hissed.

Loud groans rattled the walls and chunks of ceiling fell around him.

'And thy great mercy defend us from the evil that infests this house.' He slammed the door to the room with a loud, resonating bang and sank to his knees.

'Dear Lord, when will this end?' he whispered into the ceiling, not wishing to incur further wrath of the evil spirit for his devotions.

'Andrew?'

He heard his wife calling his name. Still muttering prayers beneath his ragged breath, he moved towards the direction of the voice. His wife stood at the threshold in her heavy shawl and coif. He wondered where she had gone so early in the morning. Seeing her children crying, she ran into the house and comforted them.

'Good day to you Mackie.'

Mackie hauled off his hat and tipped his head when he spied his landlord Charles McLellan at the door to his house.

'Good day to you, sir.' He noticed the laird held in his hands a bundle wrapped in old soiled paper. There were spots of bright red blood on it.

'Your wife came to me this morning, telling me what she had found beneath this stone.' The Laird of Colline tapped his shining boot against the loosed slab on the doorstep and opened the parcel to show his find. 'She ran the quarter mile to find me. She is deeply distressed. I took the liberty of retrieving this shocking find from your threshold.'

Mackie hung his head and squeezed the bonnet in his hands. He had been tending to the beasts in the field this morning before he heard his children yelling in terror. He gasped when the laird opened the parcel to reveal a number of bloodied bones, the bright red flesh still clinging to the alabaster surfaces.

'What does this mean?'

Colline shook his head. 'It means foul business is afoot, Mackie. Since I was told of this grisly find, I have considered the possibility that a victim to a murder seeks out the man who took his life and that he does so by disquieting this good household. By fair means and God willing, we shall find the perpetrator to this crime and silence the angry spirit inside forever.'

Mackie bowed in reverence, concealing the wildness in his eyes.

Colline turned to leave, his expensive cloak billowing behind him. 'I shall request the civil magistrate to call upon all the former residents of this property to convene at my home. There they shall touch these gruesome remains in turn. We shall let the bones speak for themselves. If the murderer is one of the former tenants, these bones will mark him.'

chapter 1

THE INTRUDER

The house was different. It was not the tangible difference experienced after moving the furniture around or widening a window to let in more light, but rather a subtle shift in time and space; a slight alteration in ambience; a faint expectation of the arrival of an unwanted guest. It was as if the house held its breath, sucking in its brittle walls and creating a vacuum of tension and unease.

MacAoidh stood amongst the boxes in the hallway, listening, his nerves twitching against the strong sensation of being watched. His eyes scanned the staircase and the sweeping balcony above his head before coming to rest at a figure in the doorway.

'Mr Mac... er, A-yo-id ... uhm, Ah-id. You reported a break-in?'

MacAoidh felt his heart leap in his chest as he stifled his yell of surprise. 'It's Armstrong, officer, MacAoidh's my Christian name and it's pronounced Mackie, as in this key that works this obviously useless door lock. The spelling's a wee bit misleading.'

'Is it Gaelic?' the young officer stepped across the threshold, his radio hissing and clicking from his shoulder, his lively blue eyes scanning the hallway for signs of criminal activity.

'Aye. My mother gave me a few surnames to juggle. I'm very grateful only one of them's in Gaelic.'

'A few?'

'My middle name's Ross. This way officer.'

'I'm police constable Callum Maxwell.'

'Pleased to meet you Callum,' MacAoidh shook the hand before the officer had a chance to present it properly. 'Where's the rest of the team?'

'I'm just here to conduct the initial report, sir. I'll take your statement and see if there's a need for a follow-up investigation.'

MacAoidh kept his thoughts on the proper procedures on reporting crime to himself and led the constable into the living room where strong sunlight blazed across the floorboards and unpacked crates, haloing the contours and softening the shadows of the room.

'Nice house.'

'Thanks. I thought so too until this morning. It's strange how something like a wee intruder can make a man feel unwelcome in his own home.' He hauled the plastic off an armchair, exposing the inviting comfort of the soft cream leather. 'Would you like some coffee or something?'

'No thanks, I had one before I came here. I'd like to take a statement, if that's OK with yourself.'

MacAoidh winced. He hated the way police officers and council officials slaughtered the reflexive pronoun.

The officer drew out his notebook as if it were a pistol in a gunfight and snapped it open before melting into the armchair. After a short struggle to free himself from its overly-enthusiastic embrace, he sat composed with his pen poised.

'Would you tell me your full name please, sir?'

MacAoidh paused for a brief moment, wondering whether he had just held a conversation or whether he'd imagined it. 'MacAoidh Ross Armstrong. That's M-A-C-A-O-I-D-H.'

'Thank you. And may I ask your date of birth?'

'The twenty first of September, nineteen eighty six.'

'And you are the owner of this property?'

'I have been since three days ago when I picked up the keys. As you can see, I've moved in but not settled in. I've got a fair bit of unpacking to do.'

The young officer gave a sympathetic smile. 'We moved a few years ago to a new house. It was definitely the most stressful time of my life. It almost caused a divorce. We're still finding boxes to unpack.'

'Aye, moving home doesn't come without its anxieties.'

Before the conversation had time to lull, the officer continued his inquiry: 'What's the address here?'

'It's The Ring Steading. That's Auchencairn. I'm sorry, but I can't remember the postcode.'

'That's OK, Mr McKie, I can look that up later. Does anyone else live with you at this address?'

MacAoidh raised an eyebrow. 'No, just me.'

'No wife?'

'Not anymore.' He crossed his arms as a signal to end the conversation.

The cue was taken. 'Can you tell me in your own words what happened?'

Believing this was going to take all afternoon, McAoidh hauled another lengthy piece of plastic sheeting off the sofa and sat down.

'I left the house this morning ...'

'What time would that be?'

'Oh, around eight-thirty. I haven't had any food in the place since I moved in, so decided to go into Castle Douglas for supplies.'

'What time did you return home?'

'About ten. I went to the bank and then drove home.'

'Was that when you noticed the house had been broken into?'

'I noticed the kitchen window was open.'

'So you came home through the front door and didn't notice anything odd until you walked into the kitchen.'

'Aye.'

He waited a while until the officer wrote the requisite notes into his pad.

'So you think the kitchen window was the point of entry? Can you show me?'

'Of course.'

MacAoidh led the constable to the front door and demonstrated how he opened and closed it. He then paced the space across the hallway and into the kitchen at the back of the house behind the staircase. 'Sorry about the mess,' he added as an afterthought.

PC Maxwell smiled in acknowledgment of the scattered miscellany of MacAoidh's life strewn across the floors and stacked up against the walls at random intervals.

'I didn't touch anything and even left the window open.' He indicated with a nod to the heavy sash window, the bottom part of which was open wide. 'It's an old catch, but it isn't broken. I was airing the place yesterday but I'm certain I locked up everything last night.'

'I can't see any sign of forced entry.' The officer duly noted this in his pad. 'Is it possible you forgot to secure the premises properly?'

'I've lived in the city too long and brought a few of those values with me. One of those values is that you never leave an open invitation to intruders or opportunist thieves. It's strange, though, there are no footprints, despite the fact we've had a few big storms and the garden's awash with mud. The window and lock are intact and nothing was taken but someone certainly came in.'

'Nothing taken.' The officer repeated slowly as he scribbled down his findings. 'How do you know someone entered the premises then?'

'Come with me.'

He led his guest into what was going to be the dining room once he brought the furniture out of storage. He pointed to the fireplace.

'Looks like a fireplace to me, Mr Mackie.'

'Excellent observation, officer, but I didn't set it. That paper and kindling were not placed there by me. Every room in this house once had a fireplace with a mantle and hearth and all but two of those were removed in the fifties, so the estate agent told me. Take a look at this.'

He moved towards the far door and into a smaller room which was stacked to the ceiling with boxes and bursting black plastic bin liners. He folded his arms and watched the officer's expression turn from curiosity to puzzlement.

'There would've been a fireplace here at some stage before the fifties but it's long gone. So why would someone want to set a fire here?' Lying on the concrete floor beside the wall was a small, neatly-stacked pile of wood and peat clods placed on scrunched-up folds of old newspaper. 'It's the same in all the rooms in this house, apart from the living room and the bedrooms above it. I've had a good think about this. That part of the house is an extension that was added about ten years ago. There are no chimneys in that part and never were any fireplaces. It's under floor heating so there would be no use for an open fire.'

'Were any of these materials set alight?'

'No. Someone just came in and set it all up. They must've taken the wood from the shed next to the barn. There's coal in there but no peat.'

'What about wood?'

'There's lots of it in there. I chopped it on my first day here. I enjoy using an axe. It helps to relieve tension.'

MacAoidh immediately regretted that statement when the officer raised his eyebrows.

'You're an outdoors type then?'

'My father's got a farm in Sutherland. I grew up there. I'm not much good in an office. That's why I bought this smallholding. It's going to be a fresh start for me.'

'What did you do before this?'

'I got a Masters degree, lived in Africa for a while and ran a business in Aberdeen on my return. Suffice it to say life was a bit too mundane for me in the city.' Feeling he was being interrogated, and worried he was giving away too much too soon, MacAoidh felt his defences rising. 'Have you got any ideas?'

'A helpful neighbour, perhaps?'

'Helpful or angry?'

The officer stopped for a moment to think. 'There's no indication that the person who did this means you harm, Mr Mackie.'

'What about the neighbouring landowner, James Black? I know he put in an offer for this farm at the same time as me. My bid was the better and he lost out. Do you think he could be bearing a grudge?'

'You say nothing's missing; there's no sign of forced entry or damage to the property. In fact, the person who allegedly did this actually left something on the premises. Burglars are usually prone to taking things away. On the face of it, I can't see that any serious crime's been committed here at all. That's not to say, however, that one hasn't been.'

'So that's it then?'

'I'll put my report together but it'll be up to the team to decide whether this incident will be screened in for further investigation. Of course, if anything else happens, let us know straight away. Is there anything else you want to show me?'

'No, that's it.'

'Would you read and sign your statement please?'

MacAoidh flicked through the policeman's notepad, scanning the large lettering as he sucked his cheeks in and let out a heavy breath to show his disappointment that the local law enforcement didn't take the incident as seriously as he.

'What if he or she comes back and puts a match to their handiwork?'

'I really don't think this is anything more than a prank or an over-enthusiastic neighbour, Mr Mackie, but I'll be asking a few questions around the neighbourhood this afternoon. This is a small and very friendly village and I'm sure whoever did this did it with only good intentions. No doubt you'll get to the bottom of this when you start integrating with the members of your local community.'

'No doubt.'

MacAoidh saw the officer to his car and watched him pull away, the gravel crunching against the wide tyres. He stood for a while, letting the strength of the afternoon sun melt the misgivings from his mind. Across the rolling countryside with its prickly gorse bushes, scattered boulders and stunted wind-warped trees piercing the landscape like giant twisted thorns, he could see the blue cloak of the Solway Firth spreading into the horizon. There was a pinch of salt in the breeze and the faintest smell of wood smoke.

He surveyed the cluster of outbuildings and tried not to think about the amount of back-breaking work it would take to turn this land around and tame it. The barn, stables and outbuildings were all but derelict but he would remain focused on his plans..

'Home sweet home,' he said to no one in particular. It wasn't quite the homely feeling he'd expected, but it was close enough and would do for now.

He would visit James Black and offer a hand of friendship and even affiliation if he would have it. A few hundred yards away, in the middle of a field, stood a dead oak tree, its skeletal branches flattened to fans from fending off the incessant thrust of a ruthless wind; its great trunk bowed and brittle with the effort. MacAoidh only hoped he wouldn't look like that after a few years of living at the steading. He laughed and turned towards the front door, his mind focused on which box he would unpack next.

A high-pitched squealing shrilled from the house and, taking a few paces backwards, he looked up to the bedroom and cursed as he saw a dark wave of smoke creeping from the open window.

chapter 2

THE INVESTIGATOR

'Well, Detective Chief Inspector Andrew Galbraith Prendergast, I deny all your accusations!'

Libby leaped across the reception desk with the athletic agility of a cat in a tree, her animated greeting almost knocking him into the plastic chairs of the waiting room.

'I'm not with the Met anymore, Libby.' He returned the hug with a burly one of his own and awkwardly patted her back. 'It's so good to see you, my dear. How's the new life?'

'Not much better than the one before, actually, but I'm working on it. I changed allegiance to the Scottish Bar and took this little job in the outbacks of Southern Scotland. The pay's crap but the work's easy and I've managed to get quite a name for myself amongst the local criminals as an excellent defence lawyer.' She shot him one of her most mischievous smiles. 'So, if you're here to plea bargain, I'm listening.'

She spun around to one of the office secretaries. 'I might be a little late back for lunch, Audrey, so please make Mr Slob comfortable and try not to giggle when he announces himself.'

'Still humiliating your clients, I see.' Prendergast's laughter was purely out of affectionate amusement.

'No, that's his name. It's spelled S-L-O-B but he pronounces it Slobe. He gets really irate when we get it wrong and I think Audrey does it on purpose.' Libby lowered her voice to a whisper as she snatched her jacket from the hook. 'She likes a bit of a drink during the day and gets a little indignant with the clients, but she means well and keeps this place together, even though she's personally falling apart.'

'That's a shame. Are her employers doing anything to help her?'

'Yes, they're ignoring the fact she's got a problem. Two of the partners are away from the office most of the time visiting various prisoners and the third sits in his office all day and rarely comes out. Some say he's been dead for years but only Audrey and a few clients have daily contact with him.'

'I hope for his clients' sakes he's not dead.'

'No, he's often spotted on the golf course during the day getting in a couple of rounds between meetings. I think he sneaks out the back window when no one's looking.'

They laughed together and walked out of the office. Libby tucked her arm into his. 'I'm so excited to see you, Prendy. I don't have much contact with my old London life and was really pleased when you told me you were coming to Scotland to visit.'

She hauled on his coat sleeve when she reached the café door. 'I know this is an art gallery but they've got a good restaurant downstairs that serves up some very respectable homemade food. I know how much you like your culture and your grub. It's not exactly London haute cuisine, but it's honest, affordable and the waiting staff don't treat you like they've just been forced to scrape you off the bottom of their shoes.'

'It sounds just like my kind of place, Libby.'

'So, tell me what all the secrecy's about.' Libby sat down on the wooden chair opposite her friend and threw him a menu. She was pleased to note he hadn't changed much apart from a bit more grey around his ears and a stone or two heavier than when she'd last seen him two years ago.

'There's no secrecy. I just wanted to tell you in person. As I said, I left the Met shortly after the Nunhead incident.'

Her acknowledging nod was heavy with sorrow. Most of that time she wanted to forget. Parts of it, however, she would remember fondly for the remainder of her life.

'But we don't want to talk about that. I've also changed allegiance and am now a private investigator with a highly respected and successful international private investigation agency.'

'What? You? A private dick?' She couldn't hide her surprise, nor her amusement. 'What about the pension?'

She let out a heavy sigh when she spied the waitress glaring at her. 'Oh no. It's her. I thought it was her day off today.'

'Who's that dear?' Prendergast was too busy studying the menu to notice Libby's obvious unease.

'She hates me.'

'Were you rude to her?'

Libby cast him a withering glower that caused him to smile. 'No. We fell out over a man. Well, that's what he calls himself. He's a fellow lawyer who works in Dumfries. I went out with him twice until I found out he had a fiancée.'

'At least he had the decency to tell you.'

'Wrong again! She told me when she marched into the restaurant while we were having a meal. She threw his red wine over his face and I got the slap!'

'Did you sue?'

'I didn't need to. I've been punishing her ever since the incident.' Libby sat back and crossed her arms tightly against her chest as the waitress moved slowly towards her with a glint of hunger in her dark eyes. 'Two special soup and sandwiches and two coffees please and thank you kindly.'

'Do you want your coffee with your lunch?'

'Well I don't want it with my breakfast.'

'Libby!' Prendergast's look was only slightly chiding.

'OK, put it in a bag and send it to my home address and I'll do the same with your tip.'

'I don't know whether I'm delighted to see you haven't changed or disappointed that you still haven't learned any manners,' he chuckled.

'I've changed in lots of ways, but I don't see why I should be polite to a woman who assaulted me for her fiancé's indiscretion. I was the innocent party.'

Prendergast diffused the highly explosive situation by changing the subject. 'I decided there's more to life than money, Libby. The pension, however, is safe. I retired from the force but didn't want to give up detective work. I'm good at it.'

'You certainly are.'

'I think, if it's OK with you, we could be working together again for a little while.'

'Oh yes, do you have a wealthy client for me to defend?'

'I have a wealthy client, yes. He's a Highland lad who recently gave up his job in Aberdeen. He's only lived in this region for a few days. He's up for assault on his neighbour but swears he didn't do it. I've been hired by the family to look into the incident. From what I'm told, it's a very unusual case. I know how you like defending the apparently indefensible so I've given him your details, if you don't mind.'

'Sounds interesting. What do you mean by unusual?'

'He thinks he's the target of some local community conspiracy that wants him out. His alleged victim is a neighbouring landowner who was beaten on my client's premises.'

'Were the alleged injuries serious?'

'A few bruises to his nose, collarbone, scapula, head and forearm but nothing that won't heal quickly. I'd say they were serious in the eyes of the law, however. The weapon, an axe, was found in my client's wood shed. The victim had been beaten with the shaft and, thankfully, not the metal head. My client identified the axe as his own. It was covered in the victim's blood and had my client's fingerprints all over it.'

'If your client identified the weapon as belonging to him, it can reasonably be assumed his fingerprints would be found on it. Did the police give a motive?'

'The police attended an incident at my client's house a few days after he moved in. It's in a beautiful spot, surrounded by a lake and a stream, and quite close to the sea.'

'Yes, that area is known locally as the Scottish Riviera. What does he want to do with the land?'

'Haven't really asked him myself, but the villagers seem to think he's turning it into a holiday centre.'

'I'm sure his venture would go down well with the tourists but not so well with the locals. Do you think the villagers have raised their pitchforks up against him because they don't relish the notion of holidaymakers in their back gardens?'

'That's what I'm here to find out.'

Libby smiled to herself as the man who had become her friend through a set of bizarre circumstances, and who had taken it upon himself to leave a job that he had loved from the onset, could not help but speak like a copper.

She watched in silence as the waitress brought them two steaming bowls of soup and freshly prepared crayfish sandwiches with side salad and crisps. Libby almost laughed as the woman gently placed Prendergast's food before him and threw the rest at Libby, splashing her hands with hot liquid.

'What's the soup?' She wiped her hands with her napkin.

'Spiced parsnip.'

'I take it that was prepared in nineteen ninety seven when that recipe was in fashion.'

'It may be old fashioned but it's a favourite here and we've never had any complaints until now.'

'I wasn't complaining. I was just trying to point out that curried parsnip went out with henna tattoos, Aly McBeal and the Tellytubbies.'

'It's not curried, it's spiced.' The waitress spat the last word.

'Are the spices Indian ones?' Libby shot her the sweetest of smiles.

'Yes.'

'I rest my case.'

'Thank you miss, the soup looks and smells wonderful. I love parsnips.' Prendergast came to the rescue for the second time in less than ten minutes. He looked exhausted. 'You'd better bring the coffee now or you'll be in the ring for round three before you can say milk and sugar.' He turned to Libby as the waitress stomped away. 'I thought Gabriel Radley knocked all that vitriolic stuff out of you and turned you into a nice person.'

'He's not here anymore, so why should I care?'

'Because I think you do.' He patted her hand. Again an awkward gesture but one that was specifically characteristic of him.

'Where were we? Oh yes, we were talking about mens rea.' She moved her hand to her soup spoon.

'As I said, the police attended an incident at my client's house …'

'What's his name?'

'MacAoidh Armstrong.'

'Nice name.'

'He's a nice enough chap too.'

'Good looking?'

'I don't believe I'm qualified to say, but I think you'd find him very pleasing to the eye.'

'This gets better all the time. So why did the police come to his house?'

'He says someone broke in and set fires around the house one morning.'

'A fire-raiser?'

'Yes, an arsonist.'

'We call it fire-raising in Scotland.'

'The modus operandi was not typical of a normal fire-raiser or arsonist.'

'Is there such a thing as a normal arsonist?'

They laughed together.

'When the constable called, the fires had only been set. They hadn't been lit. When the officer left, Mr Armstrong found one of those fires to be alight in the upstairs bedroom and the fire alarms shrieking all over the house.'

'Did the constable say he'd seen it unlit?'

'I don't believe he checked the upstairs rooms.'

'If it was fire-raising, we're looking at revenge for a motive.'

'Perhaps. Luckily there were no carpets, soft furnishings nor other combustibles in the room so the fire was contained. It was, however, fierce enough to cause smoke damage and the floorboards around the area of the fire are charred and black. Mr Armstrong was lucky the whole place didn't go up.'

'What stage in the proceedings against him are we at?'

'He's only appeared on petition. I think that's what they call arraignment here.'

'Close.'

'He wanted to plead not guilty but his lawyer tried to persuade him to strike a bargain with the prosecution, so he sacked him. I've been hired to snoop around the locality and see if there's another reason or person behind the assault that may absolve Mr Armstrong from blame. In the meantime, he needs a good defence lawyer in the area who has the stomach for a fight.'

'What's the alleged victim saying?'

'Nothing at the moment. He hasn't spoken a word since the alleged incident. Too traumatised, according to the local bobbies.'

Libby laughed. 'We don't call them bobbies round here.'

'No, I don't suppose you do.'

They left the conversation hanging.

'I don't defend people I personally believe to be guilty, Prendy. I know it's not a professional attitude but I have to keep a clear conscience. The moral high ground is a place I never step out of anymore.'

'I think our waitress would disagree with that,' he chuckled.

'Then I'll leave you to remind her that we haven't had the coffee with our meal and that it would be nice to get it sometime this century.'

'Leave it to me, Libby. I'm a professional.'

Chapter 3

THE LAWYER

'Mr Armstrong to see you Libby.'

'Give me five minutes to finish this dictation and I'll be out to greet him.'

Libby put the phone down and wiped the ink from her mouth with a testy grunt. It was never a good idea to suck on the tip of a gel pen.

'Two down. Roland's warrior friend makes a noise. Christ, these crosswords are getting more cryptic every day.' She tapped her fingers against the desk. 'Who the hell's Roland?' She scanned the boxes and then the text, searching out an easier question. 'Twelve across. Nine letters. Insipid partner draws standstill. Hmm, I could think of a number of words for that one.' She went back to two down and thought hard for a long time, her heels drumming against the desk. Eventually she threw the pen across the room. 'What planet do these crossword compilers come from?'

The phone rang again.

'Libby, it's Mr Slob on the line.'

'What does he want?'

'He wants to know whether his petition has been filed with the court yet.'

'We only spoke about it yesterday. Who does he think I am? God?'

'Do you want me to deal with it?'

'Yes please, Audrey.'

'Then do me a favour and put down that crossword. The lovely Mr Armstrong's been waiting for fifteen minutes now.'

'Is he lovely or are you being sarcastic?'

'Come out and see for yourself.'

Libby scanned her eyes around the room looking for tell-tale signs of CCTV. 'I'll be right out.'

Stuffing her feet into her shoes and smoothing down the creases in her skirt, Libby marched into the reception area and held out her hand. 'Mr Armstrong, so sorry to keep you waiting. It's been a manic couple of days and I'm way behind with my case load. Pleased to meet you.'

'I'm Susan Adams.'

Libby threw the offending hand behind her back and felt her knees buckling in embarrassment. The woman with the short cropped hair and the body of an overfed Sumo wrestler crossed her arms against her chest and frowned.

'Miss Butler?'

Libby spun around to the male voice, eager to take the focus of her insults away from a woman who was much bigger and more powerful than she.

'Mr Armstrong I presume?' Her panicked scowl turned to a smile of wanton appreciation before she checked herself quickly. 'Follow me please.' She hoped the deliberate swing of her hips didn't look like a waddle from behind as she led him into her office. 'As you can see, my entire office is one massive filing cabinet. I think you'll find some semblance of a chair under those files. Just chuck them off and have a seat.'

'I believe Andrew Prendergast has told you a little about me.' He had a soft voice with a mellow Highland lilt and rolling Rs.

'I would rather hear it from you.' Libby didn't mean her sentence to sound like an illicit proposition but she had to admit to herself that she liked the look of Mr Armstrong. Tall and powerfully built, with short, shaggy sand-coloured hair and the palest blue eyes she had only ever seen on a Siamese cat, Mr Armstrong was much more than pleasing to the eye. His dark grey suit reeked of expensive silk and he wore his red tie with the elegant grace of a male model for Karl Largerfield.

'Let's start with the boring preliminaries first. You've received your client care letter I hope?' She waited for the nod before placing a form at the end of the desk. 'This form gives me your permission to act on your behalf. If you've brought some ID with you, like a passport, driving licence and recent domestic bill with your address on it, then Audrey at the front desk will copy it and keep it on file.'

'I didn't bring anything, sorry.'

'No bother. Just drop into the office with the documents the next time you're in Kirkcudbright or bring them along to your next appointment.'

She waited in silence for him to fill out the form and to take a closer look. His countenance and demeanour were purely defensive. The dark rings under his eyes told her he hadn't slept in days and his inability to make eye contact with her was evidence he was probably losing confidence in the legal system. She'd seen this many times in helpless defendants who'd abandoned all hope of a good verdict. She noticed his hands were shaking as he scratched his details onto paper and couldn't help but feel pity for him.

'OK, may I call you MacAoidh?'

'Aye, of course.'

'A man with a trio of surnames: Highlander and Sassenach.'

'That's me.'

'I understand you're originally from Sutherland.'

'Aye, my father's a Borders man but landed his in-laws' estate in Assynt through his marriage to my mother.'

'Was she a MacAoidh by any chance?'

'How could you guess?' He almost smiled.

She paused the conversation to read the rest of the form.

'Paladin.'

'What?' She peered above the sheet of paper.

'Two down. Roland's vassal is a paladin: one of the twelve peers of Charlemagne's court. Roland, or Hruodland, was a legendary Frankish warrior whose deeds and death were spread around Europe by the songs of minstrels.'

'Oh yes. I see.' She had no idea what he was talking about.

He placed his finger on two down. 'Friend is pal and ...'

'... a din is a noise. Wow, you're clever.' She put the form down and leaned over the crossword on her desk, revealing more than a small amount of cleavage above her polka dot neckline. He looked away.

'What's twelve across then?'

He turned the paper around and narrowed his eyes at it. 'Stalemate.'

'You a cryptic crossword compiler in your spare time?'

'I don't have any spare time.'

She grabbed the paper and plopped it in the bin beside her. 'OK, Highland MacAoidh, crossword specialist, I understand what you're being prosecuted for because I've read the police report and the charge sheet but I want to hear your side of the story.'

'It's not true.'

'What isn't?' She dared him to look at her and caught her breath when he did.

'I didn't touch that man. I've never even met him so how and why would I have wanted to hurt him?'

'Do you believe he was the one who set those fires in your house? One that could've burned your new property to the ground? I understand you intimated as much to the police officer who made the preliminary investigation.'

He tore his eyes away from her again and lowered them to his hands. 'Aye, I thought it could've been him but,' that extraordinary blue focused on her and Libby felt the breath leaving her lungs, 'I was confused. I'd just moved into a new house and found someone deliberately started a fire when I was at home. The bit about the neighbour was conjecture. I was just thinking out loud when I spoke to the officer. Surely, if I was going to beat up the so-called perpetrator, I would've kept my thoughts to myself.'

'Look, MacAiodh. I'm going to be honest with you. The alleged weapon was an axe you admitted belonged to you. The victim was found on your property and his footprints led away from your house. Now, I really want to believe you and I'm prepared to take real steps in order to assure your innocence. I should tell you now, however, that I will not defend you if I personally believe you're guilty or find out you're lying to me on any relevant facts of this case. In short, you have to be honest with me at the onset. Don't hide anything from me and certainly don't lie to me. If you do, I'll send you back out into the wild and leave you to the wolves. That means, the procurator fiscal's office and the police will eat you alive and their teeth are extremely sharp. Are we clear on that?'

'I've got nothing to hide and I don't need to lie. I did not assault Jim Black.'

'Are you capable of assault on another, MacAiodh?'

'No, I don't believe I am.'

'Then we're finished here, Mr Armstrong.' She stood up. 'I am a good defence lawyer and that means I have to do my homework. I know you have a criminal record and understand you nearly killed a man a few years ago.'

'That was a long time ago and those were exceptional circumstances. Did you read the file? I mean really read it?' He did maintain eye contact this time as he slammed his hands on the desk and shouted at her.

Libby shied away from his anger. 'Look, I know you're upset, but please sit back down, take a deep breath and try to keep calm. I'll get you some coffee.' She made to lift the phone.

'I don't want coffee, Miss Butler. I just want someone to believe me and help me get through all this without treating me like a Wild West outlaw.' Calm now, he rose and towered over the desk. 'Thank you for your time. You can send your bill to my address. I've written it down on the form. You'll have to tell your accounts department to be quick though. I don't think I can pay bills from Barlinnie.'

What was it about handsome, desperate men? Libby felt fate closing in on her for a second time in her life. 'Let's take a walk.'

'Where to?'

'I don't know. The harbour, maybe. Let's get out of here, speak like two ordinary people and forget we're lawyer and client for a while. You can tell me your story and I'll tell you mine. If you convince me you're telling the truth. We can start again and I'll do my damndest to prove your innocence to the lawman.'

'And if I can't convince you?'

She shrugged. 'Then we'll talk about your options.'

They walked in silence to the harbour where the silt laden waters carved a sluggish vent in the hidden bedrock beneath the sparkling surface and rolled out to sea some miles away. It was one of those usual summer days of schizophrenic weather where the sun shone hot through intermittent bands of misty rain. Libby had grown accustomed to the Scottish weather but still felt the warmth of the sun, when it did decide to shine, healing her heavy heart as she tried in vain to forget her past and look forward to an empty future. Those precious rays of sunlight were a reminder that she was alive and the view from the harbour gave her the incentive to remain that way for as long as she could.

'Up until two years ago, I lived and worked in London.' She started carefully, daring the images of the past to invade her present. 'I was an ambitious, ruthless senior solicitor at a city law firm and specialised in causing misery to ordinary people.'

'Isn't that what all lawyers do?'

'Only the naughty ones.' Detecting a hint of humour in his response, she decided it best not to raise her defences. 'One of the cases I worked on sparked a series of horrible murders. They called him the Vampire Killer.'

'I remember the trial. He was a particularly gruesome bastard, I recall. Were you the lady lawyer he was after?'

'Yes, that was me. He killed a lot of people, one of whom was my colleague.'

'Wasn't he caught trying to murder you?'

'He didn't succeed and the police got him.'

'Now I've met you, I would say the poor man wouldn't have stood a chance.'

'What's that supposed to mean?' She wondered whether she should be taking offence.

'I can imagine you're quite a formidable woman, despite the fact you have pen all over your face.'

'What?' Libby rummaged through her handbag for her powder compact and gasped at the sight of the blue ink stains across her lips and chin. 'Why didn't you tell me?' She wanted to leap into the water and swim until she reached the bottom. 'Have you got a hankie?' She snatched the clean handkerchief he offered and spat on it before rubbing at the stains on her skin.

She snapped her head up to him.

'Is twelve across still there?'

'It's now thirteen down.'

'Damn! Never mind.' She continued despite the stinging sensation across her mouth. 'I had the chance to kill him; to really hurt him before the police arrived, but I didn't take it. I've thought about it a lot. I hated him and wanted him dead but, when I got the chance to put him out of the misery of the world for good, I just couldn't do it. I've slapped a few people in my time but I'm not a killer and I like to think I see the consequences of my actions before committing to them. I don't want blood on my hands because I don't want to go to jail. It's as simple as that.'

'When you say slapped, don't you mean assaulted?'

'Yes but, believe me, she deserved it.'

'Were there consequences?'

'A few minor ones. She didn't sue me, if that's what you mean.'

'Then you were lucky.'

'So,' refusing to ponder on the possible outcomes to her past actions, she finished off her story, 'that's why I'm now living in Castle Douglas – a place few people have ever heard of – holding down an easy job with no friends and no one to come home to at night. London taught me a lot of things and the best lesson was to feel comfortable with myself. I quite like me now and I know what I don't want out of life.'

'What *do* you want out of life then?'

'Peace of mind, happiness, contentment, a better world, an en suite bathroom, a pony, the same old rubbish that everyone else wants but are too frightened or lazy to go out and get.'

She was surprised to hear his laughter and was delighted to have, at last, caused him to smile. He had a most beautiful smile that lit up his face and caused his striking blue eyes to shine like sunlight glancing off a sparkling ocean.

'Are you happy in your solitude?' His laughter trailed.

'Yes. I don't deserve someone to share my life with. I was a really horrible person two years ago and I'm still a bit of a bitch.'

'No one deserves to be alone, Libby. We're a very social species. Loneliness changes a person for the worse. Whatever you've done in the past shouldn't be allowed to haunt the present.

'And, what about you?' Libby decided to change the focus of the conversation before she shed tears over it. 'What part of your past haunts you Mr Highlander?'

'All of it.' The swift rise in his defences took her by surprise. 'I'm sorry, I can't bring myself to talk about it. Aye, I assaulted a man and could've killed him. Yes, I was done for it and yes, I have a criminal record: a suspended sentence, but you know that already.'

'Did he deserve it?'

'Oh, aye, he really did.'

'All right, MacAoidh, I'm going to give you my decision.' She rose from the bench and planted her hands on her hips. 'I'm going to take a chance on you and help you get to the bottom of all this. You have an excellent detective working for you and believe me when I say he'll come up with your explanations. If you really didn't assault your neighbour, then he'll find out who did. In the meantime, I'm going to work on your defence. There are a few bits of circumstantial evidence I can see but nothing strong enough to secure a successful verdict. Everything hinges on what the alleged victim has to say. I understand he's found his tongue at last and the police have been questioning him all morning. If he identifies you as the assailant, then we've got our work cut out.'

'Thank you, Libby.' His handshake rattled her bones and, as she massaged the pain away, she watched him walk away from her. His shoulders appeared straighter and his confidence stronger as he disappeared around the corner.

'I hope you know what you're doing, Libby Butler.' She whispered to herself as she stared at the space on the bench he'd just vacated.

chapter 4

THE TREE

Andrew Prendergast cursed his city shoes as he trudged across the muddy field mined with wet cow pats. He hadn't found the need for a pair of wellies since he was a boy. Now he wished he'd thought a bit deeper about the nature of his work and at least looked at a map before he drove the three hundred and so miles to the wilds of Southern Scotland.

At first it seemed like a good idea to take the marked country route which circumnavigated the steading. It would give him a feel for the area and a better overview of the locality. Being unprepared for the weather and terrain, however, was a mistake. Without a rain hood, he'd seen very little, and being improperly shod had caused a number of falls and skids which had given his clothes and skin a dramatic soaking as well as a generous dousing in freshly laid manure.

It was with some enthusiastic relief he found himself once more in the village and inside its ancient pub where the patron didn't seem to mind his dishevelled and muddy appearance.

Sitting in front of an open fire, he took his time to dry out over a pint of cask ale and a mutton pie, and watch the rain from the homely comfort of the great indoors.

'See Jim's home frae the hospital.'

Prendergast heard the conversation from the public side of the oddly boat-shaped bar with its clinker-cut hull painted white. A blond woman was speaking to an elderly gent rooted to a wooden stool. He looked as though he hadn't moved from that spot by the window since the premises were built in the seventeenth century.

'Aye,' said the man, 'an' they say it's the newcomer what's gave him the hidin'. Heard he's been arrested.'

The woman took a glug from her pint and wiped her mouth on the end of her sleeve. 'Sam says there was a fire at The Ring when the newcomer moved in.'

'City folk don't ken how tae build fires, lass.'

'He's no' frae the toon, he's a Highland lad an' he thinks it wis Jim what set his hoose alight.'

'Wherever he's frae, he's got nae business beatin' up on oor good folk, nae matter whit he 'hinks they've done. Cannae see Jim settin' a man's hoose alight wi'oot good reason. The lad should tak a lesson on buildin' fires safely.'

'Sam says the Ghost Tree's deed' an' it's the poltergeist come back.'

'Nah, load of mumbo jumbo nonsense telt tae scare the weans. Ghosts don't beat men. It's the livin' we should be feart o'. Jim put a copper nail in the oak a few year ago. Wanted it for firewood.'

'He kilt it?'

'Aye, it wis deein' onyway. Sad to see ony livin' thung stuck oot ower that hull in the face o' the wind. Ahm surprised it wis still standin' after a' these years.'

'Ah blame global warmin'.'

The conversation interested Prendergast in many ways. First, he was surprised by the intimate extent of local knowledge about events around the community as soon as they happened. Second, he was intrigued by the acceptance of ancient myth as a reasonable explanation for a criminal assault. He wondered whether there was a connection.

'Sorry to bother you, but I couldn't help but be interested in your conversation …' It was a good introduction, albeit a little cliché. 'I'm just visiting the area and would be really interested to learn about the Ghost Tree, I think you called it.'

'It's yon tree oot by the al' steadin',' the woman answered him with cordial ease. 'There were three planted centuries ago, but two o' 'em deed. The last one's on its way oot tae. They say when the last o' the Ghost Trees dees, the Rerrick Parish Poltergeist wull return.'

'How interesting. Who says that then?' Although Prendergast enjoyed experiencing the broad dialect, he had trouble in understanding it, so had to listen very carefully.

The woman shrugged. 'It's a well kent fact aroon' here. The poltergeist is famous.'

'Famous fer scarin' weans,' the old man added.

'Years an' years ago, a fairmer an' his family lived in whit was once calt the Ringcroft o' Stockin'.'

'Nah, he wis a stane mason,' the old timer corrected her.

'He wis a fairmer an' the Ring Steadin' was built ower it. This fairmer, Mackie …'

'Mackie?'

'Aye, that's whit ah said he wis calt!' The woman widened her eyes at Prendergast in objection to his rude interruption to her tale.

'So sorry, please continue.'

'Well, it all stairted when fairmer…'

'Mason.'

'… Mackie noticed fires in his hoose an' aroon the steadin'. They say he was cursed by his neighbour. His animals went missin' an' he an' his family got hit wi' stanes and beaten wi' sticks by nuthin' until Mackie had enough. He calt on the local meenister an' they held an exorcism an' the ghost vanished.'

'How long ago was this?'

'Oh, hunners o' year ago.'

'Fairy tales,' the old man muttered through the bottom of his pint.

'Nah, it wis true!' the woman protested. 'The meenister wrote it a' doon. He had hunners o' witnesses. Look it up, it's all ower the internet, includin' his record o' it.'

'And do you believe it's true about the Ghost Tree?'

'Aye. It's terrifyin' tae thunk the poltergeist's back. I wouldnae be that Highland lad for ony money.'

After buying his new colleagues a pint each, Prendergast got into his car and closed the door, the woman's words ringing in his ear.

If MacAoidh Armstrong didn't commit the assault on Jim Black, then the question remained who did? Perhaps it was the same person who set the fires at The Ring steading and lit one of them in an upstairs bedroom. Perhaps the perpetrator had been in the house all morning, unbeknown to Armstrong or the visiting officer.

Prendergast liked to follow his hunches. They had rarely let him down in the past. He had a feeling that someone in the village could be using the legend of the Rerrick Parish Poltergeist to scare Armstrong out of his new home and retain the idealistic status quo of a small rural community. Conversely, Armstrong himself could be using the legend as a way of turning his new venture into a money-spinning tourist attraction.

'The world loves a good ghost story,' he muttered to himself. Either way, a few bits of research on the internet would give him a head start on the real perpetrator's next move. In the meantime, he would keep the thoughts to himself and pay a visit to The Ring. He needed to get on the internet.

As he drove through the rain towards the steading, he spied the cadaverous effigy of a tree, forlorn and stooped in the field.

The sea mist had just began to roll in from the Solway, casting an eerie glow across the hillside, and Prendergast could almost believe in the spirit world were he not such a practical man.

He pulled into the drive and, just as he was making his way towards the front door, he heard the sound of a distressed animal coming from the new barn.

The door squealed on its rollers as he pulled it across and Prendergast shuddered as memories flooded back to him of similar noisy hinges in an abandoned church in south east London.

He took a deep breath and stepped in. The barn was silent and empty save for a few bales of rotting hay in the far corner. A loud moo startled him to glance upwards and he staggered backwards choking in shock. High above his head, tied to the RSJ in the centre of the barn was a live cow. The ropes holding it had been tied securely around its body, one behind its forelegs, the other in front of its hind legs, so that all four legs dangled in mid-air.

'Good grief! How the hell did you get up there?' Was all Prendergast could muster in terms of a suitable expression.

He looked about him for a ladder but found nothing that would help him reach the animal.

He ran to the house, but Armstrong's black Land Rover was not in the drive and the door was left unanswered.

Refusing to panic, Prendergast decided to call the emergency services and punched '999' into his phone. 'Fire brigade please and the police, I suppose. Yes, I am at The Ring steading in Auchencairn. Pardon? Yes, it is an emergency. No, I don't require the ambulance service. I may need a vet though. There's a live cow tied to the ceiling of a barn and I can't get it down. Yes, I said the ceiling. Pardon? Oh, about thirty feet high.'

Chapter 5

THE HANGING COW

Macaoidh Armstrong arrived home in the early evening to be greeted by the flashing of lights in his drive and a dark army of men and women, many in uniform, swarming in and out of his barn.

'What now?' he hissed. He recognised a few neighbours and the back of Andrew Prendergast who stood beside a fire truck speaking to a tall man. 'Can someone tell me what the hell's going on here?'

Prendergast turned around to face him, his features grave. 'Where've you been?'

'Why? What's it got to do with you?'

'It's important someone can corroborate that you were somewhere else today and not at home.'

'What do they think I've done now? Murdered the treasurer of the community council over a funding application? Eaten the village's children? Raped the post mistress?'

'No, it's not that serious.'

MacAoidh tried his best to calm down but could feel his lungs filling with fury. 'I was seeing my lawyer like you told me to.'

'Libby? Where did you meet her and what time did you leave?'

MacAoidh shook the irritation from his head. 'I saw her in her Kirkcudbright offices and then we were at the harbour for a while. I left about half an hour ago. I had to stop for diesel. Can you please tell me what's going on and why half the population of Dumfries and Galloway is running around my grounds?'

'And what about the morning?'

'In Dumfries, getting the car serviced and waiting around at the bank for one of those idiots to make a decision on my stocks and shares. Usual stuff.'

'Someone tied a cow to the ceiling of your barn, son.'

He paused for a moment to take in what he'd just been told. 'Sorry, but I thought you just said someone tied a cow to the ceiling of my fucking byre!' His anger broke.

'Not the old byre, lad. The new barn.'

'What? That's thirty feet in the air.'

'Give or take a few inches.'

'Who does the beast belong to?'

'It's one of Black's cattle, one of his employees has just confirmed it.'

'It had to be didn't it?' He let out a deep, heavy breath.

'Is this your property, sir?'

MacAoidh spun around so fast to the voice of the police sergeant, he almost head-butted him. 'You know damn well it is. You arrested me here last week and hurled me into the back of a police car with my hands cuffed behind my back.'

'Had to ask, sir.'

'I'll also remind you I was out all day, with a few solid alibis, and I come home to this. Can the bold constabulary of Dumfries and Galloway tell me what's going on?'

'Calm down, sir. I'm only conducting a reasonable inquiry.'

'And you have your reasonable answer. Now get off my property and take all these people and that bloody cow with you.'

He watched in open-mouthed astonishment as the cow was led by a halter from his barn to cheers from the gathering crowd.

He marched inside and slammed the door, barring the outside world from his privacy. He stomped into the kitchen and threw his keys on the table before he stopped and slowly turned back round. Moving cautiously into the hallway, he picked up the silver framed picture sitting on one of the boxes and thought the sudden wash of anxiety would floor him.

'Not again.'

He examined the box, turning it upside down and rattling its contents. He jumped as the doorbell rang and was not surprised to see Prendergast standing at the threshold.

'They're all leaving. I've convinced the police not to bother you tonight. May I come in?'

'Now's not a good time, sorry.' He squeezed his fingers around the frame in his hand.

'I've got a theory.'

'It's too late for hypotheses, there's no tentative explanation for any of this and, in practice, I'm losing my mind.'

Prendergast stepped through the door uninvited and closed it softly behind him. 'Is that your ex?'

MacAoidh nodded distractedly.

'Can I see?'

He handed the frame to Prendergast.

'She's a beautiful woman.'

'She was.'

'Photographs are wonderful things. You can never forget a face if you have a picture.'

'I would never forget her face. Do you want a drink?'

'I'd love one, but I'm driving. You go ahead. I was wondering if I could borrow your computer and internet for a bit. They have wifi at the B and B but it's intermittent and damned frustrating.'

'Aye, sure, the laptop's on the kitchen table.'

MacAoidh examined the box again and shook his head. 'So tell me what happened here.' He carefully laid the picture on the work surface face down and poured himself a glass of red wine. He stood at the sink watching Prendergast's back.

'I spent the afternoon snooping around the grounds and village. I came here at about four o' clock to borrow your internet and heard an almighty moo coming from the barn. When I entered the building, I saw the cow hanging from the rafters.'

'Any idea how it got up there?' MacAoidh refused to show surprise.

'No idea. Do you have a ladder high enough to reach the top of that barn roof?'

'No.' He pulled off his jacket and threw it on the worktop, followed by his tie. 'Whoever did this must've brought their own ladder or a cherry picker. There's no way anyone would be able to climb up there with a thousand-pound heifer tucked under his arm.'

'The police also doubt this could be the work of one person.'

'So they at last believe there's some sort of conspiracy against me?'

'Who knows what they believe. I'll speak to the officer in charge of the case tomorrow. There's a community council meeting on Friday night in the village hall and I think you're on the agenda. Maybe you should go along and see what they have to say about you.'

'I have no interest in wasting my time in the company of self-important do-gooders who think they know best how to run the lives of other folk.'

'I take it that's a no then. In the meantime, I have some good news in that Jim Black didn't see the man who attacked him. In fact, he didn't see anyone at all.'

'Probably too dark.'

'So it would appear, but he swears he saw the axe but not its wielder.'

'Then I'm not the only mad man in this village.'

'You may find you're the only truly sane one here after I've finished investigating. Some people think it's a ghost!'

'The Rerrick Parish Poltergeist, yes I read about it before I bought the house. This house, however, is a few hundred yards away from the Ghost Tree.'

'Not according to the woman in the pub. They say your house was built over the site of the Ringcroft of ... what did they call it again?'

'The Ringcroft of Stocking.'

'Yes, that's it.' Prendergast peered into the laptop screen. 'Here it is.' He read slowly: 'Alexander Telfair, Edinburgh, December 1695 published a pamphlet entitled A True Relation of an Apparition, Expressions, and Actings of a Spirit, which infested the House of Andrew Mackie, in Ring-Croft of Stocking, in the Paroch of Rerrick, in the Stewarty of Kirkcudbright, in Scotland.'

'He was the minister of Rerrick parish who conducted the exorcism. I believe he was a local man.'

'The victim of the alleged paranormal activity was a stone mason or farmer called Mackie. Now that's a coincidence if ever I heard one.'

'He was a mason.' MacAoidh felt uncomfortable with where the conversation was going and had to speak his mind. 'Please don't tell me you're taking this seriously. I mean, hauntings, poltergeist, God and ghost trees, you don't really expect me to believe in them do you?'

'Not exactly but I do think someone believes in them or is at least trying to persuade you that the poltergeist has returned to Rerrick in the hope you'll flee the house in terror.'

'This is Scotland not Amityville. They won't get me out with a ghost story. I don't scare that easily.'

'You don't believe in God either?'

'No, never have. Do you?'

'Yes, I've seen enough strangeness in this world to believe in anything. Damn, what was that?'

'What was what?'

'Something just hit me on the top of the head.'

MacAoidh heard the small stone drop to the tiles and picked it up. Examining it in his hand he shrugged. 'The windows are all closed and I certainly didn't throw it at you.'

'It dropped on my head from above.'

They looked up together but only saw the smooth plasterwork of the ceiling.

'Damn, your internet's down!'

'Must be the poltergeist,' MacAoidh laughed and drained his glass. 'Routers do that sometimes. It's something to do with a bad network signal and nothing to do with supernatural activity.'

'I certainly hope not, or this will be the shortest investigation of my career.'

'Oh, come on Andrew, surely the dead don't scare you.'

'Maybe the dead don't but evil certainly does and good spirits don't throw stones at people.'

'Nothing threw that stone. It was probably stuck in your hair.'

Prendergast nodded but didn't look at all convinced. 'I suppose it probably was.'

'I do, however, believe in your theory that someone may be trying to emulate the poltergeist in an attempt to scare me off and they're being pretty malicious about it.'

'Why, has anything else happened to you?'

MacAoidh was loathe to say but decided it might be relevant. 'This picture of my wife,' he tapped his forefinger against the photograph he found on the box. 'I packed this picture myself. I put it at the bottom of that box. You see the one marked with a red H in the hall?'

Prendergast nodded.

'It's still sealed isn't it? Take a look,'

He followed Prendergast out of the kitchen and into the hallway. 'I taped that box up. That's my packaging, yet I found the picture sitting on top of the box when I came in tonight. Now how do explain that?'

'Someone was careful to seal it back up?'

'I can accept that but why that picture? Why choose the only memory in my possession that can still hurt me?'

'I don't know, son, but I'm going to find out.' Prendergast picked up his coat. 'It's getting late and Mrs Armitage at the B and B will be expecting me back for dinner. She's a wonderful cook, but is over-generous with the portion sizes. I think I'll need a new wardrobe by the time this is over. My own wife won't even recognise me.'

They shook hands and MacAoidh opened the door.

'Thanks for stopping by. Sorry I was rude to you this evening. It's not every day someone ties a cow to the rafters of my byre.'

'No need to apologise, lad. You've been through a lot lately. Sometimes you have to concede that last straw.'

'Consider it conceded!'

'Pardon?'

MacAoidh sighed before he swore. 'Think we'll need the fire brigade back. The shed's on fire.'

THE CONFESSION

chapter 6

'Hi, I hope you don't mind this personal call. I was in the area and have some news for you.' Libby had no idea why she felt so nervous as MacAoidh stood at the door dressed only in a towel. She averted her eyes. 'I'll come back later if now's not convenient.'

'Not at all. Come in, Libby, and make yourself at home. I'll be back in a second.'

She watched as he bounded up the stairs and out of view. Alone in the hallway, she idly flicked her fingers against a few papers and helped herself to a chocolate biscuit from a half-eaten packet on one of the boxes. She checked herself in the hall mirror and decided she wore her hair as if her ears had outgrown it, like one of those Chinese crested dogs: all fringe and startled expression.

'You've still got a lot of moving in to do, I see.' She yelled up the stairs. 'I could give you a hand if you want.' She moved into the kitchen and turned over the picture in the silver frame which was sitting face down on the work surface. A woman's face stared back at her. She looked happy. She heard him coming down the stairs and slammed the picture down on the surface.

'Decent at last.'

She let out a tinny laugh – not the one she'd hoped to hear coming from her own mouth.

'Sorry about that.'

'No, it's my fault; I should've called you first.' She watched him as he filled the water container for the coffee machine. With his back to her, she could take her time to eye him critically and decided he was beautifully built with strong forearms, a taut, muscular back and a tight backside. His casual clothes hugged the contours of his body in all the right places, especially the impressive bulge in the front of his jeans. She definitely preferred him in the towel.

'Is there something wrong?'

Libby leaped from her daydream and realised she'd been brazenly eyeing him up in all the wrong places while he'd been speaking to her. She hauled on her emergency reserves and pulled herself together. 'I was just thinking about something else. Sorry, I do that sometimes. My mind's always wandering into the next thing to do.' She breathed out slowly, hoping to God he'd swallowed all of her excuse.

He handed her the coffee in a mug. 'Milk and sugar are on the tray by the coffee maker. You said you had some news for me?'

'Yes and it's good news. You're in the clear. The PF has agreed to drop the case. Where did you say the milk was?'

'Just … here,' he scratched at his head as if he was missing something. 'I could've sworn …'

'Here it is.' Libby picked the jug up from the butcher's block in the centre of the kitchen and waggled it at him. 'Mr Black swears no one assaulted him.'

'Correction, he says he saw the axe but not the person who used it on him.'

'No, he used no one in the literal sense. He says he was beaten with the axe, although no one was holding it. In other words, he says he was attacked by an unseen entity called No One.'

'That's ridiculous, but I know why he's saying that.'

'Yes, Prendy filled me in this morning. He says there's some strange goings-on at this property and believes some of the villagers may be behind it. I heard you had another fire last night. Are you OK?'

'It was only a small one. Nothing to be alarmed about and it was obviously not intended to do much damage.'

'It's bizarre, though, that people are capable of behaving so badly. Tying a cow to a roof is an odd message to leave. I wonder what they meant by it.'

'I don't care. It wasn't my beast and I wasn't there when the deed was being done.'

'Doesn't the fact that someone's doing it at all bother you?'

'No, because that's what they want. They want all this to bother me. They want to see me throw it all in and leave, but I'm not going to give them what they want. I'm staying here until I decide to leave and nothing and no one else will make that decision for me.'

'That's the spirit,' Libby smiled and he smiled back.

'Thanks for your help.'

He surprised her once again. 'I didn't do anything.'

'You did a lot more than you think. You were considerate and showed me compassion. I'm grateful for that and forgive you for staring at my crotch.'

'I was not!'

'Hello, is anyone home?'

A middle-aged woman with a ruddy complexion and thick curly hair made her way cautiously through the boxes to the kitchen. She carried a basket of eggs and a large plastic container that Libby assumed would contain some delicious home baking. She was glad of the interruption.

'I'm Mary Hyslop from Greenbrae, along the road. I thought you deserved a proper welcome. It's Mr Armstrong, isn't it? I've brought you a housewarming present.'

She stuffed the basket and container into MacAoidh's arms and patted his bicep.

'It's a nice day for a walk, so I thought I'd take the opportunity to pay you a little visit. Are you settling in all right?'

Libby thought that was one of the most stupid questions ever asked, considering the circumstances. 'He would do if someone would only desist in setting alight to parts of his house and dangling cattle from his barn roof.'

'Oh, aye, I heard about that. Was there much damage done?'

'Only to my pride, Mary. Thank you for your kind welcome.'

'What a lovely accent you have Mr Armstrong.'

'He's from Sutherland.' Libby felt invisible.

'I'm not far from there myself. I'm originally from Hartlepool.'

'Ah, yes, Hartlepool by Durness.' Libby crossed her arms tightly around her chest and wedged her tongue in her cheek.

'Libby meant to say Sutherland, Mary, not Sunderland and please call me MacAoidh.'

'That's what I said ...' Libby protested.

'This is a friend of mine, Libby Butler.'

He shut her up with a slight shake of his head, while Mary barely acknowledged the introduction.

'Well, I best be going, but please let me know if you need anything. Enjoy the eggs and the baking. They were freshly laid this morning.'

'Crumbs, I'd love to see the hen that can lay a pan scone!'

MacAoidh saw his guest to the door and, after exchanging a few pleasantries, closed it behind her. Libby watched her shuffling down the drive from the hall window.

'If you're serious about helping me unpack this stuff, then we'd best get to it.' He stabbed a knife into the top of one of the boxes and ripped it open with his hand. 'Oh, and please don't touch the box marked with a big H.'

'Why, what's in it?'

'Things I'd rather not unpack. That one's for the loft.'

'I think your Sutherland charm must've rubbed off on Mary because she's doing the Highland Fling down the drive.' Libby giggled at the antics of the woman as she skipped down the drive, flailing her arms around her head and leaping from side to side. It was only when she saw the woman writhing on the grass that she realised something was wrong.

She threw open the door and ran down the drive towards the fallen woman who was now yelling in panic and pain. Mary lay on the grass, screaming, and acted as though she fended off an invisible attacker. Libby thought she heard the flat blows but could do little to help her. She was just about to grab Mary's arm when MacAoidh was there in front of her. He scooped the screaming woman up in his arms and ran into the house with her, yelling for Libby to follow him.

'Call an ambulance.' He lowered Mary on to a comfortable sofa in a large, light room with huge bay windows and no curtains.

'No, please, I'm all right. I'm not hurt, I promise.' Mary's protests sounded real. 'If you'd be kind enough to take me home, MacAoidh.'

MacAoidh didn't look convinced. Libby stood by the window and watched him try to compose himself. He looked so shaken, so confused. 'What do you want me to do?'

'I'm taking her home. You can stay here until I come back but I'll understand if you want to leave.'

'I'll be here.'

She sat for a while, trying to take in what she'd just witnessed. She decided she probably saw nothing. Mary did look as though she was being attacked and Libby still heard the flaps of what sounded like a flat of a large hand against Mary's skin, but there were no marks on her flesh to indicate anything untoward had taken place.

Whether it was a village conspiracy or truly a poltergeist, Libby didn't really care. What did concern her was the man whose life the natural or the supernatural were toying with. He was a good man and all this was very unfair on him.

She moved across to the baby grand in the corner which had been sparkling white in its heyday. It obviously had a lot of use over time as the keys were worn and discoloured. A few pictures sat on its dulled surface, one a portrait of a sweet looking middle-aged woman with a bashful smile and ruddy complexion. Next to the piano was an ancient ornate grandfather clock, its heavy pendulum beating out the seconds in the same way as it had probably done since the first day it was made.

'This has to be your mum. She looks really kind.'

He stopped at the door and pocketed his car keys. She noticed the streaks of gold in his hair as they blazed in the sunlight setting his eyes on fire.

'Is that what you see?'

'Is seeing believing?' She placed the picture back carefully.

'Probably.'

'Did you hear something slapping her?'

'Not sure.'

'I did.'

'I don't care.'

'So you choose to ignore it?'

He nodded.

'Supposing it gets worse?'

'Then I'll deal with it.'

'Do you mind if I smoke in here?'

'No, but try not to set the house on fire. It's becoming a domestic hazard. I'll get you an ashtray.'

Libby found the packet of cigarettes in her handbag and lit one. She pulled the smoke into her lungs slowly, savouring the sensation as if it was her very first.

'Libby, did you take that photograph out of the kitchen?'

'What photograph?' She choked on her smoke.

'The one in the kitchen you were looking at earlier. What did you do with it?'

She coughed. 'I only glanced at it. I put it back. Why? Is it gone?' Not wanting to collapse into the cushions and embarrass herself, she perched on the corner of the deep sofa.

'Mary.' He let out a low but sorrowful chuckle and sat down next to her. 'Beware of wolves in sheep's clothing.'

'You think Mary took it?'

'She's part of all this. Her speedy recovery was a bit suspicious, don't you think? She chatted all the way home as if nothing had happened. The woman didn't even look ruffled.'

'Do you believe these people can be that clever? I mean that well organised?'

'I don't know but I'm beginning to doubt my own sanity.'

'How so?'

She followed his line of vision as he indicated with his head to the sill of one of the bay windows where the silver framed picture lay face down.

'No way!'

'What's your involvement in all this, Libby? Why are you doing this? Are they paying you to confuse me, to scare me?' He didn't sound angry but the clip to his voice and stiffness of his shoulders were evidence that he was disappointed in her.

'Wait a minute. I didn't move your bloody picture.' She stubbed her cigarette out into the pristine crystal ashtray and moved away from him. 'I've got no investment in this, personal, financial or otherwise, and it both upsets and distresses me that you think I might be capable of such cowardly behaviour. I deserve better than your suspicions and hostile accusations, MacAoidh Armstrong. I'm here to help you.'

'Why?'

She bit her lip. 'Because you remind me of someone. Someone very special who I lost and will never see again. He was honest and brave like you but you don't have his surety or his confidence. I want to help you find them.'

'I don't know who to trust anymore.' He rose, snatched up the photograph from the window sill and stuffed it into her hand.

'You have yourself and that's a good start.'

They sat in silence while she studied the happy face in the photograph.

'Her name was Helen and she was my wife. I was teaching her to drive on a Sunday afternoon.' The confession came from nowhere as they sat together on the sofa and watched the world from a bay window. 'I didn't realise we'd been in a crash until someone dragged me out the car. Even standing on the road and watching the scene, seeing the blood, so much blood. Have you ever been in a car crash?'

'Only a proverbial one.'

'Shock does strange things to the head, you know. I think it's a natural protection of the mind. It shuts you down. Turns reality into a dream. You know what's happening around you, but you feel it's happening somewhere else.'

'Like a drug.'

'The emergency vehicles were suddenly there. All those lights flashing in the darkness, like some weird funfair warps into town. When someone asked me my name, I couldn't even tell them. Didn't know where I lived or how old I was.' He paused for a moment and squeezed his eyes shut as if to rid himself of the terrible visions before him.

'You don't have to go on if it's upsetting you.' Libby didn't know how to reach him and could only observe while he locked himself into an agonising memory of his past that would not let him go.

'I don't know how long I'd been standing there; it felt like days. Someone was crying. It could've been me. Helen was in the driver's seat. When I came to my senses, like someone had punched me, I tried to get to her.'

He took a breath before continuing. 'The car hit us side on and its bonnet was wedged in the driver's door. I panicked. All I could think of was getting her out of there, but there were hands holding me back. Lots of hands, hauling at my arms, bruising my shoulders. I tore away from them and felt my arm pop from its socket but strangely, looking back on it, didn't feel any pain.'

'OK, that's enough. I don't need to know anymore. I understand where this is going.' Libby was already fighting back the tears and refused to shed any more.

'Anyway,' he breathed out his despondency in a long, heavy breath. 'The guy driving the other car skipped red lights and ploughed into us. Although he'd been drinking, he agreed to plead guilty to drink driving but blamed Helen for going through a red light. After a quick plea bargain, he got off with a suspended sentence. He came to see me one day at work to tell me how sorry he was but tried to slip in something about foreigners not knowing what colour means go and what means stop.'

'So you assaulted him?'

'I beat the living crap out of him and don't regret a single blow.'

'I'm not surprised.'

'Thanks for listening. That's one story I've never told but I think it needed to come out. Sorry you had to be the one on the receiving end.'

'I'm honoured you chose me to confide in.'

'That was five years ago. I also got a suspended sentence, so now I suppose we're equal. I'm not the type to bear grudges but that bastard really got to me.'

'Although I can't condone criminal behaviour, I think, in the circumstances, your actions can be justified to stand neatly inside my little patch of moral high ground. Is there anything else you want to confess to me?'

'I don't think so.'

'Is there anything you want to ask me?'

'I'm wondering why the police didn't take the incident at my house more seriously. They sent a wean to take my statement. Believe me, I own pairs of trousers older than him. He didn't ask to be shown around the house and I don't believe he followed up the complaint. He couldn't even get my name right.'

Libby laughed at last, delighted she had managed to break this unhappy man's solitude and bring him back to reality. 'Modern day coppers will only bother to investigate burglary if it's deemed solvable using proportionate resources. That means the burglar has to practically hurl himself into the police station, admit everything and offer to pay for their inconvenience before the police will take the investigation to the next level. Like all business machines, the force is going through a drastic restructuring process that leaves them understaffed, under-resourced and undervalued. They're too busy making money from mobile speeding units and ANPR to bother about little break-ins that don't result in personal injury or death.'

'Do I detect an air of cynicism from a lawyer?' He almost smiled.

'Let's say I'm an expert in survival. Cynicism won't kill you but trust in the legal system certainly will.'

'Why do I feel safe in your hands?'

'Because I think I understand you and can empathise with your plight. We've both got a few things in common and that's violence in our past and we've both lost someone we've loved. Although neither of us want to really dwell on the past, it continues to, pardon the pun, haunt us all the same. It's time to lay our ghosts.'

'I think mine will need an exorcist.'

'Then we'll just have to go to church and find one.'

'I've got another question.'

'Shoot.'

'Since you know so much about coppers, why don't they use the personal pronoun?'

'That's easy. You don't need grammar to work a taser.'

chapter 7

THE LEGEND

'Well, I never!' Prendergast set the printed pages onto the library table and shook his head.

Sitting in the reference section of Dumfries' cosy Ewart Library, he had read everything he could on the Rerrick Parish Poltergeist and a transcript of the testament of Alexander Telfair, one of fifteen sworn witnesses to the event, in sixteen ninety five.

His research uncovered a few hints as to why Andrew Mackie and his family were being pestered by the paranormal and the rumours surrounding the incident. Some had said that Mackie was a freemason and that he'd conjured up the devil in his house by uttering the masons' 'word'. Telfair had dismissed this accusation by portraying Mackie as a man of good morals who was 'honest, civil, and harmless, beyond many of his neighbours.'

Witchcraft was also suggested and this was a time when, although the rest of the world was coming to realise there were no such things as witches, innocent people were still being strangled and burned in Galloway for the 'horrid sinne': one of them only three years after Telfair penned his account.

It appeared there had been some trouble with the supernatural at the Ring Plantation of the Ringcroft of Stocking before Mackie, and there was a submission that a man called Macknaught had failed to thrive there. In desperation, he sent his son to a witchwife in Irongray. The son, however, met up with some soldiers a short time later and ended up fighting in

Flanders. Remembering his duty to his family, however, he sent a message home with a comrade called John Redick, telling his family the witchwife's advice.

Redick visited the farmhouse but Macknaught had died and his wife gone. A man called Thomas Telfair now owned the steading and Redick related the message to him. He was to find a tooth that was lying in the house and burn it. Thomas Telfair searched the door threshold and found a tooth, just as the witchwife had said. Although he was not certain whether this tooth was from an animal or a human, he duly threw it in the fire and it apparently burned like a candle. Thomas Telfair lived at the Ringcroft of Stocking without any paranormal incident taking place.

It wasn't until February sixteen ninety five, when Andrew Mackie took over the plantation, that the strange and bizarre dominated the domestic. The trouble began in February when his cattle were set loose from their ropes and, despite making stronger bindings, he would find the beasts roaming free the next morning.

The next event, and this was the one that sent a cold chill down Prendergast's spine as he read it out loud, also concerned Mackie's cattle:

'One of them was bound with a hair-tedder to the balk of the house, so strait that the feet of the beast only touched the ground, but could not move no way else, yet it sustained no hurt.'

'Sorry, I'm late.'

Prendergast leaped from his chair with a shout as Libby plopped herself down next to him and shook the rain from her hair.

'Jumpy today?'

He scanned the tables for reproving glances but saw only curiosity hanging from the few faces who were staring at him.

'This is hair-raising stuff.'

Libby took a quick glance at the papers strewn across the table. 'Yes, I had a good look last night on the internet. Looks like someone's trying to scare the living crap out of MacAoidh by resurrecting a seventeenth century demon.'

'Or, perhaps, the legend of the Ghost Tree is true and the spirit has returned.'

'I'd rather like to believe MacAoidh's version of the truth than follow a lead that takes me beyond the grave, thanks. Strange about that cow, though.'

'Yes, very strange, but suspending a cow from the roof of a barn is not impossible. There was apparently no evidence that heavy machinery was involved. I looked around those grounds for quite a while as I waited for the emergency services and saw only the tyre tracks of MacAoidh's Discovery and my Honda.'

'So someone had to sneak in with a thirty-foot ladder and climb across the RSJ to secure the rope. Climb back down, tie up the cow and hoist it all the way up.'

'A dangerous prank for even those with the best head for heights.'

'I visited the house yesterday.'

'Yes, MacAoidh told me.'

'Did he? What did he say?'

Prendergast nodded but kept his tiny smile to himself. Libby was feigning interest and her eyes twinkled when his name was mentioned.

'He told me about Mary Hyslop from Greenbrae and the whole incident. He believes you had something to do with it.'

'I know. I think that's why he told me about his wife's death.

I think he was appealing to the compassionate side of my nature in the hope I'd repent and admit that I'm a co-conspirator. I really want him to trust me but he's so paranoid.'

'Give him time. He's stubborn but he's not stupid. I think I managed to persuade him you've no connection with Rerrick whatsoever and that you're not the type to make up stories of invisible spankings.'

'Thanks, Prendy. So what've you found out so far?'

'The case of the Mackie Poltergeist is a fascinating one, I must say, and there are some close similarities to what's been happening to our MacAoidh. The incidences in the seventeenth century began with cattle becoming untethered in the barn and roaming free. Small fires would spring up across the property and then stones were thrown at people. A stone fell on me from nowhere the night before last.' He left that thought hanging. 'That incident in MacAiodh's barn with the cow also follows the pattern. I wonder whether this is going to be the start of a very interesting case indeed.'

'It got worse, though, didn't it?'

'Much worse. Objects moving by themselves; objects disappearing then ending up somewhere else; voices; strange noises. Then the physical violence started. Listen to this:

'I was struck several times on the sides and shoulders very sharply with a great staff, so that those who were present heard the noise of the strokes. That night it threw off the bed-side, and rapped upon the chists and boards, as one calling for access.'

Libby visibly shuddered. 'That's terrifying. I'd hate to get attacked by something I couldn't see to fight.'

'Let's hope it doesn't get that far.'

'No one really got hurt, though, did they?'

'Not according to the account. Telfair reports the stones appeared half their weight and didn't do much damage. They eventually got bigger, however, and I think some drew blood. It's odd that the poltergeist seemingly became more boisterous during prayer and on the Sabbath.'

'Obviously not a Presbyterian poltergeist then!'

'Or it may not have been a poltergeist at all.'

They fell into silence, each mulling over their own personal fears.

'Telfair's account alluded to a murder which had perhaps taken place in or around the steading. Mrs Mackie apparently found some bloody bones wrapped in paper beneath a stone on the threshold to the house while the activity was at its worst. At the behest of the Laird of Colline, the magistrate called all the former residents to his house and made them touch the bones.'

'What for?'

Prendergast shrugged. 'I think they believed the earthly remains of the victim would somehow react to the murderer. They didn't, however, and the suggestion was dropped.'

'Do you think MacAoidh Armstrong could be doing all this by himself, Prendy?'

'It's possible. It's also possible he has an accomplice or two. We'll have to wait it out and see. In the meantime, against my better judgment, I'd like to spend a bit more time in that house.'

'You want it to be haunted, don't you?'

'I'd like to know either way whether the supernatural really does exist or whether it's a product of the scheming living.'

'Let me know if you find anything. I like my friends alive, thanks. If there is a real poltergeist, I don't want to be the focus of its mischief.'

'Neither do I, but I'm curious. Let's do a bit of investigating of our own. I'll check out the neighbourhood and you get close to our client.'

'How close?'

He winked. 'You're an intelligent, resourceful woman Libby, I'll leave that measure up to you.'

Chapter 8

THE VISITORS

Macaoidh was in a dark mood. Last night he'd been forced to beat out a small fire in one of the derelict stables and this morning he found his router in the upstairs bathroom smashed into a mess of broken wires and bent metal. Three mugs had been laid out rim-down on the floor in the kitchen and there were cattle roaming around his drive.

He now realised, whoever was doing this, was gaining entry into his house at will and while he was sleeping. He'd spent most of the morning on a shopping spree for security locks and a new router.

He sped across the gravel and slammed on the brakes, inches from the wide open front door. He recognised the blue Mercedes parked in the driveway without having to see the personalised number plates.

'That's all I need.' He was now very glad he'd taken the time to unpack and tidy the house

'Is this a new craze in décor or has bachelor life rendered you careless and lazy?'

His mother stood with a long brush between her perfectly manicured hands.

'Hello, Mother. What a lovely surprise.' He tried to prevent his shoulders from sagging.

'Hello darling. Since you haven't bothered to get in touch for weeks, we thought we'd take a little trip south to visit your new home and make sure you're still alive.'

'We?'

'Catherine's here too.'

'That's just grand.' His shoulders caved in with his sigh.

'Why are the beautiful boards of your hallway covered in little stones?'

He noticed the thin carpet of stones beneath her crocodile stilettos and sighed again. 'It's a very long story.' He shrugged. 'Where's Catherine?'

'She's unpacking and tidying herself up for you. I've taken the front bedroom – the only one with an assembled bed in it. Catherine rather likes the big room at the back but you'll have to put some furniture in it.'

'Later, Mother. I've got some things to do first.'

'Now, MacAoidh.'

He knew, from that stance, that look and that title, he had no choice but to pander to her whims immediately lest he suffer a verbal bashing for an hour or two. Barbara Armstrong was not a woman to be argued with and the only way was Barbara's way.

He found Catherine in front of the bathroom mirror lathering on her make-up, her thick golden hair tamed by a long plait from the crown of her head all the way down to her slim waist. He moved behind her, wrapped his arms around her body and kissed the smooth neck.

'Hi Cathy.'

She carefully placed her lipstick inside her make-up bag and turned around to face him, her hazel eyes glowing with seduction. 'I miss you, Kie.'

Her kiss was so passionate that he was forced to break away from her eventually to catch his breath. 'My mother's downstairs.' He peeled her arms from around his neck.

'Oh, come on, Kie, you're a big boy,' she raised her symmetrical eyebrows, purely to tantalise. 'Still, she's given me some chores to do now and she'll be up in a moment to make sure I've started them.'

He watched the smile turn into a churlish pout as she moved her hands underneath his shirt and hauled on his belt. 'On second thoughts, do you want to give me a hand? I'm making up our bed?'

— — —

An hour or so later, MacAoidh wandered into the kitchen where his mother sat draped upon a high stool at the butcher's block reading a magazine with a glass in her hand.

'Isn't it time for tea?'

'Yes, and I'm having a G with it, *mo ghraigh*. Would you like one?'

'No thanks, I've got some work to do.'

She peered up at him from her tortoiseshell bifocals and put the magazine down. 'Is all this really necessary, Kie? You have a beautiful house and a considerable amount of land in Assynt. Why come all this way to set up home when your people and everyone you love are hundreds of miles away? You need us.'

He sat down next to her and took her hand. He resisted the urge to raise his eyes to the ceiling when he noticed hers sparkling with unshed tears. 'I wouldn't come as far as Ullapool so long as he's alive.'

'Please don't refer to your father as if he were a stranger, Kie. He has a name. He misses you and he doesn't know how to make things right.'

'He can never make things right. He's an arrogant bigot and I will never forgive him.'

'He only wants what's right for you.'

'He only wants what's comfortable for him. Now, I don't

want to talk about him or coming home ever again. If you love me, you'll respect my wishes and leave it be.'

He groaned as his mother blotted her lids with a piece of kitchen towel and, placing her right hand against her heart, took a deep breath. He knew that meant a lecture.

'What about Catherine? Do you expect her to leave her comfortable home in Lochinver for a sheep shed in the south?'

'That's up to her.'

'No, Kie, it's up to you. The girl's a mess without you. It's such a pity you didn't meet her before ...'

'Dont!' His voice rose. 'Don't you dare.'

'... before you moved to Aberdeen. What did you think I was going to say?'

'Just drop it.' MacAoidh knew his mother well enough to know he would never get the best of her in an argument. She always played dirty by twisting his words and emotions to make him believe in the end that everything was his fault. Her mastery at manipulating the sentiments of others by resorting to subterfuge and feigning offence was remarkable. He had learned to cope with it over the years by simply ignoring her efforts as best he could.

'Are you going to marry her?'

'Who?'

'Catherine, you idiot.'

'No. We're too different.' He took a sip of his mother's drink before pouring the rest down his throat.

'You mean she's a Christian and you're an atheist.'

'There's that.'

'The sounds she was making upstairs a while ago didn't sound very Christian to me. I was forced to put kitchen towel in my ears.'

'Stop it.' He felt his face flush.

'Ha! I've made you blush.'

'No you haven't. It's the gin.' He knew she could see straight through him.

'She's hoping you'll ask her the question this weekend.'

MacAoidh slammed the glass down on the table, causing his mother to jump slightly. 'Well, it's only Friday but I doubt very much that's going to happen.' He realised he was shouting and mellowed his voice along with his temper. 'I understand you want to see me happy, Mother, and I also understand you've been grooming her for years after setting up the introduction in the first place. I know you believe Catherine to be an excellent catch for a poor bastard like me who's mourning the loss of his dead wife but …'

'That was five years ago, darling. You were very, very young. Isn't it time you moved on?'

'What do you think I'm doing now? I've moved on. I'm over it and I'll stay over it provided you stop dragging it up every time we speak.'

'Whisht. Whisht'

'Pardon?'

'What?'

'What did you just say?' Barbara stood at the kitchen window pouring herself another drink.

'I didn't say anything. You told me to whisht.'

'No. That wasn't me. I don't use the vernacular. If I wanted you to stop talking I would've said shut up.'

'Kie.'

They spun around in unison to see Catherine staggering across the hallway in her bathrobe. She held her hand to her head. There was shampoo and blood in her hair.

MacAoidh took a step towards her but she flew backwards as if she had been given a sudden and violent shove. Her back hit the front door and she crumpled to the floor, opened her mouth and screamed.

— — —

It took the remainder of the afternoon to calm Catherine down. A stone had hit her on the head while she was in the shower and made a small gash in her temple. It was only a minor injury but it bothered MacAoidh who believed, whoever was doing this, was becoming more desperate and certainly more aggressive.

They sat in the living room and talked for a while about small events MacAoidh had missed and the trivialities of the people he knew, but the conversation still kept coming back to the incident with Catherine.

'I can't help wondering why people see fit to throw stones through a bathroom window unless they want to hurt someone.' Barbara sat at the piano and tinkled some Debussy from the keys.

MacAoidh sat at the end of the sofa with Catherine's head in his lap. He stroked her hair and now and again she would touch his fingers with her own as a gesture of contentment.

'Just stop worrying about it.'

'It was probably that ghastly youth I caught staring through the kitchen window this afternoon.'

'What did he look like?' At last he had a lead.

Barbara shrugged her silk shoulders while she played. 'Blondish hair, pink cheeks, mischievous eyes. I didn't get a chance to look at him properly because he ran off when I shouted at him.'

'Which way did he run?'

'I didn't watch him go, darling. He just left and jolly good riddance, I must say. You really should put some gates up around the property. Gates, railings and a barbed wire fence.'

'What about a mine field?'

They laughed together.

'Why have neither of you spoken about what happened to me in the hallway?' Catherine, who had been silent for most of the afternoon, had obviously spent her time thinking about the implausible.

'What do you think happened to you?'

Barbara stopped playing.

'Something pushed me, Kie. It pushed me hard. So hard, in fact, that the impact threw me into the door. You saw it. Why are you both pretending you didn't?'

'You were in shock, dear, and quite frankly I really don't know what I saw. It all happened so quickly. I thought you'd tripped and fallen backwards.'

'Ten feet is a long way backwards, Barbara.'

MacAoidh gave her hand a reassuring squeeze. 'There'll be a perfectly rational explanation for it all.'

'It didn't happen to you, Kie. Maybe if it did, you'd find God at last.'

'God damn!' MacAoidh rose so quickly that Catherine tumbled to the floor with a squeal. 'There's that fire alarm again.'

He leaped into the hallway and took the stairs three at a time. A thin plume of smoke trailed from his bedroom door while the alarm shrieked. Cursing, he threw the door open to find his sheets ablaze in the centre of the bed. He managed to beat out the fire with a pillow and his temper rose with every blow.

'That's enough!' he roared and bounded back down the stairs. 'Mother, chuck a bucket of water over my mattress. I'm going out. I'll be back shortly.' His hand touched the door handle. 'And lock the door after me,' he yelled as an afterthought.

Driving through the heavy rain, his windscreen wipers

beating at the speed of his heart, MacAoidh's temper had consumed him. The Land Rover came to an abrupt halt with a screaming of tires and he slammed the door shut with such force that the bang resounded around the hillside. He marched across to the village hall, which seeped orange light and muffled voices, and he burst through the doors with the impact of an exploded grenade.

'Enough is enough!' He yelled.

Soaking wet and fuming with anger, MacAoidh stood at the door with his hands on his hips and glowered at the stunned faces around the table.

'MacAoidh Armstrong, this is a meeting of the community council,' a middle-aged man with a grey beard, probably the chairman, could not hide his outrage.

'Good, I hope you're all here because I have something to say to the committee.'

'I'm afraid you're not on the agenda, Mr Armstrong. Put your comments in writing and we'll discuss them at the next meeting.' The chairman's voice faltered half way through his sentence but he remained composed and managed to finish it without whimpering.

'You've had your fun. Now I'm telling you to leave me alone. I'm here to stay whether you like it or not and there's nothing, and I mean nothing,' his eyes flashed dangerously, 'you can do to me that will make me change my mind. Is that clear?'

'Sit doon, son, and stop makin' a dick o' yersel'. None of us hae ony idea whit yer rantin' aboot.'

MacAoidh, in his rage, didn't notice James Black at the table but his cordial words, said with sympathy and compassion, completely disarmed him.

'No thanks, Jim, best not. I've said my piece and hope that'll be the end of it.'

He turned around and left the committee to decide how they would get their shocked mouths to eventually close.

chapter 9

THE DINNER PARTY

'So run me through this again. We're not to speak of anything that's happened at The Ring and certainly not mention the poltergeist. We can't talk about the assault charge and we have to pretend that we're good friends of his?' Libby didn't think she'd be able to remember all the rules, especially after a few drinks.

'We don't have to pretend we're best friends. I think he just wants to dilute his mother for an evening. She doesn't think he has any friends here so she's been going around the locality trying to enlist a few. She's driving him mad, he says.'

'God, what an interfering old cow, and she looks so sweet in her photo. Tell me, did he really ask me to come too or did you suggest I tag along?'

'He asked for you by name.'

'Do I look all right?'

Prendergast smiled and straightened the strap on her shoulder. 'You look lovely, lass. We'll be fighting for your attention all evening.'

With a wide smile, she took the arm he offered and he rapped on the door.

'Do me a favour,' she whispered to him as she peered through the glass panel and saw MacAoidh's silhouette approaching, 'don't let me drink too much. I get a bit rude when I'm drunk.'

'What ruder than you are when you're sober? This I *have* to see!'

She caught her breath as her handsome host answered the

door with a wild smile. She was delighted to see his tie was the same colour as her sapphire blue dress, but he wore a plain white shirt and black trousers, where her dress had a plunging sweetheart neckline and its sequined bodice showed off her curves to their shameful best.

'Andrew,' his nod was respectful but not stiff as he shook his hand. 'And, wow, Libby, you look …'

'Sensational,' she decided to finish his sentence for him before he fell over. She was pleased with her choice of attire tonight which had the desired effect on her host and she wouldn't lose her momentum. She shoved the bottle of wine in his hand and her kiss lingered on his cheek. 'Nice aftershave and I'll forgive you for staring at my breasts.'

'I'm not wearing aftershave and I wasn't…' She wafted past him into the sitting room. 'This is my mother. You may call her Ma'am. Ma'am, this is Libby Butler and Andrew Prendergast, the private investigator you landed on me.' His wink told Prendergast there was no offence meant.

His mother replied with a well-practised ingratiating smile. 'It's Barbara to you.' Ignoring Libby she held a perfumed hand out to Prendergast. 'Kie's feeling a bit playful tonight.'

'Good,' the word left Libby's mouth before she could stop it. 'I mean, that's good. Playful is better than boring or dull. Isn't it? I like playful men.'

She wished she'd stayed at home when Barbara raised her smooth eyebrows. At least the woman now acknowledged she was there at all.

'How's life down on the farm?' Libby decided to swiftly move on.

'The farm?'

'Yes, MacAoidh told me you have a farm in Sutherland.'

'Did he now?'

The conversation had obviously taken a turn for the worse. 'Your photograph doesn't do you justice at all.'

'Oh?' Barbara stood at the window in a cascading pink silk dress that had more material in it than a parachute. Holding her champagne glass like a lamp in the darkness, she reminded Libby of the Statue of Liberty: tall, significant and stone cold.

'I'm not saying it doesn't look like you, because it definitely does.' She floundered in self-doubt as Barbara glared at her through ice-blue eyes. 'It's just ... I do love your dress.' She pondered on the outcome of ending the evening abruptly by leaping out the bay window and avoiding any further humiliation.

'Thank you. It's important to dress well for dinner. What on earth made you wear all those sparkly sequins? They make you look like one of those garish disco balls.'

'On second thoughts, you actually look nothing like your picture.' Libby didn't understand why Barbara felt she deserved that insult.

'Which picture would that be? Kie has so many.'

'The one on the piano.'

MacAoidh waggled the photograph at his mother, a half smile creasing his lips.

'That's Betty, Kie's nanny.'

Libby snatched the glass of fizzy from MacAoidh's hand and downed it in one gulp. He filled it up with a frown.

'I've never been to Sutherland, Barbara.' Prendergast at last came to her rescue while MacAoidh left the room. She could hear his burst of laughter as he hit the hallway. 'I've been as far as Glasgow ...'

'Hello, I'm Catherine.'

Everyone's focus of attention shifted towards the woman with the soft voice. Catherine shimmered towards her in a surge of light hair that Libby fancied was woven out of the finest strands of pure twenty-four carat gold. Her eyes shone like dark moonstones and her skin was smoother than the delicate silk of her pale pink dress. She looked like a fragile alabaster carving: smooth, well-crafted and over-exaggerated. Libby wished she'd remembered to put a hammer in her handbag.

'Catherine is Kie's partner,' Barbara trumpeted her worthy title in the style of a court herald. 'We're working on something a little more permanent, aren't we Catherine?'

'You're making me blush, Barbara.'

'That would have to be some flush to get noticed under all that war paint,' Libby muttered to Prendergast who squeezed her arm in sympathy.

'So, are you the cook?' She had to say something.

'Oh Lord, no,' Catherine's voice tinkled like a fountain in a garden centre. 'We don't go in the kitchen. Kie is a fabulous cook and he's done everything, even laid the table and washed up. It's Italian tonight. My favourite.'

'We are spoiled,' Libby bared her teeth in a semblance of a grin. 'Champagne and Italian.' She raised her glass.

'That's Prosecco.'

The poor effort to keep up the good manners was exhausting her and Libby was no longer in the mood for superficial pleasantries. 'No, yours is Prosecco, mine's empty.'

She ignored the disapproving glare from 'Mother' and concentrated her full attention on the Venus de Milo who was testing her skills on crushing her opposition with a mere flick of her false nails.

'Keep the old bitch busy, I'm going to tether another cow to the rafters.' She patted Prendergast's shoulder as she glided past him and towards her latest prey.

'Nice aftershave.' Libby now realised why MacAoidh smelled

so good as Catherine's perfume attacked the sensitive lining of her sinuses.

'So, Libby is it? How did you meet Kie?' Catherine teetered backwards on her strappy heels as Libby closed the gap between them.

Libby's eyes met with those of her host as he filled up her glass and joined the conversation with his mother and Prendergast. Now and again he would take a quick glance at her and she knew he was worried about what they would be talking about. She remembered the list of rules of what she could not say and so thought she would have some fun making up some of her own.

'Our meeting was accidental, actually, at a holiday centre on Loch Ken. He was in the next caravan to mine.'

'Caravan?'

Libby had to bite the smile from her lip as MacAoidh's head snapped towards Catherine and then to her. His eyes narrowed.

'Yes, you know those wooden things on wheels that look like a little home and are normally occupied by working class people on holiday.' She leaned forward to whisper, 'Don't be fooled by what you're told, caravans are quite comfortable really and very commodious. Some are even quite plush and a few have a porch in which to park your Hunter Wellies.'

'Really?'

'Anyway, MacAoidh and his friends were a little rowdy one night.'

'His friends?'

'Yes, the ones from the scheme in the town.'

'What's a scheme?'

'You know, those strips of urban land set aside for ugly rows of terraced houses where dirty little people who can't afford a real home live.' Libby now noticed the conversation in the room had stilled and all ears were pointed towards her. The attention only served to make her worse. 'I think they all had a few too many bottles of Buckfast and were playing their gangsta rap far too loud.'

'Gangster?'

'No gangst-A, you know that violent sub-genre of classical music called hip-hop where all the artists shoot each other before, during and after performances. Anyway, the whole camp was complaining and children were crying. I couldn't sleep, so decided to go over there and ask them to turn it down. I found MacAoidh throwing up into his Hunters with his trousers round his ankles and that's how we met. I took him to hospital that night to get his stomach pumped. We've been friends ever since.'

'Good lord, is that true?' Catherine had the look of one who had just borne witness to a miracle by the almighty.

'Brownies' honour.' Libby held up her two fingers in the appropriate salute.

'Dinner time.' MacAoidh grabbed Libby by the arm and hauled her towards the dining room. 'I heard all that and so did my mother. Are you trying to start a war?'

'What, with your snotty girlfriend? She's not worth the fight.'

'No, I mean with my mother. Now she's going to think I can't cope.'

Libby snatched her arm away from his grip. 'Grow up MacAoidh. Why should you give a damn about what your mother thinks of you? You're an adult in case you didn't notice. And what's wrong with holiday caravans? Is the thought of spending precious relaxation time in a trailer so repulsive to you? Most people can't afford an annual ski trip to Courchevel and poor folk think Necker Island is a piece of land in the middle of a motorway where underage teens go for a quickie.'

'Wo! Libby, where's this coming from?' He pulled her into the kitchen by the waist while Prendergast took the initiative to lure his hostesses into the dining room.

'I abhor snobbery.'

'So do I. What makes you think I'm pretentious?'

'You're bred from the same stable as those two snooty women in there, MacAoidh, and you're the prize stallion. The yarn I spun Catherine outraged you because it made you lose face.' She noticed he still held her by the waist, even though he had no idea where his hands were resting.

'You've read me wrong, Libby. My life's more complicated than it looks and I don't understand why you would want to disgrace me in the first place.'

'Disgrace? See what I mean. Don't posh people get drunk with peasants?'

'I meant launch a personal attack.'

'Peasants don't have nannies, MacAoidh. They also can't afford top of the range four by fours that cost four times more than their entire council house development cost to build. I'll bet you had a chauffeur, a couple of maids and a butler while you were growing up in the wilds of Sutherland.'

'You forgot to mention the wet nurse and the eunuchs who shovelled the snow from my delicate feet.' His face was now so close to hers that she felt his breath on her cheek. She didn't want to close her eyes for fear of falling. She was beginning to enjoy his sense of humour and the way those eyes sparked when he was angry was slowly disarming her.

'Can I help you serve the first course?' She felt her back pressing against the wall and the sweat dripping down her spine. She peeled his fingers from either side of her waist.

He took a step back, suddenly realising he'd breached her

personal space and obviously felt ashamed for doing so. 'No, please take a seat at the dinner table. I've whipped the slaves soundly today, so you won't be able to cause any further insurrection.'

Libby picked up a bottle on her way to the dining room and filled up one of the neatly arranged crystal glasses by her place setting. Cathy and Barbara were speaking together in Gaelic while Prendergast, locked out of the conversation, studied the bare walls and sipped at his wine in silence.

'Would anyone like some?' She couldn't understand the looks of confusion on the faces around the table. She turned her attention to the bottle and refused to feel any further humiliation when she read 'Olive Oil' on the label. 'It's extra virgin.' She took a small sip.

No one laughed.

MacAoidh removed the bottle, snatched the glass from her hand and pushed something drinkable between her fingers. He didn't say a word.

'Andrew was just saying you two worked together on a serial killer case in London. How interesting.'

Libby turned her head to her left and focused her eyes on Barbara who sat at the head of the table. 'We weren't actually working together. We started off our relationship as enemies until we realised we were fighting for the same cause.'

'Yes, former enemies do make the very best of friends.'

'Libby and I have certainly found that to be the case, Barbara.' Prendergast added with a warm smile.

'Both Catherine and I had to work very hard on Kie to grab his attention, didn't we Cathy?'

'I don't think he liked me very much at first, Barbara.' Cathy giggled.

'No, but we turned him around eventually and I must say

I've hardly seen the pair of them. They're either having sex or in the shower.'

'Cleanliness is next to godliness.' Libby curled her lip.

'Hallelujah to that. And how do you both manage a relationship, with one in Scotland and the other in London? Does your wife know of your affair, Andrew?'

MacAoidh almost dropped the platters of antipasti. Libby's lower jaw hit the table while Prendergast choked on his wine. Catherine was obviously suspicious of Libby's relationship with MacAoidh as her brown eyes now narrowed dangerously. This was one cow that certainly would not be strung up without a fight.

'You know, Catherine, contrary to popular opinion, there is such a thing as a platonic relationship between the sexes. Although I both respect and admire Andrew, I don't look on him as lover material. Conversely, he has a wonderful relationship with his wife and would never see me, nor any other woman to that matter, as a potential mistress. He's not the type to have affairs. He's wholesome, loyal and honest and I find your observation both inaccurate and highly offensive as it was purely intended to debase either me, Andrew or both of us. Now, I don't care what you think of me but I won't allow you to upset or distress my good friend.'

'Catherine meant no offence, Libby.'

It was Barbara's turn for a reckoning. 'Your son is a good man with a mind and body of his own but you treat him like an expensive thoroughbred that requires a strict retraining programme. What gives you the right to choose his friends, his lovers or his way of life, Barbara? You may be his mother but you act like his agent.'

'Sorry,' MacAoidh slammed his hands on the table sending his glass spinning into the air. 'This is too far. I can't deal with this. I'm going to bed. Libby, Andrew, thanks for coming. I hope you all manage to finish dinner without killing each other. I'll get my butler to mop the blood up in the morning.'

He left the company for the evening, leaving his astounded mother and tearful girlfriend to host their silent guests.

Chapter 10

THE TRUCE

'Ok, ok, coming, coming.'

Libby rolled out of bed, picked herself off the carpet, threw on her housecoat and pushed her feet into a pair of slippers when she heard the banging on the door. The postman was always heavy fisted with the knocker but this time he was trying to break her door down.

'Wait a minute, it's Sunday.' She threw the door open and stood inside the frame clutching the front of her housecoat. She squealed as MacAoidh rudely shouldered her out the way, his face red and twisted in rage. 'Do come in.' She closed the door behind him.

He stood with his back to her, his breathing heavy, his fists knotted into tight balls.

'What the hell was all that about?'

He spun around to face her. Shock registered on his expression but was gone in an instant. She realised she must've looked like a bag lady in her tatty gown, vertical hair and pink, fluffy slippers. All she needed to complete the look was a half empty bottle of Buckie. She wished she'd taken time to dress.

'I invite you for dinner. You come, you offend and you leave.'

'Your girlfriend and your mother were rude, so I simply returned the sentiment.'

'You started it.' His expression was one of utter disbelief. 'My mother wants to sue you for defamation.'

'Tell her to bring it on. I'll spin my defence out for a while, postpone the proceedings a couple of times and then plead veritas. I'll come out laughing and she'll get a hernia lifting her solicitor's bill off the front door mat.'

'A nice way to treat ordinary folk. I thought you'd given up on being a ruthless bitch.'

'Your mother doesn't fit into the classification of ordinary folk, MacAoidh. Anyway, I'm sure a little kiss from their best boy is all that's necessary to have Mummy-wummy and Cathy-wathy eating out of your paws again.' She crossed her arms and waited for the next yell.

'They've left, and both of them in tears, thanks to you.' MacAoidh was so angry with her, he was in danger of exploding and taking her house with him. 'Why were you so uncivil? What did any of us do to you?'

'Why did you lead me to believe you're a farmer's boy and that picture of your nanny was your mother?'

'I didn't. You just assumed it.'

'You could've corrected me and spared me the humiliation. You could also have offered some support when your mother was being outrageously rude to me.'

'You're more than capable of looking after yourself, Libby. Besides, you got to her. You actually managed to offend her. I was enjoying watching her squirm.'

'At my expense?' she didn't mean to yell.

'So that's what this is all about? I was beginning to believe you harboured some personal grudge against me.'

'Look, MacAoidh, I'm sorry I ruined your dinner party and …'

'You're not sorry. You're incapable of such fine sentiment. What gives you the right to judge the character of others when your own is so venomous, unpleasant and vindictive?'

'Is that what you came to do? Insult me? Well consider

your mission accomplished.' His words hurt. She felt her heart stinging. 'We're equal. Now, get out.' She felt the traitorous tears welling inside her eyes, but could do nothing about them. The more she tried not to cry, the harder they fell. She cursed her inability to restrain her inner emotions.

To her surprise, the effect of her tears on MacAoidh was devastating and he simply crumpled. He slid his back down the wall, landed on the ground with his legs splayed out in front of him and buried his face in his hands.

'I'm sorry, Libby. I'm very quick to rile. It's a failing of mine. It wasn't my intention to hurt you. Forgive me.'

'I think I should be the one to be dishing out the apologies. I ruined your evening and you were such a gracious host. In fact, you're a really pleasant person all round and I've got an attitude problem. I'm excellent at making enemies but not so good at keeping friends. You didn't deserve that and I'm happy to write to your mother with sycophantic, snivelling apologies before she slaps her lawyers into action. I don't want to be the reason why they've cut their stay short.'

'There's no need and you're not the only reason why they left.'

'Oh?' She sat down next to him and waited for him to formulate his words. MacAoidh Armstrong, when he wasn't in a rage, was a cautious speaker.

He brought his knees up to his chest and pulled his hand through his shaggy fringe. 'I've seen things over the past few days that've shaken my obsession with the plausible. I don't believe the spirits of the dead can rise from the grave and haunt the living but I'm beginning to believe in the existence of forces of nature beyond our ken.' He threw his head up and his laugher was shaded with bitterness.

'What's happened?' He looked so broken that she put her

hand on his. He curled his fingers around hers, obviously grateful for the comforting gesture. 'Can I get you anything? Coffee? Fruit juice? Water? A glass of olive oil?'

She made him smile at least.

'This morning I woke up to another fire in the old barn. It wasn't too fierce and I put it out easily with a blanket. When I stepped back in the house, there was a layer of small stones lying all over the hallway, hundreds of them, chuckies from the drive. I've no idea how they got there or who would've had time to throw them into the house behind my back. This is the second time something like this has happened.'

'Do you think you're in danger?'

'If a fire catches in the house when I'm asleep, then I'll burn to death. Yes, it's dangerous but, so far, I believe they've just been warnings.'

'Prendy's on the case. He's planning a stake-out to catch the perpetrators in the act.'

He didn't seem to hear her. 'Last night, I woke up to Catherine's screams. She was hysterical. She says the duvet was pulled off the bed. She says she tried to pull it back but it was yanked from her hands and hurled across the room.'

'She could've been dreaming.'

'Aye, that's true, but twice I've awoken and found my duvet lying on the other side of the room. How would she know that?'

'There's got to be an explanation, whether it be a scientific or paranormal one.'

'There's no such things as the paranormal, Libby. That's what they want me to think, don't you see? I just need to catch someone in the act and I'll sleep better at nights.'

'Look, Kie. Can I call you that?'

'Why not? Everyone else I know does.'

'I witnessed Mary Hyslop being spanked by an unseen hand. I heard those blows. I know I did. Now I've been thinking a lot about that incident. It's highly possible she used some form of trickery, perhaps even hypnosis, on us to make us believe what we saw to be true.'

'That's a good and intelligent suggestion. Why didn't I think of that?'

'Because you're too close to it and too busy losing your temper to think wisely.'

'Aye, right.'

'Now, it's also very possible there's something under the ground, some magnetic force perhaps, that's causing stones to apparently fly into your house.'

He nodded as if deep in thought.

'I have another suggestion. I'll cancel my appointments next week and Prendy and I will come and stay in the house to be your eyes and ears. We'll keep the windows and doors locked and CCTV in a couple of key places would also be a good idea.'

'Thank you, Libby, you're a good friend.'

'You know, there is a danger we may not be able to come up with a solid explanation. What then?'

'Then you can call the ghostbusters in.'

She rose and held her hand out to him. 'All right, Mr Armstrong, let's lay our ghosts by whatever means necessary. We'll start as soon as possible. I'll get Prendy out of his comfortable bed and we'll be over tomorrow afternoon. Is that too soon for you?'

She saw the sparkle in those eyes as they made contact with hers and doubted if he was taking her seriously. He rose and, with a small smile, closed the front of her gown that had fallen open leaving little of her dignity to his imagination.

'You were speaking about failings,' she choked in

embarrassment, 'mine's exposing myself to men I hardly know.'

'I'll see you tomorrow afternoon. You should bring that gown with you.'

Libby stood at the door for long moments, squeezing the mortification from her eyes and wondering how she was ever going to face him again without blushing.

Chapter 11

THE TRAP

'Oh no.' Libby spied Kie dangling from a rope and harness at the top of a tree with a chainsaw in his hand.

'What's the matter?'

'He had to have his shirt off.'

'What's wrong with that? It's a good day and he's working.'

'He's got a really lovely body,' her words fell from her lips with an appreciative sigh. 'He makes Bear Grylls look like a Cheeky Girl.'

Prendergast laughed as he parked the car in the drive. 'Don't worry, Libby, I'm sure you'll get very close to him before the week's out.'

She twisted her mouth. 'No, Prendy, everything's changed now I know he's got a girlfriend. I promised I would never take another woman's man and I'm keeping to that. Even though that woman's a snobby cow.'

'That's very noble of you, lass, but it won't last.'

They waved to Kie as he hauled himself to ground level and removed his harness on a low branch. With an athletic leap, his heavy boots sent the gravel flying in all directions as he landed.

'What are you doing?'

'I'm setting up motion sensor cameras around the steading. I needed to take some branches down to get a good view of the front of the house.'

'You're going to need a lot of wire.'

Kie picked up his T-shirt and scrubbed the sweat from his

neck with it before pulling it on. 'It's wireless. I can route the analogue cameras via CoAx to the DVR and pipe it to the TV, the laptop and even my iPad via a distribution amp. It's simple, effective and will, hopefully, catch the bastards at work.'

'I understood all that, did you?'

Prendy shook his head. 'No.'

'Neither did I actually.'

Kie laughed. 'I'll bring your bags in. Please go inside and make yourselves at home. My house is yours. I don't have any rules apart from blazing fires are forbidden inside the house and outbuildings.'

'It's a really lovely house, you know.'

Libby stood next to him facing the front aspect. It was a tall, traditionally built building in whitewashed stone with small windows in the older part. There were obvious signs of later extensions with a contemporary conservatory and huge bay windows looking out to sea. The house was flanked on one side by a neat row of derelict outbuildings which, together with a number of tall ornamental trees dotted around the grounds, gave the setting an elegant but rustic charm. Its aspect, however, was ruined by the addition of a huge modern barn that dominated the site and spoiled the views from the south facing part of the house.

'Are you going to keep that big ugly barn?'

'I could use it but I may sell it or move it to a place where I can't see it from my window. Dismantling it is just another job on my list that I've been forced to put back. I'd like it moved or gone before the autumn though.'

'Have you had any further visitations since yesterday morning?'

'Just a few things gone missing and turning up in strange places, but that could be put down to my poor state of mental health at the moment.'

'You swore you wouldn't let all this get to you.'

'Easier said.'

— — —

They spent the afternoon adding battery operated smoke alarms to the existing ones wired to the electrical system and erecting motion sensor spotlights in and around the outbuildings.

Libby had enjoyed her day working with Kie and decided there was nothing on the practical side of work he couldn't do. Everything about him impressed her. Watching him wiring a plug for her bedside lamp, she was ashamed to admit she had been wrong about him. He was not like his mother at all: a woman who was too afraid of chipping her nail polish to help her son in the kitchen when he had friends coming for dinner.

They sat in the conservatory with the view across the hills to the sea. The evening sun, captured inside all that glass, was so hot that Libby felt she was slowly melting away to a large puddle on the tiles.

'Do you want to move to somewhere cooler?' He must've noticed her sweat marks.

'No, I need to boil. It's so rare the sun comes out in this part of the world that I want to take as much advantage of it as I can. You could do with a pool on these grounds.'

'What would I do with a pool?'

'I was just thinking …' Prendergast, who sat poring over pieces of A4 print-outs and taking notes on a reporter's pad, had been silent until now. 'Your theory of hypnosis could be sound.'

'How's that then?'

'We know it can be done, Libby. We've witnessed such feats in action.'

'Yes, but please don't mention any names.'

'Don't worry,' Prendergast sighed, 'I wouldn't like to go through all that again.'

'Is this a private conversation?' Kie put down his screwdriver.

'It's a long story, son, and I'll tell it to you one day when I'm over it. It *is* possible that someone's using hypnosis on you which causes you to function at times in a sort of altered state of awareness.'

'How can that be done?'

Prendergast shrugged. 'Sometimes a word or a sound can be used to induce this altered state of mind and sometimes a light or sequence of flashes. I'm no expert, but I've been reading there are a few well-known techniques of hypnotic induction and it's possible that one or more of them are being used on you and perhaps certain members of the community.'

'So you think someone's going around clicking their fingers at people and sneaking into their subconscious?' Kie didn't look convinced. 'I think I'd know if someone was messing about in my head. I'm not the kind of man whose persuasions are easily manipulated.'

'If you were conscious it was happening, you would be able to call on your natural stubbornness to fight it off. If you're not aware of it, however, how would you defend yourself? I've heard you say at times you were going insane. Perhaps this is a symptom of flicking from normal consciousness to sub-consciousness.'

'I don't like it, but I see your reasoning. It's a perfectly logical explanation. I'd rather believe in that than believe in the return of the Rerrick Parish Poltergeist.'

'OK,' Libby joined the conversation with lively enthusiasm. 'Let's say Kie's mind is intermittently addled by third-party intervention which makes him see and hear things that are not real and let's say that some of the villagers, like Jim Black and Mary Hyslop, are compelled by hypnosis to come to The Ring and act out their spankings sub-consciously. We agree all that's plausible.' She waited for the nods. 'Who's doing it and why?'

'I wonder if it's something to do with the death of that Ghost Tree in truth.' Prendergast continued his musings. 'I heard Jim Black put a copper nail into it some years back.'

'He would need to have hammered a copper pipe into a tree that size to kill it.'

'Does copper kill trees? I thought that was a myth.' Libby was genuinely interested.

'If it gets into the root system it does. Copper damages the cell growth of a tree. If the tree's already unhealthy, it won't have much of a chance of survival after being poisoned by copper.'

'Hmmm,' Libby wondered if there was anything on the planet MacAoidh Armstrong didn't know.'

Prendergast cleared his throat. 'My point is perhaps someone is angry at Black for killing the tree. Maybe someone who's into ecology.'

'We're looking for a bunny-loving tree-hugger with homicidal tendencies then?'

'Whoever it is, with whatever motive, purposefully singled out Black and Mary Hyslop who, incidentally, is Jim Black's sister in law. Both of them have had more than their fair share of bad luck over the years. She lost a son ten years back just after Jim lost all his wintering cattle in a barn fire. He's apparently never recovered financially.'

'Did Mrs Hyslop's boy die?'

'No, he apparently disappeared.'

'How awful for her.' Libby immediately forgave the woman for her rudeness. 'So it may be that all this is happening to teach Jim Black a lesson for his bit in destroying the planet?'

'And its focus is on my property because this is where the poltergeist legend originated.'

'With all that hardware set up around the premises, we should know the identity of our perpetrator by tonight if he or she dares to strike.'

'By heavens, Mr Sherlock and Mr Holmes, this excellent piece of detective work calls for a celebratory drink. Mr Sherlock's favourite tipple!' Libby hauled the bottle of single malt from her handbag and grinned.

– – –

With all the will in the world and enough whisky in her circulation to anaesthetise a small elephant, Libby still could not sleep.

Lying awake in the early hours of the morning in a strange bed that smelled of the stockroom and new plastic, all she could think about was ghosts, rattling chains and objects moving around in the dark all by themselves. Although she didn't really believe in ghosts, she was grateful for her bedside light which remained switched on since she got into bed and she kept a firm hold of the end of her duvet, just in case some unseen hands attempted to swipe it from her.

Despite her certainty that the phenomena at The Ring could be put down to human mischief, she couldn't help but wonder if there was such a thing as the Rerrick Parish Poltergeist, whose violent antics had been recorded by an upstanding member of the church along with fourteen other eminent and dependable witnesses.

She tried her best to think of other things in her life and particularly fantasised about a steamy relationship with MacAoidh Armstrong but, every time she heard a sound, she imagined a shadow in the room.

She thought about turning off the light and trying her best to sleep, but she had to admit to herself she was far too frightened to leave her imagination to the darkness.

There had been a time when Libby had a psychotic fear of the dark, but that had left her two years ago after her encounter with Gabriel Radley.

She thought of Gabriel and allowed those wonderful memories to soothe her troubled mind. She conjured up his face and smiled, feeling at peace for the first time since she went to bed. She snuggled into the deep duvet, reached over to the light switch and turned it off.

Libby leaped from the bed in terror when strong light poured through the window in a series of loud bangs as all the floodlights came on at once.

She heard heavy footsteps running down the stairs and the front door bang open. She raced for the light on the far wall and flicked it on before beginning a frantic search for her jeans and a T-shirt in her unpacked bag. She threw on her clothes, half ran, half tumbled down the stairs and out into the light. More floodlights at the front of the house fired up like flares and she had to squint against their glare.

'Jesus Christ!' Kie's roar was like the howling of a desolate wolf.

She ran towards the sound of his voice and stopped dead when she saw the back of his figure standing alone with his legs splayed open, one hand holding on to his jeans, the other balled by his side. Haloed by the dazzling flare of floodlights, he looked like a man who had just stumbled out of a lifetime of darkness and was seeing the moon for the first time.

'Oh my god!' She choked out her disbelief.

The big barn had gone, its space filled with empty dark countryside. MacAoidh Armstrong stood high up in the centre of a sea of metal sheets and columns, neatly laid out on the ground, the black silhouettes of cattle encircling him.

chapter 12

THE DECISION

'Tae hell with this!' Kie banged his fist against the keyboard and swore again. He took another glug of black coffee, cracked his knuckles and buried his nose in the laptop for one more time. His heavy boot continued its incessant drumming against the kitchen tiles.

Libby and Prendergast exchanged concerned looks behind his back.

'You've been at it all night, Kie. There's nothing but static from those cameras. Static, me, a few cattle and you trying to stop yourself mooning at the moon.'

'There has to be something else.' He was in no mood for her humour. His fingers stabbed the cursor keys with such force he was in danger of smashing his computer.

She put her hand over his and was surprised at how cold it was. 'Give it up for today. You've had a bad shock. You need to rest.'

He snatched his hand away from her. She noticed it was shaking. 'I'll rest when I work out how this was done.'

'Is it possible to disassemble that barn in a night?'

'Not without the aid of machinery and a big work force. That barn's made of solid, extremely heavy metal. We would've heard it coming down from Glasgow.'

'So you're saying what happened last night was an impossible feat?'

'I don't know anything anymore.' He leaned back on the legs

of his chair and pulled at his hair. 'Fuck! A few stones, I can deal with, but this is too weird.' The chair legs squealed against the tiles as he suddenly rose and left the house, slamming the door behind him.

'He's right, Prendy. This *is* too weird. What are we going to do now?'

Prendergast sat at the butcher's block eating his toast. 'We may have to concede there are forces working here that we don't understand and maybe never will.'

'You'll never convince Mr Practical.'

'Not yet, anyway, but he may be forced to open his mind if this gets any worse and, if the legend of the poltergeist turns out to be real, things will get a lot worse before they get better.'

'God, that's so frightening. I'm not sure whether I'll be able to sleep in the house for another night.'

'Me neither, but we're professional, intelligent people, Libby. We'll do what we have to.'

'What do you suggest?'

'It wouldn't hurt to get a team of paranormal investigators in. You never know, they may be able to give us a vital lead.'

'There's no way he'll agree to that.'

'He may have to. We've run out of theories and, with no clear evidence of human intervention, we have to turn our minds towards the implausible, if nothing else but to rule it out.'

'I'll speak to him.'

'I'm certain you can be more persuasive than I,' he winked.

— — —

Libby found MacAoidh at the Ghost Tree. He stood at the base of the tree with his broad back leaning against the trunk and his arms folded. He was speaking to a man in a green jacket who had a strange haze around him. She trudged across the field, avoiding the muddy patches, and hoped the man he was speaking to was a real person and not a ghost.

'Thought I'd find you here.' She stopped to catch her breath. 'Hi, I'm Libby, a friend of MacAoidh's.'

'Jim Black,' the man returned. He had a haunted look in his eyes but the haze had gone. 'We'll speak mair later, lad.' He tipped his cap at Kie and ambled off across the field.

'Sorry, did I interrupt something important?'

Kie had calmed down and placed his hands flat against the dead trunk. 'Not really. We were just exchanging ghost stories.' His laughter was mirthless. 'Jim did kill this tree with a copper band. See the deep marks at the base? Now he's too frightened to chop it down and use it to keep his house warm.'

'He believes in the story?'

'He says he has every reason to believe it's true.' He dropped his arms to his sides and hung his head. 'Jim Black is a practical man with a strong body and a stout heart, yet he believes something is haunting him and he's terrified beyond his own capacity to fear.'

'Is he experiencing similar phenomena on his property?' Libby idly picked at the dead branches.

'He says he's been beaten twice and one stone that was hurled at him struck him on the side of the head and drew blood. He says the missiles are getting bigger and more painful when they hit him.'

She followed him back down the hill towards the house. 'He hears voices, has seen ghostly figures and his cattle are constantly breaking through his boundaries and wandering on to my land. He says he's tried his best to mend the fences but every morning he finds a new hole. The trouble, as he calls it, takes place mainly in his home and on the south side of his land: the side that borders mine and an area that once comprised the subjects of the Ring Plantation before it was split in two and the parts sold off to separate owners. He offered to sell off his share to me at a bargain price. Can you believe that?'

'It's very unusual for a working farmer to sell off his land, especially at below market price. If he can cope with his fears, however, you certainly will get through this.'

'Cope? Tae heck, no! He hasn't been sober for weeks.'

'Maybe that's a good idea.'

'Ghosts don't frighten me.'

'What about the unexplained?'

'That confuses me, but certainly doesn't scare me. There are many more things to be frightened of in life and a poltergeist, whatever that is, is not one of them.'

'So you're telling me you wouldn't be scared if a ghost manifested itself right in front of you?'

'Why should I? What could it do to me apart from chuck a few stones, slap me around a little and start fires in my house?'

'God, you're brave.'

'I'm not brave, just realistic.'

'Well let's see how realistic you are prepared to be. Prendy says things could get a lot worse.'

'And how's he figured that out?'

'He's been reading up about the poltergeist. I take it you've read Telfair's transcript too?'

'I had a quick look at some of the accounts out of curiosity but not in great depth. I'm just not interested in any of it.'

'Well, your alleged haunting is following a very similar pattern. Prendy says if we study the chronological events, we will at least know what to expect if and when it happens.'

They reached the house and sat outside on the patio's ornate cast iron chairs. Libby was certain she heard a few stones drop onto the old byre roof.

'Look at that. How the hell did that happen?' Kie couldn't stop shaking his head at the neat stack of metalwork of his disassembled barn lying on the concrete.

'You did say you wanted it down.'

'Aye, but in my own time and by my own hands, not with the aid of the dead.'

'So you do believe now?'

He tutted at her and leaned over the table to secure her attention. 'There are no such things as poltergeists, Libby. They just don't exist.'

'So how do you explain the barn?' She waggled her fingers playfully, and met his stare.

He sat back and crossed his arms. 'I can't, but I'd rather believe I did it myself under deep hypnosis, than believe some hobgoblin did it for me.'

'I want to ask you something but I don't want you to blow up again. Do you think you can hold back that temper, just while I explain myself?'

He eyed her suspiciously. 'I've got a strong feeling my answer's going to be no.'

'It's just a tiny request.' She shot him her sweetest of smiles.

'The answer's no.'

'I haven't asked it yet.'

'That smile tells me I'm not going to like it. It's no, Libby.'

'I would like to bring some friends here to take a look around.'

'They're ghostbusters, aren't they?'

'They are parapsychologists and one of them is a good friend of mine.'

'Ghostbuster. Shame on him.'

'He's a she and there's no shame in her research at all.' She continued her soft assault. 'She's exorcised many a fake ghost.

She and her team are trained, professional scientists. They investigate complaints of paranormal activity, independently and competently. It's vital research to them.'

'That means a lot of messy equipment in the house; doors taped up; cameras and sound equipment everywhere, not to mention a load of strangers littering the floor space for days on end. No and the answer will stay no.'

'Aw, don't be a spoil-sport. It could be fun.'

'I said no.'

'I'll cry again.'

He ended the conversation abruptly by leaving her alone on the patio.

Chapter 13

THE GHOSTBUSTERS

Kie awoke to the sound of voices he didn't recognise. He stretched his eyes, bleary with a solid night's sleep, and checked the time on the alarm clock. He was astounded to note that it was eleven forty-seven and he'd overslept for the first time in years.

He lay back on the pillows with his arms crossed behind his head, stared at the ceiling and smiled. The antics of his guests last night had amused him so much that his laughter had brought him to tears. It had been good to laugh again, even if it was at the expense of his two companions who were obviously staying at his house on sufferance.

Andrew Prendergast, a former policeman who'd enjoyed a brilliant career as one of Scotland Yard's top detectives, had become afraid of his own shadow in a matter of days. The hard-boiled inspector, who by his own admission had seen and experienced every horror that a human being could endure, was finding it difficult to investigate a series of crimes where the chief suspect was a mischievous spirit.

Kie laughed out loud and turned onto his side.

Libby Butler was an intelligent lawyer with a warped sense of humour and a self-professed sociopath. He liked Libby Butler. Perhaps he liked her more than he should, but then she was an easy woman to like. She maintained a hard outer exterior to protect the vulnerable softness inside. Kie knew she had a brittle shell and wondered why such an amazing woman could be so lacking in personal confidence.

He laughed again and thought perhaps he'd taken his teasing a little too far last night, especially when he leaped out of the cupboard of the landing with a blanket over his head as the two were going upstairs to bed. The shock could've killed them but it didn't because Kie just managed to grab Libby's arm before she tumbled down the stairs. He rubbed at the bruise on his chin and laughed again. Libby Butler had a deadly right hook.

She had a beautiful smile and some animated facial expressions that made him laugh. His thoughts turned to her impromptu wardrobe malfunction and he decided to get up or lose himself to the memory.

After a quick shower, he pulled on his jeans and clean T-shirt, and noticed the short milking stool from the old byre was sitting on his chest of drawers. It hadn't been there before he went into the bathroom.

'If you're really there, put that back where you found it.'

He felt ridiculous for even thinking out loud as he laced up his working boots.

He chuckled to himself again and wondered if his guests would be speaking to him this morning. He met Libby half way up the stairs.

'Oh, I heard you rumbling around. I was just coming up to get you. You have visitors.'

'Living or dead?'

She looked uneasy. 'I'm not sure.'

He narrowed his eyes as she skipped down the stairs and heard her whisper: 'Shhh, he's coming.'

Before he could open his mouth, Libby shoved a cup of coffee in his hand, slipped her arm into his and hauled him into the sitting room.

'This is the wonderful MacAoidh I was telling you about. Kie, this is Nora, George and Keith.'

He eyed the polite faces and gave them a cool smile. He turned his attention to Libby. 'Friends of yours?'

'Yes, well sort of.'

'Libby?'

'All right. They're a four-piece ghost hunting team from Ayrshire, if you must know and they've been kind enough to drop everything and beetle across to this neck of the woods to take a look around your house. They've promised to keep their findings to themselves and not report them in public in any shape or form without your permission. Haven't you?'

The three strangers nodded in unison.

Libby looked as if she was holding back a full bladder that was about to burst. How could he be angry with her?

'You said four.'

'Janet's in the car, she won't come out.'

'It's not that she won't come out, Libby. She feels the need to protect herself before she begins,' Nora chirped.

'Begins what?'

'Janet's the spiritualist medium of the group. She's reportedly very good.' That sweet smile again which sole purpose was to disarm him.

'She won't come in.' Prendergast took one look at Kie and panicked. 'Good morning, Kie. Er, have you met Nora …'

'I've been introduced to your team of witchwives, thanks. Let me see if I can coax Janet into my house to complete the coven.'

'Be nice, Kie, their intentions are good,' Libby trotted after him as he crossed the drive to the car.

'Was this your idea?'

'No, Prendy contacted them last night after you almost hospitalised him with your flying shoe trick.'

He tapped on the window and opened the door. 'Your

colleagues are waiting for you and I've run out of eye of newt.'

Janet didn't rise to the challenge. She held a crystal between her fingers and fondled it affectionately.

'You can bring your precious with you.'

'I can't come out.'

'Why not?'

'The spirit doesn't want me to.'

He threw his eyes up to the blue skies and hissed. 'Well the spirit doesn't own this house, I do, and I say you may enter at your peril.'

Libby placed her hand on his arm, a gesture he'd grown fond of. 'Let me handle this. Sorry about him, had a bit too much cynicism in his testosterone flakes for breakfast.' She snapped her eyes up to meet his. 'Don't be so bad-mannered. These people are trying to help you.'

'Whatever.' He crossed his arms while Libby stuck her head in the car.

'It's OK Janet, he's an unbeliever and inherited his offensive nature from his mother's side. Please come in, have a cup of tea and we'll show you around when you feel settled enough to begin.'

'Tell her we still have some blind-worm's sting, a howlet's wing and half a fillet of fenny snake left.' Kie's laughter trailed when he realised Janet had heard him.

Janet jumped from the car and slammed the door. 'If you're still laughing by the time I'm finished, I'll give you a hundred pounds. If not, then you'll owe me the same.'

Kie made a bad attempt at composing himself and averted all eye contact with Libby as the woman stopped at the threshold. She shuddered and held on to her crystal as if it were a holy cross. She touched the door frame and snatched her hand back as if it had just burned her. Instead of going inside, she turned to the outbuildings and walked across the gravel with her arms outstretched, moving like a blind person without a stick. She reached the pile of former barn.

'Oh my.'

'She doesn't look like a medium.' Libby whispered as they followed the woman into the house.

'What does a medium look like?'

'Like that little woman with the high-pitched voice in Poltergeist. You know, that movie where the little girl disappears into the television.'

'Aye, I remember it.'

'She looks more like an office bearer of the Scottish Women's Institute All teeth and hairstyle. God, I hope I don't disappear into your TV.'

'I'll find a rope and send Prendy in after you.'

'Aw, that's so sweet.' She patted his cheek.

Kie's mood remained light as Janet's team members joined her trail followed by Libby and Prendergast. The ghostbusters looked like ordinary, decent folk to him and he couldn't help but wonder why anyone would chose to pursue a hobby in the supernatural.

To everyone's surprise, a small stone flew from apparently nowhere and scratched Keith's ear.

'Sorry, I think this may become a habit.' Kie shrugged in apology.

They moved into his bedroom and Kie noticed the milking stool had gone but his chest of drawers was sitting on its side. Janet moved towards it cautiously and Keith, obviously spooked by the stoning incident, wriggled into a space between his colleagues for safety.

The company then visited Libby's room. Her clothes lay strewn around the floor and bed as if someone had picked up her suitcase and shaken out the contents from a great height.

'The ghost's been busy in here,' Kie sucked at his cheek.

She looked embarrassed. He picked up a tiny lace thong and raised his eyebrows at her. She slapped it out of his hand.

Another stone hit Keith on the back of the head as they descended the stairs and he cried out this time. It had obviously hurt him.

The four ghost hunters gasped at a layer of stones covering the hallway and became increasingly agitated as they moved from room to room. They halted to listen to a series of gentle taps seemingly coming from somewhere within the wall of the hallway.

'That's new,' Libby whispered as she sidled closer to him. She no longer found ghost hunting enjoyable and reminded him of a startled fawn. He placed his arm around her shoulder and they followed Janet into the living room, completing the sweep of the house.

Prendergast had made tea and swore he'd set out biscuits on a plate. He set about looking for them.

Janet took the seat in the middle of the sofa and told them all to sit down. Her fingers gripped her crystal as she pressed her bony knees together and closed her eyes.

Kie sat on the arm of Libby's chair.

'I feel a young presence. An adolescent boy.'

'That'll be you,' Libby whispered.

He tried not to smile.

'He is a blond boy with a ruddy complexion.' Janet continued her findings as if she were preaching to a congregation. 'He's sad and he's lost.'

'Yep, that's you all right.'

Janet threw her a stern glower and Libby bit the contrition into her lip.

'What does he want?' Prendergast asked the question burning on everyone's tongues.

They were interrupted by a sharp whistle coming from somewhere in the room. The sudden, inexplicable sound caused everyone to jump.

'He's here.' Janet remained composed as she fiddled with her crystal.

Libby moved closer towards Kie and clutched his knee.

'He's brought along a friend. She wants to speak to you.'

As Janet was speaking, Kie swore he saw her hair move. She had one of those perfect bobs that curved around her head like a china bowl. It moved again, very slightly. He watched in fascination as her hair appeared to gradually slip sideways, revealing the thin grey strands beneath, and he no longer listened to what she was saying. He felt Libby nudging his arm and realised the woman was wearing a wig but probably hadn't secured it properly to her head. He wondered if he should warn her.

The next moment, the people in the room gasped simultaneously as if someone had exploded a firework in front of their faces. Janet snatched her hands to her head too late. The wig hovered in the air just out of reach of her grasping fingers and landed with a splash in her tea cup on the low table in front of her.

MacAoidh was just trying to absorb the incident when Janet's legs straightened at the knee in front of her and she somersaulted in the air to land on her shoulders on top of George's lap, her skirt burying his face. The act would have been comical had the circumstances not been so bizarre.

At that point, the four ghost hunters were taking their leave, beating each other out the door to be first into the car and safety. MacAoidh ran after them and helped them into the car.

Before he closed the door, Janet grabbed his wrist. 'Get out, Mr Armstrong. While you're still able, get out. It's too strong for you. You'll be hurt.'

'I'm not afraid of ghosts.'

'He can't rest until he's found and it won't allow that.'

He tried to pull his arm away but she held onto it.

'Nīngwendete.'

'Pardon?'

She took a deep inhale and squeezed her eyes shut. 'She loves you and she'll come for you when it's time.' Her nails bit into his flesh. 'If you follow her, there's no coming back.'

His eyes widened and he could think of nothing to say.

'You owe me a hundred pounds.'

She released his wrist and he watched the car pull away, the driver's intention to put as much space between the Ayrshire ghost hunters and The Ring as was humanly possible.

Chapter 14

THE MILKING STOOL

'That went well.'

Libby found Kie in the old byre. He sat on the concrete next to an ancient lump of metal and wires. His hands, face and once clean clothes were smothered in black oil. In the background, Neil Young sang his haunting set of oldies from a portable stereo. Bits of the machine's filthy, rusted guts lay everywhere.

'I've cleared up the house and the chuckies are back on the drive where they belong. The stone throwing's stopped for now and I haven't found myself accidentally performing the Arabian double front in the laid out position over the settee. I thought I'd give you some personal space to let your temper settle.'

'Thanks.'

'What did you think of Winnie the Witch et al?'

'They must be fakes.' MacAoidh swiped his unruly hair from his face, leaving another dark streak across his forehead. 'She obviously undertook some research before she came.'

'Yes, I thought the same. You do realise you're covered in oil?' Libby crossed the byre floor and kneeled down next to him. 'What are you doing?'

'Fixing this old generator. Some idiot reversed the polarity and the points have welded together. I just hope the armature's not completely burned out.

'Sounds painful. Can you fix it?'

'Of course I can. Hand me that adjustable spanner would you?'

She picked up the tool he was pointing at.

'The spanner Libby, the silver thing with a head like a jaw. They're pliers.'

'Sorry.' She slapped the spanner in his hand and wiped the oil from her fingers on the back of his T-shirt. 'Why can't you just buy a new one and save yourself and your poor washing machine all this trouble?'

'Because there's nothing wrong with this lovely old lass.'

'Are you fixing it to give yourself something to focus on or do you intend to use it?' Her knees cracked when she stood up.

'Both. Did you see the way the lights were flickering? I don't want to be left in the dark. This is my insurance. I've put a torch in your room. It's by the side of your bed if you need it.'

'Thanks.' She looked around the old byre with its one tiny window blinded by eons of dusty cobwebs. All of the ambient light spilled in from the open space left by rickety double doors flapping on rusted hinges. Pieces of old machinery, harking back to a time in agriculture when elbow grease and animals did all the work, waited it out on the cracked concrete for MacAoidh Armstrong to restore them to their former glory.

'Prendy has to go to London this afternoon for a meeting. He'll be back in a couple of days. I think he misses his wife.'

'Aye.'

She heard the distractedness in that 'aye' while Harvest Moon spilled from the stereo, but decided not to allow him to wallow in old memories. She both loved and hated the way he used that word. Sometimes it would mean he was concurring with her; sometimes he would use it as a definitive ending to a conversation. 'How long did you live in Africa?'

'Who told you that?' She watched him wrestle with a stubborn bolt, the strong sinews tightening the bulging muscles on his shoulders and arms.

'Prendy.'

'Prendy's got a big mouth.'

She ignored his testy comment. 'Whereabouts?'

'Kenya mainly.'

'Do you speak Swahili?'

'Ndiyo, nasema Swahili kama mzungu.'

'I know you've said something rude!'

He cast a swift smile backwards. 'It wasn't rude.'

'What did you do in Kenya?'

'Grew coffee and learned how to fix old machinery. Can we talk about something else please?'

'Oh, I thought you might've been working in the tourist trade.'

He put down his tools and twisted his body around to face her, the unusual blue of his eyes flashing behind his jagged fringe. 'Why the hell would you think something like that?'

'Isn't that your business?'

'No!' He looked astounded by her observation.

'I thought you were turning this place into a holiday centre.' She crossed her arms and set her jaw when he laughed at her. 'That's what I heard.'

'And what do you think I would do with a holiday centre?'

She shrugged. 'Manage it. Run it. Cook. March around in a red uniform shouting Hi-de-Hi. How should I know?'

'And put a wee scheme o' smairt caravans aroon' the loch?' He laughed again, heartily this time. 'So that's what people are saying.'

'You should put them right.'

'Ach, let them talk.'

'So what *are* you going to do?'

'I'm going to farm it. Work it. Live off the land. Become self-sufficient and to hell with the rest of the world. That's my plan.'

'I thought people only did that when they're going through a mid-life crisis.'

'I'm post crisis. This is *my* time.'

'I'll bet your mother booked herself into therapy when you broke the news to her.'

'She'll come round.'

'What does your dad think about your plans for the good life?'

'I need to get on.'

She knew she'd snooped too far when he picked up the spanner and renewed his vigorous assault on the generator, leaving her question unanswered.

'I'll find a glass to polish.'

His silence was her dismissal.

'Can I borrow a car? I need to get some shopping.'

'Key's on the kitchen table.'

His curt reply annoyed her but she decided to leave him alone. MacAoidh Armstrong was a strange mixture of dourness and cordiality and that tempestuous nature reminded her of the Highlands. Like the landscape he grew up in, he was prone to sudden, violent storms preceded by mild blue skies. He had the strength of a stag, the sharp eyes of an eagle, the agility of a wildcat and...

'Are you just going to stand there and watch me work?'

'The manners of a rat!' she growled before leaving him to fester in his filthy mood.

— — —

Kie rolled the work light lead back into its reel and stretched his back. Although the sun dropped over the hills, there were still a good few hours of daylight left. He closed the byre doors, rattling them a little to test the old hinges before sliding the wooden slipbar into its iron keeps. The Discovery had gone and he was grateful for some personal space after the ghosthunters had made their sharp exit.

The thought of them angered him and he wondered why people like Janet would choose a life that duped the vulnerable into believing their long lost loved ones were hovering around inside an invisible spiritual dimension hoping to make contact with the living.

'Con artist!' He spat on the ground. 'You want to hurt me do you?' He laughed to himself and made for the house.

A familiar sound caused him to turn around. The slipbar lay on the ground in front of the byre door. He hadn't heard it fall but he was certain he did hear the sound of it sliding through its keeps.

He picked it up and hefted it in his hand before opening the door and peering into the shadowed interior.

The barn was still and silent, save for the occasional fluttering of nesting swallows flying in and out of a tiny hole beneath the slates and the soft flapping of bats in the rafters. He curled his fingers tighter around the wooden bar and stepped inside.

Out of pure natural reflex, he caught the stool in his left hand as it hurtled towards him. It was the same old milking stool he found on the chest of drawers in his room this morning.

'You want to play games?' He hurled it back into the shadows and heard it hit the wall in the far corner of the barn.

He waited.

'Shit!' He was forced to duck but only just managed to catch the stool by one of its legs before it brained him. He felt the chill creeping up his spinal column, steadily turning his back to ice, as he kept both eyes on the corner of the barn where the daylight failed to reach.

He threw the stool back at the corner with such force that

he heard it shatter against the stone wall.

He waited. He waited some more.

Realising his body was aching with tension, Kie slowly made his way between the old machinery to the corner of the barn, disappearing into the darkness with cautious but steady steps. Squinting into the black, he reached the far wall and could just make out the dark outline of the broken stool in the corner.

He knelt down in front of it and slowly allowed his hand to feel around the brittle contours of the shattered wood. It wasn't until he began to feel dizzy that he realised he was holding his breath.

A passing swallow startled him and he lost his balance, just managing to put his hands flat to prevent his head from hitting the wall. He made to stand but the pressure on his left arm would not allow him to move.

He felt panic welling as he tried to free his arm from what felt like a cold, metal vice. He could see only shadowy outlines in the darkness: shadows and his own breath freezing before his face. It was so cold.

He hauled until he felt the joint on his shoulder would tear from its socket. He brought up the wooden bar and began to beat at his imprisoned wrist until the pain became unbearable.

He threw himself to the ground, his cheek pressing against the cold concrete, and could just make out the glow of a small pale hand wrapped around his wrist.

Something hard hit him on the back of the head and he saw no more.

Chapter 15

THE MOON

Libby returned from her shopping spree and ran into the kitchen.

'God, I love that car of yours. Tinted windows, soft black leather to sink into, Alpine sunroof, a dashboard that looks like the bridge of the Starship Enterprise and, when I turned on the air con, it almost blew my head off! It's so big, I felt like a toy in it: a very posh, expensive toy.'

'It's reliable.'

She suddenly noticed Kie's poorly bandaged wrist. He held a cold compress, comprising a dishcloth and a bag of peas, to the back of his head. He was still filthy from the work on the generator. She dropped her bags and picked up the empty glass beside him. She didn't need to sniff at it to know it once contained a strong spirit 'What happened to you?'

'Ach, I was careless and fell over the beam of that old plough in the byre. I'll live.'

She passed her hand over the back of his head. 'God, that's a huge lump, you could have a cracked skull.'

'I'm fine.'

'Did you lose consciousness? Do you have a headache? Wait, let me look at your pupils. Are they dilated?' She grabbed his ears and peered into his face.

He pulled away with a testy grunt. 'I said I'm fine.'

'I suppose a head as hard as yours would take some cracking.'

'Aye.'

She had a sudden and horrible thought. 'You weren't doing any involuntary gymnastics over the generator were you?'

'No, it's been nice and quiet here until now.'

'Did you bandage that in the dark?' She set about unwrapping the loose binding to find his wrist and forearm covered in red bruises. 'God Kie, that looks really painful. It's badly swollen but I think you should give it a wash first and get all the grub off it before we can play doctors and nurses.'

'Aye, I could do with a cold shower.'

She ignored that twinkle in his eyes. 'When you come down, I have a surprise for you.'

'Don't tell me, the cast of Most Haunted are coming for supper and an all-night vigil.'

'No, I have a fabulous plan to put you in a better mood and forget all this horror for a while.'

'That sounds ominous.' He shot her a suspicious glance but, from the tiny smile, she knew he was up for a happy time.

She started placing the contents of the shopping onto the work surface by the sink. 'Prendy's not here and we could both do with some cheering up. Your Neil Young album gave me an idea. It's going to be a full moon tonight so we're going to have a picnic by the loch.'

'The burn has better places to sit.'

'If you like midges with your meal.'

'They don't bother me.' He shrugged.

'It won't be dark until about ten. I've bought an industrial-sized bottle of midge repellent and some wonderful picnicky food and drink for us to gorge ourselves on. We'll put some batteries in that portable stereo of yours and listen to music while stuffing our faces and watching the sun go down and the moon rise.'

'That's a lot of wine you've got there. Are you trying to seduce me?'

She continued with her unpacking as if he hadn't just said something that caused her hands to shake and her knees to buckle. 'Let's get this straight before there are any stupid misunderstandings. I don't hit on other women's men, Kie. You're spoken for and, anyway, you're not my type. Besides, your mother can't stand me. I thought we were friends.' She wished she'd braved the bold eye contact before delivering her sermon.

'I was kidding.'

She couldn't read his expression. 'Good, I was worried for a moment you'd done the bloke thing and taken a simple gesture of friendship the wrong way.'

'What's the bloke thing?'

'That there's no such thing as a platonic relationship between the sexes. That all women are secretly gagging for it so any positive action that shows a personal interest in a man can naturally be taken by said man as a green come-and-take-me beacon.'

'I see what you mean.'

She wondered whether he was still kidding or whether he was concurring with her. She was relieved to find him laughing eventually.

'So, if we use your syllogism as an argument, Prendy and you *are* having an affair.'

'Oh, shut up and go for a shower. I'll meet you down by the lake.'

'Loch.'

'Stretch of water that doesn't require a yes or no vote.'

He hung his head. 'I'm sorry, Libby, I'll make poor company tonight.'

'You need to put some space between you and this house, even if it's only a few hundred yards. It'll be good for you.' She came up behind him and wrapped her arms around his neck, swayed her hips and sang into his ear: 'There's a full moon on the rise and I feel like a dance.'

'On one condition. We don't talk about my family, my past or my poltergeist.'

Her good mood obviously had an effect on Kie, as he trundled up the stairs and took his shower.

By the time Libby reached the loch with the heavy picnic basket in one hand, four bottles of wine in a cool bag in the other, and a blanket over her shoulder, she was out of breath and collapsed in a heap on the shore. She looked up into an indigo blue sky and saw the full face of the moon shining down at her.

She pulled a bottle of Cava out of the stack, bit the top off with her teeth and spat out the cork. She turned on the stereo and chose Harvest Moon to get her in the mood for the evening. Laying out the blanket with the black waterproof layer grass-side, she dived into the picnic bag for the glasses.

'I could have sworn ...'

MacAiodh Armstrong stood in front of her waggling two crystal glasses sparking fire in the evening sun. His dark silhouette loomed over her, blotting out what remained of the day, and a glow of orange light haloed his tall form. Libby, for the second time in her life, believed in gods.

'Dance?'

She shied away from his waving fingers until she was persuaded to take his hand by that hallmark smile and a small persuasive nod.

She placed a tentative hand on his shoulder and folded her fingers into his broad palm. He smelled of Radox and sump oil.

They swayed together to the soft cadence of the music, their bodies keeping a close but safe distance away from each other: he studying the contours of her face with a half-smile she couldn't read; she finding a focus on the dark profile of the dead tree across the field.

'Are you still in love with her?' She had to ask the question, since Neil Young was singing it.

'Aye. What about you?' His fingers curled around the back of her neck.

She sighed as they swayed to the rhythm of wonderful memories. 'Aye. I can't forget him.' She rested her head on his chest. 'Is it realistic to still be in love with someone you know will never be part of your life again?'

He tightened his grip on her waist. 'Probably not, but love's at least a positive emotion and we should hang onto it for as long as it'll let us.'

She felt him thaw as if an enormous iceberg had just burst apart and its shattered remnants hurled across the ocean. She leaned her head instinctively towards the hot breath caressing her neck that whispered promises of desire … passion … obsession and … a girlfriend.

'Hungry?' The word had the effect of Nelly the Elephant's trumpeting call at point blank range straight through the ear canal.

'Yes, ehm, right, I haven't eaten all day.' He appeared to shake away dizziness.

She launched an airborne-style assault on the hamper, her arms and legs flailing as she hunted for items that escaped her memory.

She squealed as his hand touched hers and set her skin on fire.

'Have a drink.'

She took the glass and they sat down on the blanket beneath the moon. They ate, they drank, they talked, they laughed and they kept their emotional distances from one another. Lying with the tops of their heads touching, under a blanket of darkness peppered by millions and trillions of tiny lights and a climbing moon, Libby felt tiny and almost afraid.

'Kie?'

'What?'

'Do you ever get the feeling that someone or something's watching you from up there?'

'I can't believe, with all those stars, galaxies and universes stretching out into wide infinity, that only one little planet is capable of supporting life.'

'So do you believe in alien life forms?'

'I think, on a balance of probabilities, as you lawyers would say, that Earth couldn't possibly provide the only surface in zillions upon zillions of solar systems upon which to support life as we know it.'

'You should audition for a role in Star Trek.'

'As a Klingon?'

'No, the ridges on your forehead aren't deep enough. Maybe Romulan?

'I don't have ticks for eyebrows.'

'Do you believe in God?'

He cast his eyes up to the twinkling starlight and laughed. 'No, sorry, he's not part of all this. Aliens, I can believe in. A single, moral consciousness, separate and distinct from tangible reality? Can't see it.'

'So what about poltergeist then?'

'You promised.' He sat up.

'I forgot.' She sat up too. 'Tell me something about you that you're ashamed of.'

'No. You're more than capable of blackmailing me with the information.'

'OK, I'll go first.' She thought for a moment and squirmed.

'I had an affair with my married boss.'

'You should be ashamed of yourself!'

'I really am.' She shut her eyes and drummed her heels on the grass.

'Was he worth it?'

'I thought so at the time but, looking back, I can honestly say he really wasn't and neither was I.'

'Why do you say that?'

'I became friends with his wife after it was all over. She's a wonderful, caring woman; the kind of person who's incapable of seeing bad in others. I'm sorry for hurting her. She's the sole reason for my shame.'

'That's an honest response and a good lesson learned.'

'I swore never to come between two people ever again.'

'Never is a long time.'

'Your turn.' She ran her hands across the soft grass and raked it with her fingers.

The minutes passed like hours in his silence.

She poked his side. 'Well?'

'I'm afraid.'

His words were barely audible but had enough emotional charge in them to raise a city to the ground.

'That medium really got to you didn't she? God, you did a fantastic job of hiding it.'

'No, she was a joke. Today, when you were away and I was closing up the barn, I think I may have come into contact with the implausible.'

'So you didn't fall. Something hit you and gave you that bump on your head? Well, you've every reason to be afraid.'

'It wasn't the physical act of being attacked that scared me, Libby. It's the powerless feeling it's left me with. Whatever happened to me today was outside my control. I couldn't fight it off and I couldn't reason with it.'

'I want to know exactly what happened.'

'And I'm not going to tell you, because I don't know myself. I've decided something, though. I'm not going to bide it for much longer. I never want to feel like that again.' He rubbed at his arms as if to drive away the chill.

'How can you fight what you can't see?'

'With knowledge and answers. I'm going to try and understand what's happening at The Ring. If I can identify the rationale behind the symptoms, I'll find a cure, but first I'm going to get some answers.'

'Do you want me to call in the parapsychologists now?'

'Nah, I'm going to clean my shotgun.'

Chapter 16

THE BOY

The sound of shrill barking in her ear caused Libby to open her eyes. She closed them quickly as the sunlight stabbed its sharp shards into the sensitive optical membranes. Rolling on to her back, she yelled in surprise at the flapping of dark grey wings in the corner of her eye. The nearby heron got such a fright that it took off from an impossible vertical leap, an event never witnessed by even the keenest of ornithologists.

She groaned as the thumping in her head got heavier and more painful and she spat some grass from her dry mouth. Wrapped in the picnic blanket and Kie's Parker jacket, she remembered the dance, the food, the laughter and a few bottles of wine – most of which she'd consumed. She also recalled his eyes and the pale reflection of the moon shimmering on the surface of the dark water but not very much else. What she did get out of the evening was that his affections for her were as far away from his heart as the iridescent moon in the sky.

She trudged back to the farmhouse, her blanket trailing behind her, to find Kie in the kitchen cooking breakfast.

'Good morning.' His smile told her he was in a bright mood today.

'No it's not, it's horrible. What's that terrible fishy smell? I feel sick.'

'Kippers.'

Libby felt the contents of her stomach heaving against her diaphragm. 'No thanks, unless you're going to plop them in a glass of milk with a raw egg as a hangover cure.' Her stomach jerked violently. 'Why did I say that?' She noticed a very fancy shotgun standing against the fridge.

'Do you have a licence for that?'

'Aye.'

'What's the time?' She decided she'd neither the strength nor the inclination to lecture him on the immoralities of blood sports.

'It's only the back of seven. Thought I'd leave you to sleep.' He stopped to look at her, the fish slice dangling from his bandaged hand, 'Thanks for a grand evening. You were right, I needed that.'

'Was it grand? I can't remember most of it.' She sat down at the butchers block and dragged the mug of tea towards her. 'Did I behave myself?'

'You were on fire.'

Libby's eyes widened. 'Are you telling me we had sex?'

'Are you telling me you don't remember?' He looked hurt.

'Oh no,' she buried her face in her hands, 'I've done it again.'

'Done what?' He placed a plate with a steaming kipper under her nose and she shuddered in revulsion.

'Had an affair with another woman's man.'

'It was only sex, Libby.'

'You don't understand …'

'Cheer up.' He sat down beside her and patted her hand. There was little affection or romance in the gesture. 'Catherine will understand. We were drunk and, besides, we didn't exactly go all the way.' He launched into his breakfast.

'How far did we go?' She couldn't believe she'd ruined another good relationship.

'Far enough.' His wink told her it must've been pretty far.

'Did it involve mouths?'

'And a few other human organs.'

She groaned again. 'You took advantage of a drunk woman and I don't remember you doing it.'

He managed to look stunned. 'You were gagging for it.'

His laughter gave his playful ruse away and she slapped his arm.

'Bastard!'

She pushed her kipper around the plate, knowing her narrowed digestive tract would not allow it to enter. He chuckled beside her.

'That's a serious-looking gun.'

A tiny stone fell on to her plate and his laughter ceased.

'I want you to go home.'

His announcement came as a complete surprise.

'Why?'

'Because things are getting worse here and I don't want to be responsible for you getting hurt.'

'I'm a big girl and can take care of myself.'

'I thought that yesterday.'

'What, that you were a big girl?'

His humour had gone and in its place was the dour MacAoidh who growled a lot and took life far too seriously.

'I'm too busy to run around all day protecting you. I've too much to do.'

She felt the hackles rising on the back of her neck. MacAoidh Armstrong was the most stubborn, most infuriating man she had ever met. 'I said I would aid you and I'm not going back on my word. You're stuck with me because I'm not leaving until I've helped you to solve this enigma and get your life back on track. You need a friend, but you're too pig-headed to ask. I don't turn my back on friends, MacAoidh, even if you do.'

'Who's being stubborn now?' his voice was low but non-aggressive.

'Me.' She pushed her uneaten kipper away, jumped from her stool and kissed the side of his head. 'Besides, the prospect of going home alone with only my vivid imagination to keep me company is more daunting than staying here and facing my fears.'

'And are you frightened?'

'Why should I be? I've got a strapping Highlander to run around protecting me with a loaded gun. Now, what are we doing today?'

'Cleaning the byre.'

'But that'll take all day!'

'Aye.'

— — —

Libby fell onto her mattress fully clothed, stinking of bleach and understanding the true meaning of hard work. She'd scrubbed, scraped, cleaned, sanitised, washed, brushed, cleansed, scoured, rubbed and polished all day and now her hands, arms, legs and back were throbbing in complaint. She didn't have the energy for a quick shower. Despite her arduous tasks around the farm and irrespective of her aching limbs, she smiled to herself in contentment. She'd enjoyed every bit of her day working with Kie and had quite forgotten about the poltergeist.

She scrubbed while he spent the day knocking down the end wall of the long byre. She knew it was important to him to take a sledge hammer to the stone, but she didn't understand his reasoning. Most people would spend their time and effort securing property from the powerful forces of nature but Kie worked the entire day exposing his barn to the same. He did mutter something about the usefulness of daylight at that end and how he was going to install glass panels there, but she wasn't really listening to him. When he smashed up the concrete floor and took a shovel to the dirt beneath it, she began to worry that his obsessions had taken him away from reality and left him in that cold, lonely place professionals call psychosis.

She did notice his mood had shifted from light in the morning to black by the end of the day.

A few stones had dropped onto the roof of the barn while she was working there and she'd misplaced her mobile phone. The new router had packed in and one of the bulbs in the kitchen exploded. The worst thing that happened later in the evening was a small fire in the kitchen. Neither Libby nor Kie would've given it a second thought had the fire not been found smouldering from the plasterboard ceiling.

Whatever Kie said and whatever he thought, something was going on at The Ring Steading that stretched the conventional laws of physics to snapping point, only he would not accept it.

Libby knew she was scared but a force more powerful than terror kept her stout heart beating. From the moment Gabriel Radley left her life, she'd shown little interest in the opposite sex. Perfection, so complete, so flawless, was impossible to find again. Yet, along came a sullen Highlander with seductive eyes: MacAoidh Ross Armstrong, a walking paradox of inner strength and outer vulnerability. He was a living oxymoron of error and correctness; of righteousness and impiety; of passion and formality. He was a most unusual man and one who unwittingly manipulated her sentiments so fiercely that she found herself braving the wrath of demons because she was more frightened of the prospect of his absence in her life.

She hoped he might just feel a similar empathy towards her but guessed those eyes didn't hold much affection for her other than friendship. They'd worked together, eaten together and, at the end of the day, they'd sat on the sofa speaking softly about life until they'd almost fallen asleep. She wanted to see a longing glow in those startling eyes as they said goodnight on the landing but he'd simply gone to bed.

She heard soft footsteps padding the boards outside her room, the barely perceptible rap on the door and she suddenly wondered whether she'd been wrong about his intentions.

Libby threw her jeans off, slapped her cheeks until she felt the blood rushing to the surface and raked her fingers through her hair. She sprawled herself, as seductively as she could muster with her reluctant muscles, across the bed and thought to hell with the snotty girlfriend, this was war. 'I'm not asleep yet.' She hoped her voice had the intended alluring appeal.

She smiled, trying hard not to allow the eager anticipation to register on her expression, as she watched the handle descend and the door open with a barely audible click. The darkness from the landing spilled into the room like oily water.

She waited for his soft outline to assemble into human form. Something did come in from the darkness, but it wasn't him.

Libby's inner senses screamed at her for caution as the bedside light flickered violently before it went out with a loud crack.

The door banged shut and she found herself whimpering in the darkness in the company of a dark silhouette moving across the floor. She heard light footsteps fluttering against the carpet and her body began to fill with cold dread, starting from her fingertips.

With no light to guide her, Libby battled to find the torch on her bedside table and managed to grab it before it fell. She scrambled on hands and knees into the corner of the room, her throat letting out involuntary squealing sounds, her heart pushing against her ribs.

She punched at the button a few times and a beam of white light radiated across the room, its glare dissolving into soft shadows against the inner confines of her black prison.

With her back pressed into the corner, the breath heaving from her chest and sweat dribbling from her temples, she jerked the torchlight backwards and forwards across the room, following the quick thumps of footsteps, but their owner evaded her sight. Standing up carefully, she made for the door with slow, cautious steps, keeping the wall at hand's reach at all times. Shivering with fear, she could barely hold on to the torch.

The footsteps stopped.

She shook her head to rid her ears of the noise of her pulses banging at either side of her eyes but the room was still save for a hair-bristling awareness that someone or something was in the room with her, waiting.

A high-pitched whistle caused her to leap in the air. She shrieked for Kie but was unable to formulate a comprehensible word through a throat constricted with fear. She made for the door at a run and, keeping the light in front of her, found the handle and hauled on it. She let out a small, manic laugh as the door swung open and she jumped into the safety of the landing.

Her spine tingled again, stronger this time, and she was aware of the static haloing the back of her head as she felt a looming presence close behind her; so close she could feel its breath.

She spun around and a wan figure of a boy suddenly stepped into the beam of light, his face a few inches from hers.

Libby's body turned to stone. She wanted to run but her feet wouldn't move. She wanted to scream but her natural reflex to breathe had gone. So she stood instead, face to face with what she instinctively knew to be an anomaly of professional science. A lattice of black veins etched a thin film of translucent skin across his face. His eyes were closed and his blond hair was matted and caked in mud. He looked asleep but she heard him breathe: a ragged guttural wheeze that turned her flesh to ice. He was shivering.

She didn't have chance to ponder on it. Another shrill whistle snapped her from her trance and the boy vanished, his image replaced by a leaping mass of teeth and fur. She threw her hands in front of her face and fell backwards, screaming until her lungs were empty.

— — —

'Libby. Libby, it's OK. You're all right. It's only Jim Black's collie.'

The lights fizzed before they came on and Kie's arms enfolded her body: soft, comforting and safe.

'Where did he go?'

'He fled down the stairs and is probably gnawing at the door to get out after all that screaming.'

It took Libby a while to comprehend where she was and who was speaking to her. A sleepy Kie stood in his underpants scratching at something beneath his hair.

'No, Kie. The boy. He was here. He was …' She saw that look, half compassionate, half condescending, wholly asleep, and realised she stood alone in her beliefs.

'There's no one else in this house, Libby. You may've been dreaming. That phoney medium's playing with your head.'

'I wasn't asleep.' Her protests fell on deaf ears.

'Go back to bed and we'll talk about it in the morning. Can I get you anything?'

He looked so exhausted that Libby felt she couldn't ask him for the platoon of Green Berets and choir of seraphim to watch over her while she slept. 'No, I'll be all right. Would you leave the hall light on for me please and can I keep the dog?'

He hardly heard her as he shuffled off back to his room but

he did let out a sharp, shrill whistle that had her shuddering in fear.

She stood in the light of the landing for long moments, catching her breath and listening to her pounding heartbeat slowly returning to normal. She'd little compulsion to return to her room and the possible horrors it contained, but she also had no option. The thought of ordering Kie to move over in his bed held more terror for her than another visitation by a ghostly boy.

Jim Black's collie padded up the stairs and sat by her legs.

'Come on Rover. You and I are going to have a wonderful night together.' She patted its head and curled her fingers around the tarry leather collar.

As she moved her foot, she noticed the lacquered board beneath her toes bore deep scratches. Libby bent over and traced the contours of the indentations with her fingertips. Her eyes widened when she realised it was lettering indelibly engraved in the floor of Kie's landing. She read it out loud.

'Find me.'

Chapter 11

THE CAVALRY

'Goodness, what the blazes happened here?'

Prendergast peered through the open dining room door and noticed the Windsor chairs stacked in a pyramid on top of the long oak table like props in a macabre circus performance.

'Kie? Libby?' He cursed as a small stone hit him on the shoulder while he moved up the stairs. It was after nine in the morning and he'd just driven up from York after a full English breakfast. He was eager to tell his colleagues the results of his recent findings.

He noticed the crude scrapes on the floorboards of the landing outside Libby's room before he even reached the top few steps. Someone had carved a couple of words in the wood. He gave the door a gentle rap, but there was no answer.

'MacAoidh? He moved down the hallway towards Kie's room and ignored the next small stone that whistled past his ears to fall safely on the carpet a few feet in front of him.

'Prendy?' As Kie peered out his bedroom door, a black and white dog bounded out between his legs and fled down the hallway, its claws scraping for a foothold as it took the corner at maximum velocity.

'You've got yourself a dog?'

'No, it's Jim's collie. I think it slept on my head last night.' Kie wrestled with a stubborn hair in his mouth.

'When you get dressed, I have some news for you.'

Kie nodded wearily and, as he did, Prendergast noticed the

form of Libby stretching her arms in his bed. He didn't mean to raise his eyebrows so high.

'It's not how it looks, Prendy. The three of us have had a very bad night. The dog and I drew the short straw and lost the bed.'

'He was a gentleman and offered it to me.' Libby waggled her fingers at him in greeting. 'Hi Prendy.'

Prendergast cleared his throat. 'What you two, or indeed three, get up to behind closed doors is none of my business.'

He thought he'd wait downstairs. It was a beautiful morning as he stepped outside and took in a breath of air. Kie had obviously been busy with renovations to the old byre and the neighbour's dog was helping him to dig a hole. He watched the collie for a while, its white and black paws frantically clawing at the dirt.

'I've just realised. The barn's gone.'

'Aye,' Kie handed him a mug of tea. 'I sold it to a man in Stranraer. The pieces were cluttering up the steading so I got rid of it.'

Despite Kie's outward bravado, Prendergast knew he had a more compelling reason to rid himself of the disassembled pieces of that barn. The memories of how it was taken down would haunt any strong-headed man for a long, long time.

'Here!' Kie shouted at the collie. 'That'll do.'

The dog pressed its chest to the ground and moved backwards on all fours until it was a safe distance away from the hole. It lay staring at it, ears pricked, as if waiting in earnest for something to chase.

'What are you digging?'

'I'm just making a hole for a concrete post.'

'You'll be interested to know I stopped by an address in York on my way up. I visited the Patterson family who lived in the house ten years ago.'

'Oh, aye, what did you want with them?'

'I wanted to know if they'd encountered any strange phenomena in the house while they were there.'

'And did they?'

'They say not but they did tell me, when Mary Hyslop's son went missing, their teenage boy was suspected. He's a strange lad. I met him. The type who prefers the company of his computer to real human contact. Black eyes and greasy hair, like those emus you hear about.

'Emos?'

'Yes, that's it. There was never any evidence to suggest he had anything to do with the disappearance of the lad at the time, but the mud stuck firm and the Pattersons left to build a new life in York.'

'Can't see how I'd find that information interesting, Prendy.' MacAoidh leaned against the doorframe with his arms crossed, daring a challenge.

'Neither can I at the moment, but I have a hunch it may be important. Let's keep it on the back burner for a while and see if we can fit it into the overall puzzle when we find more pieces.'

'You're speaking in riddles, man.'

'I also spoke to the Renwicks while I was in London. You know, the couple who sold you the house. They live in Argyll now and, although they didn't want to see me, were happy to speak to me over the phone.'

'Enough!' Kie roared at the dog as it pounced on the hole. Picking up a stone from the drive, he hurled it at the animal which took off with a yelp. It took him a while to stop swearing. The stubble around his chin only served to accentuate the wildness in his eyes and Prendergast realised the man at last was beginning to harbour doubts about what was real and what was surreal. Like the great oak tree in his field, these strange inexplicable events on his property were MacAoidh's copper band and he was slowly beginning to wilt as he continued to draw in the poison. Prendergast decided to keep the rest of the news to himself until he felt Kie was strong enough to hear it.

'It's getting a lot worse, isn't it lad?'

'Nothing I can't handle.'

'I don't believe you. It's time you got some help in.'

MacAoidh laughed into the skies. 'And who do you suggest I ask for help? The police? Another medium? A shrink?'

'None of those. I want you to agree to allow a team of parapsychologists to study these phenomena as they're taking place and come up with an answer for you. I've been doing some research myself in London and all that's happening on this property could be attributed to something as simple as electromagnetic charges in the ground or in the air.'

Prendergast waited for a response but ended his conversation abruptly as MadAoidh stared behind him in wild-eyed horror.

The stalwart former detective chief inspector was forced to leap into the doorway, behind MacAoidh's back, half expecting the grim reaper to be holding a loaded rifle and pointing it straight at him.

Instead he saw the figure of Barbara Armstrong staggering up the drive in her Sunday best, the slim heels of her expensive shoes jamming intermittently in the gravel. In one hand she held her soft leather handbag; in the other a blue feathered hat. A tall elderly man walked beside her. He wore black with the grimness of an undertaker and his starched white dog collar like a holy call to arms.

— — —

'You didn't believe for one minute I would leave you alone to cope with all this did you?'

Without so much as a small greeting, Kie's mother kissed him on the cheek and pushed past him, dragging Reverend MacKenzie behind her.

Kie could only stand and watch.

'*Madainn mhath, MacAoidh, Ciamar a tha thu?*'

'I'm fine, thank you, Mr MacKenzie. How've you been keeping all these years?'

As Reverend Mackenzie crossed the threshold with wide steps, he managed a short nod of acknowledgment to Prendergast. He didn't notice the tiny stone hit him on the flap of his jacket.

'He's in for a time of it.'

'Who is he?'

'The local minister.'

Prendergast nodded in sympathy as they followed Barbara into the house.

'The minister speaks Gaelic, Macoidh. You'd do well to answer him in it when he addresses you.'

'We have guests here, Mother. Reverend MacKenzie should be polite enough to confine his language to a place where everyone understands it.'

'Catherine's booked herself into the big hotel on the bay. She's expecting you to go across as soon as you can. Our bags are in the car and the car's with her.' If she could tell he was annoyed, Barbara refused to show it.

'Where've you stationed the cavalry?'

'Don't be facetious. '

Leaving Prendergast to make his acquaintance with the minister from Sutherland, Kie made to haul his mother into the dining room. Seeing the chairs stacked up on the table, he slammed the door and decided to lecture her in the conservatory instead.

He crossed his arms and waited for her to speak.

'I won't allow my only son to handle this trouble alone.' His eyes rose to the glass ceiling as she dabbed at her tears with a lace handkerchief. 'I don't know whether this is all happening to you or because of you but I intend to be here while it's taking place and help you see it through.'

'I'm fine, Mother.'

'Carson nach èist thu rium?'

'I am listening to you.'

'You're not. Look at you. You're unshaven, sullen, distraught and exhausted and your hair's far too long. I barely recognise you. You have bruises on your arms and what have you done to your hand?'

'I hit it by accident.'

'Don't think I haven't read about the horrible things that happened here in sixteen ninety five and it's no wonder you didn't tell me about them. I'm here for as long as it takes because I love you and, whether you admit it or not, you need me.'

He folded his arms around her and kissed her on the top of her lacquered head. 'You can help me by staying away from here. Everything's under control.'

'Have you taken up smoking, MacAoidh Armstrong?' She sniffed at the air with the wrinkled nose of a bloodhound. 'This place reeks of cigarette smoke.'

'Does it? Must be the poltergeist.'

'The dead don't smoke, MacAoidh, nor do they leave cigarette ends in ashtrays.' Her eyes widened suddenly. 'Oh Lord, don't tell me you're having a relationship with that dreadful lawyer. She smokes. She stinks of it. How could you?'

'She has a name and I'm not having a relationship with Libby. She and Andrew have been staying at the house for the week. They're helping me out.'

'I'll bet she is! Where is she?'

Kie had a sudden, terrible vision of his mother catching Libby in his bed. 'She went out.'

'Did she now?'

He cursed the way his mother could see straight through him and ran after her as she took the stairs, three at a time, his protests only serving to quicken her pace. She threw the bedroom doors open as she passed them before reaching his room. He hurled himself in front of the door and barred her entry.

'So?' She crossed her arms and tapped her foot against the boards.

'It's not what you think, Mother.' He felt like a naughty child, caught with his hands in the biscuit barrel. 'She's a friend. A good friend. I'm not emotionally or physically involved with her.'

'I understand you may occasionally lack common sense, MacAoidh, but having any association with that woman is utterly foolish. Miss Butler is uncouth, uncivilised and common. What's more, she ...'

'Hello Barbara.'

Kie closed his eyes, not out of relief that Libby wasn't in his room, but more out of sympathy for her hurt feelings.

She stood in the corridor in a pair of tatty jeans and a short lace smock, rubbing her light brown hair with a towel, while a shaft of morning light illuminated her contours from behind. She looked strangely beautiful. He knew from that smile and the clip to her voice, however, that she'd heard his mother's every word.

'Oh, hello Miss Butler. We were just talking about you, weren't we Kie?'

'Yes, if you're using the Royal we.'

'Go and get my bags from the hotel, please. I wish to get

changed. Catherine's waiting for you there. She looks so pretty at the moment. Please don't disappoint her.'

The flushed cheeks and wild eyes told Kie that his mother was at least embarrassed, and perhaps even ashamed, of her outburst. That was always a good sign. Libby and he stood at the opposite ends of the hall and waited in silence for his mother to leave them. He noticed the slight falter in his mother's step as she passed Libby before disappearing back down the stairs.

'Sorry about that.'

'I've been called worse.'

He remembered his scene in her house a few days ago and felt even worse for her.

'Don't worry, Kie. I changed your mind about me and, like you said, have become a good friend. No doubt I'll manage to charm her off her broomstick before she can fly back to Assynt and turn her neighbours into frogs for pruning her rhodies on their side of the fence. How long is she staying?'

He shrugged.

'You'd better not disappoint Catherine.'

He took that as a dismissal and nodded, searching her face for signs of emotion but couldn't read her. 'I'll, ehm, be back in a wee while.'

'Take your time. I've got a pyre to build.'

'Oh, and Reverend MacKenzie's going to be staying here as well.'

'Fantastic, that's two witches to burn.'

chapter 18

THE STAND-OFF

'It was observed, that the stones which hit any person had not half their natural weight; and the throwing was more frequent on the Sabbath than at other times; and especially in time of prayer, above all other times, it was busiest, then throwing most at the person praying.'

'Do yourself a favour, Rev MacKenzie, and become an unbeliever or you'll find yourself celebrating Hallowe'en on every Sabbath day. Trick or treat?'

Libby sat down next to Prendergast at the dining room table and picked up the page he was reading.

'It's true.' Prendergast said. 'The stones being thrown around this property have quite a light projection. They certainly don't hurt much when they hit you. It feels as if they lose power when they land.'

Reverend MacKenzie sat opposite them with that wild-eyed look of a patient being told he had only days to live. He had a long, skinny face, crinkled with age, and a matching nose. His round wire spectacles dangled between his eyes like a gymnast holding on to the crucifix position on the rings for too long. It was only after a very long silence that he spoke: 'And, you say there were witnesses to this 'trouble'?'

'Fifteen in all, including Telfair. Clergy and laymen, but all upstanding members of their communities.' Prendergast was in his element, relaying the facts of his case to a new recruit.

'And this minister, was he Presbyterian?'

'I believe he was an Episcopalian chaplain.' Libby stifled her laughter as Reverend MacKenzie looked as though he was about to call for an exorcist. 'He changed his spots to Presbyterian minister after the Golden Revolution forced him to tow the Calvinist line,' she added quickly.

'Did he believe the devil was involved?'

'He says at the end of his account: 'Be sober, be vigilant, because your adversary the devil, as a roaring lion, walketh about seeking whom he may devour: Whom resist, steadfast in the faith.'

'Hmm, the words of Peter the Apostle.'

'Or Peter Peter the Pumpkin Eater.'

The minister cast Libby a withering glower. 'You're not a believer then?'

Libby shrugged. 'Not really. If I don't believe in the devil, he can't harm me.'

'Don't be fooled, lass. The devil walks amongst us in various guises. It is only through prayer, blessing and the ministry of healing that we are able to cast him out. This house needs blessed.' Libby half expected a boulder to come hurtling through the door and take the minister's head off, but it didn't. Not even a small stone dropped beside him. 'Are these,' he fought for a suitable word, '... occurrences more prevalent on the Sabbath?'

'Not to my knowledge. Monday, Tuesday and Wednesday were definitely bad days.' Libby said. 'Yesterday was OK, until last night, which was particularly horrible.'

'What do you mean by horrible?'

'Something came into my room, put out the lights and ran around. When I escaped on to the landing, I saw a boy in my torchlight, standing as close to me as Prendy is now. He disappeared and became a dog instead.'

'*Cù-Sìth*, a hound of Satan.' The minister whispered his

words into the heavens and squeezed his Bible.

'No, actually, a hound of Jim Black. The naughty dog ran around the room and scared the living daylights out of me. I can't explain the boy, though. He scratched 'find me' into the floorboards under my feet.'

Libby suddenly realised she was speaking to someone who was relatively new to ghost hunting and the devastating affect her tale was having on a good man of the cloth was evident in his slack-jawed expression.

'I saw a boy looking at me through that window.' Barbara joined the conversation from the kitchen door. 'What did your boy look like, Ms Butler?' She said her name as if it hurt.

'Blond hair. Chubby. Early teens ...'

'Ruddy complexion?'

'He was pale and unhealthy, like he'd grown up on chip butties all his life. He looked asleep, even though he was standing up. It makes me shudder just to think about it.'

'And you're still happy to stay in this house after an ordeal like that? Goodness, you must be keen.'

Libby ignored the verbal bullet, but it wounded her all the same.

'So,' Prendergast took up the conversation as if on another one of his rescue missions. 'A young male, either living or dead, has entered the premises...'

'Prendy,' Libby's voice was only slightly chiding, 'you're talking like a cop again.'

'Sorry,' Prendergast straightened his tie. 'I have a hunch that I need to explore. Bless the house by all means, Reverend MacKenzie. I'm sure a good blessing would do more good than harm. In the meantime, I think I might take a walk.'

'Where to?' Libby didn't relish the prospect of spending any amount of time in the company of Barbara Armstrong. 'Can I come with you?'

'Best not.'

'You can help me clean.'

Libby now believed in the devil when she fancied Barbara's eyes flashing red.

'So sorry, I need to work. I've got to go to court on Monday.'

'And will you be standing in front of the dock or behind it?'

— — —

Flicking through case notes and client files all afternoon, Libby was glad she at least had something to take her mind off the verbal assaults of her new-found adversary. She sat on the patio, turning the mug of cold tea around in her fingers and wondering why she hadn't stood up for herself against his mother's acerbic battering.

She hated Barbara Armstrong, with her neatly pressed suits and plastic hair-do, almost as much as Barbara Armstrong hated her. It was obvious that MacAoidh's mother didn't want her around and had taken to demonstrating that fact with loud sighs and tuts whenever they came within close proximity of one another.

With Barbara stalking her all morning, Libby had taken herself off into the garden, determined that, if a poltergeist couldn't scare her away, 'Mother' certainly wouldn't.

She was ashamed to admit to herself that Barbara's brazen hostility towards her actually hurt. She was surprised at her own truth that she wanted Barbara to like her. She tried to push the possible reasons for her rationale to the back of her mind but came to the painful conclusion that mother and son were close and shared a mutual respect, as well as a deep love. She wanted to be part of that love but Barbara would rather entertain an infestation of rats than suffer Libby sharing in the affections of her precious son.

'I hope you're not waiting for Kie to return.'

'No, I've had some work to catch up on and it's a lovely day.' She hoped Barbara wouldn't see through her.

'I very much doubt whether you'll see him until tomorrow, dear. Catherine and he are very fond of each other, you know.'

'That's nice.' She opened a folder on the patio table and pretended to study it.

Kie's mother stood her ground as if she'd been planted on that spot centuries ago.

'I understand you've been helping Kie lately and I'm extremely grateful to you for offering your hand in friendship to my son. Lord knows he could do with a few more friends.' Libby braced herself for what was coming. 'It's just that the house is a bit crowded now and Kie is surrounded by people who love him. There's really no need for you to stay anymore.'

'I promised I would help him and I want to assure him I'm willing to see that promise through. I don't like going back on my word.'

'What can you do?' Barbara's temper flared and Libby immediately saw the source of the ugly part of Kie's DNA. 'You defend criminals, not good men. You can't use your legal text books to exorcise a ghost.'

'I'm not helping him in a professional capacity.'

'Then why are you here, Ms Butler?' Those cold blue eyes narrowed until they were hidden behind tiny slits and she stressed 'Miz' with a tiny curl of her mouth.

'He's vulnerable and he's lost. I just want to help him find his way back.'

'And I suppose your charitable intentions have got nothing to do with aspirations for wealth and status?'

The words were meant to sting and Libby felt her hackles

rising. 'I've got plenty money of my own, Mrs Armstrong. I'm an independent woman who likes to be able to stand on her own two feet. I wallow in my own successes because I've striven hard to achieve them and, to my knowledge, we've never had a Caste system in Scotland. Just because you're born into money doesn't make you a better human being. In fact, if your character and personality are anything to go by, I would say that wealth dehumanises a person.'

'You didn't answer my question.'

Libby felt as though she was on trial. 'Which one? Why am I sitting on this patio or why do I not want you to be treating me like a bloody untouchable?' She didn't intend her voice to rise, but she was shouting before she could check it.

Barbara sat down on the chair opposite her and wriggled her posterior into its hard metal surface. She leaned her elbow on Libby's folders, being careful not to appear too close.

'Look, Libby,' she began with a patronising smile. 'Kie has experienced suffering in his life that no young man should ever be forced to deal with. You are right, he's vulnerable and he's broken, but I've planned very hard to fix this. He needs constancy, love and support in his life, not more pain and confusion.'

'He needs the capacity to make his own choices. You treat him like a minor.'

'You know nothing about him.'

'And, obviously, neither do you.'

They stared at each other over the patio table for long moments, Libby's heart vibrating; Barbara's nostrils flaring.

It was Barbara who ended the stand-off. 'I really don't think your staying on here will be of any benefit to my son. When Mr Prendergast returns, I'll ask him to take you home.'

Libby took a deep breath and slammed her palms on her

folders. She looked up at the colossus that was 'Mother' and held her gaze.

'Today was my last day here anyway. I've got to return to work next week and need a few days to settle back to normality. I don't need Prendy to play chauffeur for me, I'm perfectly capable of calling my own taxi.' She felt her back teeth grinding together in an effort to rein-in her anger. 'Before I go, however, I need you to know that, despite your attempts to rule his life, Kie is a free spirit and anything you do to him by way of interference in his liberty to choose how he wants to run his life will cause irreparable damage to his confidence. He loves you and he wants to please you and he's prepared to do that to the detriment of his own happiness. Now what loving mother would wish to tether her only son to a life of obedience, leaving him sad, broken and unfulfilled?'

'Now look here ...'

'He occasionally likes kippers for breakfast and will only enjoy porridge with sugar and cream; oh, and a wee pinch of salt. His favourite possession is his grandfather's old Purdey, given to him by his father. He doesn't like to shoot things with it, but he does love the feel of it in his hands and the smoothness of the trigger pull. He likes the shiny black Discovery you gave him for his last birthday because it will never get him stuck in the mud, but he prefers his vintage Series One that's rusting in the garage awaiting his eager attention. He loves his father, but is too stubborn to forgive him for whatever he's done. It hurts him that he doesn't know how to make things right. His favourite colour is blue. He likes the smell of lavender and doesn't understand why people buy expensive foreign honey. His favourite place in the world is a loch beneath the east facing peak of Quinag, called *Lochan Bealach Cornaidh*. It's cold, it's savage and it takes a bit of an effort to get there with his fishing tackle, but it captivates him with its sullen, brooding solitude because it evokes deep emotions in him that remind him of comfort and home.' Libby let out an audible, wistful sigh, unaware of the effect her words were having on the listener.

'He can speak perfect Gaelic. He was happy to make the ninety-eight mile round-trip to school every day because you couldn't bear to send him away to boarding school and he didn't want to leave home. He's quick to rile but takes his time to trust. He's headstrong but always wants to do what's right. Catherine's right, he's an excellent chef but only so because he puts his whole self into all his endeavours.'

Libby didn't know what snapped her out of her trance, but she collected up her folders and stuffed them under her arm. 'Now I've only known him for a couple of weeks. You gave birth to him and didn't know any of that. I'll get my bags.'

Barbara stood in silence, trembling, her tears eroding rivulets in her foundation.

As Libby made to pass her, Barbara caught her arm.

'You're in love with him, aren't you?' Her words were an accusation.

'He's a wonderful, gentle human being. What's not to love about him?'

chapter 17

THE MEENISTER

'There you are.'

Kie sat on the beach throwing pebbles into the high tide line as Catherine approached. He heard her footfall crunching on the shingle a long time before he heard her voice.

'They're serving breakfast, are you coming?' She leaned over his back and curled her arms around his neck.

'I'm not very hungry.'

'Well, you can't expect me to eat by myself, Kie.'

He exhaled his annoyance and stood up.

'I've been looking everywhere for you. I woke up and you were gone. I thought you'd left me without saying goodbye until I spied your Discovery in the car park.'

He didn't bother to respond as Catherine continued to talk at him all the way to the restaurant. He sat down with a bowl of citrus fruit and a glass of breakfast orange. Before he could raise his spoon to his mouth, Catherine grabbed his injured wrist.

'Shall we go back to bed after breakfast?'

He wrestled his hand away and ate his fruit, wondering why she was trying so hard to appeal to his masculine needs.

'No, I've got things to do at the steading.'

She looked taken aback. 'What will I do all day without you?'

There was something about Catherine today that was different. She sat opposite him in a dark blue v-neck sweater over a stark-white shirt, her golden hair cascading over her shoulders, her expensive string of pearls grinning under her chin. She was a beautiful woman who was eager to please herself and had a tendency to launch into nocturnal over-drive in order to feed her insatiable desires. What was there not to like about her? He noticed the hungered look in her eyes and began to worry.

'Go home, Cathy, there's nothing for you here.'

He regretted his honesty as soon as the words left his mouth. Catherine burst into tears at the breakfast table causing the other diners and the staff to cast concerned glances across the room.

'What was last night all about then? Did it mean anything to you?'

He wished she hadn't spoken so loud as he now attracted the attention of the maître D'. He kept his voice to a whisper. 'What're you talking about? We've been together for three years. What's changed?'

'You want to dump me, don't you? Don't think I'm stupid enough not to be able to see that.' She howled into the plaster ceiling and blew her nose on the starched napkin. 'You've never once told me you love me.'

He took a quick glance around the breakfast room and cursed as he now had everyone's attention. He leaned across the table in a vain attempt to be less audible. 'I don't think we're going anywhere, Cathy. We want different things in life and now live too far away from each other to continue a meaningful relationship.'

'So you were just using me for sex all this time?' Her chest heaved with every violent sob. 'You never did intend to marry me.'

'Cathy, please. I'm very fond of you and I've really tried but must admit to both of us that I don't love you. Love's very important to me.'

She wailed and MacAoidh just had to watch her, his confidence and resolve draining with each shriek of misery.

'Excuse me.'

He snapped his head around to a well-dressed, middle-aged woman who'd been sitting to their right. She carried a miniscule Yorkshire Terrier between her armpit and right breast. Both dog and woman wore the same growling snarl on their faces. Before he could ask her what she wanted, she slapped his face. 'Bastard!'

Her dog flew from her arm and bit into Kie's bandaged hand as he brought it up to protect his face. His reflexive punch sent it spinning into the air in a series of yelps before landing on the coffee trolley against the wall.

'Murderer!' The woman screamed and raced after her pet. 'George. Do something.'

Her husband, a fragile little man with years of nagging hanging from his expressionless features, rose from the table and mechanically rolled up his sleeves.

MacAoidh believed only a quick exit now would prevent another arrest.

'Go home, Cathy. I'll call you a taxi and we'll speak about this another day.'

He checked out, threw his bags and those of his mother's and the minister's into the Discovery, and sat for a while at the steering wheel. It was late morning. It had taken him a few hours to attempt to find a taxi service that would agree to take one person all the way to the sparsely populated, old crofting shire of Lochinver. In the end, he couldn't find one at such short notice and persuaded Catherine to take his mother's car home. He checked her into hotels in Loch Lomond, Fort William, Achnasheen and Ullapool to break up the journey, knowing the long haul would wear her nerves out before she even reached Abington.

After she'd finished crying, Cathy had become silent and dismissive. He'd been grateful for that and also didn't mind the scene at the breakfast table which demonised him and exonerated her as the victim of male arrogance. He shouldered the blame and felt better for having done so. There was no such thing as a painless way to finish a relationship and he was sorry for causing her hurt. His only regret was not hitting that wee dog a bit harder. He could still feel the teeth marks nipping under his bandage.

He checked his mobile phone for messages and was surprised to see he had seventeen missed calls from his mother and six from Prendy in the space of ten minutes. He decided to speak to the only one of the two he would probably get any sense out of.

'Hi, Prendy. Sorry I missed your calls. What? What do you mean something terrible's happened. How terrible? Pardon? What? Did you say the minister's dead? How? OK, I'm on my way.'

— — —

'Where is everyone?'

Kie stormed into the house and followed the sound of voices. As he hit the sitting room, his mother raced into his arms and wept. Prendy looked grim as he knelt by the minister's body and inspected it thoroughly.

Reverend MacKenzie, dressed in his Geneva gown, knelt on the floor, his knees and arms tucked underneath him, the tip of his nose just touching the ground. A bottle of holy water lay at his side, its contents spilled on the rug. His bible and crucifix lay beside him like offerings on an altar. He looked like a man at morning prayer, save that his body was stiff as a board.

Kie made to take a step forward.

'Just stay back please, lad. I want you to treat that sofa as a police line so an investigation can be made of the scene without fear of outside contaminants.'

'Fair enough.'

'I've called the police and ambulance services and both are on their way.'

'Did you have to involve the cops?'

'Afraid so. Although I don't believe the good minister's death is suspicious in any way, we don't know his medical history and he's over three hundred and fifty miles away from his own doctor. Let the police and the procurator fiscal deal with this, that's what they're paid to do.'

'How am I going to tell Alison, his wife?'

Prendy turned to Barbara. 'I understand how difficult this is for you, my dear. Please don't worry, the police will handle everything.' Prendergast had taken control of the aftermath in a relaxed and dignified manner.

'I should never have brought him here.' Still sniffling, Barbara pulled herself out of Kie's comforting arms and straightened her hair. 'I'll phone Alison. We're very dear friends and the news will be better coming from me.'

Kie shook his head and couldn't rip his eyes away from the bizarre body of the minister kneeling in the centre of his living room. 'How did he die?'

'We won't know that until the PF makes out a report. I'm no medical expert but it looks to me like a heart attack.'

'How long has he been there?'

'By the rigidity of the body, I would say he's in the early stages of rigor mortis, so would guess he died a few hours ago. He told me last night he was getting up at five to make a start. At seven hundred hours, I found him like this.'

'He died blessing this house?'

'Looks like it.'

Kie whistled. 'Are you going to tell the police that?'

'Why not? There's nothing criminal or out of the ordinary about a holidaying minister blessing the house of a family friend.'

'How are they going to get him out of here?'

'Stretcher.'

'Will they have to cart him out of here in that position?'

'Until his body relaxes, he'll stay in that position unless they cut him up.'

Kie didn't understand why he was seeing comedy in such a grim scene and put his reactions down to the unusual bizarreness of the situation.

'Where's Libby?'

'She returned home yesterday. Holiday's over and she's back at work on Monday.'

'I thought she said she was staying 'til tomorrow.'

'I think your mother spoke to her.'

'Why are you twitching?' Kie realised Prendergast was trying to warn him of something but didn't want to get hit by crossfire. Kie decided to let it drop until the shock of the minister's death had dwindled to mere astonishment.

'There's a dead body at my feet, Kie, why wouldn't I twitch?'

– – –

There were times when MacAoidh Armstrong wished he could disappear once more into some far-off corner of the world with only a passport and backpack. This was one of them.

His house was like Monday morning rush-hour on the Bombay Railway. Teeming with police, medical experts, emergency service personnel and nosey neighbours, there was nowhere he could go in the confines of his own property that didn't involve bumping into someone who wanted to ask him a question.

'Does that CCTV work, Mr Armstrong?' A fresh-faced policewoman asked him, indicating with her head to the camera above the door.

'I haven't got round to connecting it properly, sorry.'

As if locked in someone else's dream, he watched the earthly remains of Reverend MacKenzie being carted out on a wheeled stretcher by sombre bearers. His odd shape was shrouded in a blanket and reminded Kie of the Ark of the Covenant.

'Did the deceased suffer from any form of ill health that you are aware of yourself?' Another voice surprised him from behind.

Kie bit his tongue at the police speak. 'Sorry, officer, the last time I saw Reverend MacKenzie was at Sunday school when I was eleven years old. He was very well then. You'll have to ask my mother.'

'Do you have any sugar?'

'I believe the drama is over for one day and it's time you all left this family in peace.' Prendergast once again came to Kie's aid as he ushered the unwanted guests out the door.

Standing alone in the hallway at last, with the last police car disappearing across the gravel, they could both breathe a little deeper.

'Has there been any more activity while I've been away?'

Prendergast shook his head. 'Oddly enough, the house has been very quiet. When I saw Reverend MacKenzie lying dead, I did look for a random stone around the corpse, but there was none. Nothing untoward happened yesterday either, come to think of it, apart from the fact we ate your mother's cooking.'

'Oh, aye?'

'Oh, aye,' Prendergast echoed, 'and I hope I shall never be forced to suffer a similar experience in this lifetime.'

'Don't tell me. You had lamb stew.'

'That's what she called it, at least.'

'I wouldn't be at all surprised if the procurator comes up with a verdict of death by poisoning.'

'I wouldn't like to be the officer in charge of *that* investigation.'

They managed to laugh, despite the serious issues of the day.

'I have a confession, Prendy.'

'I'm listening.'

'I lied to the police.'

'About what?'

'The surveillance camera. We should have a recording of the minister's last moments.'

'Can we see it now?'

'I'm not sure if I'm ready for any more shocks today.'

'Neither am I, but I think we should take a look at least.'

They sat at the kitchen table, shoulder to shoulder, while Kie ran a remote search of the multiple camera captures from his laptop. He clicked on the image on the camera above the door of the sitting room that looked across the room to the bay windows and filled the screen with it.

'There.'

The top of Reverend MacKenzie's head came into view. With the Bible and cross in one hand and his vial of holy water in the other, he soundlessly read a passage while sprinkling the contents of the bottle across the room with sharp jerking movements.

Kie felt a strange emotion wash over him. The man died this morning, but the final and most dramatic role in his life was playing out on a computer screen as if he were still alive.

Reverend MacKenzie stepped in and out of the camera's view, his eyes closed, his lips twitching in prayer.

'What's that?'

They both brought their noses closer to the screen.

'I don't know.' Kie felt a cold sense of dread scratching at his spine.

A large black spot appeared to fall from the ceiling by the window. Kie stopped the movie and replayed it, certain at first he was seeing things. As it fell, a dark mist grew until it hovered behind the praying minister like a vertical slick of black oil, stalking his movements in perfect synchronicity. Unaware of the shadow rising behind him, the minister continued his blessing.

Kie and Prendergast gasped in unison as Reverend MacKenzie spun around suddenly, taking fright as if someone had shouted his name in his ear. He put out his arms, as if to fend off an imminent attack, then flailed at the air, shrieking. The black shape appeared to hurtle towards him, engulfed him and then dissipated so quickly that Kie was forced to replay the feed several times before he satisfied himself he wasn't delusional.

Reverend Mackenzie dropped to his knees, spilling the holy water, his precious Bible skidding from his hand. His body slumped forward, his nose hit the carpet and he never moved again.

Chapter 20

THE FLIGHT

'Let's look on the bright side, Sandy. You've got off with a fine which you can pay by weekly instalments from your dole money and that leaves you enough cash to get a carry out from the corner shop and meet your friends under the bridge. Just try not to get caught drinking in public again and don't throw your empty cans in the river.'

'Thanks, pal.'

She watched her client ambling down the street with his ill-fitting clothing barely concealing the wasted muscles of his limbs. 'I mean it. I don't want to see you here again.' She shouted after him but knew her warning shot had lost momentum and missed him.

'He'll be up next week for the same crime.'

She turned around to the sound of that soft Highland accent and tried to restrain her emotions. Kie leaned against the railings with his arms crossed, wearing his usual black jeans and plain t-shirt, red this time, and a smile that had the power to melt the remainder of the world's pack ice and cause a global disaster within minutes.

'Hello, Kie. What brings you to the steps of Dumfries Sheriff Court?' She hoped he couldn't tell her hands were shaking.

'You do. I haven't seen you for a whole week and thought I'd take you out for lunch, although it's a bit late now.'

'Well, here I am,' she spread her arms out and brought them swiftly back to her sides when she remembered the small tear in the armpit of her jacket. 'Have you been waiting here for a while?'

'About half an hour. I spoke to Audrey and she told me where you'd be this afternoon.'

'We were running late.'

'I thought it was your policy not to defend guilty criminals.'

'The only thing that man's guilty of is being an alcoholic drug user with no money, no employment skills and no prospects of ever turning his life around. It's the system that's guilty of violating his human rights and turning him into an outcast member of society. If I could bring the system to this sheriff court and point the accusing finger at it, I would.'

'Wo, Libby, get off your high horse. It's me. I agree with you.' She smiled. 'How's the trouble?'

'Gone. The place has returned to normal since Reverend MacKenzie dropped dead.'

'Yes, I heard about that. What a shock it must've been. I heard it was a heart attack.'

'He was a good age.'

'Has the grand high witch flown back to Sutherland on her broomstick?'

'Not yet but she'll have to go home for the funeral when the body's released. I hope I can persuade her to stay home this time.'

She couldn't bring herself to ask about Catherine. 'Have you got things to do in town?'

'I've done them.'

'Then could you give me a lift back to Castle Douglas? My car's in the garage and I was forced to take the bus this morning. That's the first time I've taken public transport since leaving London. It felt quite nostalgic.'

'Stay there and I'll bring the car around.'

She allowed him to take her briefcase and all her folders but drew the line when he offered to carry her handbag. She watched him run across the road and disappear around the corner.

Standing by the railings outside the court, the dark red sandstone walls looming behind her, Libby couldn't stop smiling. She'd genuinely not expected to see him again so soon, if at all. She knew Catherine had returned to Lochinver in Barbara's car, having taken four days to get there, but Prendy was vague about the circumstances surrounding her sudden departure. When asked if the relationship was over, Prendy had spluttered his ignorance and refused her plea to interrogate Kie over a few cans of beer.

She'd mulled over the argument with his mother time and time again, mentally dissecting every sentence in a meaningful attempt to find a word, or series of words, that could be translated into remote positivity. She decided in the end that 'Mother' would not tolerate any relationship, professional or personal, between her precious son and a woman who was uncouth, uncivilised and common. It would be fight or flight for Libby.

She spied the Defender in the traffic inching along Buccleuch Street and felt her spirits soar. His appearance today was purely for personal reasons. He hadn't forgotten her and perhaps he'd even missed her. What's more, his mother hadn't managed to infect him with her vitriolic poison. She decided there and then to don her armour and fight dirty for his affections.

Her plans to make an elegant step into the vehicle, with a tantalising glimpse of thigh, didn't quite work. She'd forgotten the height between the ground and the passenger seat. She felt, and certainly heard, the back seam of her skirt rip from hem to waist as she tried to gain a foothold on the floorwell. She knocked her forehead on the metal sill as she heaved herself into the seat and slammed her jacket in the door.

If Kie noticed her graceless entry, he was polite enough not to show it. He leaned across her and opened the door with a smile while she tugged at the material, feeling flushed.

'Good week?'

She stared at the river's surface, sparking oranges and yellows in the afternoon sun, as he drove across the bridge. The trailing branches of green willow stroked the lazy water. 'If defending habitual re-offenders meets with your definition of good, then my week has been filled with delirious pleasure.'

He glanced at her and smiled.

'What about your week? Do you really think the poltergeist has gone?'

'I don't believe it was a poltergeist at all, now the world's returned to normal. There were times when I felt my entire belief system was being rocked, but I think the mind can play tricks when a person's not thinking straight. I'm never going to underestimate the power of suggestion ever again.'

'So who took down that barn?'

'I don't care.'

'You're evading the important issues again, Mr Armstrong.'

'Life would be dull indeed if we had all the answers to every question, Miss Butler.'

She watched his hands on the steering wheel and gear lever and marvelled at the strength in them. He had huge masculine hands with long fingers and thick veins bulging from the straight sinews. She also noticed the crown logo on the blue face of his watch and realised it was not made of ordinary stainless steel but a white metal far more pricey.

'Libby?'

She snapped out of her musings with a jump. 'Sorry, I was just admiring your watch. Is it white gold?'

'I don't know. It was a present.' He looked embarrassed.

'From Mommy Dearest?'

'No,' his cough revealed a hint of apology, 'from Catherine.'

'Sorry, what were you saying?'

'I was just wondering what your thoughts were.'

'About what?'

He fired another quick glance at her, this one confused. 'Prendy gave up the recordings and the DVR to the police.'

'What recordings?'

'The ones I've just been telling you about. Have you been sleeping?'

'Sorry, Kie, I'm still in work mode. Tell it to me again.' She felt she'd got away with the lie this time and kept her gaze to the scenery on her left.

He showed no signs of annoyance. 'I have a recording of David MacKenzie's death. When the police came to take his body away, I told them the CCTV hadn't been hooked up.'

'Why did you tell them that?'

He shrugged those broad shoulders. 'I don't know. I was worried there would be something odd or inexplicable on them and didn't want to go through a lengthy explanation about ghosts and hauntings.'

'Still in denial.' She turned to smile at him and noticed his quick glance at her lap. Her skirt had twisted around so the long, ragged tear was now highly visible, revealing an entire right thigh and a large portion of her underwear. She wriggled into a semblance of decency and dared him to laugh. 'This is becoming a bit of a habit. It tore when I got in the car.'

'I heard it. Anyway,' he continued with a surreptitious smile, 'Prendy thought it best to come clean and hand everything over to the police who are now treating the minister's death as suspicious.'

'Are you a suspect?'

'Jings, no. I wasn't even there at the time. Luckily, a former upstanding, highly-respected member of Scotland Yard was, and he's vouched for me. Forensics have been crawling over the property all week but have come up with no explanation for a black mist attacking the meenister.'

'A black mist attacked Rev MacKenzie?'

'I've got a copy of the recording. I'll show it to you but you're not going to believe it.'

'Try me. Lately I've developed a very open mind. Who's the copper in charge of the investigation?'

'They're using Prendy as a consulting detective on the case.'

'That's going to set their budgets back to the nineteen seventies.'

'I'll admit I'm relieved this has all come out in the open. That way, I can let someone else deal with the whys and wherefores while I get on with my life.'

'You do realise, now the death is being treated as suspicious, it's fallen into the public domain. You'll have to brave the newshounds baying for a top story.'

'I've already had a few sniffing around but took Prendy's advice and gave them no comment.'

'That's very good advice but some can be very persistent.'

The natural break in the conversation gave Libby the opportunity to dig a little. 'So you're staying in Auchencairn for good?'

'Aye, why not. It's as good a place as any to settle down.'

'Does settling down include a wife, two point two children and a dog called Tiddles?'

'Aye.'

She was beginning to hate that word.

'Would you mind stopping by the house with me before I take you home?'

'I'm not dressed. My bottom's hanging out my skirt.'

'It won't take long. I'd be grateful if you would cast your lawyer's eyes over some paperwork for me. I promise not to walk behind you and I'll cook you lunch.'

Libby's heart sank. The visit hadn't been a personal one after all. He wanted her advice in a professional capacity and not her company as she'd hoped.

'I don't think so, Kie. I've got a few files to read through and some research to do on proceeds of crime. I really need to get home. If you give Audrey a ring, she'll make you an appointment and ...'

She squealed as he swerved the wheel into the verge and hit the brakes. He twisted his body around to face her. 'Has my mother scared you off?'

The question came so suddenly that she didn't know how to respond. 'No, I ...'

'She told me the two of you had *words*; are you going to tell me what those words were?'

'Ask her.'

'I'm asking you.'

'Look, Kie, I don't want to come between you and your mother.'

'You won't.' He turned the ignition off, crossed his arms and leaned back into his seat, his jaw set to stubborn.

'All right, she gave me my marching orders. I saluted, made a ninety degree pivot on one foot and did the military one step in double time into a taxi.'

He started awkwardly: 'I want you to know my mother's sentiments don't reflect mine in any way.'

That declaration was far too clinical for an apology. 'It's comforting to note you can on occasion have a mind of your own. At times I think you're nothing more than a ventriloquist's dummy and Mother's got her hand up your arse.'

'Fine.' He turned on the ignition, threw the car into gear and sped off towards Castle Douglas.

Libby slammed the door as they reached her house and just had time to leap out his path before he ran her foot over in his speedy effort to get away. Clutching her folders, briefcase and handbag to her chest, the pages spilling on to the path, she ambled towards the door, ignoring the reproachful look of a neighbour who didn't appreciate the brazen display of bare cheek smiling through her tights. Throwing herself on the couch, she let out a deep, heavy sigh to mark her continuing disastrous love life. Barbara had won an impressive victory without even having to pull out a gun.

'Have him!' she muttered out loud, 'and I hope you'll both live happily ever after.'

Chapter 21

THE EVER AFTER

'As he was at prayer he observed a black thing in the corner of the barne, and it did increase, as if it would fill the whole house. He could not discern it to have any form, but as if it had been a black cloud; it was affrighting to them all.'

'Didn't that black thing appear at the very end of the Mackie haunting?' Barbara shivered and tightened her cashmere shawl around her shoulders.

'Yes, the very day before it all ended. If this phenomenon is following a similar pattern to the seventeenth century troubles, then we have a black cloud on camera and we can expect peace at The Ring for at least another three hundred or so years.'

Prendergast, closed his folder, sat back in his chair and smiled to himself.

'You know, Barbara, I now believe in ghosts and have very little doubt the occult's involved in the strange activity that occurred on these premises. As a former policeman, however, I have to take the hard-nosed view and look for other more natural clues involving criminal activity. This house, however, is telling me the other side exists and can interact with the living. I would love to know either way. I wish your boy would agree to a proper investigation.'

Barbara put her hand to her mouth and let out a dry titter behind it. It was at that moment Prendergast realised just how controlling she was in every aspect of her life. She wouldn't even allow herself a random burst of sentiment. He suddenly felt very sorry for her son.

'We MacAoidhs have a very long and traditional history with the other side. It's part of our lives. Kie grew up in a haunted house in Assynt and saw spirits in Africa. I knew he'd inherited the *An Dà Shealladh,* or second sight, from a very young age, but he's always chosen to deny it. Perhaps he can't anymore. He'll have to accept his heritage eventually. I think that's the lesson something's trying to teach him.'

'Well, our work's almost done here.' Prendergast didn't want to give Barbara any more reason to interfere in her son's new life by discussing more lessons she believed he needed to learn.

'Yours may be, but mine's just started. I want to get Kie and this place ship-shape before I'll be satisfied he doesn't need me around.'

'I think the lad copes remarkably well. He's a hard worker and has an extremely intelligent head at the end of his neck. He'll be just fine by himself.'

Prendergast wanted to say more, but thought the better of giving his opinion when it wasn't asked for. Besides, Barbara Armstrong wouldn't ever admit to being wrong.

'But he won't be by himself, will he? That dreadful lawyer will be pushing herself into his life once my back's turned. It took me hours of phone calls to eventually persuade Catherine that Kie's not himself and didn't mean what he said. She's agreed to give it another go but this will be his very last chance. She's a very good catch for any young man but she can't wait forever. She's already twenty-six and wants a baby by next year.'

Prendergast wanted to tell Barbara that Kie was standing at the door but couldn't squeeze a word of warning between her barrage of sentences.

'Ah, MacAoidh, you're home. I have some very good news for you.'

He winced as Kie moved slowly towards them, maintaining his hooded focus on his squirming mother. He sat down in the carver at the head of the table and crossed one leg over the other, his body language open and challenging, his foot shaking violently against his knee.

Prendergast continued before a fight broke out. 'I spoke to the PF and forensics this morning and the evidence points to the fact that Reverend MacKenzie died of natural causes. He had a heart attack. It's also agreed that the black shadow on the recording, by the way it mimics the reverend's movements, is probably an anomaly either caused by the light from the bay windows or a defect in the camera or both.'

MacAoidh merely nodded as he levelled his gaze on his mother.

'The stone phenomena, the noises, the sightings, the alleged attacks, could easily be put down to paranormal activity or magnetic or electrical fields.' He fed him the information Kie wanted to hear and not Prendergast's own personal thoughts on the matter. He would never convince him anyway. 'Without a thorough investigation, we can't tell. Since there's been no further incidences in this house since the minister's death, it's highly possible that this will mark the end of a rather worrying and distressing time for all of us. Whether the blessing worked on the devil or whether the death was enough to scare the nuisance neighbours from continuing with their mischief, can only be left to conjecture.'

'Thanks, Prendy. You've done a good job.'

'I'm going home today. Wife's getting a bit upset in my absence and I must admit I miss her smile and her cooking. I'd like to come back and visit if it's OK with you.'

'That would be grand.'

'Of course, if anything further occurs, you will let me know immediately?'

'I'm not going to call you back from London for a wee stone but I will call if I think you should be further involved.'

'Good,' Prendy nodded to the pair of them. 'I'll get packed then. I should make it to London by dinner time.'

He thought about leaving MacAoidh to strangle his mother but decided to have a final word that may help the lad's situation. 'Oh, and Barbara, they're releasing the body later this morning and sending the reverend home by car. I've arranged for you to accompany him to Sutherland.'

'I'm not sharing a car with a corpse.'

'The corpse won't be driving, dear.'

'I'm not going.'

MacAoidh sprang up and grabbed his mother's arm. 'Oh, aye, I think you are and I'm going to help you pack.' He winked at Prendergast as he hauled her protesting from the room.

Prendergast sat for long moments before gathering up his papers. He closed his eyes, willing a stone to hit him or a rap on the underside of the table, but the house was still.

The birds sang outside and, now and again, the lazy buzz of a passing insect would reach his ear.

What could have dismantled a thirty-foot-high barn in a matter of hours and in the dark? He wondered if there really had been some paranormal force behind the strange occurrences at The Ring steading but decided he'd probably never know.

'Ah well, better visit Libby before I go.' He spoke to the silent house and listened for a while, half expecting a response.

As none came, he picked up his papers, stuffed them into his briefcase and climbed the stairs to begin his packing.

— — —

It was well after midnight before Kie decided to go to bed. He sat in the living room watching a subtitled Polish movie which had one of those conceptual endings that left him wondering what the story had all been about in the first place. Alone in the house, he had to admit to himself he missed the company of others, even his mother's incessant nagging.

It took him a good part of the morning to persuade his mother to leave. The effort, of course, had involved an argument about her overbearing attitude and her need to control all aspects of his life. To his surprise, she conceded to his wishes and left for Assynt with the earthly remains of Reverend MacKenzie. Prendergast left for London shortly afterwards with a promise to return in a few months.

Thinking about his list of chores in the morning, Kie put down the remote control and idly thumped the tips of his fingers on the low marble table in front of him as he thought.

His contemplations turned to Catherine and he wondered whether he should take that second chance or risk spending the remainder of his life alone.

A faint tapping on the window caused him to stop drumming his fingers. He listened but was answered with silence.

Libby then sprang to mind and he shut her out with a testy curse and a rap of knuckles on the table. That woman had blown hot and cold too many times and was beginning to annoy him. A light tapping echoed his cadence.

Cautiously, and only after a deep breath, MacAoidh rapped five times on the table and was astounded to hear the same amount of taps in return.

He moved to the window and peered out into the darkness but could see nothing but the shadows of the outbuildings. Believing the noise to have come from a crow, he turned off the light and made for the stairs.

He spun around as the tapping began in earnest and eventually turned into loud raps. By the time he reached the sitting room, the raps were now heavy bangs: rhythmic, persistent, decisive. Standing in the dark, with frantic eyes he scanned the view from the window but could see nothing.

The bangs turned to resounding thuds that shook the walls, rattled the photographs off the piano and set the grandfather clock chiming. The furniture jumped with the impact of thunderous pounding and the whole house felt like it was shaking in its foundations.

Believing he was witnessing the effects of an earthquake, MacAoidh could only stand in its epicentre and wait either for the quake to subside or the ground to open up and eat him alive. He leaped out the way with a loud curse as a heavy object fell from the ceiling and smashed against the marble table.

The banging ceased abruptly and an eerie stillness took its place but he felt the chilling sensation that he wasn't alone.

He picked a careful path across the room to the light switch, his feet crunching on fragile objects littering the floor. He turned the light on and what he saw shook his soul.

The wooden box marked H he'd put in the loft weeks ago lay in splinters over the table and floor, its colourful contents strewn across the room. MacAoidh looked up to the space in the ceiling from where it appeared to have fallen and then down to its shattered remains. Raw recollections invaded reason as he recognised the colourful jewellery, the photographs of happy times and letters with her handwriting. He took in a painful breath and let it out slowly before he began to gather up the pieces of his life he believed he'd locked away forever.

A loud bang at the window caused him to leap backwards in shock and the photographs flew from his hand. Another thump and MacAoidh could see a dark shadow in the gloaming. He moved forward to get a closer look. Squinting into the night, his face so close to the glass that his breath misted his vision, he could just make out the shape of a long, thin object swaying very slowly on the other side of the window. He rubbed the fog from the glass with his hand and tried to make out what it was. He didn't know whether it was reflex that caused him to leap backwards or an inherent survival instinct but he just managed to dive out of the way before the object came smashing through the window with such force that it took the glass pane with it and showered him with shards.

MacAoidh scrambled on his hands and knees across the floor before taking off at a run and slamming the door behind him. Grabbing his keys from the kitchen table, he rushed up the stairs and across the south hallway to the end storeroom where he kept his guns.

He could barely control the movement of his hands as he fumbled with the keys to the gun cabinet, dropping them a few times before releasing the lock. His body shaking and his teeth clattering together, he grabbed his shotgun and a packet of cartridges and flew back down the stairs, half running half falling.

His back slid down the wall opposite the sitting room door and he sat on the floor with a thump. The cartridges spilled from the box, scattering in all directions, as he tried to load his shotgun with hands that wouldn't stop trembling. The sitting room door banged, shuddering against its hinges, causing him to jump, but he managed somehow to push the cartridges into the barrel. He snapped the hinge closed, welded his cheek to the stock and waited.

Another bang and he almost jerked the trigger. He took a deep breath, maintained his aim and tried to remain calm. The door handle slowly turned, preceded by a faint whispering, and

Kie felt his nerves would break.

'I've got a loaded gun here.' He could hear his voice faltering as he wrestled with his anxiety to keep the barrel pointed at the door. His body spasmed, his pulse thumped in his temples and he felt his heart would burst from his ribcage. 'I'm not in the mood for negotiating with you and I will fire.'

The door opened slowly, the whispering became louder and he held his breath, the static caressing the back of his head.

'If you make a sudden move, I swear I'll shoot.'

He hoped his threat would be enough to scare off the person on the other side of the door but instead it continued to open, the disjointed whispers taunting him.

MacAoidh slowly moved his eyes from the shotgun sight as his jaw dropped open. Moving from the room in front of him, floating in the air at waist height as if carried by unseen hands, was the crossbar of the byre door. He blinked a few times, disbelieving his own eyes, as the old wooden bar turned towards the front door all by itself and passed across his vision. It stopped at the door, hovered there for a few brief seconds and dropped to the mat with a dull thud.

'Find me.'

He leaped in terror as the voice whispered its final words in his ear and the house went to sleep once more.

chapter 22

THE TURN

Libby found MacAoidh sitting at the front door cradling his shotgun. Haloed by the glare of floodlights, his body rigid and shaking uncontrollably, she persuaded him to get into her car and be driven to safety. He'd lost the power of speech.

She'd answered his call in the middle of the night and knew from his voice that something was very wrong. He sounded so distressed that she didn't even bother to dress, leaped in the car and rushed to his aid.

She stopped only once on the way home to wrestle the gun from his shaking hands and throw it into the boot.

Home safely, she helped him into the house and lay him down on her bed.

'Here,' she handed him a glass. 'This is the only spirit in the house, I'm afraid.' She regretted her choice of words immediately as she heard his teeth chattering. 'It's a very old brandy. So old I think it was distilled during the last Ice Age.'

He didn't hear her humour. In fact, he didn't appear to hear her words at all. He simply lay on the bed, those masculine hands taut and trembling at his chest, and stared into the ceiling. Libby doubted he even knew where he was. She lay her smooth palm in his and sat with him.

After an hour or so, Libby wondered whether or not she should call a doctor. Kie's condition, if it could be called that, had remained the same. His skin was freezing cold and his body shivered spasmodically. She couldn't get him to drink his brandy and he'd been unresponsive when she pulled his boots off. He'd obviously suffered some terrible trauma that left him speechless and, even worse, in an apparent coma. She considered taking all his clothes off but the decent side of her character told her that would be taking advantage of a vulnerable man.

She made her decision and rose from the bedside chair.

She squealed as he grabbed her wrist. 'Don't go. Please, don't go.'

'I'm not going anywhere.' She stroked his brow with her fingertips as he held on to her wrist.

She lay down next to him, nestled her head into his neck and promptly fell asleep.

— — —

When Libby awoke, Kie was sleeping. His breathing had returned to normal; his body was warm and no longer shuddered. At some time in the night he'd rolled over and wrapped his limbs around her. His face lay close to hers and his breath tickled her cheek. She wriggled free and watched him for a while, taking in the soft rise and fall of his chest, the short stubble on his chin and the heavy muscle cladding his arms. She pushed back the unruly strands of hair that had fallen over his brow and ran the palm of her hand across his cheek.

She closed her eyes and moved her finger softly along the smooth bridge of his nose to the tip; down to his lips and then his chin. She trailed it as gently as she could across the bony hump of his throat and along the centre of his sternum.

When she opened her eyes wondering whether to go further, he was staring at her, the unnatural blue of his irises blazing like cold sapphires in the morning light. His gaze shifted around the room and a shadow of consternation crossed his face before changing to confusion.

'Libby?'

She wondered whether he'd lost his memory. 'I'm relieved you remember how to speak.'

He sat up so quickly that he knocked the glass of brandy off the bedside table. After a few disorientated moments, he let out a loud, ragged breath. 'Thanks, Libby. I think you saved my life last night.' He drew his hand through his hair and settled back into the pillows.

'Do you want to talk about what happened?'

'No. I never want to go there again. I don't want to remember it. Please don't ever ask me.' He turned his face to her. 'Ever!'

'OK. Then let's take this one stage at a time. You were in terrible shock last night. I think you should see a doctor.'

'I don't need a doctor. I'm fine now, thanks to you.'

She tried not to show smugness in her smile. 'You gave me a bit of a fright too. I didn't know what to do with you, so I just lay down next to you and kept you company.'

'That was good of you.'

'Not at all. I couldn't be bothered to make up the spare room bed.'

He answered her with silence.

'What do you want to do today? You don't have to go back to The Ring if you don't want to. We could spend the day together. We could take a picnic to Rascarell Bay or even take a drive to The Rhins.'

She saw the shudder in his shoulders as she mentioned The Ring. 'That would be grand, Libby, but I have to go back. If I don't go back now, I don't believe I'll have the courage to ever return.'

'I'll come with you.'

'You've got your re-offending pals to defend.'

'It's Saturday, you dope.'

'Don't you want to stay in bed?'

She knew it was an innocent remark. 'I've got an unattended vehicle out there with a loaded gun in the boot. I could lose my practice certificate. Let's go.'

When they arrived at The Ring, the front door lay wide open. Libby couldn't remember if they'd left it like that. Kie sat in the car for a while and she left him to his personal deliberations on whether to run or face his demons.

She tripped over a wooden plank at the doorway and almost fell. She swore and kicked at it and squealed when it suddenly bounced back to hit her on the arm. Although the impact was gentle, it was enough to cause her to swear again and stamp on it a few times. The downstairs floor was covered in a blanket of small stones throughout all the rooms. Shotgun cartridges were spilled across the hallway and one of the huge bay windows of the sitting room was smashed. The piano stool lay on the sofa. Glass, wooden splinters and personal effects peppered the carpet and furniture. It looked as though someone had chucked a grenade into the room and closed the door.

Back in the kitchen, she armed herself with a long brush and a roll of plastic bin liners and decided she'd clear up the mess and save Kie from further distress. Whatever happened to him last night had hit him very hard and she saw him pacing the drive like a nervous bridegroom.

There was a terrible smell in the dining room. It reeked of rotten carcases and was so powerful that Libby was forced to pull off her T-shirt and wrap it around her face. The chairs lay stacked upside down against the hearth where a small fire blazed.

Moving back into the sitting room, she noticed the piano stool perched upside down on top of the piano. The smell in the dining room was now permeating throughout the house and she heard knocks and scratching, gentle at first, becoming increasingly louder.

'What do you want?' With the protection of broad daylight, Libby felt almost invincible.

She was answered with silence.

Deciding to use reason as a shield, she balanced on the edge of the sofa, hardly believing she was speaking to something that defied the principles of modern science. A chair cushion flipped in the corner of her eyes but she remained seated and willed herself not to notice it. She could hear voices talking as if in the next room and she was certain someone was crying.

It wasn't until she felt a sharp tug on her hair that Libby's courage broke. She rose quickly and left the room. In fact, she left the house and slammed the door behind her.

'I really don't think you should go in there.'

He didn't have to say anything, for the wildness of his eyes said it all.

'Why don't you stay away for a few days and see if this all settles down? You need a glazier, a cleaning contractor and, perhaps, you'll need an exorcist after all.'

'That bad?'

She nodded, her eyes wide. 'Believe me, it's that bad.'

He leaned against the car, battling to find his famous valour which had obviously left him. He stood for long moments with his arms crossed, staring at the house. Eventually, he made his decision.

'How fast can you get your team of ghostbusters here?'

'I told you, Kie, they're not ghostbusters, they're parapsychologists and they're all very serious about their work.'

'How fast?'

'I'll have to speak to Hannah.'

'OK, speak to her but make it quick. I'm going inside now

and I've no wish to end up like Reverend MacKenzie. If she's going to come at all, she has to come now or she'll probably have my ghost to contend with as well as whatever else is in there.'

'You're going back in?' Libby could hardly believe what she was hearing. 'After what happened to you last night and the terrible state you were in, you're going back?' Her look was incredulous. 'I saved you last night but, should you have another experience like that again, it may just tip you over the edge and only a long stint in a padded cell will be able to help you then.'

'I won't let it win.' He opened the boot of her car and hauled out his shotgun.

'Fat lot of good that big toy will do you against the forces of hell.'

'Aye.'

'Stubborn bastard!' She watched him storming into the house as if undertaking a one-man military raid.

She took a deep breath and brought her hands up to eye level. They were shaking like leaves in an autumn storm. 'I suppose someone has to protect him.'

She clutched her handbag as if it contained the last remnants of her failing courage and followed him into the house.

chapter 23

THE EXPERTS

'Ok, I've managed to persuade my bosses I'm having a nervous breakdown and need some time to recover.'

Libby found Kie in the dining room, smashing out the old marble fireplace with a heavy long-handled hammer. The air was choked with dust. He'd ditched his shirt and stood in his jeans, a paper mask and heavy work boots. A thick film of powdered plaster and brick dust covered his skin and hair.

'You didn't have to do that, Libby.' He pulled the mask from his face to reveal a broad stripe of white from his forehead to the top of his nose.

'I know, but I have and that's the end of it. Anyway, they agreed they owed me a few holidays. I've only taken three days off in the entire two years I've been working there.'

For the past few days, they'd braved the horrors of The Ring together and so far survived the ordeal. Apart from a few knocks, some whispering, a couple of strange shadows and a terrible smell, the house had been reasonably quiet during that time.

It was the expectation of a sudden violent encounter that was most nerve-wracking and they lived in a tentative peace, always expecting the worst would jump out at them at any given moment.

'Why are you wrecking the dining room?'

'That smell's coming from somewhere inside this fireplace. I need to get rid of this facing to see what's behind it.'

Libby, not for the first time in a few days, worried that Kie was falling apart. He took to strange notions of destroying parts of his property. First it was the byre wall; next the cabinets in the downstairs bathroom; and now the beautiful marble fireplace in his once elegant dining room.

She eyed him critically as he glugged down a glass of water and noticed he'd lost weight. He no longer had the brawny shape of a rugby player; his figure was now more refined and the bones of his ribcage were prominent.

'You're making yourself sick.'

'Aye.'

'Will you stop saying that?'

'What?'

'Saying aye.'

'I'm agreeing with you.'

'You're telling me to shut up and mind my own business.'

'Am I?' She noticed the impudent glint in his eyes and was pleased he hadn't lost his sense of humour.

'I'm worried about you.'

He put down his hammer and crossed the space between them, his eyes glowing.

'Don't.'

He folded his arms around her, the gesture catching her completely by surprise. She laughed and made a weak attempt to repel his advance with her fists. It was only when he hauled her off her feet by her backside, that she realised why the sudden burst of affection. Libby pushed him away and planted her hands on her hips. Her black suit was covered in white powder. She looked as though she'd had a baking disaster.

They only stopped laughing when they heard a gentle rapping.

'Here we go again,' she breathed out her misery.

'Libby?'

She leaped in fright and Kie snatched up the hammer as a woman appeared behind her. She recognised the shocking ginger curls and freckled face.

'Hannah? Wow! Hannah! You've grown.' Libby could barely get close enough to embrace her.

'You must be MacAoidh.' Hannah dropped Libby like a sack of mouldy grain and flashed her green eyes at the tall, handsome man wielding the sledge hammer. They shook hands and Libby noticed Hannah's hand lingering for a second in his while he attempted to avert his gaze from her enormous cleavage.

'Libby and I shared a few flats when we were at university together. I studied medicine and she studied law.'

'We had a lot of fun.'

'We really did.' She hugged Libby again. 'I'll go and scramble the team so we can settle in as soon as possible and before you demolish the house completely.' Her laughter sounded like a toy Gatling gun. 'I hope you don't mind but there are six of us and quite a lot of equipment. I tried to keep it down to four but, if what Libby's intimated to me is anything close to the truth, this house deserves a thorough investigation by at least twelve of us.'

'The more the merrier,' Libby shrugged before searching Kie's expression for annoyance. To his credit, she didn't find any.

'That's Hannah.'

'Which one?'

They laughed together.

'She must've had a boob job or four. I can't believe how skinny she is.'

'No living thing can grow under *that* shade, Libby.'

She didn't like the impish glint in his eye as she followed him into the hallway. 'Here, put your shirt on.' She threw him his cotton short-sleeved shirt. 'There are four women out there and they need to concentrate.'

As Kie helped the team in with their bags and equipment Libby welcomed Hannah into the house and instructed her as to where the six would sleep and where they would set up a base. She was under strict instructions to tell her nothing about the nature of the paranormal activity or where it took place. Hannah wanted to find that information out for herself.

They regrouped in the sitting room where Libby served them tea but hadn't been able to find the biscuits. Standing by the now repaired bay window, she marvelled at how her old friend hadn't appeared to have aged at all. She was still tiny, although unfeasibly top heavy. A tight dress with a low neckline only served to accentuate her enormous assets, especially when viewed from a standing position, and Libby compared her to a milking cow with mastitis.

The other members of the team consisted of a tall bald man who stood at the side of the byre, engrossed in conversation on his mobile phone. A dark-haired, heavily set young man who announced his name as Sal had Libby wondering if she'd heard right for a moment, until he explained his name was Salvatore and his father was Italian. There was a non-descript girl in her twenties who introduced herself as Andrea and another, striking but shy young woman who was called Jenny.

Completing the trio of lovely lasses was a twenty-something woman with short blond hair wearing a flimsy top and shorts so tiny and so tight, Libby imagined she could hear their contents squeaking. She shook Libby's hand and, with a strong German accent, said her name was Katja Albrecht. She then ran to take a camera from the bag and asked Libby to turn around in order to photograph the seemingly ghostly handprints on the back of her skirt.

Hannah turned to Kie and began her introductions in a light Midlands brogue she'd refined over the years. 'I want you to be

THE EXPERTS

aware we're not ghost hunters and neither do we necessarily believe in spirits of the dead. We're trained observers. We study psychic phenomena and try to look for underlying causes but we're not here to offer solutions. I'm Dr Hannah Simpson, head of this team, and I'm a doctor of medicine and a professional psychologist specialising in the personal backgrounds of people claiming to have experienced paranormal activity, especially of a polt nature. I study the behaviour of living people, Mr Armstrong, not the dead. So, I'll be keeping close to you and asking a few questions over the next few days. Is that OK?'

Libby smiled as she saw those shoulders shrugging. Dr Simpson would have her work cut out trying to get any personal information out of him.

'All right. Sal, Andrea and Jenny are brilliant fourth-year students of mine and take their work very seriously. They all have a keen interest in parapsychology and are here to study the wider aspects of your report through a series of investigations headed-up by Katja who is a very able young scientist. We're looking for reliable and, hopefully, replicable evidence. They're here to gather, test and evaluate, log the data and eventually write-up a report. Charlie's outside checking out the outbuildings and measuring the levels of electromagnetism in the immediate environment.'

Kie nodded to each team member as their names were announced, but there was no warmth in his smile.

'You'll hear a lot of acronyms bandied about like PSI, EVP, EMG, MPV but don't worry, you'll get used to the jargon and one of us will explain it along the way. I know we've got a lot of equipment, but we need to cover everything. I see you've got a surveillance system already installed but would you mind if we used our own, perhaps in conjunction with yours?'

Kie opened his mouth to say something but obviously

decided against it. He shook his head and shrugged again.

'Good, then. I understand there are a few of us but some, at least, do need to stay on the premises for the duration of the investigation. Do you want some of us to book into a nearby hotel?'

'No, there are plenty of beds here and lots of rooms. You're all welcome to stay for as long as it takes.' Libby thought she'd answer for him before he brandished his shotgun and warned them off his property. She could see the irritation building in both his expression and his body language as all focus fixed firmly on him.

'One last and very important request,' Hannah said. 'I don't want either you or Libby speaking to the team about your experiences. I want to come in completely clean, to rule out any form of auto suggestion.'

'Fine.' Kie responded at last.

'I need an EMF meter, a hand-held will do, something's just hit me.' The sixth member of the group staggered into the room, his cream shirt covered in dirt. He was obviously shaken but managed to pull himself together just enough to shake Kie's hand before sitting down with the students and telling them of his ordeal in a low, hushed voice.

'Charlie? Charlie Jones?' Libby could barely believe her eyes as a man from her long-forgotten past walked back into her life.

'Oh, yes, Libby. I forgot to tell you Charlie joined the team as a temporary member a few months ago. He's currently undertaking survival research for a doctorate.' Hannah didn't appear in the least bit perturbed that Charlie had seemingly just been attacked.

'That doesn't surprise me. Charlie's always been one of life's survivors, Haven't you Charlie?'

'That's survival of the human personality after death, Libby.'

'That figures.' Libby hadn't spoken to Charlie since he dumped her for a Spanish seductress over twelve years ago. He was the first man to ever break her heart. 'You've changed, Charlie. You've lost all your lovely blond curls.'

'I grew up, Lib. Adults do that sometimes.'

'You know each other?' Kie came to her rescue.

'Yes, Charlie's the sole reason I can't stand Welshmen.'

'Do you have a problem with him Libby? It's best to get it all out in the open now.' Hannah took a professional stance.

'Not at all. The next few days are going to be very interesting indeed.'

'What about you, Mr Armstrong, do you have any objections to Charlie living in close proximity to Libby over the next few days?'

'Can't tell yet. I'll let him know if I do.'

'All right,' Hannah sounded less confident than before, 'let's get set up and, Charlie, please analyse the location and log what you've just experienced. We'll begin this in the proper way.'

Libby stood with her arms folded tightly across her chest while Hannah and her A-Team leapt into action.

'What do you think of them?'

Kie sat on the piano stool, playing with the keys. 'I'm sure they're all very fine folk, but I don't believe they should be here.'

'Too late, MacAoidh, you're stuck with them. It's become a case of mutual necessity, I'm afraid. Besides, I feel better knowing there are more people here. The last few days have been a bit anxious.'

He nodded with a small sigh. 'What's the story behind Charlie?'

'He's an old flame. We all went to uni together. Hannah and I were conquests to him, nothing more. To think I would ever get the chance to watch him squirm.'

'Hannah too? He's a real stud, isn't he?'

'I'm not sure if that's still the case but Hannah and I intend to have some fun with him.'

'Rekindle the flame?' He drew his forefinger across the keys from treble to base before playing her a few choice bars of Chopin's Death March.'

'Play something more lively, would you?'

'I'll play the Hallelujah Chorus from Handel's Messiah on the chanter if your Spooks can make this all stop.' He shut the piano lid and dropped his head.

'They might not be able to make it stop, Kie.'

'Do you think they'll even be able to give me answers?'

'I hope so.' She brushed her hand across his shoulder. 'Just give them a chance.'

He nodded. 'Why not? I like the look of the one with the legs.'

'Who? Katja? The German girl with her arse hanging out her shorts?'

'That arse isn't capable of hanging.' He smiled to himself.

'Trust you to notice.' Libby slapped his arm playfully but really wanted to punch his face. 'You'd better get this place habitable if you're having guests. I'll help you clean up the dining room and then I suggest you take an ice-cold shower.'

THE SUBJECT

Macaoidh stepped into the conservatory and immediately felt like turning around again when he saw the camera on a tripod, a microphone on the table and a set of green eyes peering at him above a pair of tinted spectacles.

Hannah tried to put him at ease by offering her sweetest smile and gestured with her hand for him to sit. He sat on the chair opposite her and wriggled uncomfortably, trying his hardest to keep his eyes off her ample cleavage.

'Is the camera necessary?'

'Like I said, I want to get to know you and study your responses to my questions. I'll try to make it all as painless as possible. The footage is for my personal use. No one else will see it.'

He saw his reflection in the camera lens and looked away from it.

'What's this all for?'

Hannah took a small sip of her water. 'Let me ask the questions. Are you ready?'

His nod was the acceptance she needed. She leaned over to the tripod and turned on the camcorder.

After stating the date and time, she began. 'Subject, Mr A, is a twenty-eight-year-old white Caucasian. Widower. Lives alone. Healthy. No known mental health problems. No known allergies.'

'How do you know?'

'I've done my research.' She sat down and placed her hands on her lap. 'Some of the questions I'm going to ask may seem obvious to you, but please answer them to the best of your knowledge with as much information as possible. I don't want yes and no answers.'

'Fine.'

She picked up a clip board from the arm of her chair and poised her pen at the paper form. 'What's your full name?'

'Are you going to be holding any personal data on me?'

'For a while and in strictest confidence, but my report will not mention names nor any personal information that may identify you. You'll be known as Mr A or case PH-07351.'

He waited for her to say more before realising he hadn't answered the first question. 'Sorry, I'm a bit distracted at the moment, this may take all day.'

'Take your time. We have all day.' She had that ingratiating, pained expression of a nun who wanted to slap someone.

'MacAoidh Ross Armstrong.' He paused and let out a sigh of resignation. 'OK, it's MacAoidh Ross Duncan MacKenzie Armstrong but now I'm going to have to kill you.'

'When and where were you born?' She ignored his attempt at humour.

'The twenty-first of September, nineteen-eighty-six in Nairobi, Kenya.'

'Did you grow up in Africa?'

He raised his eyes to the right in order to access the visual memories of his childhood. 'I grew up on an estate in Assynt, Sutherland.'

'What were your parents doing in Africa?'

'My father dabbles in the coffee business.'

'How old were you when you settled in Sutherland?'

'A baby. We visited Kenya quite frequently, though. It was

like a second home during the winter months.'

'Do you have any brothers and sisters?'

'There's only me.'

As Hannah continued her line of questioning on the trivial facts of his life, Kie noticed her ticking boxes and writing notes against the papers on her clipboard. His answers were as mechanical and safe as her questions and he slowly began to relax.

'Not so bad is it?'

He smiled and shook his head.

'It would be good if you opened up to me a little.' Her words were only slightly chastising. 'Tell me about your childhood.'

'I lived in Sutherland, I went to school, I grew up and left home.' He shrugged.

'Did you have a happy childhood?'

'Aye.'

'Were there any times in your childhood when you perhaps felt unhappy?'

'Not that I can recall.'

He waited while she scribbled down her notes.

'Now I'm going to ask you more personal questions about you and I want you to tell me what comes into your head first. I would really appreciate it if you elucidated on your answers as much as possible.' She waited for him to nod but he simply stared at her. She asked anyway.

'Are you religious?'

'No.'

'Do you have a belief system?'

'Aye. I believe in what's real; what's fact; what can be scientifically proven or logically explained.'

'Do you have any phobias?'

He paused. 'No.'

'Have you ever experienced paranormal activity before you came to The Ring?'

He looked at her, his mouth unwilling to speak the words.

She waited for his response, but none came.

'We're not getting very far are we?' She pulled off her glasses and placed them on the table.

Kie could sense an air of tension from her.

'Do you want me to talk about my negative thoughts and feelings? My goals for the future? What do I aim to get out of this therapy session?'

'All right, MacAoidh, we'll end the questions for today.' She leaned her mouth towards the microphone on the table. 'Subject, Mr A, PH-07351, is non-cooperative ...'

'Now, wait a minute, I answered your questions.'

'This session ended at,' she glanced at her watch, 'fourteen fifty-six on the twenty sixth of July ...' She sat back, crossed her legs and watched him in silence as if waiting for him to begin the conversation again.

'Can I go now?'

'What do you think's going on here, MacAoidh?'

'I don't know. I was hoping you would be able to tell me.'

'I'm trying to but you're not taking this seriously enough.'

'Believe me, you wouldn't be sitting here now if that was the case.'

It was warm in the conservatory and Kie felt the sweat seeping down the back of his neck. He looked out the window and watched the hills.

'I'm trying to find out whether this spontaneous phenomenon is caused by a human or spirit agent. The questions I ask may appear trifling to you but the significance is in the answer. You're either being deliberately obstinate or you're too afraid to bare your soul to a stranger.'

He answered her with silence.

'Have you ever experienced psychological trauma in your life? I'm speaking about an event where you felt completely helpless, overwhelming sadness and terrible, crushing fear?'

'No.' He couldn't bring himself to tell the truth.

'Those strange blue eyes of yours deceive you, MacAoidh Ross Duncan MacKenzie Armstrong. Do you want to answer that question again?'

Could she see through his soul?

'Yes, all right. Five years ago my wife was killed in a car crash.'

'How did that make you feel?'

'Lost. Confused. Angry. Frightened.' Still watching the world from the window, he lay in the chair with his back against one arm and his legs tossed over the other. 'Alone.'

'Do you mind if I turn this back on?'

She hit the camcorder's record button and held the microphone in her hand.

'You must've been quite young.'

'I was old enough to feel the pain.'

'And do you feel what happened to your wife is holding your life back?'

'In what way?'

'Do you still feel anger?'

He blinked. 'Not anymore.'

She put on her glasses and began to write again. 'Bitterness? Regret?'

'Regret, maybe.' He wanted to talk about it. 'I met Helen in Juja. My father owns a small plantation there and I went after university, mainly to doss for a while. She was Agikuyu, one of the Bantu tribes of East Africa. She could speak perfect Swahili but very strange English.' He laughed, lost in distant happy memories. 'She preferred to be called Helen but her real name was Kakena, meaning happy. Her father called her Wangari in front of me. That, in Gĩkũyũ, or Kikuyu as we call it, means unavailable.'

'Did her father agree to the marriage?'

'Eventually. Her dowry cost me a fortune.' He laughed again. 'He was furious because I refused to go through a public circumcision.'

'Did you undergo a private one?'

'No, I don't believe in unnecessary mutilation of parts of the body unless it's for medical reasons and they'd have to be life threatening ones.'

'How did you manage to persuade him?'

'Cash.'

'Was Helen circumcised?'

'No, thankfully. Working on a coffee plantation owned by a Scotsman exposed her parents to western views.'

'Did you have any children?'

'No.'

'Do you regret that?'

'No.' He felt his answer was too quick when he saw her eyebrows arching into her hairline.

She stared at him above the rims of her glasses, her pen poised over the form. 'She wanted children but you didn't?'

He nodded but wasn't prepared to elucidate. That was between Helen and him.

'Was Helen religious?'

'What does that matter?'

'I'm just curious.'

'Aye, the Kikuyu believe in a god who lives on the top of *Kiri-nyaga*, or Mount Kenya. He's *Ngai Mwenye Hinya Wothe*, the apportioner, possessor of the brightness and all-knowing. They believe *Ngai* apportioned the Kikuyu people with the tools for farming.'

'You've just explained the religion but haven't told me whether your wife adhered to it.'

'Aye.'

'As in she did?'

'What else does aye mean?'

'Do the Kikuyu believe in an afterlife?'

'They believe when they die, they become a ghost. They're terrified of vengeful ghosts.'

'Vengeful?'

'Aye, the ones that still have bones to pick.'

She sat for long moments, simply looking at him. Kie didn't know whether she was psyching him out, or whether she was formulating her next question.

'Did you bring Helen to Scotland?'

He resented the question. 'For a while but I fell out with my father so we moved to Aberdeen.'

'Did she like Scotland?'

'No, not much. We were there a few months, then she died and that chapter of my life closed for good.'

'What did you do then?'

'I played around for a while in the export business and made a fortune but I never did enjoy the city life very much. I travelled for a year …'

'Around the world?'

'Pretty much. *Guthii ki kuona.*'

'Meaning?'

'Travelling is seeing.'

'In Gaelic?'

'No Kikuyu.'

'And did travelling help you to see?'

'Most definitely. It put my life in perspective and possibly saved me from myself. I decided a few months ago to buy this place.'

'Did you find it difficult to have other relationships with women?'

'No, I've never found that difficult. I've had plenty relationships.'

'Sexual?'

'Spiritual inspiration has always ended in bed for me. Sex is Plato's higher love, he was just too hung-up to admit it.'

'And were you physically or mentally attracted to all these women?'

'Both.'

'I see.'

He knew, from that look in her eyes and those two little words that spoke a text book in psychology, she was offended by his honesty.

'I don't think you do.'

'No?'

He left her to consider the implications of that answer.

'Did any of these relationships last?'

'The longest relationship I've had since Helen was with a woman called Catherine who I rarely saw. That recently finished under regrettable circumstances.'

'Regrettable?'

'She made a scene and I got bitten by a tetchy wee dog.'

Hannah laughed and he smiled.

'And what are your true regrets?'

'Not standing up to my father.'

'He didn't agree with the marriage?'

'He hated the very idea of it.' Feeling the anger brimming dangerously, he took a deep breath and watched a red kite soaring in the thermals against a backdrop of azure blue sky. 'It doesn't matter anymore.'

'What doesn't?'

'Like I said, I was young. I've mellowed a lot. I was content until all this started. Now I'm just thankful to get through another night.'

'Are your night times bad ones?'

'You can tell me that tomorrow morning after you've experienced a night in this house. We'll compare notes.' He laughed again. 'Libby's presence helps a lot.'

'In what way?'

'She makes me laugh. She's a constant reminder that life can still be good in the face of all this madness. I think she's braver than I am.'

'She's always been courageous. Is she still rude to people?'

'Fatally wounding.'

'Do you find it hard to let go of Helen?'

He had to think about that question. 'What do you mean by 'let go'?'

'I mean do you think you are capable of falling in love with another woman?'

'Perhaps.' He refused to play her game.

'So such an event would require circumstance or intervention?'

'Or even interference.' He crossed his arms.

'Do you feel that I'm in some way trying to manipulate your emotions?'

'I think you're digging a wee bit too deeply.'

'Do you think I'm attracted to you?' She sounded surprised and a little uncomfortable.

'I don't think your questions are aimed at 'us' at all. The answer to your questions is between Libby and me.'

'You're very smart, PH-07351.'

They sat in a silent stand-off for long moments.

'Let's go back to Helen. How did you take her death at the time?'

MacAoidh sat up and scrubbed his hands through his hair. 'I don't want to talk about that.'

'All right, but I get the feeling there's something you're holding back. It's just a hunch but ... wait, did you hear that?'

'It's just the whispering, you'll get used to it.'

Hannah stood up and looked around the conservatory. She checked to see if there was anyone outside the door but the sitting room was empty. She jumped at the sound of three clear raps coming from the direction of the low bookshelf.

'That was really clear.'

'Speak to it. It'll occasionally give you an intelligent response. One knock for yes, another for no, or whatever way round it is. Three hundred for a drum solo.'

'That's remarkable.'

'If you say so, but personally I'm sick of it and wish it, whatever it is, would go and talk to someone who wants to listen.'

She pulled a walkie-talkie out of her handbag and switched it on. The handset hissed. 'Anyone listening?'

'Yeah, Sal here.' A muffled voice scraped through the crackling.

'I'm in the conservatory. I need a MEL-8704R and a TLD-100 now. I've got auditory activity in here.'

'You won't need fancy machines, it will come to you in good time.'

Kie found the scene strangely amusing. The team rushed into the conservatory brandishing their sensitive hand-held meters like phasers set to stun.

Libby popped her head round the door, a half smile on her face.

'It's the Polt Police!'

She giggled and stepped inside. 'How did it go?'

'Badly. I think she thinks I'm completely insane.'

'An uncannily accurate diagnosis. I'm impressed.'

Chapter 25

THE CHANNEL

'Well, what do you really think?' Libby couldn't wait to hear what Kie had told Hannah.

They trudged up the cliff path and took in the view across the Solway. The brisk wind whipping the hair around their faces was warm and soothing. Across the firth, stakes of white turbines glistening in the sun stood with their arms outstretched like a naked corps de ballet and Libby felt the fresh air doing her the power of good.

'I'm afraid I'm bound by client confidentiality, Libby. Even if I wasn't, I really can't tell you much that you don't know already. He's extremely obstinate and not good at showing weakness or emotion. He wasn't particularly co-operative.'

'I think they breed them like that up in the savage north-west.'

'You may be able to help me, though. Did he tell you anything about his wife?'

'Only that she died in a car crash. It sounded horrible. He was there at the time.'

'I'm just wondering whether her death in those circumstances could've triggered a strong psychokinetic response.'

'In what way?'

They climbed a low gate and carried on walking away from the cliff and into a wide field spiked with prickly gorse and thistles. 'Polt activity is rarely believed to be caused by mischievous spirits of the dead, but can often be attributed to a human agent. If a ventriloquist can throw his voice, for example, why can't we use that same theory to throw an object?'

'A voice is inanimate.'

'Yet never underestimate the power of the mind. I won't bore you with the scientific theories, but I've come to the conclusion, after years of researching into the para side of psychology, that it's possible for the mind to physically interact with the environment to cause this apparent poltergeist activity. We call it recurrent spontaneous psychokinesis.'

'You think Kie's doing this to himself?'

'It's very possible he is. If we can find a link between his state of mind and this odd behaviour taking place around him; prove that he's the nucleus of this activity, then we may be able to come up with an explanation to fix it.'

'So you're saying all this can be put down to a physical expression of psychological trauma?'

'Yes, well put. Incidences of polt activity are not as uncommon as you think. Very often you'll find a living factor behind it. Troubled teenagers, especially girls who've reached the age of puberty, are prime culprits for inducing bursts of apparent paranormal activity in an otherwise normal household. There are loads of recorded cases which suggest that, once the human agent is forced to bring their repressed emotions into the open, the polt activity ceases.'

'He's twenty eight years old, for Christ's sake, he's hardly a pubescent teenager.'

'I have a strong feeling an event, or series of events, in his life has traumatised him emotionally and this is his subconscious way of bringing it into the open. There's more to it than losing his wife. I know that must've been bad enough but I just can't help feeling there's something else he's not telling. I'd need to perform a proper EMG under lab conditions to find out what makes him tick.'

'There's no way he'll agree to that.'

Libby had to stop and take in the views across the firth. Her lungs felt like they were about to explode and she needed to catch her breath. When her heart rate dropped to twice its normal cadence, she pulled a cigarette out of the packet in her pocket. She lit it and drew in a deep breath of smoke. ' D o n ' t you just love the fresh air?' Hannah raised her eyebrows. 'Your theory has a flaw. I've seen and heard things that only exist in those terrifying movies of the man and the woman who film themselves in the bedroom.'

'Like I said, thought can't be underestimated. Look, for instance, at the power of suggestion.'

'But lots of these disturbances took place when Kie was nowhere near the house.'

'Yes, that's the exciting part to it. If I can prove thought can also leave residual energy powerful enough to cause anomalous behaviour on its own, then I'll be famous.'

They came to a gate and climbed over it, Libby catching the hem of her silk top on barbed wire. She groaned when she heard it rip. 'This is all one big scientific experiment to you, isn't it? For me, it's a good man's sanity you're toying with.' She helped her friend jump down from the top of the gate before her enormous chest succumbed to gravity and pulled her over.

'I'm not toying with him. I'm trying to help him. You're right, he's a remarkable man. He's wholesome and straightforward, unusual traits in the male species in this day and age. He's also stunningly good looking and what a body!'

'Just you keep your filthy claws off him.'

'Why? You don't want him.'

Libby knew from that smile Hannah was teasing her. The good Doctor Simpson would never allow her professional life to cross with her personal preferences.

'Are you going to tell me about it?'

'Get me a couch and I'll bore you into a zombie. He's got a girlfriend.'

'Is her name Catherine by any chance?'

Libby sighed. 'He told you about her.'

'Libby, why don't you speak to him about how you feel? It's obvious you're completely addicted to him. You can't go on sharing the same room; staying at his house; and being a large part of his life without taking it to the next level. The effort to hold back must be killing you.'

'I'm not his type. Yes, we share a pokey little room at the end of the hall but that's because neither of us is brave enough to spend a night in any other room in that house. The gun room is the only place where there's been no whispering, no stone throwing, no bangs and no ghostly apparitions. We spend the night together and we sleep really well.'

'If it's any consolation, he spoke very highly of you. He said you made him laugh.'

'You see, he sees me as nothing more than a sister. I don't think I'll ever be anything else to him other than his personal jester. I heard him telling his mother much the same thing.'

'Ouch!'

They spent the rest of their walk laughing about old times and recalling incidents from a happy past. The subject matter then turned to Charlie and, as they planned their revenge strategy over the next few days, their screams of laughter echoed around the hillside.

When they returned to The Ring, Libby found Kie up a ladder fixing one of the outside floodlights. The leggy Katja held on to his shin with one hand and the other was fastened to his inner thigh.

'I am frightened he will fall,' Katja said in her thick German accent.

'For you? I doubt it.' Libby wafted past them with her nose in the air.

Katja ran after her. 'Are you and MacAoidh having a relationship?'

Libby was taken aback by the frank question but recovered quickly after taking a look at the magnificent blond in the skimpy clothes. 'Well, we were but it didn't work out.'

'Why not?'

'He has a really tiny willy. I wasn't supposed to laugh, but I did and he took offence.'

'You were disappointed?' The trusting blue eyes stared at her in earnest.

Libby demonstrated with her thumb and forefinger and left Katja trying to figure out whether the gesture quantified or measured her apparent disappointment.

'She's a pleasant girl and a brilliant student, Libby. Be nice to her.' Hannah pulled off her walking boots and placed them neatly outside the front door. 'I'm warning you she can also be extremely blunt. She's a bit of a sociopath with poor cognitive skills, possibly autism spectrum disorder, and she has a tendency to speak her mind without thinking of the consequences.'

'I'll remember that.'

'We're going to cook dinner together, just like old times. I bought all the ingredients with me.'

'That would be nice.'

'Let's do Charlie's favourite, Spaghetti Bolognese.'

'You know he can't eat spaghetti with any semblance of dignity and his tastes have probably never evolved from the brontosaurus burgers he used to love when he was young and unhealthy.'

'Let's treat him to a taste of nostalgia anyway.'

'Does that mean we also have to drink buckets of Lambrini?'

'We'll improvise.'

— — —

For the remainder of the afternoon, Kie sat in the sitting room, reading the paper before taking Jim Black's collie out for a very long walk over the hills.

Libby and her old friend Hannah took over the kitchen while the scientific team set up the equipment around the house. They placed what they called 'triggers' in some of the rooms. These were random objects the team designed to hopefully provoke a physical psychic response.

The team crawled around the buildings with hand-held devices searching for electromagnetic fields and base line temperature bearings which they recorded on paper forms and computers set up in Kie's bedroom.

They placed visual and audio equipment in two of the upstairs rooms, including Libby's former bedroom, and then sealed the doors shut with tape. Two monitors were placed on the marble table in the sitting room. They then tested their meters and camcorders in preparation for a long night's vigil.

Now and again there would be a rumble of excited activity as someone reported a stone falling from nowhere; hear a strange sound; or answered the odd rap on the wall with an eager one of their own. Otherwise, the house remained eerily quiet.

When Kie finally returned home, caked in mud and exhausted, the company were waiting for him in what was left of the dining room.

Libby and Hannah did their best to set an elegant dinner table and to make the dining experience a happy one. This was the team's first night on the case and living spirits were high and full of excited expectation.

'Dinner's been ready for over an hour and everyone's waiting.' She planted her hands on her hips as he made his way upstairs.

'Sorry, I got caught up with Jim's wife Margaret. Man, she's a blether. I'll be right down.'

Libby returned to the table as Hannah served the soup.

'So, Charlie, tell me about your life.'

Charlie broke his roll in half and placed a small pat of butter on the edge of his side plate. 'Well, nine years ago I married a woman who led a triple life for seven of those wonderful years, so I recently got divorced.'

'She was cheating on you?'

'Yes, with two different men and I never suspected a thing.'

'That's very sad.' Andrea, who was sitting to Charlie's right, joined the conversation. 'Did she ever explain why she sought extra-marital affairs? There must've been a reason why she took such a practical and emotional risk.'

Charlie shrugged. 'We were quite young. She was only eighteen when we married and I worked a lot. I believe she sought additional physical encounters for emotional sustenance.'

'That is a very typical response from the jilted partner.' It was Katja's turn to put her viewpoint forward. 'Your former wife was both sexually and emotionally incomplete in the marriage. She was either looking for validation of both or your sexual performance disappointed her.'

Libby was astounded by the frankness of the conversation and how Charlie took what appeared to be a vicious attack on his male prowess, straight on the chin. He had certainly changed and, to Libby's astonishment and delight, for the better.

'What about love addiction?' It was Sal's turn to give his professional opinion. Big Sal, with the East London accent, was the first to finish his soup and helped himself to more from the terrine. 'Maybe your wife felt she made a mistake in marrying you. Maybe she was a relationship addict.'

'I thought about that, but …'

'Perhaps she didn't understand herself.' Jenny cut in with her tiny voice and blotted her red lips with her napkin.

'Maybe she just wasn't in love with you.' All eyes turned to Libby. 'I mean, maybe her passion for you faded over time and she was looking to rekindle it in someone else.'

'The fact she had two separate and distinct affairs behind the back of her primary partner, suggests she was searching for the emotional and, or, sexual satisfaction that Charlie was unable to offer.' Katja placed her spoon in her empty bowl and sat back in her chair. 'That was very nice, thank you.'

'Do you always psycho-analyse each other's lives over the dinner table?' Libby took the break in the conversation to add her thoughts.

'This is the first time we have all had dinner together. It is fun.'

Libby returned Katja's comment with a curl of her lip and cleared up the first course plates and cutlery while Hannah brought the main to the table.

When she returned to the dining room, Kie had joined the company, his hair still wet from his quick shower. He seated himself at the head of the table, flanked by Jenny and Katja, and mumbled his apologies for being late. Libby noticed the narrow-eyed glances Charlie was making in his direction while Kie exchanged pleasantries with the women closest to him.

Libby sat for a while, playing with her spaghetti, and watched the interaction around the table. It felt odd to be in the company of so many people again and especially in a house which lapsed into occasional fits of volatile behaviour. Eight people sat around the table as if they had been friends for years.

She turned her attention exclusively towards Charlie and realised he bore little resemblance to the man she used to love. She didn't know whether it was the loneliness and frigidity of her existence that caused her to warm to him or the fractured memories of the moments of excitement he once induced that stirred an isolated emotion in her soul. She decided it was probably a mixture of both. Whatever the reason, she believed Charlie Jones, by the way he jealously eyed his Highland host, possibly felt the same for her.

'Libby has told me you have a very small penis.'

The food sprayed from Libby's mouth onto her hands and plate.

'Ach, Libby measures penises in accordance with the size of her big mouth. There aren't many men who can accommodate that.' If Kie was surprised, shocked or furious with Katja's blunt announcement, he deserved the utmost admiration for hiding it.

'Is your insulting remark to Libby intended to detract from your feelings of humiliation amongst the ladies?'

Charlie didn't find a humorous side to the conversation.

'Is your over-protective response to a light-hearted remark intended to detract from your feelings of inadequacy amongst the ladies?'

Neither did Kie anymore.

Libby sucked hard on her string of spaghetti and didn't notice, through the sudden heavy atmosphere, the end of it travelling across her face in a swift slapping movement, leaving her cheeks and hair spattered in Bolognese sauce.

They all jumped when Charlie's glass exploded, the sharp crystal cutting his hand, and marked an abrupt end to the conversation.

'Yes, he's definitely the channel.' Hannah whispered in her ear. 'I wouldn't want to be Charlie for love nor money.'

THE VIGIL

chapter 26

'You really didn't need to stand up to Kie, he was only kidding.'

Libby stood at the bathroom door while Charlie brushed his teeth in front of the mirror. He spat into the sink and rinsed his mouth with a deep gurgle.

'I think we're all a bit on edge tonight, Libby. This house is insane. Andrea and Sal are terrified. I don't think they'll last the night.' He wiped his face with the end of a towel.

'They haven't experienced anything yet.' She could see him shiver as her warning hit him in the back.

Andrea was just getting over a bout of hysteria after reporting her hair had been pulled very hard and one of the trigger objects placed behind a locked and sealed door was found on the butcher's block in the kitchen. On examination, the door seals were found not to have been tampered with. What was worse, Charlie and Jenny found scratch marks on their bodies, which was a completely new experience. Libby took the information very well but ran into the bathroom to carefully examine her own skin, just in case she'd been clawed by unseen talons.

Hannah refused the pleas of her team to analyse the video tapes, making the excuse that watching the recordings would only serve to amplify fear and reduce reason. Around eleven o' clock, she called everyone to the sitting room and announced they were all to camp down in the one room for their first night in order to minimise contamination of evidence and eradicate suspicions of human interference.

They sat and lay in sleeping bags and duvets chatting in low voices to each other; the lights turned down low. Kie, of course, was the last person to join them.

'There's a haar rolling in from the firth.' He threw his sleeping bag on the carpet by the piano.

Charlie, Sal and Andrea whimpered.

'He means a sea fog.' Libby translated.

'Why didn't he say that then?'

'He just did!' Kie slid into the quilted bag and wrestled with his jeans. 'It'll add to the vaporous atmospherics in here.' He turned onto his side and closed his eyes.

Hannah lay on the couch under a duvet, a glass of brandy in her hand. She watched the split screen monitors showing live surveillance feed from the upper floor rooms, outside hallway, outbuildings, kitchen, dining room and attic. 'If anything happens outside this room, we'll take it in turns to investigate. Two at a time. I just want temperature and EMF readings, nothing else. No more hysteria and no heroics. We'll take a look at the evidence tomorrow. Libby and I'll take first watch on the monitor,' she drained her glass and raised it up to Libby who answered her with a mischievous smile. 'I'll wake a couple of you up when it's time for a changeover or if anything interesting happens.'

'Which two of you want to go first?' All eyes turned towards Kie who lay in the corner. No one answered him. 'You'd better make up your minds quickly, there's a light in the barn. Must be another fire.'

The team rushed to the window and peered out into the fog. Kie groaned and wrestled his way out the sleeping bag before pulling on his jeans. He let out a long, exasperated sigh when he noticed all eyes were affixed to his groin area, each person intent on finding out whether or not Libby's report on the size of his penis was true.

'Looks like it'll be me then.' He left the room alone.

'I think I can see shadows moving in the barn.' Sal sounded panic-stricken and Libby realised Hannah's team of professional scientists was beginning to fall apart. They had become unnerved by the expectation of real exposure to the unexplainable and the fading light heightened their natural instinct to fear. That which could not be seen in the dark, therefore, was replaced by morbid imagination.

Libby sat next to Hannah on the sofa while the other guests pressed their noses against the bay window and squinted into the inky darkness.

'He's taking his time.'

'I can't see anything for the fog.'

'Wait. What's that?'

She jumped slightly at the deafening concerted bellow when Kie's face suddenly appeared at the window in front of them. He held a torch to his chin which gave his features a pallid, ghostly glow and set his eyes on fire. The men and women at the window leaped back in terror, some running for cover behind the sofa; some still screaming hysterically.

When Kie eventually returned, still laughing, he was met with angry remonstrations from his horrified victims who remained badly shaken from the terrible fright he'd given them. Only Hannah and Libby stayed calm.

'Is it raining outside?' Libby asked.

'No, it's just dreich.'

'You're a mischievous spirit, PH-07351.' Hannah sounded annoyed as he flopped down between them.

'Sorry, couldn't resist it.'

'You've nevertheless set the tone for the evening. We're going to be jumping all night, thanks to you.'

'Why would anyone wish to take part in a ghost hunt if

they're afraid of their own shadows?'

'It's not a ghost hunt, MacAoidh, it's a professional investigation into spontaneous phenomena and I don't want these observations to be blighted by errors or infected by thought transference.'

'I won't do it again.'

'Did you manage to put out the fire in the byre?'

'I left the light on, that's all.' He rose from his seat, squeezing Libby's shoulder as he stood. 'I've got work to do tomorrow. If you don't mind, I'm going to try and get some sleep.' He lumbered across the room once more to his sleeping bag and Libby and Hannah watched him in silence as he appeared to fall asleep.

As the lights went out, the remainder of the team bedded down for the night. Charlie arranged his duvet between Jenny and Katja on mattresses on the floor, while Andrea and Sal settled down on the big comfortable chairs. They spoke in nervous hushed voices to each other. After a few moments, Katja rose in her sleeping bag and waddled towards the piano. She dropped down next to Kie, complaining that it was too noisy and too crowded at the other end of the room.

'What did you mean by your remark about not wanting to be Charlie?' Libby kept her voice to the lowest whisper and sidled up closer to Hannah.

'Can't you tell? He's got the serious hots for Katja but she's told him a few times, and in public, that she's not interested. I think he's jealous of Katja's personal interest in MacAoidh and can't help but show it.'

Libby hid her disappointment as their faces glowed in the pale light cast from the monitors.

'In turn, our handsome Highlander, in his disassociated but heightened state of consciousness, is picking up the negative vibrations being thrown at him and is liable to subconsciously hurl them back with devastating force. I wouldn't be at all surprised if some of the more violent activity is directed towards Charlie in the coming days.'

'We should warn Charlie.'

'Why? He's a psychologist, he should know better than to transfer his insecurities by blaming others he feels he can't compete with. Haven't you noticed his outward displays of animosity towards Kie? He interprets Kie's physical superiority and assertive competence as disparaging, threatening and a devaluation of his own masculine ego. This has led to repressed negative feelings of self-doubt and lowered self-esteem which he attempts to hide by showing animus against the object of his ...'

'Oh, shut up!'

Libby poured them both another brandy and they chinked glasses.

'Do you think that's why I'm so rude to people? That I have low self-esteem?'

'Probably, but if you ever want to talk about it ...'

Movement in the monitor caught her eye and Libby shook Hannah's sleeve. 'The bed's moving.'

Hannah put her glasses on and leaned forwards into the glare. 'Where?'

They heard the scraping of moving furniture above them and, from the monitor, observed the double bed shudder for a few seconds before it slid across the room as if on greased casters. The sash window to the right of the wardrobe opened suddenly, followed by an enormous thud that shook the entire house.

'Sal and Katja were on their feet, while Libby knew the rest of them were pretending to sleep.

'That's one of the rooms we sealed.' Hannah said, trying to maintain a professional air of control. 'Just temperature and EMF, please. If the door's still sealed, take a picture or video of it. I don't want anyone attempting to open it or tamper with the tape. We'll do that in the morning.'

'Look!' Libby pointed at the monitor and stabbed her finger against its warm surface over the camera angle in the kitchen. The back door lay wide open.

Hannah kicked Charlie awake and shook Andrea by the shoulders. 'Kitchen, please.'

'I think someone should investigate the dining room too. Something's moving in there.'

'Come on Jenny, let's do our job.'

Libby sat at the monitor for a while and watched the silent scenes play out from a distance. The team moved cautiously into their respective areas, like the drugs squad on a raid. Some of them looked confident while others stood with hunched shoulders, barely able to move. They waved their meters around the rooms and peered under the beds and furniture. Inside the glare of the monitor, Libby saw Katja walking quickly down the corridor, now and again taking swift glances backwards. She looked disturbed and frightened. Libby felt peculiarly detached from her own emotions. Feeling as if there was a sudden drop in temperature, she wondered how Kie managed to sleep amongst the commotion. She shook him with her foot.

'What?'

She sat down beside his recumbent body.

'You're not helping with the investigation?'

'No. I'm sleeping. Besides', he rolled over on his back to face her, 'I'm just glad the focus of attention is on some other poor bastard and not us for a change. Let them enjoy what they came here for and we'll enjoy a good, uneventful rest.'

'I don't think I can sleep with all this going on around me and Hannah's in the mood for a brandy whipping tonight.'

'Do you want me to take you home?'

'Of course not. I'm not frightened. We're off duty tonight and someone else is dealing with the supernatural. I feel strangely free and am really grateful for that.'

'Then get in and go to sleep.' He pulled down the zip of his sleeping bag and patted the narrow space between his right flank and the seam. Libby slipped in giggling while he closed his long limbs around her in the way she'd come to adore.

'They'll think I've run away.' She snuggled into his chest.

'Or been spirited away.'

'Wow, Kie, there's no need to get so excited. I've got all my clothes on.' She wriggled her hips.

'What?' He fumbled around between their groins. 'You were lying on the torch!'

He threw it out of the sleeping bag and they chuckled like little children at their very first sleepover before eventually falling asleep.

chapter 27

THE EMF

'Where's Kie?' Libby shuffled into the kitchen and opened the fridge.

'He's outside showing Charlie and Katja round the steading.'

'Is he? What for?'

'Charlie's doing a thorough sweep and taking EMF readings inside and outside the house today while Katja and I are going to have a look at some of this data.'

'Sounds painful.' Libby pushed the coffee pod into the machine and turned it on.

'Now we've been here for a night and recorded some extremely rare and unusual activity, it's time we heard your accounts.' Hannah chewed on her piece of toast and picked up her cup of coffee. 'I've got some forms for the pair of you to fill in, if that's OK. It's really just ticking boxes, it shouldn't take you long.'

'Where are all the others?' Libby cursed as the bubbling coffee cascaded onto the floor from the machine. She was sure she'd placed the mug under it. She looked around for the roll of kitchen towel.

Hannah frowned. 'I'm afraid Kie had to take Andrea, Sal and Jenny to Carlisle at the crack of dawn to catch a train: any train that would take them as far away from here as possible. They've got all the recordings on disc and are going back to the university to analyse them. That's the least they could offer by way of compensation for running away from their duties.'

'I don't really blame them, this house will give them nightmares for the remainder of their lives.' She took the form and pen that were handed to her and joined Hannah at the butcher's block.

'Yes, I feel bad about that. Maybe we should've found out what we were letting ourselves in for before we came. I just didn't want to influence the team with preconceived notions. Turned out, I needn't have worried. This house is a parapsychologist's diamond mine.'

Libby turned her eyes up to the ceiling before looking at the form. 'OK, let's see. Section one. Question one. Have you or any person in your household experienced the following over the past twelve months. Hmm, that's a tick; that's also a tick. Mmm, feeling of being watched, maybe that's a tick too.'

'What is for breakfast?' Katja peeled off her brightly coloured festival raincoat and joined them in tight jeans and a very wet T-shirt.

'Did you remember to buy salami and smoked cheese at the supermarket, Kie?'

He shook the rain from his hair and shoulders as he walked through the door with Charlie. 'So now I'm psychic?'

'I like fruit and yogurt for breakfast with fruit juice.' Katja sat down on Libby's vacated stool and commandeered her coffee.

'OK, a bowl of fruit, fresh out of the tin, and a glass of liquid e-numbers coming up for Frauline Albrecht's Frühstück. I'm afraid we're out of natural yogurt but I can introduce a glass of milk to some friendly bacteria I found in the toilet bowl this morning.'

'It's OK, I will have toast.'

'Someone impervious to your sarcasm. That must be very frustrating.' Kie nudged Libby playfully with his elbow.

'We have to fill out a form each.'

He leaned over her shoulder, she could feel the warmth of his chest against her back as he took the pen from her hand.

'What's psi?'

'It's the twenty third letter of the Cyrillic alphabet.' His mouth against her hair caused her ear to tingle.

'It's also a broad term for the sentient mind,' Hannah bit into her toast, 'and a generic word we in the business use for parapsychological or psychic faculties like ESP and PK.'

'PK?'

'Sorry, that's psychokinesis.'

'Olfactory, is that smell?'

'Aye.'

'Tick that.'

Libby enjoyed the close relationship she shared with Kie, even though she doubted very much if he even noticed she was there. He wasn't afraid to touch her or invade her personal space, possibly because he felt he was welcome to get as close as was decent without receiving a slap. Her problem was, the more he closed in on the miniscule details of her life, the more she wanted him to remain by her side and all her natural barriers she'd built up over a lifetime of poor relationships had crumbled to dust before the power of his smile.

She found herself missing his laughter and his face when they were apart and was at odds with her irrepressible desire for this abnormal phenomenon in his house never to leave, despite the fact it was turning him slowly insane. While it was there, she would remain close to him and she knew this was the reason why she no longer feared the unexplained. She longed for time alone with him.

'Ach, come on! Atmokinesis, aerokinesis, chronokinesis, geokinesis, cryokinesis … that's a lot of different words for movement in response to stimuli.'

'Katja, please talk them through ...'

'No.' Libby put her hand out a bit too quickly and nearly hit Katja in the face. 'We're intelligent people. We'll work it out, just like a crossword puzzle. Come on, Kie, atmo.'

'Atmosphere, weather.'

'That's a cross. Aero is air.'

'Wind?'

'Cryo is temperature.'

'Agro, plants; chrono, time; hydro, water ... This is ridiculous. Put a cross against all of them apart from pyro.'

'What's the difference between tycho and typho?'

'One's smoke and the other's ... damn, what is it? Probability. It's probability. You can put a tick against that one too.'

'What university did you go to?' She turned her head towards him.

'Oxford, but that's not where I learned Greek.'

'You don't have to apologise for your choice of education. It's not your fault you're smart. I also went to Oxford.' Katja closed in on them while Charlie stood at the door drinking his coffee, a dejected expression on his face.

'I think we should talk about last night, Hannah. We're all a bit disgruntled.' Charlie came right out with his complaint. 'You should've warned us that the activity was of a violent nature. Some of us were attacked last night. There are only three of us now and a lot of work to do.'

'You volunteered for this opportunity, Charlie.' Hannah's voice was cool and firm. 'You said yourself that you weren't hurt but I'm sure you did get a fright and I'm sorry for that. If it's any consolation, I also had no prior knowledge of the goings-on in this house but I think it's time we found out. You are, of course welcome to leave at any time if you feel it's all too much for you. As are you Katja.'

'I wish to stay.'

'I just hope none of us gets hurt.' Charlie voiced his reluctance.

'The incidents so far have been pretty benign. To my knowledge, there's no extant record of polt activity ever causing serious harm.'

'There's always a first time.' Charlie rumbled. 'I'd better get on or we could be here for months.'

— — —

'I've been put out the house for the afternoon. Thought you could do with this.'

Kie found Charlie in the field wielding a hand-held meter of sorts and trying to write on the soggy paper forms drooping from his clipboard. His clothes were saturated and plastered to his skin and his suede shoes were ruined. Kie handed him a wax cotton jacket as the rain came down upon them in a vertical shower.

'Thanks.' Charlie continued with his work.

'What are you doing?'

'Taking EMF readings of the area. Measuring magnetic field density and looking for possible pollution by human-made or natural sources; anything that may cause a spike. Is there a library in the village?'

'The nearest one's about seven miles away. What do you want to know?'

'I just want to take a look at the geology of the area, but I suppose I can do that on the internet.' Charlie pulled his hood up in an effort to keep the heavy rain from pounding his bald head.

'Carboniferous limestone, sandstone, granite, so far as I'm aware. There must be a few mineral seams around here because there's an old copper mine down the road.'

'Ah, limestone's a prime conduit for supernatural behaviour. It's the underground streams that are usually to blame or metal ore and magnetite.'

Kie's tiny nod showed he wasn't convinced. He wasn't sure he liked Charlie. Shaking his hand was like waggling a dead herring and the man couldn't maintain eye contact for more than a few seconds. It surprised him that vociferous and confident women like Libby and Hannah considered themselves his 'conquests' and wondered what positive qualities they could see in him that Kie could not.

'It's possible that anything under this grass made up of ionic compounds could be affecting the environment above.'

'Do you think there may be a correlation between electromagnetic fields and the things going on in my house?'

'It's very possible. Electromagnetic fields, or EMFs as we call them, have a lot to answer for in cases of apparent paranormal behaviour. EMFs act on objects with a ferrous content, so affect circuitry. Strong power surges will pop light bulbs, turn TVs on and off, drain batteries, all the normal sort of polt activity you hear on TV shows. Sudden drops in current flowing through a magnetic field can cause sound waves called magnetostrictive acoustics which can take the form of taps, knocks and bangs.'

'So all this could be exclusively caused by some metal mine or subterranean burn beneath my property or even a power line?'

'Not exclusively, but exposure to strong field sources could possibly be causing some of it.'

'And are you ruling EMF out or into your particular line of research?'

'Trying to rule it out. I believe in ghosts. God, this rain's bloody awful. Fancy a walk to the pub?'

'Aye, why not.'

Kie regretted taking Charlie on a shortcut across the fields to the village. Apart from the wax cotton jacket, he wasn't dressed for the great outdoors and obviously had spent little time exploring the countryside in his youth. Charlie ripped his trousers scrambling over a dyke to get to the road and then fell in the burn when he slipped on a rock. By the time they got to the pub, he looked as though he'd been pulled out of a river by his ears. He sat Charlie close to the open fire at the side of the boat-shaped bar and placed a pint in front of him. It was gratefully received.

'I could get used to country life if the bloody rain would stop.'

'I thought you were a Welshman?'

'I'm from Cardiff.'

'*Lechyd da.*' Kie raised his glass.

'You know something, MacAoidh, I think you're the bravest bloody man on Earth. I wouldn't ever want to live in that house. You look like you're not short of a bob or two, why don't you just sell up and live somewhere quiet and sunny?'

'I like it here. Besides, if the activity can be put down to something as simple as electromagnetic interference, then I can live with that.'

'EMI, doesn't beat people up. It doesn't cause bite and scratch marks on the skin. It doesn't write messages on the floorboards and doesn't talk to you. Have you ever seen an apparition in the house?'

'What? A ghost?'

Charlie nodded and Kie was surprised he maintained eye contact with him this time. He put it down to the pint of beer he'd just downed in record time.

'No, not a whole one. I saw a wee pair of hands, but I've come to the conclusion that was my imagination. Mind you,

I was playing ball with a milking stool with something or someone in the byre.'

Charlie stood at the bar getting another round in. 'What do you mean?'

'I threw a stool in the byre and something threw it back at me. Twice.'

'That's amazing. Do you think we can recreate the incident when we get back?'

'I'm no' doing that again. One time was bad enough.'

'Has any of the activity really frightened you? I mean, have you ever felt as if you were in danger?' Charlie sat down again, his clothes showing some dry patches in front of the lively fire in the hearth.

'Fire's dangerous, even under controlled conditions, but that answer will have to be no. I was terrified into a stupor at one point when a wooden slipbar crashed through my sitting room window and walked past me all by itself.'

'Did it look like it was hovering in the air?'

'It moved through the air, slowly, as if someone was carrying it.'

'How long did it travel for?'

'About twenty seconds.'

'That's fantastic.'

'You weren't the one who was forced to witness it.'

'All these incidences, these inexplicable phenomena that can't be replicated through logic or science, strongly suggest that some paranormal force is causing them.'

'Like a ghost?' Kie didn't look converted but allowed Charlie to freely voice his theories.

'Yes, like a ghost. I'm trying to prove that there's no such thing as death of the personality. That's what the survival theory's all about. Human beings manipulate energy by simply being alive and energy, as you know, can't be destroyed. This force can be benign or active.'

'What's the difference?'

'Benign or residual activity is where the living person has left a residue of his life on the Earth: under certain conditions, that residue can be seen by the living eye as a playback of an event. A bit like a movie. That's why certain entities are seen in certain places, like the White Lady coming down the staircase; dead old Uncle Albert sitting on a chair; or the man in black standing at a window. Footsteps are also a common trait of benign energy. It's like a small capture of the force they created when they were alive and doing those things. This type of residual energy phenomena is often associated with hauntings.'

'And active?'

'That's your poltergeist. The spirit is active in its environment. It can interact with and touch the physical world, move objects, throw stones, start fires, write on walls and poke people. I want to find out, first, how it can be done and, second, why. Hey, thanks.'

He wrapped his hand around his third pint of the day in less than half an hour.

'Hannah believes in the living agent theory, that someone inside the environment is the cause of these disturbances through, perhaps, some form of repressed anxiety.'

'I find that explanation more palatable.'

'But I believe, in some cases, it is a spirit agent that's causing the trouble.'

'I believe we just die and that's the end of it.'

'Then how do you account for what you've seen and heard?'

'That's your job.'

'A psycho-psi realm exists, MacAoidh, and it's a realm that we haven't even begun to understand. There's a spirit in your house: a mischievous, angry personality that's using the energy fields of the living environment to scare and possibly harm you. It's using you. Do you feel it's getting stronger?'

'Maybe.'

'Then maybe one day it'll be strong enough to do some serious damage. It's living off your energy. It could possibly kill you.'

Kie laughed into his glass. 'I don't believe the dead can come back and kill the living. What would be the point? They'd have a very angry dead person to contend with for eternity if that was the case.'

'Have you even thought that it wants you to notice it and perhaps your choice to ignore it is making it even angrier?'

'All it has to do is ask,' Kie wasn't taking this conversation very seriously at all.

'It already has, you just haven't been attentive enough. It's obvious. It wants you to find it.'

'Here ye go, MacAoidh,' the barman planted two more pints on the table. 'That's the coach in. It's going tae get awfy busy in here for the next couple o' hoors, but dinnae let that drive ye away, son. I'll see tae ye. How's the ghost?'

'Thanks, Callum. Fine.'

'What language was that?'

'Scots. They tend tae speak it aroon' here.'

'To the Scots! I love 'em all.' Charlie thrust his glass into the air.

'To find what?'

'What?'

'Aye, what does it want me to find?'

'Oh,' the alcohol was beginning to take effect on both of them. 'Earthly remains, its energy source, who knows? Shit!' Charlie's pint spilled across his shirt as someone knocked into him from behind. The public bar was filling up with an assortment of people from a social club on a coach-driven pub crawl.

'Sorry, darlin',' a burly woman in a tight satin dress flopped her arms around Charlie's shoulders and drooled.

'Gerrof him, ya big tairt,' another woman gracelessly staggered towards their table on the sides of her buckling four-inch heels. 'Let a man enjoy his pint in peace. Sorry aboot her.' Before he could turn away, she spied Kie. 'Ooh, hiya gorgeous. You wearin' them fancy tinted contact lenses?' She grabbed Kie by the hair and thrust her fingers into his eye. 'Na', they're real. See this man's eyes, Carol?' She patted his cheek. 'This seat taken?'

'Aye.' Kie nursed his injured eye.

Charlie peeled the woman's hands off his chest and the pair teetered off into the dining room, screeching with laughter.

'So what's the score between Lib and you then?'

'We're friends.'

'Ah, that's not what I see. I think she likes you.' Charlie's wink exposed the measure of his perception of 'like'.

'I'm not her type.'

'Know what you mean, boyo. I'm not Katja's type either. Bloody wish I was.'

'Maybe you should be a wee bit more direct with her. Subtlety isn't one of her finest qualities.'

'She's got so many good qualities,' Charlie sighed.

'That's what you should be saying to her. Be affirmative. Look her in the eyes and just tell her.'

'She'd punch me.'

'That's a risk you'll have to take. It's better than walking around with a long face in her company. That'll hardly endear her to you.'

'I think she fancies her chances with you.'

'Nah, that's just a physical thing, a visceral lust, and purely transient. She'll drop the challenge after a while when she's certain I'm not interested.'

'Are you interested?'

'No. I've had enough of women lately.'

'You're so bloody sure of yourself, aren't you?' There was no challenge in Charlie's tone, just wonder and admiration. 'You've got every eligible bird in this pub staring at you and the women back in your house running after you, wanting to please you and get into your pants. That's some powerful magnetic field you must be giving off.'

Kie leaned forward across the table, almost knocking the glasses over. 'I've got my back to the room, Charlie. You sure it's me the lassies are eyeing-up?'

They laughed for a while until the alcohol in their bloodstreams began to infect all reasonable emotion.

'Sorry about your wife, mate.'

Kie nodded. 'Sorry about yours.'

'Hey, that was a lifetime ago for both of us. I'll get another pint in.'

'Mine's a whisky.'

Charlie stood up, saluted and staggered off to the bar through the crush of bodies.

'Here you go, mate.' He returned after a while with a couple more pints and some shots. 'Complements of the department of parapsychology. Nice bunch of people in here. I've just been speaking to a couple of lovely Irish girls at the bar. I've asked them to join us. They've got a bottle of Irish whiskey back at their tent on the bay. They've invited us over later for a nightcap. Must have some animal attraction after all.'

'Shouldn't we be conducting experiments or something?'

'Nah, we've taken the rest of the day off. Time to work on our Celtic connections. *Lechyd da!*'

Kie smiled and raised his glass. '*Slàinte!*'

chapter 28

THE EVP

'GET OUT!' Libby threw open the car door and slammed her fists against her hips. The sudden release of alcohol fumes into the fresh air made her stagger backwards and she was relieved she wasn't holding a lit cigarette. MacAoidh and Charlie slept like babies in the back passenger seats. Smothered in sand, which clung to their hair, their clothes and their dry lips. They sat cuddled into each other like a pair of newlyweds, the same gormless smile hanging from both their faces.

'I couldn't get them out of the car, so I left them there.' Katja handed Libby the car keys.

'Where were they?'

'On the beach. I found MacAoidh lying face down in the sand and Charlie's feet sticking out of one of the tents.'

'Tents?'

Katja shrugged. 'I think there were women and whisky involved. There always is when Charlie's around. He is a very bad influence.'

Libby's temper flared. She marched into the barn, filled up a bucket of water and threw it over the pair of them, bucket and all. They woke up spluttering and gasping for air.

'Get out of the car, right now!' She growled.

To her fury, they could only see the funny side of her anger. They burst into laughter, pointing at her and laughing even more. She realised they were still very drunk. She turned to Katja who stood in the early morning sun shaking her head in disgust. 'You get Charlie and I'll take lover boy here.' She hauled on his arm. 'OK, soldier, out you get.'

'If it's not the lovely Liberty Belle Butler,' he slurred her title as he rocked himself from the seat and staggered into the morning air. 'Jings, the groond's spinnin'.' He fell to his knees after taking a deep breath and threw his arms around her waist. 'You've grown.'

She helped him inside and had to haul him up the stairs while Katja carried Charlie into the house in a wheelbarrow, making sure she knocked his head against the doorframe a few times.

'Where the hell were you?' Libby threw Kie on his bed and his head bounced off the wall with a dull thud.

'In the pub and then I don't know …' His voice trailed off as he hit the soft pillows. She sat down beside him and pulled off his muddy wellies.

'We were really worried when you didn't come home. We phoned the pub just after midnight and they said you'd left. We even phoned the bloody hospitals to see if you'd both been admitted. We've been searching for you since dawn and were beginning to think the worst until Katja said she'd found you.' She scrubbed at his hair and face with her sleeve and brushed the sand off his pillow.

He opened his eyes and dazzled her. 'Aw, you were worried about me?' He flopped his hand on her lap. 'I love those wee flecks of green in your eyes.'

'Well, I don't love the wee strands of red in yours.' She picked his hand off her lap like a dirty handkerchief.

'I love you Libby Butler.' He collapsed his upper body into her lap.

She felt her heart leap. 'Then never do that to me again.'

'And I really love Charlie, the gorgeous wee Welsh bastard.'

She sat for a while listening to his deep, regular breathing. 'I love you too, MacAoidh Armstrong, but I wish to God I'd never met you. You've ruined my life.'

— — —

'OK, Sal, just upload the files onto the cloud now and I'll take a look at them.' Hannah spoke into her laptop as Libby joined her on the patio.

Libby waggled her fingers at Sal's pixelated image and he returned the gesture with a wide grin. 'Are you sleeping with the light on now, Sal?'

'Nah, I'm over it. I'm not coming back, though, no way.'

Hannah said her goodbyes and turned off the video link. 'We've got some fabulous evidence of psi activity, Libby. The best I've ever seen or experienced. This house has kicked some of Newton's theories in the arse. I'd love to get my hands on MacAoidh and do some more tests in a controlled environment. I think he may be harbouring some very special psychic powers.'

'You think he's a medium?'

'In the sense that he's a channel for psychic activity, yes.'

'Well, you'll have your work cut out, he's in an alcoholic coma upstairs and, by the look of him, may be lying in that state for another day or so.'

'That may be to our advantage. Alcohol's a depressant and affects the neurotransmitters in the brain. Haven't you noticed there's been no paranormal behaviour recorded here since Sunday morning and it's very quiet now.'

'There are long spells of quiet, even when Kie's here. He doesn't normally drink very much.'

'Charlie said something interesting just now. I caught him throwing up in the toilet but he was babbling on about his Celtic brother and about how his, and I quote, 'animal attraction' got them …', she glanced at Libby, a shadow of sympathy crossing her expression, '… never mind about that. I think he's hit on something very important.'

'What? He fancies Kie too?'

'No, that MacAoidh has a very strong personal magnetism that affects people he comes into contact with. I must admit, I was struck by his sheer presence at our first meeting.'

'That's because he had his shirt off and a sledge hammer in his hand. You probably thought you'd walked into the house of Conan's more barbaric brother.'

'No, it's more than physical. He's pleasing to the eye of any objective beholder, but there's a prevailing mental aura around him that also attracts people like iron filings to a magnet: it's his charisma, it's very unusual. He has a quiet confidence which has an irresistible pull, in a sensual rather than sexual way. When he speaks, I believe what he says; I have confidence in his convictions. He projects fearlessness, trustworthiness and charm and those traits have a powerful influence on others.'

'I'm sure Hitler had similar traits.'

'No, he utilised coercion and propaganda to a demoralised and desperate public to attract a nation to his cause. That's different.'

'I was joking.'

Hannah shook her fiery-red curls. 'Sorry, I'm going off again on one of my lectures, aren't I?'

'It's an interesting subject. So, you think Kie is both causing this psychic activity, subliminally of course, and somehow infecting the minds of those around him via a form of telepathy?'

Hannah laughed. 'I forget how smart you are, Libby. Yes, it's called telepathic overlay where the dominant mind can infect or induce the sympathies of the subordinate mind through a telepathic connection. It's therefore possible what we think we're experiencing may not be truly taking place. Like I said, however, I would have to put him through all the right tests to prove this. God, I'd love to get him to the labs, just for a few days.'

'I'll work on him if you want, but I don't think I've got his magnetic charm. I can't even persuade him to go to the shops for me.'

'We'll carry on, regardless. Katja's working on the field research; Charlie, when and if he ever rises, will carry on with the spirit agent side of things; and I'll get into MacAiodh's head and try and work out why he's doing all this.'

'There's another flaw in your theory,' Libby crossed her arms as Hannah sat back down in her chair. 'We have some compelling evidence on video of your so-called polt activity. Are you also saying that Kie can manipulate electronic devices?'

'Why not? We are all part of the same energy field, whether we're animate or inanimate. That's a truly interesting question which would require an even more fascinating answer. There was a time not long ago when the invention of radio waves, photographs and movies were considered an impossibility. Now we know all these once inexplicable phenomenon can be put down to a few scientific equations of light and electromagnetism, which is exactly what we're studying now. Ironically, the inventors of all those wonderful contraptions we take for granted today, all stumbled upon them while they were looking for ways to contact the dead.'

'Can you stop this, Hannah? Can you bring the status quo back?'

'I'm going to try, but that depends on how co-operative our charismatic Mr Armstrong will be. If he started it, he can stop it. Come on, let's see what Sal's sent us.'

Libby followed Hannah to Kie's bedroom where three

computers were set up. Behind them, Kie slept under his duvet.

'Sal's sent us some audio and a few video clips he wants us to look at. He's worked overnight on the data.' Katja sat at the centre screen and kept her voice low while Libby and Hannah clustered behind her.

Hannah explained: 'I asked Sal just to look for stuff that wasn't obvious to the naked eye or ear. We've got some footage of a bed moving, a window opening and my team members walking around, so we're looking for the things we haven't seen. This is the first of three video clips.'

'Anyone brought the popcorn?' Libby felt like she was at the premiere of a top-billed movie starring her.

'Sal says the action happens at 24:14.'

'This isn't going to make me pee myself again, is it?' Libby watched the screen with trepidation. She'd seen too many of those joke videos where, right at the end, the girl from The Exorcist pops up screaming in front of the camera. The video showed the camera angle from the bedroom which had been taped and sealed.

'Wow! Did you see that?'

'See what?' Libby didn't see anything at all.

'Rewind. Watch the end of the bed, Libby. Right hand side.'

She saw the same view of the room but concentrated on the part of the bed. The end of the duvet moved a little and an imprint appeared at the foot of the bed as if someone was sitting there. 'Oh, my God!'

'Let's see the next one. Quick,' Hannah couldn't contain her excitement.

The next video, which provoked orchestrated oohs and aahs was more obvious. One of the trigger objects in the byre simply vanished before their eyes and reappeared on the concrete a few seconds later.

'Sal says you're going to like this one, Libby.'

'Me?'

The last video played out and Libby recognised the scene in the sitting room after the team had gone to investigate the sudden burst of activity around the house on their first night. She watched as if from a high vantage point looking down at herself living in the past. It was an odd sensation. The other Libby sat on the sofa watching the monitors, drained her glass and looked over towards the piano. She rubbed at her arms before moving across the room to Kie. The footage stopped just as she nudged him with her foot.

'What was that all about? I look really fat!'

'Play it again.' Hannah sounded puzzled. 'Let's concentrate on the room and not the subject this time.'

It began again, the other Libby from the past watching the monitors.

'There!' Katja cried out and Libby leaped with fright. Katja hit the rewind and, after a few seconds, froze the frame. 'Look.'

'Did you feel a drop in temperature then?'

Libby sat mesmerised to the screen. 'Yes, I remember feeling cold.'

'Perhaps that's why.'

Rising behind the settee was a small black shadow in vague human form which crept slowly towards her. The moment Libby felt cold was the moment it appeared to wrap around her.

'They look like arms.' She shuddered in shock.

'We've got two EVPs. Unaware of the trauma the video had caused to a non-professional, Katja moved on to the sound files.

'Here's the first. Sal says this one was taken in the conservatory after the interview with MacAiodh when you called us in.'

They listened carefully. Libby heard, or thought she heard a voice during the spike on the graph but couldn't make out what it was saying. She shook her head after the third playing. That's not a voice.

'I think it said 'Charlie paid'.'

'Play it again?'

Libby could hear the name 'Charlie' but nothing much else.

'I don't think there's anything significant in that file. We're just guessing. Play the next one Katja.'

Katja hit play with the mouse and Libby heard Kie's voice.

'That's during the interview,' Hannah said.

'I don't want to talk about that.'

'All right, but I get the feeling there's something you're holding back. It's just a hunch but … wait, did you hear that?'

'It's just the whispering, you'll get used to it.'

A voice came over clearly on top of Kie's last sentence.

'That's most definitely a voice.'

'That's a Class A.'

'What's it saying?'

'It's saying something.'

'I don't understand the language.'

'It's African.'

The three women spun around to the sound of Kie's voice. He flopped down in the chair next to Katja and leaned on the table, watching the monitor as if witnessing an execution.

'Play it again.'

He brought a shaking hand up to the screen and touched it with his fingertips.

'It's Kikuyu. She says *ni ndirarira*. I am crying.'

THE PAST

chapter 29

A terrible commotion in the kitchen sent Libby hurtling downstairs.

Hannah and Katje had gone out for lunch to discuss their findings in a neutral environment, while Charlie slept upstairs. Kie went out for a long walk and Libby had stayed in his room, catching up on some of her case files. Libby found Kie sitting on the floor of a devastated kitchen, his spine pressed against the back door, his head in one hand and the other thrust behind him. The cupboard, fridge and freezer doors lay open, their contents spilled and smashed across the tiles. Chairs and stools had been hurled across the room and the kitchen window was smashed.

'Kie?' She crossed the room carefully, trying not to tread on the breakages.

'I didn't do this, Libby.'

She sat down next to him and wanted to put a reassuring hand on his shoulder but his body was rigid and shaking.

'It's OK to let out your anger.'

'I didn't do this,' he yelled at her. 'You can watch the fucking tape and see for yourself.'

Libby was taken aback by his antagonism. 'All right, the poltergeist did.'

'It's getting worse. It's driving me mad. How can I make this stop?'

She sighed and rested her head against the door. 'I don't know.

I don't even believe myself anymore. Who would've thought one day I'd be staying in a haunted house with an entity that throws things around and hits people?'

'She thinks it's me, doesn't she?'

'Who, Hannah?' In his lost and vulnerable state, Libby didn't know how much to tell him.

'Aye, she thinks I'm doing all this with my mind.' She noticed his hand was shaking violently as he passed his fingers through his hair.

'What do you think?'

'I don't know. Maybe she's right. Maybe I need to face my past and get it all over with.'

'What are you scared of, Kie?'

'I'm scared that someone will get hurt. I mean really hurt. They all need to leave. You need to leave too. I'd never forgive myself if I hurt someone.'

'I know you would never deliberately hurt anyone.' She took his big hand in hers and held on to it.

'She didn't want to drive, she was scared of cars.'

'Pardon?'

'I bullied her into learning because I was fed-up with chauffeuring her everywhere. She had a dream when she was a wee girl about being killed in a car crash – the lights, the blood, the terror – she was so frightened of cars.'

'It's hardly your fault …'

'There was barely anything left of her.

'What?'

'Blood and brains splattered over the windscreen. Her eye hanging from its socket against her shattered cheekbone. Her body crushed to the width of my arm. She wasn't human. She wasn't Helen.'

Libby suddenly realised he was finishing off his story in an attempt to bring his feelings out into the open. 'Someone had taken her away and replaced her with a broken thing, oozing lung tissue and entrails from a shattered mass of jagged bone. She smelled of blood and human waste. It made me vomit.'

'God, Kie, I'm so sorry.'

It was a long time before he spoke again.

'She looked at me. She was terrified. Terrible, terrible fear, pleading with me to stay with her. She was so scared.' His body began to quake as he rocked backwards and forwards, cradling his knees with his arm.

'So she wasn't killed outright, despite the extent of her injuries? That's so awful.'

'The sight of her disgusted me. It made me feel sick, like my stomach had exploded inside and wanted to burst out through my mouth. I had to get away. I couldn't look at her. I saw the tear but I ran and left her to die alone and I'll never forgive myself.'

'Kie, the brain can stay alive for only a few seconds after the heart stops beating. Hasn't it occurred to you she was already technically dead on impact? By the time you went back for her, she was already gone.'

'That may be true but there was still some emotional recognition there. I could see it. I knew her.'

'You may think it was wrong of you to run away but what else could you have done?'

'I could have waited with her until the end. Provided some form of comfort. Till death us do part and all that crap.'

'It was the end, Kie. It ended when someone else's car hit yours and killed her. Wouldn't you have given anything not to have seen her in that state? Don't you wish now those people who held you back, held on to you a little more firmly so your last memories of Helen were happy ones? There isn't a person on this planet that, with the benefit of hindsight, wouldn't do things differently given the chance. You've got to stop beating yourself up over the what-ifs in your life. It's done. It's over. There's absolutely nothing you can do about it now and you have nothing to feel ashamed about. You were in shock. It was a natural reaction, like an impulse, and you followed it. Instinct has a way of making people react in certain ways for a good reason. Now maybe it's time you stopped brooding over the past and let Helen go.'

'She won't let me.'

'What?'

'You heard that voice. That was her and now she wants to punish me.'

Libby felt her spine tingling. 'Kie? What are you talking about?'

'When she was in a temper, she wrecked the kitchen. That was her way of letting off steam.'

'You think Helen did this?'

'Either her or me. Whoever's doing it hasn't stopped since she died.'

'You've experienced paranormal activity before you came here, haven't you?' She could see through his confusion.

He nodded. 'Nothing like this though. It was just the odd thing: her picture and belongings turning up in strange places; her voice in my ear; strange dreams of her. It was as if she didn't want me to forget her. Didn't want to let me go. I put all her things in a box and the activity stopped until I came here.'

Libby wanted to hug him; to reassure him that everything would be all right. He looked so lost, so miserable, so weak. It was only when she moved a little closer to him that she realised something was very wrong.

'Kie, I can smell blood.'

'Aye, that's me.' He showed her his hand. It was covered in sticky blood.

With a squeal she stood up and examined his back to find the handle of a knife jutting between his middle ribs, dangerously close to his spine.

– – –

'Yes, that's exactly what he said. Pardon? No, he's fine. The knife didn't go in very deeply. They say he's lucky his lung wasn't punctured. I think the doctors think I did it! They're all giving me really funny looks and the nurses are making a fuss of him and handed me leaflets on anger management and domestic violence. I'm going to wait around here until he wakes up and they discharge him, then I don't think I'll bring him back to the house tonight. He's still got a thudding hangover to get over and could do with a good rest. I'm going to persuade him to stay at my house tonight. OK, well tell me if anything else happens. See you.'

Libby hit the red button on the keypad and leaped out of the way of the ambulance as she paced the car park. Hannah had been insistent on hearing everything Kie told her and Libby felt like a traitor.

She didn't know whether she'd helped Kie or caused him to lapse into some psychotic state of torment. At that particular moment in time, however, nothing else mattered but his safety and his sanity.

She dosed off in the waiting room after she was told that, because she wasn't family, she was to sit outside the ward and wait.

'You been waitin' long?' A young woman with a friend who couldn't stop throwing up into a grey cardboard bowl, asked her politely.

'I was sixteen when I arrived.'

She slept for a while in the car, her dreams fevered with nightmares about moving objects and a ghostly boy asking her to find him. She then returned to the waiting room where she was once again refused admission to the casualty ward where Kie was being held.

'Mr Andrews?' A nurse called out a name from the door. 'Ross Andrews?' She had that look of one who knew they were wasting their breath.

'He was here a while ago,' Libby thought she would put the nurse out of her misery. 'But he died of old age and slowly crumbled into dust.'

The nurse's irritated glower caused Libby to laugh at her own joke.

Realising she'd upset the nursing staff and worried they'd take their frustrations out on Kie, Libby moved to the safety of her car once more and dozed off again at the driver's wheel. A tap on the window caused her to scream in panic and she realised her own nerves were shattered. She opened the door just wide enough to speak to the man in the tracksuit.

'Miss Butler isn't it? Hello, Libby. May I call you that? Just in case you're interested, here's the number for a confidential helpline for domestic violence perpetrators. We offer information, advice and support to help stop the violence and change abusive behaviours.'

'Fuck off arsehole, or I'll scream rape after beating the shit out of you.'

The man backed away, dissolving into the car park with a horror-stricken expression hanging from his open mouth. 'I've got your number,' he yelled when he was a safe distance away, 'I know where you live!'

Libby regretted her instant sardonic reaction and knew she utilised derision as a weapon to conceal her more melancholic emotions. She settled back into her dreams with her mobile phone in her hand.

She awoke with a start at another rap on her windscreen.

'You don't look disabled to me,' the woman in the green overall of a domestic health service worker shoved her head into the open window and grimaced at her. 'Where's your blue badge?'

Libby decided to behave herself and apologise. 'So sorry, I've been here for rather a long time and fell asleep. Mine was the only car in this car park when I arrived. There are loads of spaces and they're all allocated to the disabled. Surely you don't want mine as well?'

'You've no right to park here. The car park for the able bodied is over there. It's only a short walk and you're lucky you've got a good pair of legs to accomplish that task.'

Libby bit her tongue. She'd made too many enemies today. 'If you get your snout out of my car, I'll move.'

The woman sniffed and turned away.

The sun was beginning to set as Libby wandered into the accident and emergency department once more, its comforting lights shining like a safety beacon on a stormy sea.

'I'm here to take Mr Armstrong home.'

'Yes, please take a seat in the waiting room. The doctor's just about to see him.'

'But he's been in there for three hours.'

'We're very busy today.'

'Busy doing what? There's only one more patient in the ward. He started off here as an infant and was moved to geriatrics a few minutes ago.'

The nurse crossed her arms tightly against her chest and tapped her foot. Libby sighed and returned to the waiting room. When she felt she'd spent long enough reading the boards and posters on the dangers of alcohol, she slipped into the ward when she felt no one was looking.

'Where've you been?' Kie hauled the blue curtain to his cubicle back and stepped into the corridor. Although a little wobbly on his legs, he stood tall and defiant.

'Get in the car and shut it. You've made enough trouble for me for one day!' She couldn't resist one last dramatic finale in front of the reception desk. The medical staff gasped and they were almost thrown out of casualty by a burly male nurse who quoted the hospital's no-tolerance policy before the automatic doors closed between them.

'How are you feeling?' The windscreen wipers on the car were lulling Libby to sleep. The extent of her exhaustion both surprised and overwhelmed her.

'Fine.'

'Your fancy education didn't teach you the difference between adjectives and interjections then?'

'Aye.'

'I rest my case.'

They drove in silence, the rain lashing against the windscreen, the dark countryside shrouded in mist and shadow. Kie fell in and out of sleep, the painkillers obviously making a difference, but there was also a strange calm about him that Libby had never seen before. She wondered whether it was the drugs or the hangover. She hoped it was the case that he'd come to terms with his past and buried the dead for good.

She parked the car outside her house and waited for him to wake up.

'Where are we?' He spoke at last, his voice sleepy.

'We're at my house. I'm not taking you back to The Ring tonight. You need to rest and a space to clear your head. That place is killing you and I won't be an accomplice to your death or your eventual lunacy.'

'Grand.'

Once inside, Libby marched him to the spare room and ordered him onto the bed. 'I'm going to run you a nice hot bath and then you're going to sleep for as long as I think you need. That may take hours and it may take weeks, but you will not get up unless I say so, is that clear?'

'Yes nurse.' He collapsed on the bed on his front. 'Thanks, Libby, you always seem to be saving my soul these days.'

He held out his hand for her to take and she wrapped her fingers around it.

'That's OK, yours is a soul worth saving.'

He tightened his grip. 'Sorry.'

'What for?'

'For getting you involved in all this and ruining your life.'

She wondered if he'd heard her after all or whether he was, indeed, psychic. She felt the alarm bells clanging in her head and wished for once she'd kept her mouth shut and her thoughts to herself.

'You haven't ruined my life, Kie. I'm perfectly capable of doing that without the aid of you or your haunted house.'

He turned over on his side to face her. 'Lay with me for a while.'

She sat instead, too worried about misunderstanding his intentions and embarrassing herself yet again. 'Are you going to tell me a story?'

'If you want.'

'I'd love that.' Using that as a cue to get closer, she settled down into the pillows beside him.

After a few moments to gather his words together, he began with his tale, his eyes fixed to the ceiling. 'There's a place in the far north-west called Inchnadamph. It means the Meadow of the Stag and it's where the remnants of the former home of two powerful Highland families sits on the side of a deep loch. The cold stone ruins of Ardvreck Castle jut into the sky like a giant broken obelisk but mark a proud and important history that, through time and the elements, has become a mere whisper of the past.'

'Wow! I love the way you tell it.' Mesmerised by his words and his soft lilting accent, Libby locked in to Kie's fascinating tale like a child listening to a bedtime story.

'In sixteen fifty, James Graham, Marquis of Montrose, found himself fleeing from the Covenanter Army after losing the battle of Carbisdale. Montrose was the Old Pretender's Lieutenant-Governor of Scotland and Captain General of his Royalist army and so was not a welcome personality amongst the kirk supporters.'

'I'll bet he wasn't.'

'He was wounded and, disguised as a shepherd, he came upon the home of Neil MacLeod, Laird of Assynt, who he'd fought alongside at Inverness a few years before.'

'Someone fighting for the Royalist cause should've known better than to show up in the western Highlands behind enemy lines.' Libby said.

'Aye,' Kie laughed and idly played with a lock of her hair, 'and his trust in a Sutherland man proved to be his downfall. One story says that, when Montrose got to the castle, MacLeod wasn't in but his wife, a Monro and an enemy of the clan, cast him into the castle dungeon. Some say it was MacLeod himself who committed the treachery and sold Montrose to General Leslie for twenty five thousand Scots pounds; twenty thousand of that in cash and the rest in oatmeal.'

'Why oatmeal?'

'Have you ever tried to grow oats in Sutherland?'

'I've never tried to grow oats anywhere.'

'The oatmeal was sour anyway.'

'What? It was inedible?'

Kie nodded. 'Rancid.'

'MacLeod should've sued.'

He laughed and placed his hand on her back, pulling her body closer into his. Libby knew the gesture was made out of affection but it caused her to smile anyway. 'The Covenanters turned up at Ardvreck, tied Montrose to a horse and took him away to Edinburgh.'

'Did he go shopping in Princes Street and see a show after taking in a couple of museums?'

'No, the king's man suffered the death of a traitor. He was hung, drawn and quartered and his head adorned the city's Tolbooth gate for eleven years.'

'That's horrible.'

'They say the ghost of a man in grey stalks the ruins of Ardvreck. Some say it's Montrose himself whose spirit can't rest because of his betrayal.'

Libby felt her heart pounding as Kie widened his eyes and whispered his words for full dramatic effect.

'And is it him?'

'No one kens, but he apparently talks to anyone who can speak Gaelic.'

'Even if your name's MacLeod?'

Kie smiled at her again, his face within kissing distance to hers. 'That's not all. Ardvreck has a second ghost, a young lass called Eimhir. When the first MacLeod of Assynt built the castle in the late sixteenth century, it's said he enlisted the aid of the devil and offered his daughter's hand in return for his help in the building's construction. On her wedding day, the fair Eimhir realised she was to become old Cluitie's bride and hurled herself off the battlements.'

'Why do all fair maidens of Scottish castles end up leaping from the parapets?' Swept away by his story, she couldn't help but interrupt him again. 'Cluitie's a euphemism for the devil, right?'

Kie shrugged. 'I suppose it was fashionable in those days and, aye, it means little hoof. Some say the devil was so angry he sent a thunderbolt across the mountains and changed the geology of Inchnadamph forever. Some say the lassie didn't die but fell into the loch instead and, over the years, turned into a mermaid. Whichever story you wish to take, they say the maiden can be seen in the moonlight weeping by the side of the loch.'

'Which one do you believe?'

'I like the idea of the mermaid.'

'Don't all men?'

'A wee way down the road is Calda House, a great MacKenzie stronghold, and another ruin which is said to be haunted by a white lady. People say they've seen strange lights on the road at night.'

'Why are you telling me all these ghost stories?'

'Because I was raised in Assynt amongst tales of devils and faery beasts. The Western Highlanders are a fey, superstitious lot and accept the paranormal as part of everyday life. I grew up with tales of haunted ruins by Loch Assynt, Lochan Dubh and Achmore; strange beasts in the water in Lochan Feith an Leothaid; dead sailors walking and mermaids at Sandwood Bay. I also believed the legend of the black hellhound of Creag an Ordain that has eyes like glowing peats and spits fire from its jaw. Those who hear the hound bark three times, are said to be doomed. My pals and I used to cycle past the loch with our fingers in our ears.'

'Yet, as an adult, you chose to disbelieve.'

'They're tales passed down from generations of fading memories and eventually the truth becomes so obscure that only legend remains.'

'So you consider the presence of powers that violate natural forces just too far-fetched to endorse unless there is irrefutable proof to the contrary?'

'Aye, but since the dawn of time, man has held an enthusiastic reverence for the spiritual side of existence. Whether through morbid curiosity, a love of the thrill, a compulsion to disprove, or simply a need to be comforted by the thought the soul is eternal, an existence of something that can't be explained by natural law or conventional science is an accepted part of our culture. It's like believing in God.'

'Are you suddenly becoming a believer, Kie?' With gentle fingers, she swiped away the thick lock of hair that had fallen over his face.

'I don't know anything anymore. I feel like a child who's just learned the facts of life for the first time.' He caught her hand and held it in front of their faces. 'This is going to end now. I promise. One way or another, this is all going to stop and both of us will be able to live normal lives again.'

Somehow she believed him. 'Then I won't have an excuse to sleep with you anymore. What will become of me?'

'Do you need an excuse?'

Was he joking with her again or was he trying to tell her his feelings ran deeper than friendship? Libby wished she didn't always feel the need to use sarcasm to hide her true emotions but, should she interpret his words in the wrong way, she would lose a companionship she'd come to cherish and enjoy.

She panicked.

'You need a bath, I'll help you undress.'

'Fine.'

She hated that teasing smile.

'Damn, that's not what I meant. You take your clothes off and I'll … oh God, that sounds so much worse.'

'Why don't we both take our clothes off and get in the bath together?'

Libby wasn't quite sure what he was trying to say as she stood at the door ready to flee. 'Are you still drunk?'

'No, I just love watching you squirm.'

Although it was wonderful to see Kie laughing, she didn't like to be the object of his humour, certainly not under such serious circumstances. She hid her disappointment by displaying two fingers in his direction and secretly hoped he would drown in the bath. Libby's problem was that she'd fallen in love with a man she'd only known for a few weeks, but felt as if she'd grown up with him. She didn't know when it happened or how it could have happened in such a short space of time, but she knew she could neither help nor prevent it. As luck would have it, he just didn't feel the same towards her and that left Libby in a terrible predicament: to live her life in solitude by his side or try and get over him in the hope she would one day look upon him only as a friend. Her heart broke when she saw that smile filled with affection.

'I'll run my own bath, thanks Libby. I don't need you to run around after me.'

She nodded and returned his smile with a small one of her own.

'Can I get a cup of tea?'

Chapter 30

THE CALM

'Stop playing solitaire on your computer or I'll get systems to take the games off. It's your lucky day. The lovely Mr Armstrong's in reception to see you.'

'Thanks, Audrey.' Libby yelled into the receiver and looked around the office. 'You've got a camera hidden in here somewhere and I'm going to find it and shove it up your ...'

'Ah, he's brought me some flowers.'

Libby skipped to reception to see Kie standing in his suit and tie amongst the plastic chairs. She embraced him like an old aunt but savoured his familiar feel and smell like a long lost lover.

'Hi Kie, have you come alone or have you brought along a spirit of the dead with you?'

Kie laughed. 'I don't have any spirit friends anymore.'

'I was coming to see you today after work. Hannah says they're wrapping-up the investigation this afternoon and going home tomorrow morning.'

'Aye, it's going to feel strange to be alone again. Since it's everyone's last night, I was hoping you'd come for dinner.'

'I'd love to. Did you manage to finish the dining room?'

'Just about, but it still smells of paint, so I'm taking you all out.'

'What a treat.'

Libby hadn't seen Kie for three days and those days had felt like an eternity. She'd made a decision to bow out of being a constant in his life because she didn't feel strong enough to take the strain or the misery of an unrequited love. She used the excuse she had to return to work or get fired and he'd accepted it with his usual grace and warm concern. Hannah agreed she was doing the right thing during a tearful lunch session that lasted four hours. The only good news of the entire sorry affair was that there had been no paranormal activity at MacAoidh's house since the incident in the kitchen and Hannah suspected he no longer haunted himself.

Charlie, of course, was not convinced that Kie was responsible for the abnormal activity at all, but rather he was the victim of some mischievous entity whose time at The Ring had maybe become spent.

'Lunch?'

'I've eaten, thanks.'

'Fancy a walk then?'

She took a step back, unable to meet those eyes. 'I've got a client ...'

'In twenty minutes,' Audrey leaned across the desk with her head in her hand, a bored expression on her face. 'Go on,' she winked.

'Why not?'

They walked to the harbour in silence and sat on the familiar bench. This had become Libby's favourite place in Kirkcudbright because of its connection with the day she first met Kie.

'All right, Libby. What's wrong?'

'What ...'

'You don't answer my calls and you haven't come around to the house for days. I understand you have to keep a job down, but you could at least let me know you're fine.'

'I'm fine thanks, Kie. I just thought you wanted some space

now your life's returning to normal.'

'I miss you.' He crossed his arms and slouched on the bench. 'I miss your humour and I miss your smile. I even miss you snoring next to me.'

'Then I'll give you a picture of me for your bedside table and an EVP of the eerie nocturnal noises coming from my nose.'

'How do you know I haven't got all that already?'

She laughed at his cheeky wink.

'I don't know, maybe I need some space too. The past few weeks have been very full-on and we've been practically living together. I don't want to ruin our friendship by having too much too soon and leaving nothing for the middle bit.' She felt like crying.

'The stuff I told you about Helen. You shouldn't have had to listen to all that. I'm sorry.'

'Do you think that's the reason I've been staying away from you? What an idiot! I may be daft sometimes, but I'm certainly not shallow and you should know by now that I don't scare easily.'

'You certainly don't.' That smile again sent her heart racing.

'You were angry with me for getting drunk with Charlie.'

'For God's sake, Kie, what's this all about? Yes, I was cross with you ...'

'Why?'

She was forced to think. 'Because you both behaved very irresponsibly. We didn't know where you'd got to and thought something horrible had happened.'

'I apologise.'

'Accepted.'

'Thank you.'

'What did happen to you that night?' She had to know. She'd been agonising over the different scenarios for days. She posed the question in a manner suggesting she didn't care either way what the answer was.

He shrugged. 'Too much beer; too much whiskey; empty stomach. I passed out.'

'On the sand?'

'Must've been. I think I decided to walk home but only made a few paces and probably not even in the right direction. I'm lucky it was low tide.'

'That must've disappointed the lovely buxom Irish lasses who picked you up in the pub.'

He shot her a questioning glance and Libby realised she'd allowed herself to voice her own fantasies of what happened to Kie that night.

'Those Irish lasses had Irish lads with them.'

'Charlie said …'

'Charlie's full o' shite.'

'So what's going to happen now to MacAoidh Armstrong? Are you going to eventually allow Mother to settle you down to a life of wedded bliss with Catherine?'

'Catherine? Didn't I tell you that was over?'

Her heart skipped a beat. 'Sorry, no you didn't. What happened?'

'She just wasn't my type.'

'She wasn't your type.' Libby echoed his words with a snarl and felt her face flushing with anger. Did he realise how much hurt and damage he caused with that seemingly innocent little remark that let him off the hook of emotional responsibility? She suddenly wanted to punch him. 'And that poor woman has had to wait three years for you to eventually decide her character didn't suit your personal preferences?'

'I'm a slow learner.' He obviously was insensible to her rising annoyance.

'Don't you think telling someone they're not your type is arrogant, presumptuous and cruel?'

'Aye.'

'You're a bastard, MacAoidh.'

'Why?' He kept his cool against her outward display of hostility.

'For telling women they're not your type.'

'I've never told a woman that.'

'Not to her face, that is. That would be worse, wouldn't it? That might even humiliate her and perhaps hurt her feelings, now wouldn't it?' She gulped as she saw his eyes narrowing and knew his famous temper was slowly coming to simmering point.

'That depends on *her*. I seem to recall being taken aback when you told me, to my face, I wasn't your type.'

Libby opened her mouth and closed it again, she couldn't remember ever saying that to him or why she would ever need to. Her anger fled with her words. 'I didn't say that to you ... did I?'

'Aye, you did.'

'You didn't believe me, did you?'

'Why the hell wouldn't I? Are you telling me that sometimes you don't mean what you say?' She was pleased to see his expression mellow.

'Are you telling me you expect honesty from a lawyer?'

She forced a laugh from him.

'You told your mother you'd never be emotionally or physically involved with me.'

'No, I told my mother that I wasn't emotionally or physically involved with you and I was telling her the truth at that time. Why, do you want to get involved with me?'

'No I don't, you're nothing but trouble.'

'You're lying.'

'Or is it a double bluff?'

They sat for a while not speaking, both attempting to analyse the conversation in the hope of getting to the truth. It was Kie who eventually broke the silence.

'I'm a simple man, Libby. I don't get prevarication and am very bad at guessing games. I tend to take people at their word. That may be naive but it's the way I'm made. If I tell you I miss you, I mean it.'

'What do you miss about me, Kie? My smile, my laughter, my idiotic behaviour?'

'Amongst other things. I also miss your warmth and your affection. I miss the way you hold my hand when you think my confidence needs bolstering and your reassuring words. What I'm trying to say, very badly, is I miss your friendship.'

'You'll always have that.'

'I miss you lying beside me in the morning.'

'Come on, we only had drunken virtual sex once at the loch.'

'We didn't go all the way, remember?'

'That may be so, but I think I'm pregnant.'

'How do you know it's mine? We could've been hacked.'

Libby liked the way this conversation was going as they laughed together and she slipped her hand into his.

'So, what's your type then?' He asked her through a tiny smile that let little away.

'Tall, handsome, intelligent. The strong, silent type. Oh, and there must be an accompanying poltergeist. There's nothing more appealing to a woman than a man with spirit.'

'Your twenty minutes is almost up.'

Libby felt the disappointment rising once more, she'd said too much again. 'What time do you want me around tonight?'

'Seven? I'll pick you up from your house.'

'See you at seven then.'

She left him sitting on the bench watching the harbour and wondered what had just happened between them. Kie told her he was a simple man who didn't like guessing games but he played them so well nevertheless.

When she returned to the office, her clients were waiting for her. Mrs Pullman sat on the plastic chair, wriggling now and again in an effort to get comfortable while she read a magazine. Mr Pullman sat a few chairs away from her staring into space. She was large and he was small; she was dark and he was fair; she had that derisive snarl on her face that told Libby who wore the trousers in the relationship; and he had that pained look of bitter defeat hanging from his bushy brows.

'Mr and Mrs Pullman, please come this way.'

The Pullmans had been clients of Libby's since the wife of the marriage came to her a few weeks ago with a request to file for divorce on the grounds of unreasonable behaviour. There were no children to the marriage, so no ugly separation agreement, but there was a very special bond between the two of them that only Libby saw. Mr P adored his wife but Mrs P had become so fat and unattractive that she no longer felt worthy of anyone's affection. Unfortunately for the Ps, they were emotionally incompetent and incapable of exhibiting their true feelings to an audience, let alone each other. They sat at the end of the desk, Mrs P with her arms crossed over her ample bosom; Mr P wringing his bony hands together at his lap. Kie's flowers sat in a vase by the window and their sweet, heady scent pervaded the room.

She started mechanically. 'Mr and Mrs Pullman, you've both come to me by mutual agreement to seek a divorce because one of you believes the marriage to have irretrievably broken down.'

'Damn right,' Mrs P fired the first shot, leaving Mr P cowering.

'You may remember a few weeks ago, I suggested you go to relationship counselling first in an effort to sort out your misunderstandings of each other? How did that go?'

'He fancied the skinny coonsellor!' Mrs P said. 'Uh hud tae drag hum awa' frae the meetin'.'

'I see.' She turned to Mr P: 'Mr Pullman, do you want this twelve-year-old marriage to end?'

'Uf that's whit she wants,' he shrugged.

A sharp rap on the door caused Libby to jump. 'I'm busy!' she yelled.

She was shocked to see Kie standing in the door frame. 'Mr Armstrong, please wait for your appointment.'

He nodded to Mr and Mrs P. 'Pleased to meet you but would you be kind enough to come back another day?'

'We got an appointment,' Mrs P protested.

'But I need to speak to your lawyer and don't want to lose my momentum. Please? You won't be charged for this meeting, I promise, and Libby will meet your expenses for coming here.'

His smile was so appealing that Mrs P visibly shrivelled. 'Ah wis in love yince,' her body juddered when she sighed. She grabbed Mr P by the collar and stood up. 'Mak the most o' it, lad, it wullnae last.'

'Aye it will.'

She turned to Mr P, a small crease in the side of her mouth. 'Come on you, lets gahn hame.'

Libby's back pressed against her chair as Kie shut the door behind the Ps.

'I think I need a lawyer.'

'Why, what have you done?'

'Nothing yet. I couldn't wait until seven. It's four thirty

and I think we have some catching-up to do. I'm tired of waiting.'

Libby moved across the messy office towards him, her desk no longer a barricade between their two hearts.

He grabbed her by the back of the head and kissed her.

Time, troubles and a lifetime of wearisome emotion were lost to that one kiss.

She felt her back slamming on the desk and, as her fingers clawed against a mountain of paperwork and plastic, sending it flying in all directions, her brittle resolve shattered and her mouth melted into his as if it were fashioned to fit.

It wasn't until she heard the shrill shriek of the phone that she became vaguely aware of the world around her. She broke away from him with a feeling she'd let out her first breath in centuries.

Libby scrambled towards the noise on her hands and knees and snatched the receiver from the floor.

'Yes, Audrey?'

'It's home time. Get a room,' Audrey's voice shrilled from the handset.

'It's five thirty already?'

'Aye, stop snoggin' an' take him hame.'

Libby let the receiver fall to the carpet, having no idea where the base unit lay amid the mess of her office. She rose from the floor slowly, testing her twitching muscles for breaks.

'Very well, Mr Armstrong, you've managed to convince me your case is well worth defending. I'll see you at seven?'

She loved that impudent grin.

chapter 31

THE CELTIC CONNECTION

'Here's to the best haunting we've ever investigated. *Slàinte mhath*, MacAoidh Armstrong.'

Kie raised his glass to Charlie's toast. '*Lechyd da*, Charlie Jones.'

'It's bad luck to toast without alcohol in your glass.' Charlie feigned a frown. 'You've now brought misfortune on the people around this table, especially the one to whom the empty toast was directed.'

'Nah, I've just fated you to a season of drought and failed crops. Anyway, I'm not superstitious and remember who's driving to allow you to fill that glass with wine.'

'I think you are superstitious.' Kie turned his eyes to Libby who sat across the restaurant table next to Charlie. Napkins were now on the table and the waiting staff cleared away the remnants of an excellent seafood meal. 'Not in the gullible sense.' She returned his smile, her eyes sparkling. 'I don't see how you can't be superstitious having grown up in the far north with all that Celtic myth and folklore. You people are born believing in supernatural influences, like kelpies, selpies, sith and witchwives.'

'It's selkies and *sith* is pronounced shee,' he laughed. 'Aye, we wash our faces in the May dew and lock our doors at night from the *bean sìth*.'

'Did you say banshee?' Hannah put her glass down on the table and took out a notebook from her handbag.

Kie nodded. '*Bean* is a woman and *sìth* the general term for a fairy.'

'You know, Germany has similar superstitions.' Katja joined the conversation. 'Like your toast with water, MacAoidh, means you are wishing death on your friends. It is very bad luck.'

'Sorry.' He picked up Hannah's glass and raised it. '*Prost!*'

'We also have theriomorphs like the *Aufhoker* that can shape shift into anything it likes and rips the throats out of its victims and the *Drude* which is a particularly malicious nocturnal spirit. There is also the *Nachzehrer*, a vampire that lives off the flesh of the dead.'

'Wales has a fair amount of its own legends too.' Charlie said as he allowed the waiter to top-up his glass. 'The *Afanc* is like your Loch Ness Monster, only it's considered to be an evil demon that kills its victims with poisoned darts. *Angelystor* is a spirit in a churchyard tree who announces the names of parishioners who will die that year.'

'It's the Celtic connection.' Libby said. 'The Celts are an ancient Germanic tribe and their belief in the supernatural was as much a part of their social structure as work and domestic life. Their tales have been passed down through the generations to become, like Kie said the other day,' she shot him another one of her affectionate smiles, 'a whisper of history. I don't think there's ever been a civilisation that doesn't embrace some element of superstition in its faith and culture. Even the most remote tribes who've had no contact with contemporary society believe in gods, spirits and bad luck. The reason why our respective legends bear so much similarity is because we probably all came from the same people.'

Hannah stopped writing to add her thoughts. 'Do you believe superstition is inherently part of our genetic make-up?'

'I think human beings need order in their lives and to

neatly place facts and fiction in their proper places in the mind. Where fact falls short, fiction will fill in the gaps. You have to admit that some of the phenomena that occurred at The Ring during your investigations cannot be explained by logic or science.' Libby put her hand up to stay Hannah's impending interruption, 'OK, some day science may make a break-through and have a mathematical equation for unnatural or even supernatural activity but, at the moment, no such equation exists.'

'What's your point?'

'My point comes back to Kie. He's from a small, close-knit rural community where life is almost solely dependent upon the elements and the good will of neighbours. If crops fail, there's a famine. If there's a storm out at sea, fishermen will drown. Humans naturally react to calamity by blaming dominant forces outside their control and often translate those forces into anthropomorphic entities. Superstition is a life-line to hope. That's why they believe in fairies and demons and are ritualistic in their customs and practices. God's not enough because he doesn't prevent misfortune from occurring. The supernatural fills in for the harsh realities of life. When something goes wrong, they blame it on bad luck or angry spirits; when it comes good, they put it down to lucky charms and their ritualistic efforts in casting out demons.'

'And what about God and the Devil?'

'Anthropomorphic entities.' Kie shrugged. 'Libby's right, for some reason, mankind finds it necessary to place the liability for his existence on invisible omnipotent powers of a supreme moral quality. Faith supplements reason. It's a cop-out for taking ultimate responsibility for our own deeds. It's easier to blame gods, the devil, demons and evil for the misfortunate events in our lives and even on our own bad behaviour. I don't believe saying three hail Marys every night for a month will absolve a man from sin.'

'There is more to absolution than simple confession.' Katja sat back in her chair and crossed her arms. 'To be properly absolved from sin and escape purgatory and hell, the penitent must also show true repentance and live a life of good.'

'Good is dull,' Charlie said.

'Dominus noster Jesus Christus te absolvat.' Kie drew the sign of the cross in the air. 'You are forgiven, my son.'

'Thank you, father!'

The company laughed together and Kie's eyes fell on Libby. She pulled a face at him and looked away, obviously uncomfortable at being the focus of his attention.

He wondered where they would go to next. Would they take their association to a higher level or would it be better to remain friends and preserve what had become a close and mutually pleasant relationship? That was some kiss but, then again, it was only a kiss and hadn't come with any promises. He watched her squirming in her chair under his scrutiny and he smiled. Miss Butler was a bright woman with a mind as sharp as a razor. She had an opinion on everything and a knack for conveying her thoughts to others with eloquence and clarity, without being bombastic. He didn't know whether it was her training as a lawyer or simply her unique character that commanded the close attention of her colleagues around the table but they obviously respected her opinions. In matters of the heart, however, she blethered like an idiot.

He knew she wanted more from him but he wasn't at all certain whether he could meet her aspirations. The events of the past few weeks had brought them very close but could they maintain that intense proximity when normality returned to their lives? Were either of them prepared to take the risk of destroying a perfectly good relationship with excess emotion?

She nervously sipped at her wine and Kie felt a weighty surge of affection rising in his chest. He liked the way her hair fell around her face, despite her efforts to train it. He liked her natural awkwardness and the cutting, witty remarks she made in order to conceal it. He did feel immense warmth towards her and also a steadily increasing passion. Could he live without her? Probably, but did he want to?

'MacAoidh. Is there anybody there?'

Hannah's nudge hauled him from his inner thoughts. 'Sorry, what was that?'

'I said it's very possible you're psychic.'

'Oh aye, which clinical rational deduction brought you to that conclusion then?'

'The EVP of the woman's voice, for a start. Only you amongst us could speak Swahili.'

'Kikuyu.'

'Whatever. The fact that the voice clearly spoke in a language only you understood could mean it was created by you. The brain is a very complex organ and most of us underutilise it. Some of us are able to use the mind to do wonderful things like precognition, presentiment, telepathy and psychokinesis. Others just haven't developed those skills.'

'So you're saying psychic ability can be learned?'

'Most definitely.'

'Does that mean I can see into the future?'

'Yes and even the past. I'd like to believe the activity that took place at The Ring over the past few weeks could've been caused by your ability to somehow re-enact the past: to alter your environment via fluctuations of electron activity in your brain. It's quantum physics.'

'So you think I created some sort of sub-atomic event in an Einsteinium space-time continuum?'

Hannah's delighted laughter amused him. 'Yes, exactly. I would dearly love to get you into the lab and run some tests.'

'I'm no lab rat.'

'Are any of your family members psychic?'

'Aye, all of them. I come from a long line of seers, soothsayers and hedge witches. Why?'

'He's being sarcastic,' Libby cut in before Hannah had a chance to write Kie's words down in her little notebook. 'Does psychic ability tend to run in families?'

'Yes, it can be genetic just like eye colour and nose size. My theory goes wider than that, though. I believe entire communities can develop a collective conscience. That's why places like the Scottish Highlands tend to have had more than their fair share of precognitive personalities. It's called second sight. What's that in Gaelic, Kie?'

'*An Dà Shealladh.*'

'Wasn't the Brahan Seer from your area?'

'No he was from the Isle of Lewis, across the Minch.'

'I read about him,' Charlie added. 'Kenneth Mackenzie is said to have foreseen the Highland Clearances; Aberdeen's prosperity from oil in the North Sea; and the fields of Culloden stained with the best blood of the Highlands. He apparently saw all this through a hole in a stone.'

'*Coinneach Odhar* was burned to death in a spiked tar barrel for his final prophesy. He obviously didn't see that one coming through his wee hole.' Kie's comment made everyone laugh.

'My granny claimed she could see shrouds around people who were going to imminently die.' Libby said.

'Claims of paroptic vision are common amongst older generations. Perhaps we all get more psychic with age.' As

Charlie answered her, Kie noticed the strange look Libby gave him. It was gone the next instant and replaced by her usual wide smile.

'Unless they can be proved, your theories will always remain just theories.' Kie ended the conversation abruptly. 'I know this is your work, but I've personally had my fill of paranormal talk and would like to put it all behind me now.' He poured some of Hannah's red wine into his empty glass and raised it. 'To a future of peace, happiness and no more bloody poltergeist.'

– – –

It was well after midnight before Kie and the three scientists neared The Ring after dropping Libby home.

Heavy rain pelted from the dark skies and ricocheted off the windscreen and tarmac. In the glare of the headlights, it looked like a vertical wall of smoking silver.

The passengers shrieked as Kie was forced to turn the wheel sharply and the car swerved onto the grass banking. It stopped inches before the stone dyke. He leaped out into the rain.

'Mary? What are you doing out here? I almost killed you.' He was forced to shout against the howl of the storm.

'Oh, MacAoidh, Jim's gone missing. Margaret's beside herself.' Mary Hyslop stood in the middle of the road in her wellies and raincoat, the frills of her soggy nightdress peeking out from beneath the coat's hem. She was soaking wet and shivering. 'We're all out looking for him.'

'Could he not be tending his beasts or perhaps he's down the pub?'

'No, we tried the pub. They haven't seen him in days. We're very worried he may've done something stupid.'

'Have you called the police?'

'Aye, and a fat lot of good they are. They say to wait until tomorrow morning because he's low risk.'

'Has he ever done anything like this before?'

'A couple of times but Margaret says it's different this time. He's been depressed lately.'

'Get in the car, Mary, I'll take you home and I'll go out and look for him. You're soaked and these dark roads are no place for a woman to be out so late at night.'

'You have a kind heart, MacAoidh Armstrong.'

Kie didn't relish the prospect of looking for a man in the rain and in the pitch black of night, but Jim was his friend and neighbour. After dropping the women home, Charlie and he visited Margaret and managed to calm her down. Kie persuaded her to try the police again and mention his recent depression. He was also alarmed to hear that Jim's Remington shotgun was missing. Kie didn't know whether it was instinct that pulled him to the Ghost Tree or its association with Jim Black, but the impending feeling of dread began to crush him as Charlie and he trudged across the field in the rain. As they neared the solitary tree, standing dead and alone in the midst of the shrieking gale, their torch lights fell on a figure slumped against the trunk.

'Good grief!' Charlie yelled. 'Is that him?'

Kie caught his breath while Charlie threw up on the grass. Lying against the tree in a pool of his own blood, the body of Jim Black looked like a sack of filthy rags. The gun lay on the soaking ground in front of him, having flown from his hands as a single shot was discharged. Most of his head was gone and part of the devastated tree trunk behind him was peppered with pieces of embedded shot, bone, blood and brain tissue. The shattered remnants of his lower jaw were all that remained affixed to his neck. It was as if his entire head had exploded from the inside out. Kie smelled the gunpowder and the blood. He felt the static raising the hair on his body and the nausea stomach. He wanted to run, but his feet remained ⎯e ground.

are we going to do?' Charlie couldn't stop gagging ⎯ed off his torch so he wouldn't be tempted to take anotⁿ look at the sorry end of Jim Black.

'We'll have to leave him here for the police. There's nothing we can do, apart from tell his wife.'

'Oh God, that poor woman. Can't we let the police do that?'

'No. This is one responsibility I'm not going to run from. I'll tell her.'

Chapter 32

THE INSTINCT

'I knocked but guessed you were out the back.'

Andrew Prendergast put his suitcase down and turned on the light to the sitting room. MacAoidh sat alone on the sofa in the dark with his head in his hands. Jim Black's collie sat at his feet.

'Sorry, Prendy, I was thinking. Come in. It's good to see you.'

'Are you alright?'

In answer to MacAoidh's latest call, Prendergast packed hastily and got straight into his car. The journey from London took him longer than expected with road works and a crash on the M6 bringing traffic to a near standstill for thirty miles. It was after ten in the evening and dusk had just given way to another black night in the Solway Hills.

'Aye, I'm fine. How's the wife?'

Prendergast laughed. 'Cross that I'm spending less time with her and more time chasing ghosts in Scotland again. She'll get over it when she sees the pay packet at the end of the month. She's a good woman with excellent priorities.'

'I need to find out why Jim Black took his own life five nights ago. I've tried speaking to Margaret but she's very tight-lipped and in denial about the events that led up to this tragedy.'

'Suicide brings a very different type of bereavement. Shock, anger, guilt and so many unanswered questions make it a complicated process to struggle through. The passing of time heals most of the feelings eventually, but it's hard for the one left behind to come to terms with the deceased's reasons for wanting to leave the world behind and taking such drastic measures to make it happen.'

'This is the second death at this property in a few weeks.'

'The minister had a heart attack.'

'And have you ever considered what may have brought it on?'

Prendergast nodded. He had, indeed, wondered whether the black cloud falling on Mr MacKenzie at the point of his death held some significance. 'It's possible, even though the trouble ended at this house with the help of the parapsychologists, it continued with Jim Black. Perhaps he simply couldn't cope.'

'Well, something made a good man kill himself and leave a loving wife destitute. It just doesn't make any sense.'

'Suicide rarely does, son.' Prendergast poured himself a drink from a bottle in the large oak cabinet and sat down on the chair opposite MacAoidh. 'I keep expecting a stone to hit me or a voice to whisper in my ear. The house feels strangely quiet.'

'It's a golden silence. I like it better this way.'

'Me too.' Prendergast chuckled. 'Did the scientists give you any reasons for all this trouble?'

'Many, but nothing conclusive. One of them blamed natural electromagnetic fields; another thought I was doing it all through psychic ability; and the other, Charlie, believed it was a noisy spirit of a dead person. They've gone back to their labs in Leicester to analyse all the data. Charlie wants to come back to investigate Jim Black's house, if Margaret will let him.'

'What's your gut instinct?'

MacAoidh looked at him with those extraordinary blue eyes. 'I've been doing a lot of soul searching over the past few days and I'm going to summarise my thoughts to you. I never thought I would ever hear myself saying this, but I believe things happened here that go far beyond the conventional rules of science or empirical observation. It's possible that all three theories apply equally to the recent behaviour here. I'm beginning to think it was powerful enough to stop the sick heart of an old man and cause the suicide of another. I think I got off lightly, considering.'

Prendergast took a sip of his whisky. 'My, my, that's delicious.'

'It ought to be, it's a fifty-year-old Highland Park.'

Prendergast sprayed the whisky from his mouth. 'So sorry, I didn't realise …'

MacAoidh laughed. 'It's there to be drunk. You're welcome to it. There's a fifty-five-year-old Macallan in there too. Help yourself.'

'I'm going to enjoy my little stay here.' He settled into his chair with a contented smile on his face. 'So, what made you change your mind and finally believe in ghosts?'

'I didn't say I'd changed my mind, I've just opened it a wee bit.'

'I see.'

'It was a conversation with Libby that got me thinking …'

'How is Libby?'

'She's grand. I haven't seen her for a few days. I really should get in touch.'

His eyes became distant and Prendergast smiled to himself. 'Yes, Miss Butler does have a way of getting under one's skin.'

'Libby and the team were discussing the fact the occult is deep-rooted in all human cultures. The Kenyans, for example, strongly believe in the existence of dark powers and evil. The Witchcraft Act, banning the use of spells and witchcraft, was revised only a few years ago. It's only through the conservative rules of science and Christianisation that we, as a modern race, have stopped believing in anything that can't be plausibly predicted by mathematical formulas or the Bible. What if we're wrong? Those parapsychologists were genuinely interested in finding answers through science and put their reputations on the line by trying to establish that the paranormal, in whatever form that takes, exists alongside natural laws. I know it's not the neighbours nor any form of communal hypnosis. I'm willing to go with the scientists' theories for now.'

'You've come a long way, young Armstrong.'

'It's been a hard journey and I'm not entirely converted but I'm running out of choices.'

'It's a pity we'll never really find out what caused all this. Your poltergeist has fled so now we'll never know.'

'I'm not convinced that it's gone and neither do I think I was causing this activity. I believe I was simply, as Hannah said, viewing it remotely.'

'Oh? Has anything happened to help you reach that conclusion?'

'No, it's just a gut feeling.'

'Yes, your mother said you would give into instinct eventually.'

Kie laughed. 'Has she been telling you her ghost stories?'

'She intimated you may have inherited your family's psychic abilities.'

'I'm trying to open my mind to them and following my hunches to see where they'll lead me. If I'm really psychic, then ending this is going to be easy. First, I need you to help me find some answers.'

'I'm at your disposal. What do you want me to do?' Prendergast believed in following hunches. The police had been working with psychics for years.

'Do you remember Mary Hyslop's missing boy?'

'Of course, that was one of my hunches also. I spoke to her about him and followed-up leads with a few of the former residents of this house. I didn't get very far though.'

'He wants me to find him.'

'Do you think his dead spirit seeks peace in resolution?'

'No, that's ridiculous. It's possible he's still alive but his personality is haunting these grounds. It's also possible, if he is dead, his particular energy will continue to be played back until the matter's resolved.'

'And how shall we start this boy hunt?'

'You're the detective, you figure it out. I can give you a lead, though. Both Libby and my mother said they saw a fair-haired boy. I was at Mary Hyslop's house the other day and the picture of her thirteen-year-old missing child fitted the description of their vision, or whatever you want to call it.'

'And you think Mary's boy is the one asking for help?'

'I don't know. That's what I need to find out.'

'Short of holding a séance and asking him ourselves, there's nothing much we can do. The case is stone cold now.'

'I'm sure you can persuade your ex-colleagues at the force to heat it back up. Tell them it may have something to do with Jim's suicide.'

'That's a very long shot.'

'It's all we've got.'

Prendergast laughed. 'Yes, I can't see me telling the local constabulary that a boy who's been missing for ten years is trying to contact us from the grave or through the ether with his mind. They'd pack me off to the local nut house and throw away the key.'

'You know, Prendy, I'm going to follow my instinct. I believe this is just the calm before the howling tempest to come.'

'You're beginning to sound like a psychic.'

'I'm a Sutherland man, I'm told it's in the blood.'

— — —

'I'm busy!'

Libby made to slam the front door but Kie put his big boot in the gap just in time.

'I've got something to show you.'

'Bring it to my office tomorrow morning.'

'I want you to look at it now.'

His smile was so appealing that her resolve melted. In the next instant she was fighting off the panic. 'I don't have time. Can you come back tomorrow?'

'What's wrong with now?'

'I'm entertaining. I've got guests.'

'It won't take a moment. I promise.'

'Libby, where's the bottle opener?' She closed her eyes and sighed as the male voice called from the kitchen.

'Ah, that kind of busy.' He gave her a teasing wink. 'Two minutes and I'll let you get back to your, ehm, guests.'

She felt her lips tightening against her teeth. He could at least have looked a little disappointed.

'Do come in.' She curled her lip behind his back and followed him into the kitchen. 'MacAoidh Armstrong, Paul Hamilton. Paul Hamilton, MacAoidh Armstrong.'

'Pleased to meet you.'

Libby winced as Kie gave Paul one of his Bam Bam handshakes: rattling him like a rag doll, almost snapping the delicate bones in his hand and bending his wrist into an impossible angle.

After the embarrassing slapping incident by his fiancée in a restaurant, Paul had been pestering Libby to go out with him for months but she'd easily resisted his charms. When she hadn't heard a word from Kie for over four days, she decided to get over her misery and give Paul another try. Seeing him cradling his injured hand with tears in his eyes, she wished she hadn't bothered.

'You've got something to show me?'

'Aye, but not in front of him. It could be embarrassing.'

Libby's eyes narrowed.

'What's she cooking you for dinner?'

'*Bâtonnets de poisson pané.*' Libby grabbed Kie by the arm. 'Out!'

'She'll burn them. She burns everything.'

'Is there a problem here, Libby?' Paul found his backbone as she marched Kie from the kitchen.

Kie turned his six-foot four-inch powerhouse frame of muscle and brawn towards him. 'Not at the moment. Why, are you thinking of developing one?'

'Who is this guy?' Paul, shrinking into the dish washer door, resorted to feigning humour in an effort to hide his terror.

'I'm her husband. While she's gallivanting around with her fancy men and feeding them incinerated fish fingers, I get to deal with the hungry weans.'

'You never told me you had children, Libby.'

She crossed her arms, keeping her glower on Kie. 'Must've slipped my mind. Besides, you never told me you had a fiancée, so now we're even.'

'And a husband with a previous record for assault on the last man who tried it on with her.' Kie added.

'Look, pal, I don't want any trouble.'

'Then get out while you still have one good hand … pal!'

Libby stood in the kitchen while Paul beat a swift retreat out the front door.

'That's better. How are you?'

No laughter, no smile, no explanation for such bad behaviour. Just down to business as if he hadn't just ruined her cosy evening.

'What just happened there?'

He shrugged. 'I got rid of him for you.'

'For me?'

'Aye, he has shifty eyes, a weak handshake and a lumbering gait.'

'So now you're an expert in human behaviour?'

'Just Darwinism and I can tell you your boyfriend hasn't evolved since the Neolithic era.'

'That's it, get out!' She grabbed his arm again and hauled him towards the door.

'Come on, Libby, I did you a favour. You don't even like him.' He stood in the doorframe, blocking her way to the handle.

'Oh? And how could you possibly tell?'

'Your stiff body language. The fact you let me in without a fight. The way you introduced me to him; the way you didn't make eye contact with him when he spoke to you and, the most telling evidence, you put up no resistance when I got rid of him. In fact, you look relieved.'

'I had no idea I made it so obvious.' She kept her composure, albeit with a sardonic clip to her voice.

'Prendy's back. Do you want to come over for the evening?'

'No thanks. I've got burned fish fingers to eat all by myself.'

'Bring them, it'll save me from cooking.'

'I don't feel like company tonight.'

He sighed. 'I'm sorry I didn't call you. Jim Black took his shotgun on a walk and blew his head off under the Ghost Tree the night I last saw you. We came home from the restaurant and his family were out searching for him in the storm. Charlie and I found him dead beneath the tree and the pieces of his head all over the field. I've been pre-occupied with coming to terms with two deaths on my property in about the same amount of weeks. I told Hannah not to tell you because I thought you'd been through enough lately.'

Libby forgave him immediately.

'God, Kie, I'm really sorry.'

She gave him a hug and he wrapped his arms around her. She stood inside the safest place in the world.

'It's actually chicken fricassee with tarragon; moules mariniere for starters; and a pear tatin with crème Anglaise for dessert.'

'So, you'll come?'

'It's not as if I've got anything better to do now you've terrorised my hot date and sent him packing. By the way, what did you want to show me?'

'It can wait until after dinner.'

'Oh yes?'

'Let's get the formalities over with before we settle down to the intimacies.'

'Are you being presumptuous?'

'Aye, I hope so.'

Chapter 33

THE HEADWIND

'Lovely meal, Libby. Thank you.' Prendergast placed his cutlery in his bowl and sat back, patting his rounded stomach. 'I'd no idea you were such a good cook.'

'Anyone can follow a recipe, Prendy.' Libby understated her efforts. 'I've been practising.'

Kie returned to the table with a photograph and placed it in her hand. 'I want you to take a look at this picture and tell me if you recognise the face.'

'Is this your idea of after-dinner entertainment?'

'Aye, just look at it would you?'

Libby saw a portrait of a young, overweight, fair-haired youth with smiling eyes and a ruddy complexion. 'Am I to guess his name?'

'Do you recognise him at all?'

She knew from the earnest expression that this was important to Kie but wasn't sure what he expected of her. 'No, should I?'

'Another theory flies out the window!' Kie sighed and sat down.

'Did I pass?'

Prendergast patted her hand. 'We were hoping you'd recognise him from somewhere.'

A light suddenly went on at the back of Libby's eyes. 'Ah, I see. You were hoping this was the boy I saw on the landing.' She took another look at the photograph. 'My boy had his eyes closed. His hair, I think, was a bit longer, wet and plastered to the side of his head. He didn't have those lovely rosy cheeks but the shape of the face, that little angular chin …' She handed the photo to Prendy. 'All wee boys have angular chins.'

She saw the disappointment in Kie's face.

'Have you e-mailed a copy to your mother?'

'Mother's never touched a computer in her life. She's under the impression if she presses a button, she'll blow up the world by mistake. I sent her a copy of the picture today by post.'

'That'll take a while to get to her. Don't they still use the Pony Express in Sutherland?'

'There's a gale coming. I'd better batten down the hatches and get that dog in.'

Libby and Prendergast sat in silence for a few moments while Kie left the dining room to tend to his chores.

'He's got some very good ideas for this place.' Prendergast began the conversation with a safe subject.

'Yes, he's a regular Old Macdonald. He's going to turn it into a working homestead, breed pedigree animals and grow things.'

'It must be a nice feeling to be entirely self-sufficient.'

'No one's entirely self-contained, Prendy. Everyone needs aid, support and interaction with others at some stage in their lives. He's not off the grid here. In fact, he probably consumes more electricity than the collective households in Kirkcudbright. I can't see him knocking down this beautiful home and building one of those passive photovoltaic earth houses that look like something out of Hobbiton.'

'I don't think his personal impact on the environment is his major concern. I believe the man just wants some order in his life and to live off the rewards of his own efforts. He's lucky he's rich enough not to require a regular job to sustain his daily needs like the rest of us. At the same time, he doesn't like to sit idle. A smallholding will suit his temperament. I hope he finds the happiness he deserves. He's a good, resourceful man is MacAoidh Armstrong.'

'I don't think he'll ever be happy here after all that's happened. He's had a very bad start and first impressions, unfortunately, are the ones that tend to stick.'

'He's as stubborn as a mule. I doubt a little haunting will put him off his future goals.'

'He really wanted me to recognise the boy in that photo, didn't he?'

'Yes, I'm afraid he did. He was trying to rely on intuition; to prove that hunches can work.

'Are you telling me that Kie believes in premonitions now?'

'Not exactly.' Kie stood at the door and pulled off his jacket.

'Is it windy out there?'

'Aye, there's a strong headwind knocking against the front of the house.' He sat down again next to Libby.

'I can tell by the mess it's made of your hair.' She smoothed the hair away from his face with her palms.

'Well, I do and I don't. I do believe that we're born with natural instinct that alerts us to danger and even helps us choose a mate. It's part of a genetic survival code. It could be as simple as a heightened sense of smell we're not aware of. In the savannah, you can always tell there's a lion around because every animal that could be considered prey is looking in his direction. The animals sense danger whether up or downwind of it.'

'I've read loads of stuff on prophetic dreams which turned out to be forewarnings of disasters.'

'But wouldn't that mean the future is already mapped out for us, that it already exists even though it hasn't happened yet?' Prendergast loved these philosophical evening conversations.

'That depends on whether you believe the world is a three-dimensional space of past, present, and future, all modified by the passing of time; or whether the universe is a four-dimensional block where there's no distinction between now, then and what will be.'

'Sorry, Kie, you've lost me.' Prendergast said. 'I now wish I'd remained awake during my school physics lessons.'

'What Einstein Armstrong means is that some physicists believe past, present and future are an illusion and the flow of time can't be accurately measured by man. They're all equally real. Someone once told me that and I didn't understand a word of what he was talking about until now.'

'I can guess who that was,' Prendergast laughed.

'I can't.'

Libby snapped herself back to the present, or what was called the present, as Kie gave her one of his questioning looks that demanded an immediate answer.

'I once had a very strange client.'

'Strange in what way?'

'Suffice it to say, he was a very interesting and unusual young man.' Prendergast leaped to Libby's aid.

'What do you mean by interesting, strange and unusual?'

'It's difficult to explain.' Libby didn't understand why Kie wouldn't let the subject drop.

'Try me.'

'OK, for a start, he could read your thoughts. He'd tell you what you were going to say before you opened your mouth to say it.'

'You couldn't hide anything from the lad, it was very frustrating at times. He also chose his words carefully, he gave nothing of himself away.' Prendergast added. 'Maybe his natural powers of precognition were strong.'

'So what else could Yoda do that was interesting, strange and unusual?' Kie appeared vaguely fascinated.

'He affected electrical currents and blew circuitry.'

'With his mind?'

'Well, it wasn't with his bloody ears!' Libby didn't know why she felt so defensive. 'He was also strong, I mean not like Kie Armstrong strong, but he had a power to him that was almost superhuman. However, he didn't abuse that strength and used it sparingly to chastise rather than hurt. He was actually a very gentle human being. People expected him to be some kind of kick-ass American hero-type character, but he was above all that. He didn't need to prove himself or his prowess in a fight; he didn't consider any of his enemies a challenge or a threat so he refused to hurt them. He had that ability. It was extraordinary.'

'Did he wear his underpants outside his tights or on the inside?'

Libby felt a rush of indignation flushing her cheeks. 'It's impossible to explain who or what he was because none of us really got to know him properly. What I do know, however, is that his soul was untainted with the trivialities of life and he brought the best out in everyone he touched. He was perfect in every way perfection can be defined and you wouldn't be sitting there ridiculing him now if you'd met him. In fact, you'd probably be kissing his boots.' She didn't realise she was shouting until she noticed the expressions on the faces of the two men at the table: Prendy looked embarrassed and Kie looked puzzled.

'Sorry, didn't mean to hit a nerve. I'm sure Jesus and I would've got along fine.'

'Talking of after-dinner entertainment, who wants a game of Scrabble?' Prendergast once again diffused a highly explosive situation as he pulled the board game from the oak cabinet.

Her anger swiftly spent, Libby felt a pang of contrition as Kie sat quietly digesting her sudden tantrum. 'OK but you can't have bummy or wowza again, they're not in the dictionary.'

'That last one made me a good twenty points.'

'You were cheating and I'm watching you very closely now.'

— — —

'That was a really nice evening. Sorry for losing my temper with you earlier.' Libby lay on the carpet on her front, her shoeless feet waving in the air behind her.

'It's OK, I probably deserved it. I intentionally riled you.' Kie cleared up the Scrabble board, carefully placing the plastic letters face down in their box.

'Why?' She folded the board and handed it to him.

'His memory made you sad. I wanted to alter that emotion to anything else but sorrow. I've been there too many times to know that wallowing in misery is not the answer.'

'It worked. I felt an over-riding urge to slap you. How would you've felt if I'd attacked your memory of Helen in a similar way?'

He shrugged in the way that MacAoidh Armstrong shrugged when he felt confident. 'Your opinion of her wouldn't affect my memories. You didn't know her.'

'Then tell me a bit about her.'

'No.'

'Why?'

'Because you'll attempt to taint my recollections of her solely for the purposes of vengeance. I was simply trying to help you.'

'No you weren't. You felt threatened.' She braved that crossing of boundaries: that line where good behaviour ended and bad behaviour began.

To her utter surprise, he laughed. 'All right, the depth of your sentiment towards him made me feel jealous.'

'Jealous that you felt my admiration for him compromised your ego?'

THE HEADWIND

'No, jealous as in you weren't saying the same of me.'

'You're nothing like him, Kie. And I'm nothing like Helen.'

'Helen's dead.' The raw emotion she saw in his eyes was not drawn from what was past. Libby finally felt she was getting to him.

'But have you really let her go?'

'Aye. What about you?'

She smiled out of pure affection. 'Aye, Kie Armstrong, I believe I've finally learned to live again. There's something about the very special relationship I have with you that makes everything worthwhile. You make me feel whole and safe but you can also make me feel alone and lost. You're so brutally honest that, ironically, I never know where I am with you. In your efforts to be genial and predictable, you're often distant and erratic.'

'Wow, we're doing this intellectually. OK, I'll have a go.' He paused for a few moments to formulate his words. 'I'm lured by your astonishing impulsiveness like a sailor to a Siren.'

He waited for the smile but she shook her head. 'Too soppy.'

'OK,' he turned his eyes to the ceiling, drawing on his hidden imaginative side. 'I've been built into an existence of certainty and confidence, but you're spontaneity and the way you challenge life intrigues me and compels me to always want to protect you.' He nodded to himself, happy with that. 'Despite the odds, and notwithstanding your overriding impulse to run or hide, you charge head on into the breach of the unknown, not knowing whether you'll fail or fall. I find myself leaping to your defence, hoping to always give you a soft landing. You're probably the most unusual, most human person I've ever met, Libby Butler, and I want to grow old knowing you.'

'That did it! That was beautiful.' She felt like crying and her bottom lip quivered.

'Do you want me to take you home now?'

She pulled herself together after his wonderful eulogy. 'No, I'd quite like to stay, if that's OK with you. I haven't slept in this house while it's been peaceful. It'll be a new experience. Has Prendy gone to bed?'

'Aye, since you expurgated all his dubious words on the board, he didn't want to appear a bad loser, so took off to bed with the dictionary, a notepad and a mug of malted milk.'

Libby giggled. 'What do you want to do now?'

'Fancy a game of strip Scrabble?'

She narrowed her eyes and pushed her chin into her hands. 'You know, I can never tell when you're joking or when you're being serious.'

'I was joking in that instance.' Sitting on the floor, he leaned back on the chair and rested his arms on the seat. 'But I'm warming to the idea.'

'Let's just talk.' She sat up and pulled her skirt over her knees

'All right, what do you want to talk about?'

'You start.'

'Instinct.' He didn't even hesitate to think of a subject.

'As in the inborn pattern of fixed behaviour in response to certain stimuli?'

'As in the natural desire that makes animals behave in a certain way against all reason.'

'You mean that basic reaction below the level of consciousness?'

His nod was barely perceptible as his eyes dazzled her.

She shot him a sly smile. 'What's your first instinct?'

'To run.'

'That's called primitive instinct. And your second?'

'To run faster. What about you?'

'To stand and fight.'

'That's called killer instinct.' He moved his back from the chair and leaned closer towards her.

'I can't help it, it's involuntary.' She felt her body pulling towards him.

'You must learn to control those sensory motors.' He brushed his lips across hers while his hands caressed her back.

'I can't. They're purely reflexive and happen naturally.'

'That's hyperbole, but you're beautiful anyway.'

That kiss again. That soft, passionate kiss that caused her to forget where and who she was. It was a kiss that made promises of an infinity of love and unfettered emotion. It was as if she held her breath inside his personal definition of eternalism; tenseless and unchanging. Half awake and half in dream, she felt weightless as he lifted her into his strong arms and carried her up the stairs, all the while locked together as one in that ardent, timeless kiss.

— — —

When Libby finally awoke from her dreams, the morning light stabbed at her eyes like carrion birds pecking at road kill. She lay on her front, sticking between the sheets of Kie's bed, and felt she'd been a contender in an all-night wrestling match. She heard the door open and she groaned.

'I've brought you some tea.'

Her muscles spasmed involuntarily when she felt his mouth between her shoulder blades. It would have been a wonderful sensation had every part of Libby's body not felt drowsy and over-sensitive.

'Go away. I never want to have sex again. Ever.'

'Aw, come on Libby. That was just a warm-up!' He threw his jeans off and leapt into bed with the enthusiasm of an Olympic athlete after that coveted gold medal.

'I've got work in a minute and I haven't slept all night. Come back later when all my internal organs have stopped throbbing.' She allowed him to press his body into hers and brush his mouth against the back of her neck. The sensation was akin to an electric shock in her groin and she couldn't help but react on pure animal impulse. 'I sense you're in a playful mood this morning.'

'Why wouldn't I be? I have my gorgeous lawyer lying naked in my bed: a vision I've fantasised about for a very long time.'

'Since when?' Libby didn't have the strength to turn around and face him.

'Since you exposed yourself to me at your house and perhaps even before.'

'Perhaps?' She did turn around and noticed the unusual hue of his eyes. 'You've just ruined an excellent precedent.'

She couldn't turn away from the power of his stare and misplaced herself once more in time. She heard the hands of the clock moving forwards but the noise was somewhere else: somewhere in a different dimension to the place where she was lost. She was vaguely aware of the space around her – the bed, the side tables and the constant tick of the clock – and the affirmative movement of his hands against her skin, his mouth against hers and the deep, deep penetrating force between her legs: smooth, searing and unyielding.

'Libby, ssshhh, Prendy'll think we've awakened the poltergeist.'

She woke up once more to Kie's hand pressing gently against her mouth, his expression bursting with affection and amusement.

'God, Kie, what have you done to me?'

The windows rattled and she felt she should be scared.

'It's just the wind whistling against the panes.' He curled his body around hers.

'But is it blowing in our direction or against us?'

'That's a strange question.'

Libby smiled and focused her attention on the hands of Kie's bedside clock. It wasn't until she'd been staring at it for a few minutes that she realised something was wrong. The second hand was moving backwards. She sat up in the bed and looked down at Kie who appeared to be sleeping. She saw the rise and fall of his back as he breathed and took a moment to marvel at the sight. It wasn't until she saw dark figures crowding the room that she realised she was still sleeping. She tried to call out his name but could hear herself squeaking in panic as if she'd suddenly shrunk to inaudible proportions.

Jimmy Black had a shroud around him. Charlie at the restaurant had a similar aura. She saw her granny who shot her a sweet, toothless smile. Rocking in a chair, knitting needles poised at the ready, Granny Munro – from her mother's side – had the second sight and Libby wondered whether there was such a thing as auras.

She awoke again, panting.

Kie had dozed off. She could hear Prendy rumbling around in the hallway and she quietly slipped from the bed. The gale outside was stronger. It shook the glass panes in their wooden frames and whined beneath the gaps in the door.

She shuffled to the bathroom and pulled the shower cord, but the light in the ceiling switch wouldn't come on. She tried the mirror light but that didn't work either.

'Kie,' she shook his shoulder gently. 'The power's out.'

'It's just the wind.'

'You're going to have to take me home. I need a shower before I go to work.'

'OK, I'm coming.'

He rolled from the bed, the need to sleep catching up with

him at last. Pulling on his clothes, he followed her from the bedroom and down the stairs. He spoke briefly to Prendergast in the kitchen and picked up his electronic car key. Libby waited for him by the car trying to stay on the lee side to prevent the strong gusts of wind from knocking her over. Leaves and debris swirled and eddied around the garden, flying past her eyes like miniature banshees. She smiled as she watched him amble towards her like a sleepwalker, his hair in disarray, the laces of his boots trailing behind him, his T-shirt on back to front, the gale shrieking around him.

'Maybe you'll need that generator after all.' She yelled over the noise of the wind.

She got in the car and waited for him to throw himself into the driver's seat, but something distracted him. He stood with his back pressed against her window so she was unable to open the door to ask him what the delay was all about.

It wasn't until she saw Prendergast trotting out of the house and momentarily glancing back as if he was being chased by a rabid dog that she realised something was wrong. The look on his face was one of undisguised horror.

Libby sprang across the seats to the driver's side and fell out of the car door. Scrambling on the gravel, she eventually managed to upright herself and stand beside Kie. He put his arm around her shoulder but didn't take his eyes off the house.

She caught her breath and was certain her heart skipped a few beats when she realised what the two of them were staring at.

Every window in the house, even the skylight in the roof, gaped wide open like a silent screaming choir. The curtains flapped and snapped from their poles, licking the frames before being carried off into the turbulent ether. Interior doors banged and squealed against the full force of the invading tempest. And, while the storm blasted against the outside walls threatening to tear them down, a distorted human voice howled in fury from within, bellowing its final challenge.

chapter 34

THE PRESS

'Can I help you?'

Libby was surprised to find a tall thirtyish or, if she was being unreasonably mean, fortyish woman in her office. The first thing she saw was the black suit with white trim on the neck, sleeves and hem. Libby had a suit just like it. The woman threw the diary on the desk and grinned. She placed her hands behind her back as if the gesture would conceal the fact she'd been snooping.

'Hi, Miss Butler isn't it? There was no one at reception, so I came right through to your office. I'm Mandy Rutherford.'

'And what can I tell you Miss Rutherford that you haven't already gleaned from my diary?' The woman didn't have to state the nature of her business, Libby could smell a reporter from miles away.

'I swear I picked up the book because I liked the colour of the cover. I didn't open it.'

'Oh?'

'I have a dress like that.'

'Lime green faux leather, a little scuffed around the edges? You must look sensational in it.' Libby sat down at her desk, placed the diary in the top drawer and fumbled about for a pen.

'No, like the one you're wearing.' Miss Rutherford didn't so much as squirm as she parked her large bottom on the clients' chair. 'I love the simplicity of black and white, they look so elegant on tall people.'

'But one has to have a slim figure to carry off a dress like this with any real style.'

'Yes, otherwise one can look a bit lumpy in it. Can't one?'

What was the woman insinuating? Libby took a deep breath. 'Do you need a lawyer or do you want me to make up a story for you to fill the news holes in your paper?'

'OK, I'm rumbled,' Miss Rutherford made her Cheshire Cat grin again. 'I actually need your help.' She waited for Libby to say something but was disappointed. 'I understand you have a client …'

'Sorry, I'm not at liberty to talk about any of my clients. That information is confidential.'

'I just want to speak to him, that's all.'

'Then why aren't you asking him?'

'I tried. He's ex-directory so I went round to his house this morning and left him my card but that ex-policeman threw me off the premises. He's the one who caught that London serial killer two years ago, isn't he?'

'Really?' Libby took a long look at Miss Rutherford and decided she didn't like her.

'Anyway, I'd like to speak to Mr Armstrong about the two deaths that occurred on his property a few weeks ago. I understand from some of the locals that a team of ghost hunters spent a week there and the Rerrick Parish Poltergeist has returned.'

'Is that so?'

'Can you tell me why a former Scotland Yard detective is staying at The Ring?'

Libby shrugged. 'No, I can't.'

'He's apparently been asking a lot of questions around the village.'

'Yes, coppers like to ask questions. I believe it's part of their job.'

'What's going on there Miss Butler? I know you spend a lot of time at the house. Is MacAoidh Armstrong's house really haunted?'

'I'm not qualified to answer that question. You'll have to ask a parapsychologist.'

Miss Rutherford's cheeks flushed slightly beneath her foundation. 'All I want is permission to stay a night in the house along with a photographer. It's just one night.'

I'm not the owner of the house so I don't have the authority to grant that permission. You would have to request that directly from the owners.'

Exasperated by Libby's answers, the reporter leaned into the desk. 'Look, Libby, I'll be perfectly straight with you. I know all about client confidentiality and I also know about the solicitors' code of practice. Are lawyers allowed to have affairs with their clients?'

Libby laughed. 'This is Scotland, not America. Are you trying to accuse me of impropriety?' She picked up a ballpoint pen and idly tapped it against the desk top.

'Absolutely not. I was just pointing out how embarrassing this could all get for you and MacAoidh if word happened to slip out of your illicit relations. Things like that happen when a journalist is forced to use conjecture as the basis for a storyline.'

'Wow! You're really thick, aren't you?'

'Pardon?'

'First, Mr Armstrong is no longer my client, but the confidentiality rule still stands. Second, I don't know where you're getting your information from but you'd better be able to plead veritas before I wipe the court floors with your bad hairstyle.'

'So you deny having sexual relations with MacAoidh?'

'First, I have no idea who you're talking about and second,

my sex life has absolutely nothing to do with you or the rest of the world.'

'We've got photos of you kissing outside your front door this morning.'

'A kiss hardly amounts to sexual relations. You'd better make very sure of your facts before opening your mouth again, Miss Rutherford, or I might just leap down it with a summons.'

'You should've made sure no one was pointing a camera at you before opening yours, Miss Butler.'

Libby narrowed her eyes and dug the tip of the pen into the desk. 'I hope I don't need to quote Article Eight to you. As a journalist, you should be painfully aware of an individual's right to private life under the Human Rights Convention.'

'These pictures were taken on a pavement in full view of the public. If you didn't want anyone seeing you with his tongue down your throat, you should've waited until you were inside. There's no reasonable expectation of privacy in a public place.'

Miss Rutherford had obviously been listening at her training sessions in law and journalism. 'I hardly think my private life, or even that of Mr Armstrong's, can be considered a matter of public interest. I'm neither a super model nor a high profile footballer, after all.'

'I'm absolutely certain the public will be interested to hear how the intended victim of an infamous London serial killer has moved on with her life only to find herself hooked up with a man who's haunted by a seventeenth century spirit.'

'From killer to chiller, I can see the headline.'

'Hey, that's brilliant. I'm going to use it!'

Libby took a casual stance, although she really felt like strangling the woman. 'You couldn't justify the pursuit of a legitimate aim by publishing those pictures, the purpose of which would be purely salacious. Plus, the benefits a story like that would bring to your publication are not proportionate to the harm my privacy would suffer. You have the editor's code to consider.'

'Freedom of the press is also in the public interest, Miss Butler. That's in the editor's code too. Give me just one night and we'll forget the whole affair.' She sat back and crossed her arms, delighted that she'd won a small victory against a member of the mighty legal profession.

'All right Miss Rutherford, just so there's no misunderstanding between us. You've just told me you'll desist in publishing digital images of Mr Armstrong and me in a passionate embrace outside my private home this morning, if I will facilitate entry for you and one photographer into Mr Armstrong's house for one night in order for you to secure a news story for your paper? Is that correct.'

'Just one night.'

'And, if I fail?'

'Then you may read about your public affair in the tabloids tomorrow. Paranormal romance is a very popular genre at the moment.'

'I see. So you're in effect compelling me to act against my will by the use of threats and psychological pressure, thereby forcibly removing my right to make a decision against my better judgment?'

'You really do need to stop talking like a lawyer, Libby, it's getting boring.'

'Thankfully, I *am* a lawyer.' Libby took in a deep, satisfied breath and waggled the voice recorder at her opponent. She'd turned it on when she placed her diary in the drawer. 'Game, set and tournament.'

'That's a covert device and not admissible in evidence.'

'As you can see from that big sign on the pin board behind

me, some client interviews may be recorded for training and monitoring purposes.' Libby's grin was wider than Miss Rutherford's frown. 'I believe I'm a victim of media harassment and intimidation. We'll just see what comments the Press Complaints Commission want to make when I put in my grievance.' She made sure she shouted her words into her hand-held device.

'Bitch. I'm going to ruin you!'

'What was that?' Libby leaned an ear towards the seething journalist at the end of her desk. 'I believe that's called a verbal assault. Sorry, Mandy but you'll just have to reserve the headline 'MacAoidh returns to old haunt' for a story you can print.'

– – –

'Mr Prendergast, how lovely to see you, please come in.'

Mary Hyslop stood by the door of her cottage in her pinafore and slippers. 'You're back in Scotland?' Her Geordie accent didn't sound so strong today.

'Yes, Mary, thank you. It's very nice to see you too.' The pleasantries fell clumsily from his lips as he stepped across the low threshold and allowed Mary to lead him into her kitchen. 'Sorry, if you're busy ...'

'Not at all. I'm just making scones.' Prendergast averted his eyes as she bent over and placed the tray in the oven.

'For the rural competition?'

'Oh, my goodness, no. The season's closed 'til September and we're not called the rural anymore. It's the WI. Even ladies need to take time off you know.'

'Yes, my wife would agree with that.' His attempts at humour had the desired effect as Mary let out a high-pitched cackle.

As she wiped down the kitchen table with a pristine cloth, he looked around the room. The kitchen was a scene straight from the nineteen thirties with stand-alone pieces of vintage furniture, comprising a tallboy and wooden table with two drawers and a marble slab slapped on top, sitting against the wall. There was a crazed butler's sink beneath the window hemmed with a check-patterned curtain. An ancient armchair, dilapidated and threadbare in places, loafed beside the old range. There was a homely, wholesome feel to Mary's house which mirrored her no-fuss, simple character.

'I've come to give you the photograph back. Thank you for letting us borrow it.'

She wiped her hands on her apron and pulled the photograph from his fingers. She looked at it once and placed it face down on the table. 'Has it helped with your inquiries?'

'I'm afraid not.' He wanted to broach the subject of the missing son, but needed to lead in gently. 'He's a fine looking young man. Did you have him very late in life?'

'I was twenty six. His sister is a good bit older. She's married and has two kids of her own. She lives in Portpatrick now.'

Prendergast could hardly believe Mary was not even fifty. She had the look of a pensioner complete with a tight perm and support stockings. He hoped he hadn't sounded rude.

'How old was Peter when he, er, went missing?'

'Thirteen and it's all right Mr Prendergast, I've come to terms with the fact he's not coming back.'

'Now, you can't tell that for certain, Mary. The case isn't completely closed.'

'Oh, I know. He's gone and I'll not see him again in this life.' She set down a porcelain cup and saucer with a matching plate at his place on the table and filled his cup up with tea from an industrial-sized chipped enamel pot. She needed two hands to hold it and a strong grasp reflex to keep it steady.

'May I ask you how it happened?'

'He went to school on the twentieth of June, ten years ago. The bus dropped him at the bottom of the road as usual but he never got home. The school says he won a wee writing competition that day but he never got the chance to tell me.'

'Were there any suspects at the time?'

'The village didn't like Aaron Patterson. He was a strange young man, but gentle. I don't think he would've done a thing like that.'

'Like what, Mary?'

She hesitated while opening the biscuit barrel. 'Abducted my Peter and killed him. They were good friends.'

Prendergast's laugh concealed his anxiety. 'Now we don't know if Peter was abducted or killed, Mary. He may yet walk back into your life.'

'He's dead. Ella told me how. I used to see him sometimes.'

'You saw Peter and who's Ella?'

'Peter used to come home to see me now and then: all pale and wet and shivering. He stopped coming a few years back and I haven't seen him since. Ella MacAleavey's got the gift.'

'Are you saying Peter's not dead now?' There was too much information to handle all at once and Prendergast tried to keep his questions at a comprehensible level.

'He's dead. He's just in spirit form. Someone drowned him. Ella saw it all. She has visions.'

Prendergast was forced to hide his alarm at her depiction of the boy: it was exactly how Libby had described him. 'I understand police divers made a thorough sweep of the loch and found nothing.'

'They won't find his body. Not even my Peter knows where it is.'

'Perhaps this Ella can tell you.'

'She's tried, but he won't speak to her.'

Andrew Prendergast barely believed what he was hearing but had to admit he actually believed Mary's story as she saw it. He didn't know whether it was the events at The Ring that had rattled the strong chains of his pragmatism or whether, deep down in his subconscious, he'd always thought the supernatural was simply a quirky aspect of normal life. He'd come across some odd and inexplicable cases in his career, but this was by far the most bizarre.

'What did Ella say happened to him?'

'She saw him walking home from school with his piece box and his rucksack and then she saw someone grab him.' There were tears in Mary's eyes, despite the realistic tone of her words. She'd clearly told this story many times before. 'Someone did terrible things to my boy before he was drowned.'

'Did Ella give a description of the alleged perpetrator?'

'We told the police, but they just laughed at us.'

'Was the perpetrator male? Female?' He took a sip of his weak tea and graciously accepted a large slice of chocolate cake and a piece of homemade shortcake.

'She says something's blocking her. She can't tell.'

'Blocking her?'

'Ella held a séance here in this house a few years ago in the hope we'd find out for good, but Peter didn't turn up to it. Janet Henderson's father did instead. He said Peter couldn't come any more because he was somewhere else now.'

'Wait, wait.' He put his hand up to stay the next piece of garbled information. 'You're saying you held a séance?'

'Yes, you know, the thingy that helps you speak to departed loved ones on the other side.'

'I'm quite familiar with the term, thank you Mary. Are you, Ella and Janet part of a religious spiritualist group?'

'No, I'm Episcopalian and the rest of us are Presbyterian.

We hold evenings occasionally where we visit our relatives. You know,' she pointed to the ceiling, 'from up there.'

'I see.' Prendergast's eyes naturally turned upwards, half expecting to find a face peering down at him. 'How many of you are involved?'

'Just six now. There used to be ten of us but one of us passed away; one moved from the area; Caroline Baxter was asked to leave.' She leaned over the table and whispered, 'It was her nerves. Far too delicate.' She sat back in her chair, 'And Jessie Jacobs got too scared to come after her sister told her to stop dabbling.'

'Her sister may have had a good point. Sometimes it's better to maintain a solid mental wall between life and death in the hope we'll never know the answers.'

'Her sister's from up there.'

'Did Mrs Henderson's father intimate where Peter might have gone?' He tried to prevent his eyes from widening.

'I think he's left and maybe gone to heaven.'

'He's been seen at The Ring by two independent witnesses.' Prendergast didn't know what made him say it, but the information left his mouth before he could stop it. He gagged himself with a large piece of cake.

To his complete surprise, Mary appeared delighted.

'Then we must speak to him. I'll get Ella and a few of the girls around and we'll see what he has to say. He may even name his murderer and you can take the credit for solving the case.'

Prendergast waited until he'd swallowed his cake before raising his misgivings. 'Now, Mary, I understand why you wish to see Peter but perhaps a séance is not such a good idea. These things can be dangerous and …'

'Nonsense. Ella's been doing them for over fifty years and she's never met the devil yet. She's got a gift for these kinds of things, since she was almost killed by a heifer in her teens.'

'Nevertheless, I really must protest …'

'Please, Mr Prendergast, you have no idea how important this is to me. Tell MacAoidh we're coming around. We'll bring supper.'

'I'm not going to tell him…'

'He's a lovely lad, he won't say no to us.'

Prendergast couldn't understand why he, as a seasoned lawman who'd dealt with hardened criminals all his career, was allowing himself to be bullied by a woman half his height and intellect. He felt his shoulders sagging.

'What about Mr Hyslop. What does he have to say about all this?'

'He's been gone for years.'

'He left you?'

'Aye, he died in an accident. Fell into Jim's silo.'

'Oh, how tragic. I'm so sorry.'

'Don't be, he was a useless lump of lard. Mind you, if he turns up at the séance I'll tell him to go right back to wherever he came from and take his mother with him.'

'Your mother-in-law's dead too?'

'No, she lives down the road.'

Chapter 35

THE MEEDJUM

'Prendy, I'd like a word in private please.'

Kie returned home to find a gaggle of women sitting in his living room and a cold buffet spread across the low marble table. They chatted excitedly amongst themselves and clashed tea cups.

He eyed the private detective coolly as they stepped out of the room and into the kitchen.

'I understand from Mary Hyslop that she and some of the local ladies are holding a séance in my sitting room tonight.' He crossed his arms and waited for the man to stop shuffling his feet. 'There's a ministry of angels occupying my house and you let them in.'

'I did try to tell her you wouldn't be happy but ...'

'A séance, Prendy? Have you not lost your wits? Haven't we got enough trouble here without stirring-up even more?'

'I'm sorry, she was very persistent.'

'I'll just pop the kettle on.' A tiny woman shuffled past them. 'Hello MacAoidh. How's your mother?'

'She's grand, Mrs Renwicks. How are you?' Her hug took him by surprise and he was forced to fold his arms around her and give her narrow back a pat. He looked over to Prendergast and silently shook his head at him.

'Ach, the wind blew the roof aff the coal shed this mornin' an' my neighbour's hoose is leakin'.

'Aye, I was up on his roof all afternoon fixing the slates back in that wind.'

'You're a good soul, MacAoidh.' She looked down and gasped. 'Get those boots off, lad, you've trailed mud all through the hoose.'

They waited for Mrs Renwicks to fill the kettle and switch it on before Kie rounded on Prendergast again. 'Get rid of them. There's going to be no séance here tonight nor any other night.'

'With all due respect, lad, it's your house. It's not my place to turf the ladies out into the night.'

'You invited them.'

'That's not exactly the truth. Had you not been playing good Samaritan with your neighbours for most of the afternoon with your phone switched off, you would've been here to head them off. Now we're stuck with them.'

Kie realised the bold detective was incapable of defying a small group of ladies. They were kindly, gentle, affectionate women but would never take no for an answer and Kie reluctantly admitted to himself he was also loathe to disappoint them.

'Well, you can entertain them. I'm going for a bath then I'm off to see Libby.'

'You're no' goin' anywhere, MacAoidh Armstrong,' another woman's voice barked behind him. 'We'll need both of ye here, just in case, so we will.'

'Good evening Mrs MacAleavey.'

She pushed her ample body into his and clung on to him.

'I dinnae like this hoose, MacAoidh, I've never liked it. This hoose holds very bad energies. It's evil, so it is.'

He tried to pull away, but she wouldn't let him go.

'Then maybe you shouldn't be holding a séance here. You don't want to stir up the de'il with your magic tricks.' He winked at Prendergast.

'He's here already, MacAoidh, so he is. He's in the wa's, in the floors and in the bones o' this hoose. Let's see whit he has tae say fer himsel'.

'I don't like this idea at all.'

'Ye'll like it even less if ye dinnae fin' oot what it is he wants, so ye will.'

'Is this even safe?' He appealed to Prendergast who merely shrugged.

'Hae yer bath. We'll be ready when ye come doon.'

'Suppose something happens to one or all of them? Who'll take the responsibility for that?' He felt his temper flaring.

'Since the open window incident this morning, the house has been very quiet.'

'We're not talking about the house, Prendy. We're talking about six gullible ladies, most of them elderly, who may suffer the same fate as the meenister.'

'Bear with me, Kie. I have a hunch. Ella appears to know quite a lot about the missing boy. She says he was abducted and murdered. Now, I don't know whether she's making this all up and sensationalising stories for personal praise or whether she's a genuine medium with real precognitive insight, but it might be worth listening in to.'

'Come on, man, you can't believe Mrs MacAleavy's some kind of organic celestial telegraph pole.'

'I believe there's such a thing as mediums. I've even used a few for police work in the past.'

'And?'

'Mixed successes but one or two of them in particular were uncannily accurate and helped solve the cases.'

'These aren't police mediums, Prendy, they're ordinary wee women wanting to play Victorian parlour games for a bit of evening entertainment while the rural's oot.'

'They don't call it the rural anymore. It's the WI.'

Kie shot him a look of utter incredulity. 'This isn't a bingo evening down the social. This is serious stuff. Those women have no idea what they're letting themselves in for and we're being very irresponsible in allowing them to even be here.'

'You'd better explain that to them.'

'They won't listen to me, I'm a man.' Kie let out a deep, heavy sigh.

'I'll give Libby a ring.'

'Good idea.'

– – –

'You must be joking, the silly old bag can't stand me. She even warned me off him and told him I was common. She's a snotty old ... Hi Kie.'

'Talking about my mother again?'

He heard the loud cackles of laughter from the top of the stairs but was now faced with a wall of silence. Libby sat on the floor between the two sofas, entertaining his unwanted female guests who all stared at him in reproach. Amused by the expressions of embarrassment and unease on Libby's face, he gave her a wink and smiled. She visibly relaxed and the women laughed once more.

'The ladies want you to know that they've all done this many times before and aren't afraid of spirits, dark clouds, flying stones or being slapped around a bit. Mary, in particular, has been spanked on a number of occasions. Haven't you Mary?'

'It's frightening at first, Libby, but you get used to it.'

The ladies shook their heads and muttered in consolation.

'Ella's a very good meedjum.' Mrs Henderson announced in her stern baritone voice. 'You've been up there fer ower an 'oor, MacAoidh Armstrong, an' kept us a' waitin'.'

'Sorry, Mrs Henderson, I dozed off in the bath.'

'He didn't get much sleep last night.' Libby came to his rescue but he felt the heat searing his cheeks when the ladies burst into hysterical laughter and nudged each other.

'Do you have a round table, MacAoidh?' Mary spared him further humiliation by getting straight down to business.

'No, I've got a rectangular one in the dining room. I gave the round one to King Arthur.'

'We need to conduct the séance here, in a happy living atmosphere.' She either ignored his sarcasm or wasn't aware of it.

'Lost spirits like to bide by the livin', so they do,' Ella added. 'Reminds them o' hame an' comfort. Get the table in here now, it'll have to do.'

'It's made of solid oak and it's ten feet long. It weighs a ton.'

'I'm sure Mr Prendergast will gi' ye a hon'. I'll need twa connels tae.'

'Come on, Prendy, let's do what the meedjum says.'

'Connels?'

'Candles.'

'I've never experienced a séance before.'

'Neither have I and I don't intend to. I want no part in this. I'll sit in the car if I have to.'

'I think you'll do whit ye're telt, boy,' Prendergast made a poor attempt at a Scottish accent that caused Kie to laugh.

'I'd like to see Ella MacAleavey trying to tilt this one with her knee!'

They heaved it up off the floor. By the time they'd moved the table across the hallway and into the living room, Prendergast was out of breath and Kie was sweating. The ladies had cleared a wide space to accommodate it and then sent them back for the chairs and two candles. The only ones Kie could find were huge cathedral candles on ornate silver holders. He put up with the teasing about having more money than sense with his lavish taste in antiques and didn't bother to explain they were family heirlooms. He was chastised by all the ladies for not having a Bible in the house and resisted telling them about his views on religion. On a few occasions, he felt he was the defendant at a witch trial.

When they were all seated around the table, Ella explained the procedure for the evening, making it sound like a pagan ritual. She pulled out her Bible and even placed a little bell on the table which, she said, would be rung if she needed to repel an evil spirit. When he tried to ask a question about the necessity for the other objects like the candles, a large crystal, a plastic children's game from the 1980s and why the Bible was to lay open at One Samuel Chapter Twenty Eight, he was quietened with a barrage of impatient tuts.

Kie was struck by the stark contrast between the seriousness of the process and the ladies' enthusiasm to be part of it. Rather than fearing the unknown, they embraced it with the breathless anticipation of mischievous children.

'So is this something you ladies do in your spare time?' The silence irritated him as he slouched on his seat and needed sensible conversation to cut through the tension in the room. Ella sat in deep concentration, while the women spoke between themselves in hushed voices.

'Not often.' Mary said. 'Séances take a lot out of Ella. The spirits use her energy and leave her feeling very tired afterwards. She's meditating at the moment, to get herself in tune.'

He shot Prendergast a worried glance and was answered with a mirrored expression. Libby gave his hand a reassuring squeeze under the table.

'Is this dangerous for her?'

'Only if the circle is broken and she hasn't come out of her trance properly.'

'Her trance?' Kie didn't mean to raise his voice.

'I'll have quiet from you, MacAoidh Armstrong,' Ella snapped, 'an' someone'll hae' tae sit ootside this circle. Can't hae an uneven number o' folk at the table.'

'That'll be me then.' He made to rise.

'Sit back doon MacAoidh. This is yer hoose an' it's you the spirits want tae speak tae. Mr Prendergast'll sit quietly in the far corner o' the room.'

Prendy couldn't hide his disappointment.

'I'm a sceptic, Mrs MacAleavey. I'll sit out and not block your communications. If the spirits want to speak to me, they'll find me in a far corner.' Kie rose from the table and ignored the ladies' disdainful sniffs for his blatant disobedience.

'Do you want to go through with this?' He gave Libby a kiss on the side of her head.

'I wouldn't miss it for the world.'

'We need tae concentrate noo. We need tae empty oor minds of a' negative thoughts an' just think o' the good things in life: o' laughter, happiness an' love.'

'Wait a minute, what's that for?' Kie had to interrupt when he saw the glint of a sharp blade in Ella's hand.

'Will you sit doon and whisht!' Ella's concentration broke. 'The spirits dinnae care fer sharp edges or steel. It's fer oor protection. Now no' another word, MacAoidh Armstrong, or I'll hurl ye frae the room mysel'.'

'We can hold hands now,' Mary said to Libby. 'Whatever happens, no one's allowed to speak, that includes you MacAoidh,' she shouted across the room, 'and the circle must not be broken until Ella says it can be.'

'Turn off the lights please.'

'No, I'll dim them a little for you but I'm not sitting here in the dark wondering if one of you've had a heart attack. If the spirits want to show themselves, a bit of tungsten lighting won't stop them.'

'Dae as ye're telt an' put the lights oot, MacAoidh Armstrong. You can light the connels.' Ella was so exasperated with him that Kie withdrew some of his personal defences. He put a match to the candles, dimmed the lights and sat down in the corner by the piano, his unease rising with every second of the old clock's swinging pendulum. Of course, he didn't believe for one minute that Ella MacAleavey could summon the dead with a few sandwiches, a wee bell and a sharp knife. What worried him was everyone else believed she could and, if he applied the clinical theories, that amount of collective hysteria in one room could spark a fire or a flying object. He only hoped Ella kept a good hold on that knife.

– – –

Libby closed her eyes and tried not to giggle as the silence closed in on her. They huddled round the edge of the enormous Jacobean refectory table. She and Prendergast sat opposite each other on the inside of the table and had to stretch across it to hold hands. She opened one eye to look around the room. Prendy and the ladies had their eyes shut tight, the candle light flicking shadows across their faces. In the gloom, she could just make out the figure of Kie sitting with his arms folded tightly against his chest.

'Call him, Mary.'

'Peter. Are you with us? It's me. Mum. Peter, love, I've brought you Operation. Your favourite game. Can you make the man's nose light up for us?'

Prendergast's eyes were open now and he cast a professional glance over the scene.

Libby's heart leaped and she felt Prendy's hand tighten as the door to the room squealed open. They both breathed a sigh of relief when Jim Black's dog padded across the carpet and sat at Kie's feet. That dog had taken a serious liking to Kie and never left his side since Jim died. She knew how it felt as she heard him sigh from the other side of the room. She wished this was over so she could spend some quality private time with him.

'Call him again.'

'Peter, love. It's me. Mum. Are you there?'

Ella took a deep, audible breath through her mouth, then out again through her nose, her nostrils flaring with the effort. 'Away ye go, Bill, it's no' you we want tae speak tae. If Mary's boy's there wi' ye', run an' get him.'

Libby felt Prendy's hand squeezing hers as she giggled.

'The spirits dinnae onerstan' yer humour, keep your scepticism tae yersel' until the session's ower. You wouldn't want tae offend onyone.'

Long moments passed and all Libby could hear was the women breathing and the creaking of the ancient pendulum of the old grandfather clock. Her arm began to ache and she wanted to shake it. Her attention was alerted to tiny taps that seemed to be coming from the big bay window.

'Peter, is that you?'

After a long silence, the taps came again, louder this time, and Jim Black's collie trotted across the room to sit by the window, wagging its tail. Everyone leapt as a heavy thud hit the table and one of the candles went out. Kie sprung from his chair and moved around the sitters, searching above and beneath the tables and chairs for a culprit.

'Hold the circle, dinnae let go,' Ella's voice cut through the gasps and oohs as the table shuddered violently before settling back to neutral.

Kie put a match to the extinguished candle and it flared into light once more.

Libby felt a chill sweeping across her back and then a biting cold. It was as if she sat at the top of a northern glacier in the middle of winter. Her breath froze in the air before her and she felt herself shivering. She thought she heard something. There it was again. A tiny voice called out. Someone sounded as though they were speaking from a radio placed in a far-off land, its audibleness falling in and out of range.

'*Muuuuuuuuum.*'

'Peter? Is that you love?'

'*Muuuuuuuuum.*' That disjointed voice again.

Suddenly, the red light buzzed on and off on the surface of the game and the board shuddered, spilling the contents of the white plastic bones across the table. The ladies gasped as one. Libby tried to break free of Prendy's grip but he held her fast. The buzzing slowly ceased and the light flickered weakly until it too was still. Libby noticed a strange mist, just like smoke, appearing behind Ella. It rolled softly across the women, caressing each one for a brief moment before moving on to the next.

'It's Maigret,' Ella chuckled.

Libby felt the panic rising. She didn't want the mist of dead Maigret to touch her. She tried to pull her hand away from Prendergast but he grabbed onto her wrist and wouldn't let her leave the circle. Mrs Henderson held on to her other wrist in a vice-like grip. Libby closed her eyes as the smoke hit her and she felt a million tiny feathers tickling her skin. She smelled roses. The aroma was so strong that she wondered if someone had just sprayed perfume up her nose.

She didn't know whether it was the sensation of being touched by the occult or the penetrating cold that caused her to shake, but she felt her body had been encased in a block of ice, although Prendergast's hand felt warm and alive against her wrist.

The mist passed Prendy and then disappeared behind him.

The heavy dining chair next to Libby moved and she wanted to run screaming from the room.

'Hiya Jim.'

Ella's voice snapped her back to the present and Libby noticed the dog. It sat beside her: tail wagging, ears down, staring at the vacant chair. It whined and trotted off, before returning again and answering a silent command to sit. Its ears pricked up before it lay on its belly, it's eyes shining with obedience. She turned to Kie who now stood behind her, ready to protect her should something bad happen. She was grateful for his presence. She indicated with her head to the dog. He nodded.

'I'm scared,' she mouthed her words to him.

'I'm here,' she saw him reply. Grabbing the animal by its collar, he hauled it back to his corner.

'Jim wants tae speak tae us.'

'It's not his turn,' Mary protested.

'Jim wants tae say he's sorry.'

'Tell him to get in the queue and let my Peter speak.'

The table shuddered again and rocked from side to side with such force that the candles rattled from their silver holders and clattered onto the surface, snuffing out on impact. The Bible leaped in the air, hovered there for a moment, before crashing against the window. Loud thumps echoed across the room, sending shudders through the floor. Disjointed voices wailed in unison, whistling, whispering and shouting all at once.

'Ring the bell, MacAoidh. Ring it noo!' Ella's voice thundered through the turbulence as she gripped the dagger in her hand. 'Begone, foul spirit.'

Kie leaped from his chair while Jim Black's dog growled, barked, then ran from the room yelping with its tail between its legs. Kie grabbed the bell and shook it.

A long silence ensued, only broken by the tick, tick, tick of the pendulum, and then it too was still. The clock had stopped and a crushing silence threatened to consume them.

'There's something else here.' Ella's words tolled like a funeral bell.

'What was that?' Libby heard a male voice coming through the ether, disjointed, eerie but lucid in some places.

'... warn the land to repent; ... judgement ... Praise me ... worship me, ... no more.'

'Get you gone,' Ella yelled, 'de'ils hae nae business in the world o' good God-fearing folk. Leave us be an' we'll no' think any the worse for you comin'.'

'*Meddler,*' the voice mocked and, to Libby's shock, Ella rose off her chair as if lifted by the unseen hands of the divine.

Libby truly thought she was locked in a very bad dream as Ella MacAleavey, all sixteen stone of her, floated towards the high ceiling like a rogue balloon. The woman didn't appear to notice as she drifted at least five feet above her seat and hovered over her horrified friends, her long bloomers on full display above their disbelieving eyes.

'The circle's broken,' someone screamed in the distance.

'Get her doon from there,' another yelled.

Prendergast grabbed the woman by the foot before Kie could reach her and they both just managed to catch her before she fell and injured herself. The impact of her fall knocked Kie into the chair. He groaned in complaint as he took the entire brunt of her dead weight on his lap.

'Meditate, meditate.' Mary urged. 'Link hands again. MacAoidh, give me your hand.'

The sitters touched fingers once more, Kie taking the place of an unconscious Ella who remained on his lap for the remainder of the session. The communal meditation lasted at least half an hour. Libby felt she could breathe again as Ella looked around the room as if suddenly awoken from a trance. She shot Kie a curious but stern glower before she stood up and smoothed out the creases of her skirt with her palms.

'You've got a demon in this hoose, MacAoidh Armstrong, an' it wants rid o' ye.' Her announcement was as impartial as a weather forecast. 'There's nothin' mair I can de fer ye, apart from persuade ye to leave.'

'What about my Peter?' Mary appeared shaken by the evening's events.

'The de'il has him in its clutches. We need to fin' his bones.'

Chapter 36

THE UNWANTED GUEST

Libby traced her finger along the small scar on Kie's back where the blade of the kitchen knife had embedded itself a few weeks ago. She marvelled at the strength and endurance of the human body and its ability to heal itself, leaving only a small red scar to remind man of his own mortality.

He shuddered beneath her touch and she pressed her body into his, revelling in his warmth. His mobile rattled on the bedside table and he groaned.

'Shall I get it for you?'

'It'll be Mother. Let it ring.'

She slapped her hand against the wooden surface and found the phone. 'It's an unknown caller.' She pressed the green button. 'Hello?' She turned on the loud speaker.

'Can I speak to MacAoidh please?'

Kie chuckled.

'I'm afraid there's no one here by that name, Miss Rutherford, and now I'm going to have to punish you for stealing my personal data.' Libby sat up in bed.

'Libby, I think we got off on the wrong footing yesterday. Sorry about that. Please don't hang up, I've got a very interesting proposition.'

'If you want to talk about a settlement, then come to my office in two weeks' time.'

'Look, when I was doing some research on The Ring, I came across a man who claimed he'd seen what happened to a boy called Peter Hyslop. He's agreed to speak to MacAoidh.'

'Then you should be escorting him to the police station as a suspect in a murder case and not phoning me at...' she glanced at the clock, '... eight thirty in the morning. I've had a very bad night.'

Kie turned around with a moan and snuggled into her back.

'He tried to tell the police at the time, but they were too sceptical. They treated him as a suspect instead and he had quite an ordeal of it.'

'Sorry to hear that, but coppers have a lot of suspects to eliminate from their inquiries. Your man should've kept his mouth shut and spared himself the misery.'

'Please let me speak to MacAoidh.'

'Sorry, Miss Rutherford, he's busy.' She squealed as he playfully jerked her hips into his.

'It may interest you to know this man lives in Carlisle. He's a psychic and what's called a rescue medium. He's got no investment in this and says, through a series of visions, he witnessed the murder of a young boy called Peter by a man who tormented him and drowned him in the nearby burn. I've done a bit of research and know Peter Hyslop went missing ten years ago and hasn't been found.'

Kie shook his head.

Libby felt the warning bells clanging and peeled Kie's arms from her torso. 'Sorry, Miss Rutherford, have to go.' She disconnected the line and drummed her fingers against Kie's forearm, knowing full well this particular newshound would not take 'piss off' for an answer.

'How did she get my number?' His voice was sleepy but Libby knew his brain cells would all be on red alert.

'She was in my office yesterday. I caught her snooping around. She would've got it from my diary.'

'Isn't there a law against that?'

'Yes, but I'll deal with that later. She wants to spend a night here with a photographer.'

'I hope you told her where to go.'

'In no uncertain terms, but she's the persistent type. Some reporters use gentle persuasion to lull you into speaking to them and others leap straight for the throat and rip the words out taking quite a lot of flesh with it. She's the latter kind. She's got pictures of us kissing outside my house yesterday morning.' She tensed in full expectation he would leap out of bed yelling for the executioner.

'So?'

'She tried to blackmail me with them.'

He sat up and rubbed the sleep from his eyes. 'Blackmail?'

'I didn't want your face spread across the tabloids of Great Britain.'

'Why would anyone be interested in me?'

'It's not you, Kie. It's this house and me. That case two years ago was very high profile and sold papers. Miss Rutherford's storyline would be to link me, the woman who caught a serial killer, to a haunted house and a seventeenth century poltergeist. That would drag you and your privacy out in the open. The Ring would be crowded out with members of the press, ghost hunters, spiritualists, theologians, scientists, religious fanatics, unbelievers, ghouls and exorcists all aspiring to become a part of history.'

'Fuck!' He leaped out of bed shouting. 'Get her back on the phone. I'll speak to her alright. Arrange a meeting. No photographers. We'll meet her in the pub. I'll bring my shotgun.'

'Are you sure you want to meet her?' She didn't believe the bit about the gun.

'Aye, I'm bloody positive.'

'I think she'll insist she comes here. She's desperate to look over the house.'

'That's too bad.'

'What about the Carlisle man?'

He stopped to think as he threw a towel over his shoulder. 'All right, let's play this game her way. Tell her there's no meeting unless she calls her man and gives him Prendy's number. No phone call; no meeting. Once contact is made, we'll send Prendy off to Carlisle and she can come here.'

'Do you want me to be around for the meeting?'

'I think that would be a good idea. I don't want to say anything incriminating, you'll put me right.'

He walked into the bathroom and Libby got out of bed. She heard him laughing as he switched on the shower.

'What's so funny?'

'If Cluitie's really in this house and this activity centres around me, then I'm going to whip him up into a frenzy and allow him to descend all his wrath on her. That'll give her something to publish, that's if she survives her ordeal.'

- - -

'She's outside taking pictures of the house with her phone.' Libby peeked from the curtain. 'Ha! A stone's just hit her hand. She's dropped the phone. Hope it's broken. She's looking around now.' Libby ducked. 'She's coming.'

'She's late. It's past nine.'

Kie waited for the tap before he threw the door open with a violent jerk and the woman screamed in shock. He stood to his full height with his arms crossed, like a brutal giant sentinel barring the gateway to hell.

'MacAoidh?' The woman made a poor attempt at collecting her composure as she clutched her handbag to her chest as if it were a shield. 'I came as soon as your lawyer called. It's been quite a journey from Glasgow. I hope I'm not too late for you. Thank you for agreeing to meet with me.' She swallowed some of her words with little gulps. 'I'm Mandy Rutherford.'

'Did you give me any choice?'

The woman tried to peer behind him. 'Can I come in?'

He stepped aside and allowed her through.

'Hi Libby.' She removed her coat and handed it to Kie.

They both gasped as they saw each other. Libby and Mandy wore exactly the same red linen dress with a short black cardigan. 'Are you stalking me?' Libby hid her irritation behind her usual humour.

Mandy Rutherford stood in the hallway squirming. 'What paper did you say you were from?' Libby took off her cardigan and threw it on the hall chair.

'I'm a freelancer.'

'So you're a mercenary. You sell stories to whoever will pay you the most for them?'

'Something like that.' She cast the silent Kie a quick submissive glance before turning her attention to the sound of footsteps on the stairs, just in front of her. A board creaked and she jumped. 'Wow, this house is quite creepy, isn't it.'

'I'll take that as an insult.' Kie stomped off into the sitting room and the women followed him.

Sitting on the comfortable cushions, the warm rays of the last of the evening's falling sun lighting her space, Mandy Rutherford looked more relaxed. She used his silence to pull a notebook and pen from her bag but placed them on her knee.

'Look, I understand you may be angry about the photographs, but ...'

'I don't give a damn about the photographs, it's your intention behind them I find offensive.' Kie sat with his chest splayed out and open, his arms stretching their full length across the back of the sofa, his right foot drumming against his knee.

'I don't intend to use them …'

'Oh no? I understand you already have. You've used them to extort this interview.'

Libby perched herself on the seat beside him, delighting in the woman's discomfort.

'And I apologise for that. Since, I'm here, however, do you think you can perhaps find it in your heart to make me feel a little less bloody uncomfortable?'

'Let's get down to business, then. Why are you here?'

Libby watched the transformation in the reporter as she immediately switched gear. Her countenance suddenly turned from prickly to raptorial as if someone had pushed the button on her remote control. Miss Rutherford wriggled to the edge of her seat, the seams of her red dress groaning in complaint, her notebook and pen remained in their neutral position on her lap.

'As you know, the case of the Mackie poltergeist in sixteen ninety five inspires the imaginations of paranormal fanatics across the world. No one's able to make sense of the strange events that took place in front of fifteen respected members of the clergy and community who all signed Telfair's testament.'

'Wow! You've started writing your story already!' Libby interrupted while Kie began his rant.

'Aye, but you also have to remember this was a time when people believed in the devil and his demonic hoards. James the Sixth whipped Scotland's Christians up into a frenzy with his obsession with witchcraft. For over a hundred years, the church tortured, hanged and burned innocent members of their communities for little more than brewing herbal tea, simply because a demented king's dogmas dominated rational policy. The Rerrick Poltergeist wasn't the only reported incidence of evil spirits in this region. Around the same time, there was also the Devil of Glenluce, a demon who apparently took up home in a weaver's cottage and terrorised the household. People were hysterical about witches and demons and murdered people on a regular basis for colluding with and conjuring-up evil spirits. It was a load of nonsense that cost many innocent people their lives.'

'People still believe in the devil, MacAoidh.'

'But this is the twenty first century where the established canons of science are more persuasive than religious doctrines and old superstitions. We live in the practical world of a postmodern culture, Miss Rutherford, where the devil is considered delusion and we don't burn people for simply trying to survive on the fringes of society anymore.'

'Please call me Mandy.' She snatched up her notebook, opened it and scribbled something down. 'So, you don't believe in an afterlife either?'

'If there are such things as ghosts and invisible psychic forces, then I'll believe in them only if I have conclusive evidence of their existence.'

A photo frame rattled on the piano and Mandy spun her body around just in time to see it fall face down on the gleaming surface. Her shoulders shuddered as if she'd been unexpectedly touched. Libby bit back the smile but was impressed when the woman chose to ignore it and turned back to Kie with hungry eyes.

'What would you say if I told you the last of the Ghost Trees has died and the Rerrick Parish Poltergeist is back?'

'I would say you're living in the wrong century.' He crossed his arms again, which was always a sign he was on the defensive.

'But that's what people are saying round here, MacAoidh. They say this house has been experiencing some very unusual paranormal activity since you moved in a few months ago and that you're at the epicentre of it all.'

'Conjecture and village gossip are hardly strong foundations for a sensible story, Mandy.' Libby thought it time to butt in before the drumming of that foot caused him to levitate. 'MacAoidh is trying his best to settle into this community, but …'

Mandy rounded on Kie, rudely interrupting Libby in mid-sentence: 'Have you witnessed any form of paranormal activity in this house since you moved in? OK, I understand your stance on psychic phenomena, but has anything happened in this house that you've considered strange or implausible?'

'No.'

Libby had to place her hand on his juddering foot.

'Then the police report of a cow tethered to the roof of your barn was not strange in your opinion? You don't consider a similar report of fire-raising on two occasions to be unusual? The death of a minister who was trying to bless this house wasn't a bit weird? Your neighbour chose your land on which to commit suicide? I'm told you stormed into a community council meeting accusing the committee of tormenting you? You …' She yelped and leaped off her chair, clutching at her side. 'Something just poked me.'

'Aye, it was your conscience.'

Mandy stood beside the chair in a state of confusion. 'No, I swear I felt the sharp jab of a finger in my side.'

'A finger normally carries a body and head with it and there's no one else in the house but us.'

'Was that the poltergeist, MacAoidh? Have I just been touched by a dead person?' She stood for a few seconds before her eyes narrowed. She planted her fists against her wide hips. 'All right, that's a very nice touch. You're playing with me.' She pushed her hands down the sides of the chair and inspected it thoroughly. 'That stone, those footsteps on the stairs, the picture on the piano. That's a very dirty game.'

'Is it?' He relaxed into a smile. 'Has anything happened to you in this house that you would consider strange or implausible?'

'Fuck off! It's not funny.'

'That's hardly a professional response, Mandy.' Libby joined in the fun.

'Do you think we can quit the games and behave like adults for the rest of this interview?'

Mandy thumped her rump down on the chair with such force that the seam of her dress gave way. She cursed her luck and Libby almost felt a pang of empathy towards her. She was also pleased she'd bought that dress in a larger size. She had a feeling the stitching would eventually humiliate her.

'OK, let's try a different line. The man Mr Prendergast has gone to see is a psychic. He's worked with the police and a few other government departments on cases where help of a psychic nature is required.' She stopped to give Kie a withering glower when he yawned. 'Ten years ago, Stephen Mitchell says he saw, in a series of visions, a boy being murdered by a stream.'

'A stream murdered a boy?'

'You know what I mean.'

'Do I?'

She put up with his impertinence. 'He says he gets glimpses of events, visual clues that piece together like a puzzle.'

'Oh aye?'

She clutched at the side of her head as if her hair had just been pulled. She took a deep, exasperated breath before continuing. She fumbled through the pages of her notebook again until she came to the page she'd been looking for. She continued: 'He described the boy getting off a school bus and walking down a country road when he was grabbed by a man and dragged to a solitary tree on a rocky outcrop. He described, in graphic detail, the horrible attack on the child beneath the tree. Thereafter the child was dragged again by his hair, across a narrow road, to a stream where he was subjected to a further torturous assault. The man then held his face under the water until he was still.'

Mesmerised by the ghastly tale, Libby felt the rage and sorrow rising in her chest. If this was the boy she saw outside her room, then perhaps he was trying his best to tell her his story. She felt ashamed for being so frightened of him.

'Can Stephen Mitchell describe the man?'

'No and just after the boy went missing, he wanted to come here to see if it would conjure up any more images for him. The police, however, found his testimony highly suspicious and interrogated him until he lost confidence. They couldn't place him at the scene of the crime, however, so let him go.'

'Did he have a good alibi?'

'He has absolutely no connection to this region nor the child and he was at work in a board meeting that afternoon which lasted well past eight in the evening. Those people in the meeting can testify that, at about four thirty, Stephen had a sort of funny turn where he apparently lost consciousness.' Mandy kept her right arm tucked tightly against her open seam while she jotted down notes and spoke at the same time.

'What? He passed out?'

'No, it was apparently more like a petit mal epileptic fit where he just shut down for a while. They thought he'd fallen asleep with his eyes open.'

'Yes, I've been to a few board meetings in my time and know how he feels.'

'Anyway, to fill the blanks in his visual puzzle, he would need to come to the premises and have a look around.'

'Wouldn't all the traces have gone after ten years?'

'Maybe not, I understand the boy may still haunt his locality. I spoke to a ...,' she flicked through her notes again before finding the page, '... Mary Hyslop, the missing boy's mother, this morning who told me you held a séance here last night.'

Kie groaned.

'I'll qualify that information if I may.' Libby leaped to his aid. 'Mrs Hyslop and her friends held a séance here last night. Kie had nothing to do with the decision but was too kind to throw them out.'

'She says a lot of interesting things happened during the session and that ...,' she dug her nose into her own shorthand, '... sixty-two-year-old Ella MacAleavey levitated about five feet into the air.' She directed her question at Kie who answered her with a silent glare.

'The same Ella MacAleavey also told Mrs Hyslop how she thought the boy had died. Don't you think it strange and unusual that Mrs MacAleavey and Stephen Mitchell's description of what they believe happened to the boy are uncannily similar, considering they know nothing about each other?'

'I'll admit ...'

'I was asking MacAoidh.' Mandy's challenge was like the bellowing of a bugle before the charge.

'I'm not a man who believes parlour tricks form the bases for fact, Miss Rutherford. Nor do I believe imponderable acts are caused by discarnate spirits. Science has proved that empty space can support matter, even though electromagnetic forces don't tend to obey any of its obvious laws. As for the relationship between mind and matter, that's something I'll leave to the scientists.'

'I wasn't asking you whether you believe it or not, just whether you saw it.'

His silence irritated her.

'All right, MacAoidh, would you give me permission and grace to stay a night in this house with a photographer? Just one little night?'

'Why?'

'So I can experience things first hand. Unlike you, I tend to go by the premise seeing is believing. I want to know either way whether there's such a place as the afterlife and whether or not the spirits of the dead can come back to haunt us. Whether that's spirits over three hundred years old or three seconds old.'

'And what would you do with the information?'

'Publish it.'

'Then I'll have to decline your request.'

'Why?'

'Because every journalist and ghost buster in the world will be asking the same questions. This house and my good will are not generous enough to accommodate that level of invasiveness.'

'It would be up to you to let them in or not.'

'Sorry, no.'

'Well, if you haven't got any other questions for MacAoidh, then it's getting late and we'd like some private time.'

'Of course you would.' Mandy raised her hairless eyebrows.

It was Libby who saw her to the door.

'I hope this will be the end of it, Mandy. As you can see, Kie's a very private man and doesn't enjoy the limelight. He just wants to be left alone.'

'I'm afraid that's not possible, Libby. There's a really good story here and someone's going to tell it eventually. Wouldn't you rather that someone was me who has an open mind or someone else who doesn't?'

'He'll take his chances.'

As Libby watched the tail lights disappearing out the gate, Kie joined her outside.

'She reminds me of you.' He put his arm around her shoulder.

'She's nothing like me. I'm at least a foot shorter and a foot narrower than her and I don't pencil in my eyebrows like that.'

'I don't mean in looks. She's feisty and sharp like you and doesn't let go once she's got a hold of the reins.'

'That dress looks a lot better on me though.'

He kissed her. 'It certainly does.'

She felt a gentle tickle on her ankle and looked down. Before she could grasp what was happening to her, the pressure on her ankle tightened into a grip and she was dragged at great speed across the gravel. The sharp stones tore at her dress and grazed her skin and she helplessly screamed Kie's name as he raced after her. Kicking, shrieking and flailing her arms, Libby was hurled into the woodshed with such force that she hit the opposite wall. The doors slammed shut behind her, plunging her into darkness.

Libby groaned and shook the dizziness from her head. Kie called her name on the other side of the door, rattling and shaking it and banging on the wood with his fists.

'Libby? Are you all right? Are you hurt? I can't get the door open.'

'I'm all right.' She managed a small whimper. 'Well, I think I am, everything hurts.' In shock, it took a while for her brain to analyse the last few moments. She tried to rise, but her feet slipped against the logs stacked up at the back of the wall and she fell with a shriek.

'Libby? What's happening? Libby open the door.'

'I just slipped. I'm coming.'

'See if there's anything jarring the door on your side. I can't get it to open.'

THE UNWANTED GUEST

'I can't see anything.'

She picked herself up, her body bruised and aching, and putting her hands out before her, shuffled slowly across the concrete ground. She let out a yell when she stumbled on something and was forced to calm a frantic Kie down on the other side of the door.

'I think I've found the axe.' Her hands hit the door and she fumbled around for a handle or lock.

It was then she felt the static bristling against her back and the sudden and violent drop in temperature causing her body to shake.

'Kie?'

'I'm here, I'm going for some tools to get you out.'

'Kie,' she kept her voice to a whisper and pressed her cheek against the door. 'There's something in here with me. Kie, please get me out of here.'

She squeezed her eyes shut and dared to look over her shoulder but saw only dark and the impenetrable blackness of a shadow shifting slowly towards her. Something was burning.

Chapter 31

THE RECOVERY

'A castle Douglas woman was taken to hospital by ambulance on Monday evening after being trapped inside a burning woodshed. Emergency services attended the incident at The Ring, in Auchencairn at eleven thirty, by which time the victim had been pulled to safety. The thirty-year-old woman suffered smoke inhalation, cuts and bruises. Hospital officials say her condition is serious but stable. Police confirm a twenty-eight-year-old man has been taken into custody following the incident.'

Prendergast folded the newspaper and shook the demons from his head. He'd only been gone for two days and returned across the border to be faced with Libby in hospital and Kie under arrest. It took all his powers of persuasion to satisfy the local boys in blue to release MacAoidh on police bail until Libby was strong enough to speak for herself. This was all a terrible mess.

'OK, boss, you can take him away.'

MacAoidh looked every bit like a haunted man. The dark circles beneath his eyes and the stubble on his chin were tell–tale signs that he'd not settled into life in a police cell. His forearms were covered in black bruises and cuts that had been freshly cleaned. The young female officer made to take his arm but he shrugged her off with a testy grunt. When he saw Prendergast, the relief washed some of the severity from his expression.

'How is she? Is she going to be all right?'

'I visited the hospital last night when I got back from Carlisle. The doctors hope she'll be fine but she'll need to be closely monitored. She inhaled a lot of smoke but, fortunately, it appears you pulled her out in time. She's intubated and on a ventilator, just for precaution. She's awake but can't speak and those eyes don't look at all happy.'

Kie let out an audible sigh. 'I've got to see her, Prendy.'

'Of course.'

They stepped out of the main doors of the station and Kie breathed in the air like a free man.

'That's the last time I want to visit that place again. I'm going to have nightmares about red bricks and blue signs from now on.'

He got into the passenger seat of the car and crossed his arms.

'I see you've been making my life very difficult.' Prendergast thought it best to get the chastisement over with first while he drove. 'Struggling with police officers?'

'They were trying to arrest me for something I would never do…'

'… To which, I understand you put up a physically and verbally aggressive resistance.'

'They wouldn't let me go with the ambulance.'

'You could've been the suspect of an attempted murder, Kie, look at it their way.'

'Their way? Those bastards were the ones who were heavy handed. They never once told me how Libby was nor whether she was even alive. I only found out this morning she was recovering. Can you imagine how that feels?'

'You would've made life a bit easier for yourself if you'd answered at least some of the officers' questions. It's all right to give your name and address, they already know that anyway.'

'And what do you think I should've said to them? That an invisible psychic force that's been dogging my house for months, grabbed Libby by the foot, dragged her along the garden and threw her into a woodshed and set alight to it in front of my eyes?'

'Is that what happened?' Prendergast shuddered as he changed gear.

'Aye, and what was worse, she was locked in there with smoke billowing under the door. I couldn't break it down. It was as if it were made of solid steel.'

'How did you get her out?'

'I knocked through the roof with the sledge hammer and pulled her out.'

'Well you saved her from a very painful death. At least she didn't suffer any burn injuries, thank God.'

'God had nothing to do with it. The fire flared up when I opened the roof. I just leaped in there and grabbed her.'

'You could've both been burned alive.'

'Aye.'

They held that thought for long moments while they drove through the town towards the hospital, each man lost in his own version of the what ifs.

'I've had a hard time of it convincing the police to let you go. You should've told me about your little incident with the knife.'

'What knife?'

'The one in your back.'

'Ach, that wasn't important.'

'Well it certainly was important to the casualty staff who pulled a small kitchen knife from between your shoulder blades a few weeks back. They suspected you to be a victim of domestic violence and Libby to be the prime culprit. She allegedly made violent threats to one of the charity workers in the hospital car park.'

Kie's laugh was bleak.

'And now, the perpetrator of said violent attack is lying in a hospital ward with cuts, abrasions and injuries conducive to being dragged along the ground and locked inside a burning woodshed.'

'And what do you believe, Prendy?'

'My gut feeling? I believe it's getting too dangerous at The Ring. One of us was almost killed and I, for one, don't want to be the next victim.'

They arrived at the hospital car park. Prendergast switched the engine off and turned his body to face Kie. His reprimand duly delivered, it was time for some home truths.

'This is getting ugly, Kie. Very ugly. Whether you like it or not, it's time to face the facts. If you didn't attack Libby, and I don't for one moment believe you did, then some intelligent consciousness, in whatever form you choose to believe, is deliberately going out of its way to hurt us. It can interact with its environment and is powerful enough to target its victims and cause physical injury to them. Why or how it's doing it are questions we need to find out, but we can't continue ignoring the fact that one of us may end up dead before we have our answers. We need help.'

'Please don't tell me you believe in demons now.'

'It may be a demon, it may be something far more palatable, and we can't rule out the possibility of a human agent. Whatever it is, it's capable of throwing a woman inside a burning building with intent to murder and, in my book, its presence is no longer tolerable.'

He took Kie's ensuing silence to mean he was at least listening.

'I've spent the past few days speaking to Stephen Mitchell, the psychic in Carlisle. He has some very interesting theories and suggestions for a possible solution to the problem. He's agreed to visit The Ring at a mutually convenient time. I suggest he does so during the daylight hours when the trouble is more benign. Will you agree to that?'

'Do I have a choice?'

'There's always a choice, MacAoidh, but you'll have to decide for yourself whether or not to ignore what's staring you in the face or whether you want a solution, no matter what it takes to reach it.'

'I'll think about it.'

Prendergast resisted the urge to roll his eyes to the skies as he stepped out the car. This man was exasperatingly stubborn.

'Well, hurry up about it, won't you? We need to act, and now.' He placed a reassuring hand on Kie's shoulder. 'I don't think it's safe to return to The Ring at night time and it may not even be safe during the day.'

'Are you suggesting I leave home?'

'For a while, yes. It's a war zone and not worth risking your life for. When Libby comes out of hospital, I suggest you stay with her for the evenings. I'll book myself into a bed and breakfast close by. Will you promise me you'll do that?'

'It's my home, Prendy.'

'I know, son, but I've become rather fond of you and don't want to end up facing your mother at your funeral. Now go and see Libby. I'll wait here.'

— — —

'Can I help you?'

'Aye, sorry I understand it's not visiting time, but I'd like to see Libby Butler, a patient on your ward.'

'Are you a relative?'

'No.'

'A friend?'

'Aye, a very close one.'

'I see.'

The nurse scrubbed some information off the whiteboard behind the desk and levelled her gaze at him through the thick lenses of her spectacles.

'The doctor's with her now.'

'Is she going to be all right?'

'This is her third day here, you know.'

Kie didn't know whether to take her choice of phrase as a challenge or a simple statement of fact.

'Does that mean she's recovering?'

'She's going to be fine.'

He didn't wait to hear the nurse's opinion as he walked down the corridor, peering into the wards for signs of a familiar face. He found Libby with her arms crossed tightly against her chest, telling the doctor off. Her sharp eyes mellowed as they fell on his.

'I don't have any flowers for you.' He held his hands out to prove they were empty. It made him miserable to see her so frail and helpless in a hospital bed. 'How is she, doctor?'

'She's feeling much better,' Libby rasped, her voice not yet recovered from the smoke inhalation and the tube down her throat. 'I'm trying to persuade this nice houseman that there's nothing wrong with me and I'm fit to be discharged, but he has other plans.' She leaned forward on her pillow and coughed, 'I think he wants my body for medical science.'

'The medical team know what's best for you, Libby.' He sat down on the chair beside her bed and took her hand.

'Miss Butler is a very lucky woman,' the doctor had an

Eastern bloc accent. 'We check for carbon monoxide poisoning and give her oxygen therapy. Her carboxyhaemoglobin levels fall to two per cent but she is still coughing carbonaceous sputum, which is concern. We like to keep her in for another day just in case she develop more symptoms.'

'I want to go home. I hate it in here.'

'It's a cigarette she wants, doctor. If I were you, I'd tie her to the bed, just in case she sneaks out to the smoking area in the rain with that drip attached to her arm.'

Libby lay back on the pillow and cursed. 'You don't know what it's like to be addicted to drugs.'

'No, and neither should you.'

'No smoking,' the doctor warned as he left them to tend to the patient in the next bed.

'Where've you been?' She crossed her arms and looked out the window.

'In the jail. They arrested me for your attempted murder.'

'You're joking!'

'I've been hanging around the custody suite at Her Majesty's pleasure for the last two days. I didn't know whether you were dead or alive. Prendy brought me straight here.'

'Don't go back to The Ring, Kie.' She grabbed his wrist and hauled him towards her.

'I have to, it's my home.'

'That thing wants to harm us. It's got much stronger. Look at the state of us! I'm lying in a hospital bed after almost being burned to a crisp and you look as though you've been wrestling with Godzilla. I'm so scared it'll kill you.'

'What would be the point of that?'

'Perhaps it is a demon and wants your soul.'

He laughed. 'You've been listening to Prendy's horror stories.'

'Promise me you won't go back. Take my keys and stay at my

house until I get out of here. We'll brave this thing together, but please promise me you won't do it alone.'

She threw her arms around his neck: he brought his protectively around her back and kissed her. 'You're all I've thought about these past few days. I thought I'd lost you.'

'Well you didn't. You saved me from a very excruciating combustion. I do remember that bit.' She smiled and pressed her palm against his cheek. 'My problem is that I'm stuck here and so can't support you. I want you and Prendy, therefore, to stay at my house until I get out of here. Will you promise me, please?'

He simply nodded. 'I'll be back later. I need to get a few things together.'

'Don't forget my flowers.'

'I won't.' He kissed the side of her head and she held onto his hand playfully.

'And would you bring me a packet of cigarettes? I'm gasping.'

He ignored her plea with a small smile and left the ward. As the lift doors opened, he crashed into Prendergast.

'Careful Prendy, what's the hurry?'

'More trouble, I'm afraid. I've just been speaking to one of the detectives at the station. Something very bad's happened.'

'What have I done now?' Kie let out an exasperated breath.

'Nothing, lad, nothing. It's not you. There's been another death at The Ring. Looks like a man's fallen off the roof and broken his neck.'

'The roof?' Kie didn't mean to yell as Prendy hit the lift button for the ground floor. 'What the hell was he doing on my roof?'

'I don't have the information, but Mary Hyslop found him there this morning. They think he's been dead for at least twenty four hours.'

'That rules me out as a suspect then. The police know where I was. Do they know who the man is?'

'No, he hasn't been identified yet. Is there access to the roof from the inside of the house?'

'Only through the skylight in the attic.'

'So the man gained access to the roof through the attic?'

'Aye, that's what I said.'

'Did you lock the house up before you were arrested?'

'That would've been a bit difficult to do with my hands cuffed behind my back.'

'So, we can only suspect he was an intruder. I wouldn't be at all surprised if he was running from something.'

'We won't know until we go there and see for ourselves.'

'If it's OK with you, I want to get over there and take a look before they take the body away.'

'No problem.'

'You don't mind the thought of seeing a dead body do you?'

'I've seen a few in my time. I doubt whether one more will disturb me.'

Chapter 38

THE TURNING POINT

'Hell's teeth!'

Prendergast winced as Kie barged across the police tape and choked out the vomit, the scene before him too much for even his strong stomach to digest. The body lay against the wall by the front door as if the victim had been dropped in a straight vertical line from a great height and landed on his neck. The head lay at right angles to the torso, the neck stretched out beneath the heavy shoulder blades that had crushed it in the fall. His hands were pressed against the ground on either side of his torso and his legs flopped across each other in a macabre acrobatic pose. The impact had popped his eyes out of their sockets and they dangled from the optic nerves like a pair of Christmas tree baubles. He'd also bitten his tongue in half. It was without doubt the strangest looking corpse Prendergast had ever seen. Equally as odd, was a plastic container and a box of eggs spilled and smashed respectively on the gravel.

'Just take deep breaths, lad. You'll be fine.' He patted Kie on the back as he walked past him to take a closer look at the body.

'Sorry, sir, you'll have to step back to the other side of the police line.'

Prendergast spun around to the familiar sergeant who was coming out the house. 'Since I'm a police consultant here and Mr Armstrong's the owner of the property, I doubt very much either of us will oblige your request.' The blatant disregard of police procedures offended him. 'I take it you have a warrant to enter the property, sergeant?'

The officer paled. 'The door was open, sir. I just had a quick look around, just in case there were any witnesses in the house.'

'I see.'

'I didn't go in very far. Just into the hallway. Don't like the idea of a haunted house, sir.'

Prendergast pulled out his notebook and wrote down the officer's number from his badge. 'I won't need to use this if you continue your investigations within your legal parameters.'

'Of course, sir.'

'Good then, any ideas?'

'Forensics are on their way. Looks like he was climbing on the roof and fell.'

'Don't go in there without an escort.' Prendergast tried to warn Kie as he stepped across the threshold. His concern was met with a very dangerous glower. Prendy just shrugged and turned back to the sergeant. 'Has he been IDd?'

'His name's Martin Landell. He is, or rather was, a freelance photographer from Glasgow. His wallet was still in his jacket pocket. He could've been taking advantage of the owner's absence to take a few sneaky pictures of the ghost.'

'So where's his camera then?'

'Maybe in the house, sir.'

'How did he get here?'

'There's no vehicle here, other than those belonging to the owner. We're checking the taxi services and some of the officers are out making house to house inquiries.'

'The neighbour found the body?'

'Aye, Mrs Hyslop at Greenbrae Cottage, said she was bringing round some eggs and baking for Mr Armstrong this morning when she saw the body. You can see where she dropped them. She says she fled and rang the police.'

'Did she say she recognised the victim?'

'No, sir. He's a stranger to her too.'

'So he could be an opportunist thief or just a very unfortunate visitor.'

'He dropped his camera in the attic.' Kie held a professional-looking camera by its strap and handed it over to the sergeant. As more emergency vehicles arrived in his drive, he took Prendergast by the arm and pulled him away out of official earshot. 'There were a few boxes piled up underneath the skylight. I think he deliberately used the roof as an escape route.'

'Was he trying to get away from something perhaps?'

'Looks like it. The loft ladder was folded and the hatch closed. Who closes a loft hatch after them?'

'Perhaps he thought he was preventing something from following him up there.'

'Well he's dead and can't tell us but maybe someone else can. I think I may be able to help you with your inquiries.'

'You know who this man is?'

'No, but I know who can tell us. A reporter called Mandy Rutherford visited the house just before Libby's accident. She wanted permission to stay for a night with a photographer in the hope she would catch a few spirits on camera for a story.'

'Did you give her permission?'

'Of course not but it's possible she came along anyway after hearing I'd been arrested and knowing you were in Carlisle and Libby in hospital. I have her number on my phone. Do you want me to give her a ring?'

'This is now police business, MacAoidh. Let them deal with it. There's no harm, however, in giving me the number.'

'And what about the images on that camera?'

'No doubt I'll get to see them at some point in the distant future. If there's anything of a paranormal nature on them, however, I doubt they'll ever see the light of day.'

'You can see them now. I downloaded the entire contents of the card onto my laptop before I handed the camera over.'

Prendergast had to laugh. MacAoidh had the makings of an excellent detective. 'Let's take a look then.'

They left the officials to deal with the body outside and shut the door on them. In the conservatory, they buried their noses into the screen while Kie played the images one at a time, scrolling past the group photographs of people in suits at a conference and a few head shots of men and women with cheesy grins sitting at their desks.

'Here we go,' Prendergast pointed to the first image of The Ring. It was an outside shot of the house. More outdoor scenes followed, including images of the outbuildings and gardens. These were all taken during the day but the angle of the sun, low in the sky, told them it was late afternoon.

'That's Mandy Rutherford.' Kie said as he lingered on a picture of the reporter with the house in the background. 'Look, the upstairs windows are all open. I didn't leave them that way.'

Mandy and her colleague, who they now knew to be called Martin Landell, then moved into the house. Landell took wide angle shots of most of the downstairs rooms but there were a few close-ups too, mainly of the photographic frames on the piano, two of which were lying face down, and a lot of shots of the staircase. There were also one or two of the ceiling in the dining room and the butcher's block in the kitchen.

There were more images of the upstairs landing and hallways and each of the bedrooms and bathrooms.

'They certainly were thorough,' Prendy said.

'Look,' Kie hissed, 'the windows in my room are shut now.'

'Either they closed them or there was some activity going on while they were snooping around.'

There was another photograph of Mandy sitting in the living room and laughing. She looked relaxed, but her eyes sparkled with excitement. The remainder of the images were obviously taken at night time. They were the same shots of the exterior and interior of the house. They'd followed their footsteps from room to room with little differences in the content, save for a lack of ambient light.

'Good grief.' Prendy gasped. 'Either there's a lot of dust in the sitting room or they've captured clouds of spirit orbs.'

'Orbs?'

'Yes, you see them on those ghost hunting programmes. Orbs are said to be the first manifestation of spirits. Since digital cameras were invented, there have been a lot of snaps of them. See the rounded shape and the different densities of matter inside the spheres? That's typical of the form they take, but there are so many of them.'

'Come on Prendy, that's perception. It's the same as seeing Mother Theresa in a potato or Jesus in the clouds. Those orbs, as you call them, are just dust particles caught in the flash or some kind of chromatic aberration.'

'Yes, you could be right.' Prendergast gave the photograph a second glance and felt a chill in his spine.

Kie flicked past more pictures of orbs and a series of photos of a chair in the dining room which showed it moving at least a foot by itself in the sequence. There were further orbs on the staircase and a misty cloud on the landing that also appeared to move.

'Well, they wanted evidence and it looks as though they got what they came for.'

There was an image taken from across the upstairs hallway showing Kie's bedroom door open. The next one saw it shut. By this time, all the lights in the house had been turned on, clearly by the two unwanted guests who were probably feeling very frightened. A photograph of the back of Mandy running down the stairs with her arms over her head as if fending off a swarm of wasps shocked Prendergast. There was another frozen moment as she turned onto the stairs: her face was a mask of terror.

'That's the last one.'

Prendy didn't know whether it was something he had seen but wasn't immediately aware of or that famous instinct that told him to turn back to one of the photographs in particular. 'Can I have another look at that one with the cloud in the sitting room?'

'You mean the dust.' Kie laughed.

'Yes, you really need to get yourself a cleaner if that's dust!' He joined him in his good humour and pushed his glasses over his eyes with a poke of his forefinger. 'Can you zoom in for me, I'd like to see one of them close up.'

As soon as the enlargement came into view, both men leaped from their seats with a yell.

'Away tae hell!' Kie stamped the floor and raked his fingers through his hair. 'Do you see what I'm seeing?'

'You don't need a cleaner, you need an exorcist.' Prendy slammed the laptop lid down, too terrorised by what he saw to have any wish to look more closely.

'They're not orbs, Kie, they're faces. Thousands of them.'

— — —

As evening settled in the skies over the Solway, Kie and Prendergast decided it best to take up Libby's offer to stay at her house for a few nights and at least get a decent sleep. Kie sat on the sofa trying to read a paper but couldn't get the images of the photographer and the faces out of his head. Prendergast had gone to a meeting with the local constabulary at Dumfries station and wasn't expected back until late. Jim Black's dog lay on the carpet at his feet. MacAoidh was a man who didn't like sitting about. He'd fixed a loose door on Libby's coal shed, washed the car and replaced a broken shower head. Her car was as new as her house and there was little to do save sit around and read a paper. He'd telephoned his mother and visited Libby with the promised flowers. He was relieved to find she was to be discharged in the morning.

When his mobile rang, he was surprised to see a number he recognised.

'Hello, MacAoidh. Is that MacAoidh Armstrong?'

'What can I do for you Mandy?'

'I'm in a hotel on King Street. Please would you meet me without the police and without your lawyer? Now?'

She had that hysterical, nervous tone to her voice of a jail-breaker on the run.

'I'll meet you by the loch at the bottom of Whitepark Drive.'

'I don't know where that is.' She sounded frantic.

'OK, just start walking towards Carlingwark Loch and stay on the main road. I'll meet you somewhere along the street. I'll leave now.'

'Promise me you'll come right now?'

'Aye, I'm already out the door.'

He spied her coming before she saw him and he sat on a low wall as she approached. The confident, poised Miss Rutherford had been replaced by a fretful and distressed woman who staggered along the road as if she were being pursued by an axe murderer. She was so relieved to see him that she flung her arms around his neck.

'Thank you so much for being here. I know you don't like me very much but I didn't know who to turn to or what to do.'

He peeled her arms away and held her by the wrists. 'First things first. Are you all right?'

She hung her head and nodded before the tears fell. 'I have never, and I mean *never*, been so scared in all my life. How can you live there?'

'I'm thrawn.'

'Martin fell off the roof, MacAoidh. What the hell was he doing on the roof? I got locked in the cupboard under the stairs all night. I'm certain it was responsible for Martin's death. Did you see his body?'

'What do you mean by 'it'?'

'That thing in your house. Martin saw it. He saw it before he died.' He could only watch while she sobbed in the middle of the street. 'I haven't gone home; I haven't gone into work. I don't know what to do or where to go, so I stayed here hoping you could make some sense of all this. I know the police will want to ask me questions but I don't know what to tell them.'

'Slow down. Let's talk about this and get things in perspective.'

She dried her eyes on the handkerchief he offered. 'Thanks for seeing me. I know I'm not your favourite person, but I hoped your heart was big enough to rescue a damsel in distress. Can we go somewhere to eat? I haven't eaten all day.'

'Aye, there's a pub just down the road.'

They walked in silence to the restaurant and took a seat in the courtyard. A vibrant green magnolia tree cascaded over the blue walls of the cosy enclosure. There were a few patrons sitting underneath grey sun umbrellas, but none close enough to be within listening distance.

'I'm not going to ask you what you were doing in the house because I've already figured that one out. I've got copies of all the pictures Martin Landell took that night.' He set her double vodka and coke down on the table.

'How …?'

He finished her sentence for her. 'He dropped his camera in the house.'

She breathed out her misery with an audible sigh. 'At first I thought it might be you. I thought maybe you'd taken your ghostly jokes a bit far but I also knew you were locked away in the Dumfries custody suite at the material time and Libby Butler was in hospital.'

'So you took advantage of our absence?' He was only slightly chiding.

'I'm sorry.'

'Aye, I can imagine just how sorry you are.' The tears fell again and he relented. 'You weren't to know this would end in your colleague's death. No one could've forecast that. Tell me what happened.'

She took a deep breath. 'He took photos and I made notes. We waited until dark and then took more photos and I took more notes. Odd things happened like photo frames falling on their faces; there was whistling and whispering and there were footsteps on the stairs.' She only stopped to shudder. 'It got a lot worse after dark. We saw a chair move all by itself and there were strange mists and cold spots shifting around the house. Something was scratching in the attic. Like a big rat. Things got out of hand when Martin started screaming he'd seen an apparition at the top of the stairs. He ran after it and I ran after him because I didn't want to be left alone in the house. But the doors kept banging, windows kept opening and the voices got louder. Something grabbed me by the hair and I had enough. The power went out, fusing all the lights, and I ran away. I fell down the stairs and crawled to the door but couldn't get out so I hid in the cupboard under the stairs. I got trapped inside. The door wouldn't budge.'

'Did Martin come looking for you?'

She shook her head and downed her drink flat. 'The house was completely silent on the other side of that door. I lost my voice calling for him.'

Kie raised his eyebrows. Her voice had certainly made a remarkable recovery as the words fell from her mouth leaving little space to take a breath.

'After a while, I even felt safe. Sitting there curled up in the dark was, I suppose, like being back in the womb. I must've eventually fallen asleep because, when I woke up, all the doors in the house were open, including my cupboard door. I didn't want to look over the house again, especially by myself, and thought, if Martin was still around, I'd meet him outside. It was then I saw him. Like that. Do you think the police will arrest me?'

'I don't know. Libby's the lawyer. I do, however, think they'll want to question you at length. You should offer the information before they decide to come and take it from you. If I were you, I would go to Andrew Prendergast. He's a police consultant looking into the recent deaths at The Ring. He's the type who'll help you rather than hinder you.'

'So the police do think the deaths are suspicious?'

'All deaths are suspicious to policemen.' His guard came up in a flash when he witnessed that vulturine glint in her reporter's eye. He marvelled at the professionalism of the woman. She'd just suffered the most traumatic experience of her life, but she switched it off at the sniff of a good story.

'So you didn't see what happened to Martin?'

She shook her head and didn't meet his gaze.

His eyes narrowed.

'Let's order.'

They ate and she drank enough to drown out the horrors

of her recent ordeal. Kie kept the conversation light and the subject of The Ring to a modicum level. As the evening passed, she spoke about herself: how she'd become a reporter; of her two failed marriages; and her thoughts on why her kids preferred to stay with their fathers. Although she confessed to knowing Martin Landell for over six years, she never once spoke about how his family would be feeling or how she would miss him in her life. Kie realised she was nothing like Libby after all. Save for a similar dress sense, they had little in common, especially where sentiment and sensitivity towards others was concerned. Mandy Rutherford was a ruthless and self-centred woman who was accustomed to getting her own way. He'd never met anyone quite like her and didn't know whether he found her pitiless nature fascinating or abhorrent.

'You know, you terrified me when I first met you.' She slurred her words through the bottom of her glass.

'Oh aye?'

'Yes,' she giggled. 'You were really mean to me.'

'You deserved it.'

She flicked her dark hair back with her hand and laughed. 'I suppose I did. Are we friends now?' She shot him an alluring smile. 'You're devilishly handsome, you know, intelligent and really quite charming. I'm very impressed.'

He felt immediately uncomfortable. He knew where this was going. 'It's late and I've got things to do in the morning. I'll walk you back to the hotel and then we should go to bed.' Those words didn't come out quite how he'd planned. He saw the seduction smiling from behind the red lip gloss. 'I mean to my bed.'

'I really don't mind whose bed we use.' She stood up and immediately sat down again as the dizziness hit her. He brought her a glass of water after he paid the bill and managed to haul her to her feet.

The walk back to her hotel was the longest few hundred metres he'd ever crossed as she clung on to him, swaying and staggering against his arm. Outside the hotel, she tried one last time.

'Fancy a night cap?'

'I think you've had enough.'

'I've only just started.' She curled her fingers around the back of his neck and waggled her hips. 'I'll make it worth your while.'

'Sorry, Mandy, I've got to go. I've got to be up early to see someone.'

Those predacious eyes turned carnivorous within a blink. 'Does that someone happen to be Stephen Mitchell?'

'Stephen who?' He cursed his inability to lie with any conviction and just hoped she would be too drunk to remember the conversation. Somehow he knew she would recall every little word that was said during the evening.

'Thanks for dinner.'

'You're welcome.' He turned to leave.

'Are you sure …'

'Positive. Good night, Mandy.'

She waggled her fingers at him and he left her swaying on her high heels.

When he returned home, Prendergast stood in his pyjamas with his hands on his hips, a deep scowl furrowing his forehead. He delivered Kie a stern lecture about leaving without a note to say where he was going and not answering his mobile. Prendy then ambled off to bed with a cup of hot chocolate.

Kie felt the warmth of attachment healing his wounds, despite his friend's animosity. He drew parallels with his former life when he would get home after midnight to be greeted with a similar outburst from his father. He was loathe to admit that he missed his dad but couldn't find a way to forgive him. Andrew Prendergast, over the past few weeks, had shown him the concern and fondness of a loving parent and that left Kie feeling hopelessly homesick.

He went to bed dreaming of love and familiar voices.

chapter 39

THE CONNECTION

As Libby got into her comfortable jeans and favourite ethnic print cotton top, she hoped she'd hidden her disappointment from Prendy when she realised he'd come to collect her from the hospital. She'd been expecting Kie but apparently he was busy. She waved to Prendy from the window after she heard the toot of his horn and decided that looking gorgeous took precedence over his impatience to get to The Ring and hear what the psychic had to say.

She stuffed her feet into a brand new pair of black feather and jewelled strappy gladiator sandals and snatched up the matching handbag. She took one last look at herself in the full length mirror and, although she knew she should really drop a stone or two, was pleased with what she saw. She slammed the front door and ran down the drive to Prendy's car.

'How do I look?' She flopped into the passenger seat.

'Lovely.'

Libby forgave him for the slight clip to his voice. He had, after all, been waiting in the car for over an hour and a half while she took her promised 'ten minutes' to slip into something a little more socially acceptable than a backless hospital gown.

As they drove the eight or so miles to Auchencairn, Libby felt the trepidation steadily rising as they neared The Ring. Lying in a hospital bed with snoring, groaning patients and noisy medical staff keeping her awake for most nights, she wondered whether she would ever have the courage to stay at the chamber of horrors ever again. Time, though, healed most wounds and she'd face The Ring and all its horrors if Kie needed her.

She took in a few deep breaths as the car pulled into the drive.

'What the hell's he up to now?' Prendy leaped out of the car when he saw a pile of doors on the concrete and Kie fighting with a screwdriver and the hinges of the byre door. 'What are you doing?'

'Taking off all the doors to the outbuildings and the house. No one's going to get trapped inside a building ever again.' He threw the byre door across the concrete and it slammed on top of the others with a loud, resounding thud.

'You'll need your front and back doors.'

'Not at the moment, I don't. I've got big wrought iron gates coming for the front of the drive. That should keep out the undesirables.'

'Like reporters and snoopers?'

'And the police.'

'Where's Stephen Mitchell?'

'Taking a walk down the road and following the boy's last footsteps. I left him to it. Can't abide all that drivel about spirit energies talking to him. He says he speaks to a Native American Sioux chief who's been dead for centuries. I thought I'd make myself useful and get as far away from him as I could before I whittled myself a tomahawk and hit him over the head with it.'

He suddenly noticed Libby standing on the drive and he put down his tools to greet her. She noticed, with some satisfaction, the affection and concern in that overwhelming gaze.

'What are you doing here?'

'Visiting an old haunt.'

'You shouldn't be here, Libby. You should be resting.' He grabbed the back of her neck beneath her hair and pushed his body into hers. 'I like the croaky voice. It's sexy.' His kissed her in an open display of affection. 'Come on. I'm taking you home.'

'No you won't. Apart from breathing in a bit of smoke, there's nothing wrong with me. I was ready to come out of that hospital a couple of days ago, but medical practitioners always think they know what's best for everyone. They call it caution. I call it hysteria. I really am fine, Kie. If I thought I needed a rest, I'd book myself into a spa hotel and have a manicure.' She kissed him back, passionately. 'There, you see, there's really nothing to worry about, but you can take me home for a while if you really want.'

Prendergast coughed for attention. 'I think we're reasonably safe here during the day. Which way did Mr Mitchell go? I'd quite like to hear what he has to say.'

'No doubt you'll read about it in the papers tomorrow. Mandy Rutherford's here with him.'

'Oh no! What's she wearing?'

Kie shrugged. 'African-style top, light blue calf-length jeans, black sandals with gems and feathers.'

Libby shrieked.

'I'm kidding. She's wearing a floral dress with wee white shoes.'

'What does she want?' Prendergast couldn't hide his displeasure.

'I think I let it slip last night I was having a visitor. She put two and two together and came up with the right sum. The good news is, she's limited herself to the public paths and neighbours' grounds. She says she never wants to step foot in the house again.'

'You saw her last night?'

Libby saw Prendergast sneaking off and crossed her arms against her ethnic print chest.

'We had dinner.'

'Did you now?'

'Aye.' There wasn't a hint of shame or apology in his answer. 'Why?'

'Didn't Prendy tell you about the photographer?'

'Yes, but he didn't tell me you shared an amuse bouche with his accomplice.'

'It was only a meal. We didn't indulge in any after dinner sex, if that's what you're insinuating.'

'What you do with your body after dinner is entirely your business. I now understand why you were too busy to pick me up from hospital this morning.'

'Libby?'

She spun around and stomped off after Prendergast who was just jumping the farm gate to gain access to the field. She left Kie to ponder on why she could possibly be upset with him.

'Nothing happened between them, you know that. He's very loyal. It's in his nature.' Prendy puffed as they trudged across the uneven grass, being careful to avoid the mine fields of thistles, nettles and cow pats.

'Loyal to who, Prendy? I haven't known him long enough to warrant his undivided devotion.'

'All the same, you'll have it as long as he's with you. He's an unusual young man in that he's wholly honourable and didn't think twice about resisting her charms last night.'

'She tried it on with him?'

She saw Prendy's shoulders freeze and she snarled.

'Don't cause any trouble, Libby. We don't want her writing about Kie in the negative. He's the one who'll suffer in the end.'

They found Mr Mitchell and the reporter at the Ghost Tree. He held his plump hands against the devastated trunk and stood with his eyes closed and his ear pressed to the bark as if listening for its heartbeat. Although it was a reasonably bright day, there was a cold wind blowing across the hills and Libby wished she'd dressed in warmer clothes. She noticed Mandy rubbing her bare arms and trying to stop the skirt of her flowery dress from blowing above her thighs and she smiled inwardly.

'Stephen says the boy was dragged here and …'

'I understand Mr Armstrong's asked you to stay away from his land.'

'I'm exercising my right to roam.' Mandy looked taken aback.

'So are you simply travailing around the hillside, or are you here to cause further harassment to the owner of this property?'

'Harassment?'

'Yes, as in persistent pursuit.'

'Your animosity is disturbing the spirits,' Stephen Mitchell hissed in a high-pitched voice, his eyes still shut tight.

'I'm pleased to hear that, Mr Mitchell, for those same spirits have been disturbing me for a couple of months now and I'm delighted to be able to return the sentiment and give them a taste of their own medicine. Show me one and I'll grab it by the ankles and drag it into the nearest flaming shed.'

'Libby!' Prendy hissed.

'The spirits don't take kindly to your mocking tone, miss'

'There's no law of trespass in Scotland,' Mandy retorted with an angry clip to her voice.

'As a general rule, that's correct but section two, subsection two, of the Land Reform Scotland Act twenty thirteen, says those rights must be exercised responsibly – that's defined in subsection one – and harassment, Miss Rutherford, is not a responsible action. In fact, it's a breach of the peace and a criminal offence, thereby precluding you from the freedoms granted by said act under section nine, paragraph B.'

'For goodness' sake, will you please…' Stephen Mitchell

turned to Prendergast for support. 'Please take her away, she's interfering with my communications. I've lost them.'

Libby spun around to the psychic whose eyes were now wide with frustration. 'Here, use my mobile.'

'Come on Libby, let's allow the man to work.'

She ignored Prendy's plea and rounded on Mandy Rutherford once more. 'I should also advise you that entering a private building without permission is trespass, especially when the owner has expressly refused to grant his permission.'

'Prove it.'

'You've done it for me. We are in possession of all the images taken from Mr Landell's camera, including a few of you lounging around the house when the owner was away and who expressly denied you access to his property.' She was answered with a filthy glare. 'I can't believe you're out working so soon after you precipitated the death of your close colleague.'

Mandy Rutherford burst into tears.

'It's no good, loves. I'll take a break.' Stephen Mitchell released his hands from the tree and ambled away down the hill.

Libby knew she'd gone too far, but couldn't help her reaction. She wanted to destroy Mandy Rutherford for her presumptuous behaviour, for her arrogance and for the icy callousness of her personality. Moreover, she wanted to punish her for last night's impromptu dinner date.

'What's wrong with you today?' Prendergast shot her a stern glare, took the wailing Mandy by the arm, and followed the psychic back to the house.

She stood for a while at the tree. A soft rain began to fall across the hills and settled as fine mist on her hair and skin. She knew what was wrong with her and believed the others too thoughtless to realise that her bad behaviour was a natural reaction to their insensitivity. She'd just been through a terrible ordeal that nearly took her life and she came out of hospital today to find she'd taken the bronze medal behind a scheming female reporter and a man who conversed with dead people.

She ran her fingers across the deep scars in the flaking bark where the shotgun had expelled its load at point blank range. The tree stood like a tortured man, its cadaverous branches groping the air in its desperate hunger for sustenance; its trunk twisted and bent in the agony of starvation.

Libby felt a deep, deep sorrow consuming her. The Ghost Tree had withstood the centuries in a place where no tree grew naturally. It was the last of a hardy, enduring species but its memory would now become lost through time. It didn't fall foul to the ravages of the ages or elements, but rather it was killed on a whim and the selfish demands of men. Did it protect these lands from the return of a mischievous paranormal entity? Could trees repel the devil? Her questions were lost in the falling rain. She spread her arms around the Ghost Tree and pressed her cheek against the crusty bark, hoping to hear a heartbeat, just like the psychic had done. She closed her eyes and imagined the tree alive. What would it have seen if it had eyes?

'What're you doing?'

She jumped from her musings and scratched her ear on the brittle bark. Kie's silhouette blotted out the light as he stood with his hands in his pockets.

'I'm talking to the tree.'

'And what did it say?'

'Nothing, it's a tree, it hasn't got a mouth. Don't you have guests to ingratiate?'

'Aye, but it's you I want to see.'

'If you're going to tell me off for upsetting Miss Rutherford, then don't bother. She deserves everything she gets.'

'She turns the tears on at will. You justly reminded her of her guilt, that's all. She'll get over it. I think the police gave her a hard time this morning. She's a different woman today.'

'Yes, you have that kind of effect on women.'

He shook his head.

'What's Mystic Mitchell saying?'

'Nothing. He says he doesn't want to reveal any information until he's got the whole picture. He's asked me to keep you away from him while he traces the boy's 'essence' as he calls it. He says you send out too many negative vibes.'

'I've only just started.' She crossed her arms, leaned against the tree and lit a cigarette. 'This poor tree's seen a lot in its long past, including the violent assault on a young boy. Do you think trees have a memory?'

She sniffed at the derisory click of his tongue but was relieved he didn't tell her off for smoking.

'Some scientists believe water has a memory, inasmuch as it's able to retain an imprint of the energies it's been exposed to over the passing of time. Since most of us, this tree and even the world are composed of a higher percentage of water than any other substance, then perhaps we're all part of the same energy. Maybe the memory of this tree is also our own memory: one giant universal force shared amongst all things present, past and future.'

'You've lost me.'

'No, I think I'm on to something.' She saw that brain working as if a bright light had just been switched on inside that complex mind of his. 'It's basic physics. Energy has to be transferred in order to cause movement. Kinetic energy begins as a potential power source. It needs to be stored. Like heat, sound and vibration, it falls off from its store point because magnetic field strength decreases the further you get away from the source.'

He paced the ground with his hands behind his back, looking every bit like a mad scientist.

'Electricity requires high voltage power lines to transfer it over long distances and transformers to distribute it locally. What if The Ring, its land, or even the bedrock it's built on is behaving like a kind of store point and transformer: a device that can store and then transfer energy between circuits: the then, the now and the what's to come?'

'Or the living, the dead and the unborn?' She followed his theories. 'So what are the power lines?'

'Us. We are. We are the conduits. It is our energy that's being used to manifest this potential power that's been somehow stored up in this location over the centuries of man.' He sat down on the grass with a thump and raked his fingers through his hair in the characteristic way of Kie when he felt confounded.

'Now you're scaring me.'

'Did Prendy tell you about the photographer's images?'

She nodded.

'Those translucent particles he said were orbs were faces: thousands of separate and distinct personalities. Some were thin, some fat, some happy, some sad. Old, young, blue-eyed, dark-eyed, bearded, clean shaven, blonde, brunette, red … None of those faces was the same, but all of them stared straight into the camera as if they knew their portraits were being taken.'

'Yes, Prendy told me about it. The police have apparently buried the evidence.'

'I'm not surprised.' His laugh was grave as a random ray of sunshine haloed his form in shimmering multi-coloured hues. It was as if a rainbow had burst from his back but couldn't free itself from his powerful frame.

Libby's eyes widened in panic. She'd seen a similar aura on Jim Black and Charlie and worried that the vision carried some ominous portent.

'I'm cold and I'm hungry.'

He smiled, that warm, affectionate Kie smile that invaded her dreams. 'I can fix both your afflictions if you'll let me and stop fantasising about my bogus affair with a woman I don't even like.'

'Sorry.'

She allowed him to wrap his arms around her and she stood for long moments in that comforting embrace; listening in tender silence to the steady beat of his heart under the dead limbs of the Ghost Tree.

They laughed as Kie's mobile shuddered in the back pocket of his jeans.

'It's Hannah.' He passed the phone to her.

Libby felt numb as Hannah's disjointed voice brought her bad news. She'd ended the call before she had a chance to take in the information.

'Libby?'

'It's Charlie.'

'Wasn't that Hannah?'

'She said Charlie's dead. He died in a car crash on the M4 last night. She thought we should know.'

chapter 40

THE PSYCHIC

'This Charlie was bald, brown eyes. I see a red dragon.'

'He was We…'

'… a friend.'

Libby realised Kie wanted to test the man for his accuracy. She couldn't believe she spoke of Charlie in the past tense and wondered why his death hadn't floored her. She decided she'd seen so much death over the past few years that she'd become desensitised to it. She couldn't help worrying, however, about seeing a similar halo around Kie today. Could she see death before it happened? She really hoped not.

They sat in the conservatory, a place where the paranormal activity of the house had a tendency to bypass. It was early afternoon and the man she called Mystic Mitchell, even to his face, sat next to her on the sofa. He'd finished his rounds and called them all together to discuss his findings. He sat back with his legs apart and his heavy stomach sitting on the tops of his thighs. His belly poked out underneath his striped shirt, concealing the top of his trousers.

Kie lounged in the chair opposite them, one of his long legs thrown over the arm and swinging in annoyance. Prendy was still outside speaking at length to Mandy Rutherford who refused to enter the house.

Stephen turned his gaze towards Libby: calm, compassionate, unemotional. She felt her back shrinking into the cushions.

'He's left a residue of himself within these walls, love. It's not a powerful force, but he wanted to prove something.'

Libby was just about to open her mouth when Prendy walked in with a very fearful, but contrite-looking, still snivelling Mandy.

'What's she doing here?'

'Mandy's agreed to help with the research.'

'We don't need her help.'

'Nevertheless, she wants to be involved. She wants to know what happened to her and her colleague the other night. It's only fair. She did, after all, find Mr Mitchell.'

'Do you have any objections?' she asked Kie.

He shrugged. 'Not at the moment.'

'All right, Miss Rutherford, you may attend this meeting but don't let that mislead you into believing you have a right to any further involvement in this matter. I have those photographs and a recording of your failed attempt to blackmail me, and I will use both of them against you if you push your luck. Should I draw up a contract now?'

'That won't be necessary, Libby.' Prendy laughed.

Mandy simply looked at her.

'Have a seat.' Libby rose and offered her position on the sofa with a flurry of arms. She then wriggled a space on the chair with Kie and felt dizzy delight when he slid his hand across her stomach. Mandy appeared to get the message and looked away.

'He wanted to prove he was still here. Even after the body has gone, the spirit lives on. Only it exists in a different form. That's what spiritualism is all about.'

'Did he leave any messages?'

'His essence is the message, my love.' She didn't like the condescending smile he shot her, as if she were stupid.

'Well I didn't expect him to leave me a shopping list!' Kie gave her a squeeze as a soft urge to keep her annoyance at bay.

Stephen began with the formalities. 'Before I tell you what I've seen and what happened to the boy, I want to introduce myself to you properly. Forgive me, Mandy love, if you've already heard this all before, but it's important we all have a clear idea of who I am and what I can do for you.'

Libby nudged Kie with her elbow as she heard him snort.

Stephen continued his performance, his words flowing fast and his hands gesticulating for maximum dramatic effect: 'As you know, I'm a psychic. Psychics are people who are able to peek behind what I term the veil of the usual human senses and see and hear things beyond the observable universe. We do this through extrasensory perception, or ESP as we call it in the trade.'

'Lord, not more antonyms!'

Libby had to give Kie another nudge and he grunted as her sharp elbow hit a vulnerable spot between his ribs.

Stephen ignored the comment. 'Now you probably want to know what I mean by the veil, my loves, so I'll tell you. The veil is a general term I invented to explain the border between the living world and the spirit realm. Some psychics just see and hear things behind the veil: they pick up residues left by those who have passed away which is translated through visions or feelings. Others are able to communicate with and interact with spirits and that's the kind of psychic I am. As well as being clairvoyant, clairaudient and clairsentient…'

'More like Clairfraudulent,' Kie mumbled.

'… I am an internationally renowned psychic detective but I'm also a rescue medium, a shepherd of the dead, if you like.'

'And what do you rescue?' Prendergast had his note book out and scribbled on it with his expensive fountain pen.

'I rescue lost souls, restless spirits and those who've found it either difficult or impossible to move on.'

'Move on to where?' Kie didn't sound convinced.

'To the next spiritual dimension and, ultimately, to heaven.'

'And what about hell?'

'Hell is a Christian concept. I'm not religious so don't believe in it.'

'I'm beginning to like this man.' Kie sat back, almost knocking Libby off the chair.

'I do believe, however, that this universe has many dimensions. In a way, we all exist on a spiritual plane in relation to our multi-faceted cosmos. The one we're living and breathing on at the moment, is just one of many our spirits will travel through until we reach that definitive dimension of rest and peace we call heaven. We belong to this world at this particular point of our spiritual journey and we're bound to it until the state we call death. When our bodies die, our spirits simply move on. Some, however, for various reasons, become trapped inside this world in a state of consciousness that's part of it but not, if you see what I mean. Does that make sense?'

'No, sorry, it doesn't make any sense to me at all.'

Stephen showed no exasperation at Kie's obstinacy. 'Some of us, when we die, can't or won't cross over to the next dimension. Whether it's through fear, trauma or simple reluctance, some of us find ourselves bound to the earth, watching life go by upon it, but without being able to be a part of it.'

'So where are all these earth-bound spirits? Why can't we all see them?' Mandy, who had been quiet throughout, also had her notebook out.

'Like the living, my love, the spirit tends to stay at a familiar location which reminds them of comfort, home, family and all the good things they enjoyed when they were alive and could interact with their world. Others bind themselves to places where the veils of the dimensions are weak. Like this house and its grounds. Like I said, psychics have developed the gift to see through the veils. Everyone has the ability, it's a matter of opening your mind to the seemingly implausible.'

'What about the stories you hear about seeing a big white light and, when you cross through, all your long-lost relatives are there to greet you?' Libby thought she'd add her thoughts to the conversation.

'Some believe that, love. I, personally, don't believe the light is necessary. It's just a guide. The crossing points are always there, it's up to the spirit to choose whether to go through or not. As for the relatives on the other side,' he shrugged his rounded shoulders, 'why not? We take the love with us when we pass over and love is a difficult emotion to let go of. It's only natural to want to be with a loved one in times of crisis or tragedy, so sometimes the spirit will come back to provide aid or comfort.'

'What do you mean by 'like this house'? Do you consider this house some sort of holding pen for lost souls?'

'That's a good description, Libby love. Yes, spirits are drawn to this place for some reason. I feel very many presences here but, first things first. I'm going to deal with the boy before I speak to the poor souls trapped around me.'

'Can you just shut them out like that?' Libby clicked her fingers.

'Some are very persistent but, yes. Like our cynical but lovely Mr Armstrong here, I can just shut them out. My ability comes through a lot of experience; his is a natural defensive mechanism.' He glanced at Kie's dark glower and decided it best to move on. 'I'm channelling all my focus into the boy's last few moments on this world as a living person and then I intend to speak with him and help him cross over. Does that make sense?'

'No.'

Libby resisted the compulsion to put her hand over Kie's

mouth. 'You think he's still here? In spirit, I mean?'

'You've seen him yourself, love. He's attached himself to you. He likes you.' Stephen leaned forward and winked. 'I think he has a bit of a crush!'

Libby felt a cold chill creeping across her back. 'Where is he now?'

'Oh, he's standing beside you. He's cold and he's shivering. Poor kid, he really needs to move on.'

'All right, that's enough.' Kie stood up and moved to the back of the chair. 'An adolescent spirit with a schoolboy crush? Come on man, that makes no sense at all.'

'Our personalities come from the spirit, MacAiodh, my lovely, not from the body. We bring them with us when we're born and we cross over with them when we leave this world in corporeal form. We are who were are. Fortunately, Mr Prendergast told me you were a sceptic, so I brought some things along with me that may help convince you what I'm saying may possibly be the truth.'

He hauled out a cardboard folder from his briefcase and placed it on his lap. He then pulled a number of sheets of paper from its interior.

'I did some homework before I came here, in the psychic sense, of course. You see, I have premonitions before I come to work and I write down and draw the first things that spring to mind. I'm going to say something I feel has a connection to you or to this place and I want you to answer whether I'm right or wrong. I don't want you to elaborate on your answers or put images into my mind that aren't already there. Just a yes or no will do. Are you ready?'

The absence of a nod only served to demonstrate Kie's reluctance.

Stephen didn't look down at his notes, but eyed Kie with

a warm reverence. 'You have a strong connection with the Highlands.'

Kie's laughter burst out before he could check it. 'It's the accent that gives that one away.'

'I see a loch and a ruined castle that you also have a close association with.'

'That narrows me down to just about every Scotsman on the planet.'

'There's a house, a few miles away, by the side of a horse shoe-shaped lake. It's surrounded by a barren landscape and dark stretches of water and there's a waterfall, a very high waterfall, plunging down a steep slope. There's snow on the mountains to the east and crazy-paved ice lakes scattered about a bleak, boggy wasteland. The house has a blue front door. It's a large stone mansion with a big conservatory facing south. The house is in a dark glen? Does that make sense? You belong there.'

Libby noticed Kie's jaw was firmly set.

'Am I right?'

'Close.'

'Coffee. Does that make sense?'

Libby thought Kie looked as though he was about to make a run for it.

'There's a woman. Her name's Corina? Kareena? No Kakena. She's African.'

'That's enough. I'm off.'

Everyone was left astounded as Kie marched from the room.

'Where did you get that information from, Stephen?'

'The spirits surrounding him told me, my love. He has a lot of souls around him. They're drawn to his life force. He makes them feel safe. Does that make sense?'

'I thought you wrote the information down before you came here.'

'I did, but that's not what I saw.'

'What's your version then?'

'OK,' Stephen flicked through the pages and, after licking the tips of his thumb and forefinger, pulled one of them to the top of the pile. 'I do a bit of psychic drawing. Do you recognise this face?'

He handed the sketch to her and Libby saw the boy as he appeared in Mary's picture. The pencil drawing was not exactly made by a professional artist, but it was a reasonable likeness that identified the face as belonging to Peter Hyslop. She pushed it back into his hand feeling disappointed in him. 'You know I do. You could've got that from any newspaper clipping.'

'Look at the date, pet. I drew this four days before the boy disappeared.'

'Anyone can write a date on a piece of paper. I'm a lawyer, Stephen, I'll need better evidence than that.'

'OK then. Auras. Haloes around people's heads. You see them.'

'I may have seen a few lately.'

'It's a gift that's always been dormant in you, my love, but one that you've now come to accept. All this paranormal activity surrounding you has brought it to the fore.'

'It's a curse. Two people have died. I saw the shroud on both of them.'

'What shroud?' Mandy's ears pricked up.

'Sometimes people can see death. As the spirit is drawn to its next dimension, it's trail becomes more visible.'

'Does it always mean death?' Libby felt the lump in her throat slowly choking her.

'That depends on what you see.'

She didn't want to say anything more in front of Mandy but her heart felt leaden.

Stephen put his hand on her arm. 'Death is a part of life, as marriage and birth. Don't try to interpret what you don't understand.'

She nodded. 'Anything else to show me?'

'What about this then?'

He handed her another rough pencil sketch and Libby paled. 'Where did you get this?' She felt her hands shaking.

'Do you know her?'

She could only nod.

'She's in the spirit world, isn't she?'

'Who is she?' Mandy was desperate to know.

'She's my mother.' Libby sat down with a thump. 'How could you know?'

'I didn't, my lovely. I was told.' He smiled in self-gratification. 'Now I have your attention, my lovely darling, perhaps you'll be a bit less scathing towards me when I tell you what I know about Peter Hyslop. Please get everyone together, we're all going for a little walk.'

— — —

It took Libby and Prendy all their powers of persuasion to convince Kie to join them on Stephen's impromptu ghost walk, following the final footsteps of Peter Hyslop. He eventually agreed but strictly forbade any further talk of premonitory observation. Stephen concurred but also imposed a sanction on anyone speaking while he was 'working' as he called it.

They stood together at the bottom of the lane joining the main road to Auchencairn and listened to Stephen as he talked them through what he saw. To Libby's disgust, Mandy wore Kie's wax cotton jacket over her skimpy floral dress. Always the gentleman, he'd offered it to her when he saw her shivering. She snuggled into it as if his own arms were wrapped around her.

'He got off the bus here. He was excited. Something nice had happened that day at school.' They followed Stephen up the lane. 'He came this way. He was looking forward to seeing his mum. He wanted to tell his mum something.'

He stopped as the Ghost Tree came in sight on the left at the top of the hill and lowered his voice to a hushed whisper. 'Someone was coming towards him from over there. He knew him. He was frightened. He'd been naughty and the man was coming to tell him off. He tried to run but the man caught up with him and grabbed him.' Stephen left the path and ran up the hill towards the solitary tree. 'He dragged him to here.' Panting, he stopped at the base of the tree. 'He hit him with his fist and was shouting bad words at him. Fire! Fire! It hurts. Mum, he's hitting me. His big boot. Ow, my stomach hurts. It hurts. Muuuuuum!'

Libby was so swept away by Stephen's outstanding performance that she barely noticed Kie's comforting arm around her shoulder. The psychic re-enacted the violent scene as if it were happening to him. He lay on his side on the stony ground, covered in sheep droppings and mud. He curled into a ball and spasmed, his head snapping from left to right, his back jerking at random intervals. It was as if he was being repeatedly kicked. When Stephen threw himself onto his front and screamed, Libby had to look away.

She held her breath as the psychic detective eventually lay still and she wondered if he would need resuscitation. She breathed a sigh of relief when he rose from the ground and dusted himself off. He took a deep breath and moved on.

'He was dragged unconscious across the field and past the house, across a road and towards the stream over there.' He continued his story as if speaking to a group of tourists. They followed the course he took and eventually gathered at a spot by the burn beneath a clump of overhanging trees. 'Peter Hyslop woke up here. He was screaming. He was covered in his own blood, his bones were broken and his arms had been torn from their sockets. His skull was cracked but he was still alive. He was alive enough to scream and alive enough to feel another beating.' Stephen pointed to a deep pool on a gentle bend in the burn. 'The man jumped into the water and held his head under here until Peter stopped screaming.'

He took another deep breath as if pushing the misery out of his lungs. 'Peter Hyslop died here and doesn't know where his body was buried. He wants us to find it. He wants you to find it and he can't rest until he comes home. He wants you to know that he didn't mean to frighten you, Libby. He just wants you to notice him. He's a boy and he's lost and confused. You must find his bones.'

'Are you saying it was Peter who dragged me into the woodshed and lit a fire?'

'No, that wasn't him. He would never do that to you. That was something else. No one must know.'

To everyone's surprise, Stephen threw up on the grass. 'Sorry, I'm having a bad reaction. The nausea will pass. We just have to get away from this place. I could do with a nice cold glass of milk and some biscuits. Do you have any chocolate ones?'

They began walking back towards the house and had to stop again for Stephen to vomit.

'Are you all right?'

He shook his head violently. 'There's something else with him. Something that doesn't want you to find out the secrets of this house and something that will attempt murder to keep it safe.'

'Who is he?' Libby didn't like the wildness in his eyes.

'He's a demon.'

Chapter 41

THE RESCUE MEDIUM

'A demon? Come on!' Kie lay back on the bed and placed his hands behind his head.

'That's what he said.'

'He said he doesn't believe in hell. Isn't hell the home of demons?'

'I don't know. Maybe it's just a word that represents a nasty spirit.'

They lay on Kie's bed with their clothes on while Stephen was taking an hour's rest in the conservatory. With no door to the bedroom, neither of them wanted to take the chance of being caught in a compromising position. Mandy and Prendy were downstairs mulling over the psychic's information and Libby and Kie took the lull in the proceedings to find some private space. He'd insisted she got some rest after having just left hospital.

'He's a fake. I don't know where he got the information from, like the name of my house, but he would've got it from somewhere.'

'Yes, what was that all about?'

'The house is called *Gleann Dubh*, it means dark glen. His description of the home I grew up in was spot on. That waterfall he was talking about is *Eas a' Chual Alainn*, the highest waterfall in the British Isles.'

'Is it really as bleak, barren and boggy as he says?'

'Aye, and he forgot to mention inhospitable and cold.'

She let out a little sigh. 'He drew a picture of my mother. That freaked me out completely.'

'It's possible he got all that information from various printed or digital sources. Both of us will have a footprint.'

'Maybe Mandy's helping him with his inquiries.'

'My only misgiving is, how did he get Helen's real name? I'm not on any genealogy site.'

'A couple of phone calls would've done it. It's not hard to find a person in the twenty first century.'

'Tell that to Peter Hyslop's mother.'

They lapsed into silence.

'He reminds me of a Blackpool children's entertainer: all cheesy smiles and flamboyant posturing, does that make sense?' she giggled.

'Aye, my lovely, he speaks like a clown.'

'He's got the wobbly belly and the big red nose too.'

They laughed.

'I don't care what Clairbonkers says, I don't think we should stay here after dark. Why do all mediums want to work in the dark? Ghosts come out in the day too.'

'I asked Charlie the same question when we were at the pub that time. He said it was something to do with ionisation of the atmosphere after sunset and all those solar atoms losing their electrons and turning into ions at night. Maybe spirits, if there are such things, get a better reception at night. That theory has certainly worked for this place.'

'Poor Charlie.'

'Aye. I got quite fond of Charlie. I really hope his death wasn't precipitated by my empty toast.'

'Don't be ridiculous.'

They left the question hanging.

Libby turned over and nestled into the crook of his arm, her

THE RESCUE MEDIUM

scent pervading his space. 'Do you think the ghost whisperer can protect us from violent activity tonight, like he says?'

'Maybe he can talk them down like a police negotiator.' He laughed at the visual scenario. 'Prendy seems to trust him and even Mandy's agreed to stay for a while after dark and she's the one who has most cause to fear. Apart from you, that is. I've got to say, I have my misgivings. At the first sign of trouble, we're out and I'm not letting you go this time if something decides to grab you.'

'I don't fear anything so long as I'm lying next to you.'

He moved his position to bring his face level with hers on the pillow. 'I'd like to hear what he has to say,' he whispered through his smile.

'I think you've become a believer after all.'

'Not really. I wish I could believe this is all being caused by souls of the dead. It would certainly make life a lot easier for me. But there's that practical voice inside me telling me this is all a big hoax and the joke's on me.'

'Are you scared of losing face in that eventuality?'

'Maybe. I don't know. Perhaps I'm scared of letting go of my own sense of reality that's grounded me throughout my life. It's difficult to lose conviction once it's been established. It's like giving away your strength.'

'No one will feel any the worse of you for opening your mind a little bit. I certainly wouldn't. I love the way your mind works and the way you attempt to seek out rational conclusion by taking in all the evidence first and applying it to the existing tenets of natural law. You're so wise and your knowledge base is very wide. You would either make a fantastic lawyer or be everyone's favourite partner in a pub quiz.'

They lay gazing at each other for a while in the way that lovers do before a kiss: when the eyes and a smile express so much more than words. Kie now wished he hadn't taken the door to his room away.

'That reconstruction was obscene.'

He played with a lock of her hair. 'He put on a very good show, but I'm not converted. He told the story in graphic detail but couldn't identify the assailant. He re-enacted the whole event from the boy's perspective and even said the boy knew who his attacker was. I think he's just forced us to bear witness to his own fantasies and that leaves me feeling sullied and even a wee bit duped.'

'He said the murderer was preventing the boy from telling tales.'

'Aye, that's a grand excuse.'

'Remember Ella MacAleavey at the séance? She also said there was someone there with him. She called it a devil and that we had to find his bones.'

'Whose bones was she talking about?'

'Peter's obviously. Maybe we should speak to her. Let's go and see her.'

'She'll find some chore for me to do that'll take all day.'

'You can always say no.' She moved her body closer to his.

'Ye ken I cannae say no tae a guid wummin!' He kissed her neck.

'Not even to Mandy Rutherford?'

'There's nought guid aboot Mary Rutherford, apart from her dress sense.'

Libby laughed as he playfully buried his mouth in her neck and his hands found the sensitive skin beneath her blouse.

'Besides,' he pressed his nose against hers, his eyes sultry, 'Mandy probably got that information from Mary Hyslop and Mystic Mitchell just repeated it to us.'

Libby squealed when she saw a figure in the door frame.

Fortunately it was Prendy who stood with his eyes shut closed and his fist balled in front of him as if knocking on an imaginary door. His face was flushed with embarrassment.

'It's OK, Prendy, we're decent.' She slapped Kie's hands away from her sides. 'You may open your eyes.'

'Sorry to bother you, but the psychic's had his glass of milk, been for his nap and …'

'… eaten his body weight in chocolate biscuits?' Kie interrupted.

'Yes, there's that, and he also wants to see us all in the sitting room before it gets too late.'

'Mr Mitchell, in the sitting room, with the lead piping!' Libby stood up and walked across the bed in the manner of a member of the undead rising from a grave.

'Tell Graymalkin we're coming.' Kie left the comfort of his mattress with an athletic leap, threw Libby over his shoulder and carried her, shrieking, down the stairs into the sitting room.

'I'm going to leave Peter Hyslop for now, loves, and move on to this house and its spirits because I've a good idea there's a strong connection between him and the rest of *them*.' Stephen Mitchell stressed the last word. 'I'm switching from psychic detective to rescue medium and that requires a big shift in the way I conduct the proceedings and needs you all to open your minds.' He stood by the low table delivering his next lesson as if he were speaking to primary school children. 'Psychic detective work only requires me to see and listen behind the veil. Mediumship asks a lot more of me. It requires me to force a connection with the spirit world and communicate with it; interact with it; and ask the spirits to perform certain behaviours. Does that make sense?'

'No.'

'What? Like circus tricks?'

'Not like circus tricks, Libby love. I'm going to clean-up this house and ask them all to move on. There are so many spirits here that I can't single any one of them out. It's an infestation. Something's holding them here, bonding them to this place, and they're unable to cross over. Some are angry, some complacent and a good few of them feel rage.'

'Can you tell what it is that's holding them all here?'

'I feel there's someone, in spirit form of course, behind them all, hiding in the shadows and telling them what to do. This amount of paranormal activity's rarely caused by one spirit. It's using the others, pooling their energies, to haunt this place and run amok. It's the ring-leader if you wish. Does that make sense?'

Libby shrugged and nudged Kie before he could say no again.

'It's an ancient, malevolent spirit and, quite possibly, the same force that pestered this place over three hundred years ago. We need to bring it out into the open.'

'The last time someone tried to do that, it dangled her five feet in the air.' Prendergast added his thoughts.

'Fortunately, I'm protected by my spirit guide and by my own strength of will. I won't allow anything to levitate me nor anyone else here to that matter. You must trust me. I can feel all of you have had run-ins with some of the nastier members of this otherworldly crew, but I won't let anything happen to you during my watch. You have my word.'

'I'll hold you to that.'

Kie waited for the flash of worry in the psychic's eyes, but it wasn't there. He decided he'd wait and see what happened and, if the evening became dangerous, he'd get everyone out.

— — —

They sat around the sitting room with the lights down low. The last of the sun's rays had just dropped over the eastern horizon and the hills were shrouded in a translucent blanket of murky mist. Stephen began the evening by closing his eyes and meditating for twenty minutes, sighing now and again and letting out intermittent cooing noises. He'd told them it was his way of protecting both himself and the living around him from any unwanted attention from the other side's more unsavoury characters. He said he was communicating with his spirit guide to help him.

Kie became more and more impatient as the minutes dragged on and wagged his foot. Prendy watched the psychic with forensic intensity and Mandy sat on the edge of her seat, becoming increasingly nervous at each sway of the pendulum of the old grandfather clock.

'Right!' They all jumped as Stephen suddenly woke from his contemplations. 'I'm ready. You may all follow me.' As if answering a silent call, he swept across the floor and skipped into the hall. 'There's a lady here. Hello, my love. She's in spirit form and she likes to walk up and down this staircase.'

'Who is she?' Libby, like the other two, appeared mesmerised by the man's performance and Kie wanted to throw him from the house by the scruff of his neck.

'Just a lost soul. Poor dear. Ah! Here's another one. He's new to this house.' Stephen floated up the stairs as if staging a dance routine. He ran on tiptoe across the upstairs hallway to the loft hatch.

Kie shrugged off Libby's hand as she tried to haul him after the psychic. 'He's completely taken you in, hasn't he?'

'I'm enjoying this but Mandy isn't. Look at her.'

The reporter was in tears again. She looked terrified and clung on to Prendergast as if he were the last piece of flotsam of a sinking ship in the middle of a cold ocean.

'Can you get that ladder down for me?'

Kie sighed and grabbed the pole from the side of the wall where he'd left it. He'd found it on the floor after the photographer died.

'No, don't open it!' Mandy was now hysterical.

The folding ladder came down with a squeal of hinges.

'Do you want me to go up and put the light on?' Kie put his foot on the ladder, but Stephen shook his head.

He pressed his palms against the metal rungs and turned to Mandy. 'Martin,' he put his hand to his ear as if listening to a radio turned down too low for him to hear properly. 'What's that, my love? Yes. Yes. All right, I'll ask.' He turned to Mandy. 'Martin wants to know why you folded the ladder up and locked him in the attic.'

All eyes turned to her for an answer. She shrank away from them. 'I didn't.'

'That's not what he says. He says he called you for help but you folded the ladder up and locked him in the attic.'

'It wasn't me, it was the ghost!'

'Martin asks if you're calling him a liar.'

'This is ridiculous!' Kie's temper was close to breaking point. He didn't know whether he was angry at the empty theatrics or at himself for allowing them to be staged in the first place. He felt like a fool following an imbecile.

'No, of course not.'

'Then why did you lock him in?'

'I just wanted to get away,' she sobbed. 'He was screaming and I thought I'd be next. Whatever it was up there with him, terrified him. I didn't want it coming after me so I took the pole and closed the hatch. I didn't think he would be locked in. I thought he could get out. I ran and hid under the stairs.' Mandy sank to her knees and wept.

'Martin climbed out of the skylight but slipped and fell off the roof.' Stephen delivered his words like a prayer at a funeral service. 'He doesn't blame you, Mandy. He's not going to take his anger with him to the next life. I've spoken to him and he's passed over.'

'What? He's passed over just like that?' Kie had heard enough. 'All these thousands of spirits locked inside these walls for centuries and one manages to break free after only floating around here for a couple of days? Come on, man, you take us all for idiots. Enough's enough. Get the hell out of my house!'

'Now there, lad. Let's just see what happens.' Prendergast patted his back.

'He's a fraud, Prendy, and he's got you all sucked into his theatrics. Look at him! He's loving this. It's his finest performance yet.'

'It's all right, Andrew love. I'm more than accustomed to this kind of outburst. It's the evil spirits controlling his emotions. They feed off anger and negative energies. It makes them stronger. I don't take it personally.'

'You can feed off my fucking fist! Now, that does make sense.'

An enormous thud above their heads finished the argument. Kie clambered up the ladder with a few choice oaths and pulled the light cord. The strip light fizzed on. He hauled himself into the attic, ignoring the frantic cries for caution from the people below. The attic was filled with boxes which were placed in neat stacks just as he'd left them. He moved across to the space where he thought the thump had come from, ducking his head under the rafters' wooden beams. Another thud behind him caused him to spin around.

'It's OK, it's just a fallen box of books.' He called down to answer the shrieks of concern.

He was alerted to the sound of faint scratching in the far corner of the room and moved around the boxes to see what was causing it. He managed to duck just in time as one of the books from the box hurtled past his head and landed against the wall. He felt the static bristling against the back of his neck and moved back slowly, having no wish to repeat the incident in the byre. The skylight window slammed open and Kie launched himself at the ladder and slid down it with the agility of a Chinese acrobat, remembering to pull the light switch during his descent. He landed on his feet, picked up the pole and closed the hatch with a slam.

'Nothing up there.'

Stephen shot him a narrow-eyed glance. 'Shall we continue or are you going to throw another tantrum?'

Kie set his jaw.

'It's very important we all remain calm and keep our emotions in neutral. That way, we won't give negative spirits fuel for their fire.'

'Your pants are on fire.'

'Pardon?'

'I think your spirit guide's attempting to send you signals. There's smoke coming from your trouser leg.'

Kie crossed his arms and bit back the smile as Prendy took his cardigan off and patted out the burning material before it could catch. At last, the psychic medium lost his supercilious grin and substituted it for an expression that could only be described as anxiety.

'I'm all right. I'm all right.' Stephen repeated, shaken by the realisation that he wasn't as invincible as he'd first believed. 'It's only Peter. He's a little tyke. He likes to start fires. That's what got him into trouble in the first place.'

'What do you mean?' Libby sidled up to Kie and slipped

her hand into his. He held it tightly, fearful that something bad was just about to happen that the medium would not be able to prevent.

'He likes to set fires. He likes to see the flames. He burned down a cow shed while the cattle were still in it. He didn't mean to but he was punished for it and paid the ultimate price.'

Stephen suddenly sat on the ground holding his stomach. 'Oh, there's a gentleman outside.' He held his arms up for assistance and Kie grabbed a wrist and hauled him to his feet. The psychic's face was pale and he looked as though he was about to vomit. They followed him downstairs as he staggered to the front door and stepped outside. The floodlights came on, lighting up the house and garden like a football stadium. 'He's not a pretty sight. He doesn't have a head.' He threw up on the ground.

Kie felt the blood in his veins freeze and, from the look on Prendy's face, knew he was thinking exactly the same thing.

'I think we should call it a night.'

'But I've only just started.' Stephen protested. 'I'll be all right. This gentleman is in spirit form. He keeps Peter very close. He has a secret.'

One of the floodlights exploded, plunging part of the garden into darkness.

'If I book you into a hotel tonight, would you come back tomorrow morning?' Prendy made a bold attempt to get the man to safety.

'Well, I suppose …'

'I'll pay the food and bar tab too.'

'He's filled with rage and sorrow. He did something very bad.'

Another light popped.

'I'll throw in a couple of barrels of biscuits.'

'Stephen, this is getting dangerous.' Libby couldn't hide her concern and Mandy rushed to the safety of the parked cars.

'It's OK, Peter, you can tell me. Come over here. He can't hurt you anymore.'

Kie didn't know whether it was reflex that caused him to push Stephen to the ground or whether he heard it coming, but the old four-bottom plough that had been sitting in the byre for decades, crash landed where Stephen had been standing. The noise of its impact was deafening and it left a deep furrow in the ground beneath it and showered them with turf and stones.

'Time to go.' He hauled a quaking psychic from the ground for the second time in less than three minutes and bundled him into the back of the Discovery. 'Get in the car!' He yelled to Libby and Prendy as he raced back into the house to get the keys and his wallet from the kitchen.

The hallway was once again covered in stones and the walls shook around him. He snatched up the keys and watched in astonishment as a kitchen knife hovered in the air between his eyes. He grabbed the handle and felt the resistance before it was pulled from his hand and clattered safely to the tiles. Something hit him on the back before smashing and he spun around again to find a ceramic milk jug in pieces on the floor. There was whispering close to his ear and disjointed voices wailed around him. The knocking, thudding and banging reached a deafening crescendo and Kie pressed his hands against his ears. He tried to walk but his legs felt leaden and wouldn't move to his will. He felt stinging pressure on his forearm and noticed a bite mark appearing on the skin. The pain caused his anger to rise and, very soon, it consumed him.

'Get the fuck out of my house! You're not welcome here. This is my home and I've had enough of this.' He roared across the emptiness. 'Get out all of you!'

He was answered by a sudden stillness that was even more overwhelming than the noisy assault. Time simply seemed to stop. His footsteps echoed across the hallway, resonating around the walls and ceiling to return to his ears, as he stepped cautiously towards the front door.

That sense of dread again hit him like a club and he turned around. A dark shape hovered at the top of the staircase. It had a vague human form but the similarities to anything earthly ended there. Parts of it were blacker than the darkest night. It pulsed with menace and exuded an evil so violent that Kie felt every hair in his body rising. His skin stung.

He resisted the urge to run and the effort caused the sweat to bead across his body, rendering his clothes sodden. He stood, aching with cold, his feet rooted to the boards, hearing only the steady beat of his own heart and the air flowing in and out of his lungs.

The shape, its mass like a roiling thunder cloud, shimmered in the gloom on the landing above him in front of a gently swaying chandelier. Like the smoking remnants of a snuffed candle, the mist billowed outwards and spiralled into the air, parting in the centre to reveal a small figure. It wore a cape made of sacking with the cowl pulled up and stood with its back to him.

With one foot on the staircase, the other unable to move, Kie thought he'd turned to stone. He felt the challenge growling inside his head but held his ground.

'Thought I'd made myself clear. Get out!' he hissed into the space between them and dragged his trailing leg forwards and up.

With an almighty bellow, the figure spun around and Kie obeyed his inherent survival instinct: he ran. Sprinting across the gravel towards the car, he felt the entity close on his heels.

He sensed the rage and the violence infecting his soul and devouring all the goodness around it; swallowing it whole; feeding off it. He threw himself into the driver's seat and tried to fit the key into the ignition, but his hands were by now shaking uncontrollably. His passengers screamed at him as one, joining the unearthly voices raging inside his head.

'Kie, it's a push button start.' Libby's voice called him back.

At last he heard the roar of the engine as it fired up and he threw the car into gear, speeding off into the night and away from the terrors it contained.

'What were you running from? You scared the living daylights out of us.' Prendergast clutched at his chest.

'I thought I saw something. It was nothing.'

In the mirror, his eyes met those of Stephen Mitchell sitting quietly in the back. He was smiling.

chapter 42

THE SUMMONING

'Hello again, Mary, may I come in?'

'Of course, Mr Prendergast, please excuse the way I look.' Mary Hyslop blushed and smoothed her hair down with her floured hands, streaking her soft curls with sticky dough. 'I haven't seen you around here for a while. Aren't you staying at The Ring anymore?'

'We feel it provident to stay away at night times at the moment, Mary. I've got lodgings in Castle Douglas quite close to where Libby lives. Kie's staying with her until further notice.'

'We're going to miss that lad around here. I hope this stops soon for selfish reasons. We've all grown very fond of him.'

Prendergast cleared his throat and followed her into her homely kitchen where he guessed she spent most of her days idling away her time in domestic activity rather than seeking out the lessons of life from beyond her front door.

'I'd like to ask you a few questions, if I may.' He began awkwardly. 'It's police business this time.'

'Certainly, Mr Prendergast.'

'Come now, Mary, we know each other well enough for you to call me Andrew.' He hoped the cordiality would put her at her ease as she fussed over the mess on the kitchen table and worktops, her plump cheeks glowing red.

'Andrew it is then,' she giggled. 'Have a seat. I'll put the kettle on.'

'Mary, I'm going to ask you a few questions about Peter.

Would that be all right?'

She gave him a cheerful nod.

'Have you kept anything by of his?'

'His room's just as he left it ten years ago.' She sighed. 'Call me sentimental if you must, but I haven't had the heart to change it.' She washed her hands in the old butler's sink, scrubbing at her fingernails with a large nailbrush, before wiping them on her apron. 'Never know when he'll come back to visit.'

'Would you mind if I took a look around?'

'Not at all.'

She led her guest up the narrow staircase where an old stair carpet, threadbare with years of scrupulous scrubbing, clung on to its last remaining nails and one or two brass runners.

'Watch you don't trip now. I don't have a man to do the handiwork here and the place is falling 'round about my ears. I was going to ask MacAoidh to fix the runners back for me before an accident happens.'

'I'm certain he'd be happy to oblige. He's a good lad.'

'Aye, he certainly is.'

Peter's room sat to the left of the small landing, it's narrow windows facing the back of the house. Like the rest of Mary's home, the room was a shrine to a bygone past with few signs of contemporary living. The thick curtains were of a ghastly brown and orange floral design, popular in the fifties, and hung from an aged brass rail. The simple oak bed was dressed with real woollen blankets and a light blue candlewick bedspread. There were no posters on the walls and a few toys, including that grisly Operation game, were neatly placed inside a large wooden-railed toy box, dating back to the last century.

'Don't know what you're looking for.' Mary rearranged the ornately designed vanity set on the lace mat before placing them back to their former position.

'There's a lot of looking around in police work,' Prendy said as he opened the door to the tiny wardrobe. 'A person's room is very special. It tells you a lot about that person.'

'So what does Peter's room tell you then?'

'Oh, that he was a simple, quiet boy with a doting mother.' He really wanted to substitute 'doting' for 'controlling', but thought the better of it. 'Was Peter a good son?'

'Of course he was. What do you mean by that, Andrew?'

He detected an element of defensiveness in her answer. 'I've got two sons of my own, Mary. They're grown up now but, believe me, they were challenging teenagers: always falling in and out of trouble.' He laughed in order to reassure her of the apparent innocence of his question. 'In my experience, kids turn into monsters when they reach that magical age of puberty.'

'Well, my Peter never gave me any trouble.'

'What about your neighbours? Did he ever cause trouble with them?'

Mary changed from innocuous sap to fiery defender within a blink. 'You know what neighbours are like. The first sign of trouble and they blame the young.'

Prendergast already knew Peter's story, but wanted Mary to tell it to him. 'Was your son blamed for something that happened to one of the neighbours?'

She waved her hand at him, her mild manner returning cautiously. 'Jim and Margaret thought he was responsible for setting alight to their byre and burning it down with the cattle inside.'

'Why would they believe Peter was the perpetrator?'

'Because Aaron Patterson liked to burn things. He was one of those pie-maniacs.'

'Pyromaniacs?'

'Aye, that's it. He went to the doctors about it and got some medicine.'

'So you believe Aaron Patterson burned down the byre and Peter was in some way implicated in the crime?'

'My Peter had nothing to do with it.' She crossed her arms against the front of her well-worn apron.

'Can we sit down somewhere please, Mary? I'd like to speak to you.'

'I'm very busy today, Andrew. Maybe another time.'

'It's not a question, Mary. I'm going to have to insist. Now either we do it here, in the comfort of your own home, or we go for a little drive to the police station. You're withholding very important information that won't do either you or the memory of your son any good at all.'

He followed her down the stairs once more, almost tripping on the lumpy stair carpet. She led him into her tiny sitting room which smelled of polishing spray and stale talcum powder. The crowded surfaces of the tables and cupboards told her family's life story over the generations. Prendergast perched on the edge of one of the mismatched chairs with crocheted arm covers and waited for her to sit down.

He began gently. 'I've just come from Margaret Black's house.'

'Marge is a big gossip. I wouldn't believe anything she tells you.' Mary crossed her arms and legs at random intervals as if she couldn't get comfortable.

'That may be so, but I'm trained well enough to weed out the rumour in order to get to the truth. As I understand it, the night Jim Black's byre burned down, Jim found Peter stuck on a barbed wire fence, seemingly running away from the scene. I was told the boy managed to free himself before he was caught and ran off into the night. I also understand, from Margaret's testimony today, that both you and the Pattersons told the police both boys were in Aaron's room that night until you went over to The Ring to get Peter at seven forty-five.'

'Aye, that's right. Aaron and Peter were good friends. It was ten years ago, though, I can't really remember the exact time.' She uncrossed her legs and wedged her fingers between her knees. Prendergast noticed her hands were shaking.

'The police report claims the barn was burned down at about eight in the evening, so yours and the Pattersons' statements ruled out any guilt on the boys' part for the crime of fire-raising.'

'I told you, he was a good boy.'

'I have a hunch, Mary, and my hunches rarely let me down.' She now pressed her shoulders into the back of her chair.

'I'll put it to you frankly. Aaron and Peter went out that night looking for mischief. Whether they intended such extensive damage or not, they set alight to the straw of the byre and the fire got out of hand. All that methane and dry material amongst the wintering cattle in that byre caused an enormous explosion and Jim Black's life went up in flames. With no one else to blame, the insurance company believed Jim started the fire deliberately in order to defraud them and Jim lost his livelihood, and everything he and your father had spent their lives working towards, in the course of one night. All this loss and suffering was caused by a prank by two naughty teenage boys looking for a bit of excitement to counteract their boredom.'

'The police questioned my Peter. He knew nothing about the fire.' There was no hint of shame in her expression.

'He was your brother, Mary. You lied to save your son from a stern telling off from the children's panel and possibly a spell of counselling, but that same lie caused your brother's ultimate ruin. Now, I know you want to do the right thing. You don't strike me as a bad woman. I want you to tell me truthfully your version of the events.'

'Will I be arrested?'

'I'll be honest with you. That depends on whether the police and procurator fiscal decide to punish you for withholding evidence and giving false statements, thereby perverting the course of justice. In view of the subsequent events, however, it's possible they may agree to look away. I'll speak to them on your behalf. Of course, I can't speak for your sister-in-law who may decide to take the matter further, in view of your brother's subsequent suicide.'

'She won't take it further.'

Prendergast was taken aback by her certainty. 'Oh?'

'No, she's too ashamed. This is a small community, Andrew, and people don't like the notion of others knowing their business. Yes, I lied to the police and to Jim when he came 'round my door in the middle of the night, stinking of whisky and raging about how he saw Peter running away from the burning shed. I made my statement and the Pattersons made theirs and we hoped that would be the end of it. But Jim's got a nasty temper and he took matters into his own hands.'

'In what way, Mary?'

'Jim killed Peter. My own brother did those terrible things to my boy and then drowned him in the burn. We all know it, but can't prove it in this world. Margaret's always known but she's too ashamed to admit it. Instead of burying my Peter's body like we should've, we've buried the secret instead and we're all being punished for our sin. Every one of us.'

– – –

'He's fixing the lawn mower.'

'There's nothing wrong with it.' Libby put her bag down and looked out of the kitchen window into her garden. Her eyes widened when she saw Kie beating the electric mower with a spanner. 'All right, there probably is now.' She turned around to Prendergast. 'He's like a caged animal. We'll either have to let him go or sedate him.'

'It's not safe, Libby. Maybe you should take yourselves off somewhere. Take a holiday. Get him out of here and give him a break.'

'I've tried suggesting that but he doesn't want to leave. He just wants to go back and face whatever it is that's taken up residence in his home. The only trouble is, he doesn't know how to defeat it and that's what's frustrating him the most.'

Three days had passed since they fled from The Ring with the psychic and none of them had any wish to return there, even during the day. The psychic had gone back to Carlisle, blaming Kie for feeding the negative energies with his foul temper. Mandy had returned to Glasgow, finally facing her shame for causing the untimely death of her work colleague through her cowardly actions before his death. Kie had spent the three days at Libby's house which, although was not cramped, didn't enjoy the same open spaces as The Ring afforded and he was slowly going stir crazy.

Prendergast sat at the kitchen table pouring through some paperwork. Libby had just returned from a day's work at the office and felt physically drained.

'I've had quite an eventful day. I've only just got here myself,' he said.

'Oh yes?'

'I've had some very interesting conversations with The Ring's former residents and neighbours. I even managed to speak to the couple who sold Kie the house. You know, the Renwicks who now live in Lochgilphead?'

'What did they say?' Kie came through the back door, said

hello to Prendy, gave Libby a quick kiss and washed his hands in the kitchen sink.

'Libby, that twig on the window sill needs watering.'

'Drown it for me would you?'

'I think it's dead.' Kie trickled water into the soil from a glass.

'No it's not, it's just thirsty.'

'Like the other plants in this house?'

'No, they're dead.'

'They admitted that paranormal activity in the house was one of the main reasons why they left.' Prendergast waited for the outburst but it didn't come. Kie remained strangely calm.

'You could sue them, you know.'

'Who?'

'Stambovsky versus Ackley in nineteen ninety one. It's an American case where the purchasers of a haunted house successfully sued the seller for failing to tell them in the particulars the house had noisy ghosts. The appellate court allowed the buyers rescission of the contract, notwithstanding the doctrine of caveat emptor.'

'That's the same country that awarded thousands of dollars' worth of damages to a woman who crashed her brand new camper van. She threw it into cruise control, then went into the back of it and made herself a sandwich!' Kie almost smiled.

'Good grief,' Prendergast looked astonished, 'she was awarded damages for that?'

'Aye, and she was given a considerable sum for her injuries plus a new van because the handbook didn't tell her she actually had to be behind the wheel when operating the vehicle in cruise control. You wouldn't get away with that in Scotland.'

'You might get away with suing the seller of the house, nevertheless. I think I could put up a very good argument based on the Strambovsky principles.'

Kie's laugh was bitter. 'I don't want rescission, I just want the right to live there. Could I sue the dead for breaching my human right to respect for private life?'

'Only if you can identify the potential defendant. A black blob is not descriptive enough to prove identity. Sorry, Prendy, you were saying?'

'Oh yes. Their strange activity wasn't anything like as serious as ours, but objects would go missing to turn up later on in odd places. There were a couple of small fires, but nothing very serious. Their little girl apparently spoke to an invisible child at night and, apart from the usual knocks, bangs and a few flying stones, that was the extent of their haunting. What was interesting is they blamed the Pattersons for unleashing the spirits into the house. Apparently, Aaron was fond of the Ouija board.'

'And what bearing does that have on all this?'

Prendy shrugged. 'I've heard Ouija boards, if used by people who don't know what they're doing or who don't know how to protect themselves, can summon much more than a few curious spirits.'

'Summon?'

'Yes, as in call up from the grave.'

'Right.'

Since their last experience at The Ring, Libby noticed a distinct shift in Kie's attitude towards dialogue on the paranormal. He no longer questioned the theories of spirit agents or supernatural forces, but tended to go quiet instead when they were being discussed. She wondered what he'd seen in the house and what made him flee it in such panic that night. She hadn't asked him because she really didn't want to know. She trusted he'd finally come to terms with the implausible but wasn't at all at ease with it. That made him sullen and withdrawn and she wished she could snap him out of his bleak mood.

'There's more. I meant to tell you after my visit to York, but there was so much going on that it slipped my mind. The Pattersons told me they'd lived for years at The Ring without any trouble of a supernatural nature. That changed, however, when the Hyslop boy died. Aarron Patterson apparently tried to reach him through a Ouija board and that seems to be when the first of the trouble started. Although it was at the time pretty benign and gentle.'

'So Aaron and his toy telephone to the dead started all this?'

'Looks like it, Libby.'

She cast a quick glance over at Kie as he drank a glass of water. He didn't appear at all interested in the conversation.

'There's even more.' Prendergast also eyed Kie and waited for his attention. 'Jim Black killed Peter Hyslop. Unable to live with the shame, Black then killed himself.'

'Tell me something we don't know.'

'Mary Hyslop and Margaret Black knew about it, as well as some of their closer friends. They agreed between them to keep the secret until the boy's body turned up and they could prove he'd been murdered. Mary believes they're being punished for their sins. She believes the spirits are angry with them, that Peter's angry with them, and wants a proper burial. To do that, we need to find out what Jim did with his body.'

'Find his bones,' Libby echoed.

To her surprise, Kie laughed. 'Mary thinks she's being punished for her sins? That's just grand.' He gritted his teeth, trying to keep his temper at bay. 'So why am I being punished? What sin did I commit to warrant the unwanted attention of the dead?' He slammed the glass down in the sink with an angry curse.

'You're not being punished, MacAoidh, you're just caught in the crossfire of two incompatible worlds. I'll get a team together and see if we can find that body. Jim must've buried it nearby; perhaps he even buried it under the Ghost Tree. If it's there, we'll find it and hopefully put this trouble to bed for good.'

Kie placed his hands on the sink and gripped its edge, his head hung below his shoulders. 'I don't think it will make much difference whether we find the lad's bones or not. *Domhnall Dubh* doesn't care about bones.'

Prendy was just about to ask him to elucidate on the Gaelic words, but Libby put her hand on his arm. Kie was trying to say something he'd been deliberating about for days and was already finding it difficult.

He kept his voice low and level. 'You want to know what I saw in the house the last night we were there? You want to know why I haven't been back?' He shook his head as if he didn't quite believe himself what he was about to tell them. He took a deep, heavy breath. 'I met *Domhnall Dubh*, the devil. He stood on my stairs and challenged me to fight him. I ran instead.' He raised his head and looked at them through those astonishing eyes. 'I want you to persuade Stephen Mitchell to come back. I need to speak with him.'

Chapter 43

THE DEMON

'I've no idea what you did here, my dearest boy, or what you've said to them, but the spirits are gone.'

'What do you mean by gone?'

'They've left, departed, vamoosed.' Stephen Mitchell held his hands out in the air and flicked his wrists as if shooing off birds from his garden. They stood in the sitting room with the morning light spilling in a blaze of glory across the walls and floor. 'This house, to coin a Holywood phrase, is clean.'

He sat down, picked up his coffee mug and gorged himself on the plate of biscuits on the marble table.

'Where are your partners in crime this morning?'

Kie felt a wave of elation wash across him, but kept it in reserve. 'Libby's working and Prendy's at the police station with Mary Hyslop and Margaret Black. They're changing their statements and the polis are opening up Peter's case again.'

'Woops! You've done it now, my love. I feel the presence of the boy and his headless killer outside. Sometimes it's best not to speak about them.' He gave Kie a knowing wink.

'Speaking about them brings them back?'

'Those two never left and there's still something lurking in the shadows. I can smell it there like a bad breath, but I can't see it. I believe it comes and goes at will. At the moment, it's not here. Possibly the daylight helps to keep it at bay. It'll be stronger in the dark. I'm afraid this little trio of lost souls are here to stay until they're persuaded to leave.'

'And I thought you said the place was clean.' Kie sat down, the sudden wave of euphoria broken against the negative qualification of the psychic's announcement.

'It's certainly a lot cleaner than it was.'

'But three of them are still here.'

'The big one's holding the other two here.'

'Why?'

'Like in life, no one wants to be alone. You got rid of his playmates, he's not going to let the other two get away from him if he can help it. He'll keep them very close; he'll hide the secret for as long as he can.'

'What secret?'

'Oh, come on love, where've you been for the past couple of days? I thought I made it clear that finding the boy's grave with him in it will tell the world what happened to him. Everyone's ignoring him and he's very sad and frustrated.'

'Couldn't I just tell him to get out?'

'It's not as easy as that, love.'

'That's what I did the other night.'

'What did you say to them?'

Kie shrugged. 'I told them to leave.' He raked his hand through his hair. 'I wasn't very polite about it.'

'That's sometimes all that's necessary.' Stephen picked up another biscuit and stuffed it into his mouth. 'You see, like I said, love, we're the same people whether we're living or dead. If you gatecrash a party and the owner of the house tells you to beat it, then that's what you'll do politely and without any fuss. No one wants to be somewhere they're not welcome. Spirits are just the same as us. Does that make sense? Peter, Jim Black and the naughty spirit are the exception to the rule.' He threw his arms and eyes to the skies to dramatise the tragedy, 'there's always one! Or three in our case,' he laughed as if he'd just told a very witty joke.

'Remember that ancient spirit you spoke of a few days ago? The one you said may have been the Rerrick Parish Poltergeist? I met it.'

'Yes, I know, pet. I saw it in your eyes. Evil spirits are unfortunately a bugbear in my business. They attach themselves to people normally and feed off their energies. At first I believed it was feeding off yours, but I don't think it singled you out until now. You're strong, MacAoidh. Your life force is very powerful and it's testing that strength. It sees you as a challenge and a threat.'

'How did it get here?'

'Maybe it's been lying dormant here for hundreds, even thousands, of years. Maybe the murder, which would've caused a big spike in the energy fields in the immediate environment, helped to bring it to the surface.'

'What about a Ouija board?'

Stephen stopped munching, his masticated biscuit stored in his swollen cheek, and gave MacAoidh a stern glare. 'Please don't tell me you've been playing with that awful device, love. They can be very dangerous in the hands of amateurs.'

'No, not me. I heard someone used a Ouija board in this house over a decade ago and that's when the trouble started.'

Kie could barely believe he was speaking to an outrageously effeminate psychic about demons in his house. At that point in time, his entire world had gone insane.

'Then that's how it got here. It was invited, which makes our task to get rid of it even harder. Evil spirits, or demons as we like to call them, are very good at pretending they're someone else. They take on the guise of a friendly or familiar spirit in order to lull the living and even other spirits into a false sense of security and invite them to come and play. Once they're established, they're a massive pain in the bum to get rid of.'

'Can you get rid of it?'

'I could try, love, but I doubt it'll listen to me. I'm a shepherd, not a hunter.'

'Meaning?'

'I use gentle persuasion on the spirit world. I'm their friend. I don't work with hostile haunts if the evil spirit doesn't want to leave.'

'Is that what you call this? A hostile haunt?'

'Very much so.' Stephen leaned forwards as far as his belly would allow. 'Look, my love, I understand your world has been rocked and you can barely comprehend what's happening to you, but I'm going to give you some good advice. You're strong and you're sharp. You've got a temper on you and know how to use it to intimidate. These demons are only human spirits. They're not, as Christians will tell you, some evil entity stirred up from the bowels of hell to wreak havoc on the world of the living. As people are bad in life, so are they also bad in the spirit world. Just because a murderer has left his earthly body, doesn't mean he's not still a murderer in spirit. Does that make sense?'

'I think so.' Kie hated the way the man always asked that question after delivering his information.

'Good, then I'll tell you something else.' He popped the last biscuit in his mouth and dabbed at the crumbs on the plate with his forefinger. 'There are loads of reasons why these evil spirits infest houses like yours. Some want retribution for wrongs done to them when they were alive; others simply don't know where else to go. Some are mischievous and want to play; while others are harmful and want to offend. This spirit, I feel, is a man who wants to do nothing else but control. He's latched on to this place and sees it as his. He wants you to kneel to him, worship him as you would a god. He wants to break you. It's up to you to not allow that. Does that make …'

'Aye, it makes bloody sense,' Kie didn't mean to snap. He slumped back in his chair and breathed out his frustration. 'Tell me how to fight it.'

'It's hard to fight off a psychic attack of something that resentful and malevolent. He's set up home here and you're standing in his way. It's bollocks to say dark spirits fear the light or certain religious symbols burn them and send them screaming into the hills. If you're an unbeliever in the living world, then you're not going to suddenly find god when you're a spirit. The only thing that can get rid of it is probably another spirit and, since you've got rid of them all, we'll be hard pushed persuading the boy or Jim Black to guide it over. It's too strong for them. So we're left with you, my love. Positive energy is the only weapon you have. Whatever you do, however, don't enter into a conversation with it.'

'Don't worry, I won't.'

'Be forceful with him; love him if you have to. It'll confuse him.'

'And provoke it further. That thing came after me.'

'That *thing* wanted to scare you and it did. Didn't it, love? Try being a bit more forthright when you next meet him. Stand your ground and don't let him get the better of you.'

'That's not so easily said when it's howling down the stairs towards you. That thing almost killed Libby.'

'That *thing* simply wanted to frighten you by attacking the people you care for. It's only dangerous if you're weak.'

'It's caused the deaths of three people.'

'It's just helped them along, that's all. How I understand it, the minister had a weak heart; Jim Black was a heavy drinker with suicidal tendencies; and the photographer, poor sweetheart, was so frightened he made a bad decision to escape through the skylight, slipped on the slates and plunged to his death. Had that horrible, cowardly Mandy not closed the attic hatch in her terror, he would still be alive.'

'I want you to take me to it, wherever it is.'

'What? Now?'

'I'm not waiting for night when it's at its strongest. I want to meet it when I'm at my best and that's during the daytime. Find it for me now, Stephen. Please.'

Stephen sat for a while, apparently pondering on the probabilities of his own survival in the event of finding the entity. In the end he conceded with a dramatic sigh. 'You're lucky you've got such gorgeous eyes. I'm afraid I can't resist them. I'll have to meditate for a while. I need to protect both of us if this gets ugly.'

'Fine.'

'Then I'll need another packet of biscuits and a nice milky coffee afterwards.'

Kie laughed and left the greedy psychic to his contemplations. He felt a difference in the house as he walked around it. There was a levity about the atmosphere he hadn't experienced before. Those rooms where the sunlight poured through were washed with a calm serenity and sensation of peace. He dared the staircase, the landing and the bedrooms, half expecting a shadow to cross his vision, a piece of furniture to move or an object to hit him, but the house was still. Inspecting each room in turn, he reflected on the probability of ridding the property of its mischievous spirits, simply by telling them to go. It had gone quiet before, but that lull never quite managed to conceal the breath of the storm that was to follow. This time, the house was bathed in beauty and Kie felt at last he was winning this battle and ending the poltergeist's reign of terror for another three hundred years at least.

He sat in the kitchen for a while, reading a paper, his coffee going cold. He then went outside to inspect the outbuildings and was joined by Jim Black's collie. The dog came and went as it pleased. Sometimes it would get in his car if it fancied going with him to Libby's, the shops or the neighbours and other times it would take off back home to Margaret but rarely entered her house, or so Margaret claimed. If Kie decided to go for a walk in the hills, the dog would always be there beside him. The animal had a sharp sense of smell and almost a sixth sense for knowing when it was time for a walk. It was only when he sat on the patio chair, patting its head that he realised he didn't even know its name. He'd never thought to ask.

'That dog's seen more than it should.' Stephen stood with his arms outstretched and his heavy stomach hanging out as he took a huge yawn in the late morning breeze.

'Now you speak to dogs?'

'And why not? Dogs like being spoken to and they speak back. Don't you boy?'

'Well, you're obviously not listening properly because he's a she.'

'Sorry girl, Stevie Weavie's a bad boy,' Stephen bent down to the dog and allowed its long, pink tongue to lick his mouth.

Kie shuddered in disgust. 'I wouldn't let her do that, if I were you.'

'Why not? She just wants a little kissy wissy, don't you girl? Good girl.'

'Aye, she's just been licking her arse.'

Stephen scrubbed his sleeve against his mouth and spat a few times on the ground. 'I'm ready. Let's go and find your demon.'

They returned to the bottom of the stairs where Stephen stood for long moments, listening to the silence with his head to one side. Kie followed as the psychic swept up the stairs again,

THE DEMON

bounding on his tip toes with the enthusiasm of the Sugar Plum Fairy on steroids. He stopped below the attic hatch.

'He's upstairs.' He pointed upwards with his podgy finger.

'Why does it always have to be the worst place in the house?' Kie sighed and grabbed the pole to the ladder.

Stephen laid his hand on his arm and shook his head. 'Hold strong, MacAoidh, love. Why should you go to him? Let him come and get you.'

'Are you sure you know what you're doing?' Kie gripped the pole and decided not to put it down.

'Trust me.'

'The last time I trusted you, I was forced to save you from a flying plough.'

'He's not as strong in the light.'

'I thought you said the light couldn't harm him.'

'That's not the light I was talking about.'

'Why are we whispering?'

'Because we don't want him,' Stephen pointed to the ceiling again, 'to hear us.'

'If he can't hear us, how the hell is he going to know we're here?'

A loud thump in the attic caused them both to jump.

'He knows.'

'This is ridiculous.'

Kie stabbed the pole into the catch and hauled on the ladder. It dropped with a scream. Fighting back the trepidation and willing his courage not to fail him, he scrambled up the ladder and pulled the light cord. The string came away in his hand but the light didn't come on.

'*A mhic na galla!*'

'Is that rude?'

'Very. I'll get a torch. Wait here.'

Kie ran across the hallway and down the stairs. He snatched his head torch hanging at the back of the kitchen door and raced up the stairs again. When he reached the ladder, Stephen was nowhere to be seen. He heard the adrenaline pumping in his temples and felt his heart violently beating against his ribs as he stared up into the darkness of the loft through the hatch above his head. He heard a faint scratching and wanted nothing more than to take flight: to back away from the menace waiting for him in the black space above his head. He already sensed the claustrophobic veil of night squeezing the breath from his lungs.

'Time to slay a demon.'

He secured the torch to his head, turned it on and put a foot on the ladder. The bright ray from his forehead was devoured by the shadows. He breathed away the ensuing panic and hauled what remained of his courage, kicking and screaming, into the light.

'AAAAAARGH!'

He leaped around as something grabbed his shoulder and yelled again as the screaming mouth of a horrified Stephen bellowed back at him.

'What the fuck are you trying to do to me?' Kie was shaking so much he was certain he heard his own bones rattling.

Stephen clamped his hands to his right breast as if to prevent his own heart from bursting out of his chest. 'You've just given me the fright of my life.' He tried to control his breathing by panting, his lips pursing and grimacing consecutively with every three or so exhales.

'I gave *you* a fright? What were you doing sneaking up behind me?'

'I thought I saw something in that bedroom. I went to investigate.'

The pallor had drained from the psychic's face as he tried in vain to bring his breathing under control. His terror dissipating, Kie suddenly saw the funny side of the last few moments and began to laugh. Still wheezing Stephen slapped him playfully on the arm and joined him in his amusement.

'Sometimes I think the only demons on this earth are the ones inside our heads.'

Kie stopped laughing and Stephen spun around to see what he was staring at.

'OK, Joe, get us safely out of here.'

'Joe?' Kie kept his gaze locked on the dark shape by the banister at the top of the stairs. It had begun as just a small shadow but was steadily growing in size to fill the upper landing.

'My spirit guide.'

'A Native American called Joe?' Kie began to lose all confidence once more.

'Yes and he's working on it.'

'Tell him to hurry up about it, that's the only way out unless you want to brave the roof and end up looking like a burst sack of tatties in the flower border.' Kie picked up the metal pole and hefted it in his hands.

'Put that down, you're aggravating it.'

'No. You told me yourself, I should make a stand and that's what I'm making. Come on.'

Kie stepped forwards, cautiously at first; Stephen shuffling behind him, clinging to the back of his T-shirt.

'When I say run, you run.'

'What? We're not going through that thing.'

'Run!'

With the pole held aloft in his hands, and bellowing his challenge as if in the front line of battle, Kie charged at the black shape and leapt at it. He felt Stephen's hands let go of his clothes as he sailed through the darkness and gritted his teeth against the terrible sensation of torment and rage he felt cloying at his skin as he passed through to the other side. The next thing he knew, he was tumbling down the stairs with an even louder yell. His head hit the floor and the wind flew from his lungs as a heavy pressure landed on his torso. When he eventually came to his senses, he groaned.

THE STALKER

'That's the very last time I'm ever going in there. If you break anything else, you're on your own.'

'I didn't break anything, I've got two fractured ribs and a lump on my skull that's all.'

'That's all?'

Libby helped Kie into the car and slammed the passenger door. She spun around to stick two fingers up at the nurses who were watching her from Kie's empty wheelchair at the entrance to the emergency department. He'd refused to get into it but they followed him out anyway.

'Do you know that bitch actually accused me to my face of deliberately fracturing your ribs and giving you that bump on your head? How did she think I did that? Jumped all over you when you were asleep?'

'Calm down, Libby.'

'What part of her tiny brain decided that a woman who's a foot shorter than you and whose thighs have a smaller circumference than your forearm, has managed to smash you up into little bits?'

'She's only doing her job.'

'Well, I'm considering suing the hospital for defamation. Everyone in that ward heard her accusations.'

'Get over it, Libby, you're making my headache worse.'

She turned to face him before putting the key in the ignition. 'Are you going to tell me how you got into this state?'

Kie's breathing was shallow and laboured. She lifted his T-shirt and sighed at the dark bands of horizontal bruising on his chest. She felt a pang of contrition as he closed his eyes, still bleary from the amount of pain killers the medical staff had pumped into his body.

'We were fetching a pail of water and fell down the stairs.' He looked at her and smiled through his pain. 'Don't make me laugh. It hurts.'

'You're the one telling the jokes. So how did you manage to break your crown?' The smile twitched against the side of her lips and he growled in pain.

'Stephen Mitchell and I had an accident. We took a tumble down the stairs and I hit my head.'

'And fractured your ribs? What did Jill break when he came tumbling after you?'

'My ribs broke his fall.' He wriggled his body beneath the seatbelt and tried not to sound so amused.

'He landed on top of you?' The laughter burst from her mouth before she could check it.

'Aye, they say the bruising was caused by a crush injury. Stop it, will you?' She saw the tears streaming down his cheeks and didn't know whether the reaction was caused by the effort to contain his laughter or whether his ribs were truly on fire.

The drive to Castle Douglas took longer than usual as Libby was forced to stop the car a few times to allow Kie to throw up on the verge. She gave him a few more painkillers that he washed down with a six-month-or-so-old half empty bottle of juice she'd found under the driver's seat.

By the time they reached her house, he was fast asleep. She took some time to examine him and wondered whether his nightmare would ever truly end. He looked so peaceful for a haunted man. She stole a small kiss from his lips and gently closed the car door, allowing him some rare moments of calm for a while.

'Aw, that's nice. You two an item now?'

'Hannah!' Libby flung her arms around her friend. 'It's so good to see you.'

'I went to The Ring but there was no one at home. The neighbour told me Kie was staying with you. What's PH-07351 done with all the doors?'

'It's a long story, so I hope you've got time.'

'I have a few days. There are some things I need to speak about to both of you.'

'He's sleeping at the moment. He took a tumble down the stairs with a psychic medium. I don't really know the whole story, but I don't want to wake him just yet. He hit his thick skull again but it didn't fracture. Two of his ribs, however, did.'

'Poor darling's been in the wars lately. He'll need plenty of pain killers and don't give into the urge to bandage his chest. He needs to be able to open those lungs, no matter how much it hurts. He's going to be in quite a lot of pain over the next few weeks and he'll need to rest.'

'He's one of life's copers.'

'I take it the property is still very active.'

'Yes and no, but let's talk about that over a glass of wine. You're staying here with us, right?'

'Us? I'd love to.' Hannah laughed that Gatling gun titter that Libby had missed.

By the time Libby was half way through her tale, it was well after dark. Hannah had listened with forensic concentration and taken copious notes down in her little black book.

'I must say, I'd love to meet this Stephen bloke.'

'No doubt you will tomorrow. He's staying at the same hotel as Prendy for the next day or so. You can give him the MI5 treatment then.' Libby pulled back the curtain and peered out at the car. Kie was still sleeping.

'You're horribly in love with him, aren't you?'

'He's the man I've been waiting for all my life, Hannah. He's warm, affectionate, strong-willed and so intelligent. He's also a man of honour with my kind of sense of humour. There's nothing about him I don't admire and respect. I really do love him and I think that was a certainty from the moment I met him.'

'Wow! That's a deep plunge you've taken. Will you survive it if it doesn't work out?'

'No, I don't think I'd live after that one.'

'Has he told you he loves you yet?'

'He's too cautious. He's not the kind of man who takes love lightly.'

'Nor says words he doesn't feel?'

Libby sighed. 'I hope one day I'll wake up and he'll whisper those three little words in my ear, even in Gaelic: *tha gaol agam ort.*'

'That's four words.'

'Who's counting?'

'Maybe he is.'

'I've learned that phrase in the hope I'll recognise it if he utters it in his sleep.'

'I really wish you the best. He's a great catch.'

'He's not a salmon, Hannah.' She had to laugh at the pragmatism her friend always adhered to. Hannah was a realist. There was little that was sentimental about her.

'You know. We had a good listen to some of those EVPs we recorded at The Ring during our investigations. Remember the one we thought mentioned Charlie?'

'Yes, poor Charlie. Did you go to his funeral?'

'It was lovely. We gave him a great send-off and I miss him in my life.'

'Sorry, I interrupted you there.'

'We ran some white noise across the EVP to eliminate the background and static. You know what it said?'

'Humour me.'

'It said 'Charlie's dead' and, you know what's even more surreal?' Libby could only shake her head. 'It was my voice on that recording. It came over loud and clear.'

'Good god! Why would you say that before it happened?'

'I didn't, Libby. But I did say those two words to you when I broke the news to you over the phone. As soon as they left my mouth, I could hear myself. I said 'Charlie's dead' just like the voice on the EVP. How the hell can I explain that?'

'You'll have to study the eternalism theory for that one.'

'Yes, we're looking into that. There's also auto suggestion: that I heard it on the EVP before I said it but reproduced it in exactly the same way subliminally. Yet, there's something niggling me. I have dreams about Charlie and The Ring. I dream he's trapped amongst a multitude of spirits of the dead in some kind of multi-dimensional time warp and there's someone controlling them all. Someone who won't let them go. Katja has similar dreams. We're trying to analyse them at the moment.' Libby felt the familiar chill in her spine that she'd come to know as fear. She hadn't got around to telling Hannah that bit. 'It's as if The Ring has infected us in some way, or perhaps your Highland laddie has taken control of all of our minds and turned us into his bitches!'

'That's mean.'

'I'm kidding.'

Libby peered through the curtain again and looked for movement in the car. The street lights shone on Kie's sleeping face and she wondered whether or not she should go out there and wake him.

'I've got so much more to tell you, but I think we should wait until Kie wakes up to finish the story. You can get the rest from Prendy and Stephen tomorrow.'

She peeked out the curtain again and her eyes were drawn to the beam of the street light. It looked different in some way and she could no longer see Kie's face.

'Just go and wake him up.'

'Wait a minute, Hannah, there's a strange shadow.'

Libby noticed the shadow at the side of the car was darkening. Hannah joined her at the window and they watched together.

'What are you looking at? You're scaring me.'

'That shadow, see it? Is it getting bigger? God, is it moving?'

'Get him out of there, Libby.' Hannah was already running to the front door.

By the time they reached the car, it was rocking on its wheels, the dark mist surrounding it like a death shroud. The alarm shrieked, the lights blinked on and off, and the neighbours crowded their doors as Libby's car swung violently on its spongy axles. She tried to open the door and, to her misery, was not surprised it was stuck fast. She rattled on the door handle as the car swung dangerously towards her, causing her to leap out of the way before it hit her.

'What, by the grace of God, is going on here?'

The shadow fled and the car, which had risen in the air off its wheels, crashed to the tarmac, trembled for a few moments and became still. A man in dark clothing rushed up to the car and opened the driver's door.

'Who the hell are you?' She didn't mean to sound so offensive, but the incident had rattled her good manners.

'I'm Father Michael, who the hell are you?'

'I'm Libby Butler. Sorry, Father, didn't mean to be so rude. I couldn't get the car door open.'

'You're strong for such a little woman, Libby Butler.' He had a Northern Irish accent. 'Perhaps you should make better use of your car keys in future. That's what you open the door with. You've upset the whole neighbourhood.'

Libby stood gawking at the plain clothed Catholic priest in his checked shirt and brown corduroy trousers. He didn't need his clerical garb to blurt out his profession; his dress sense said it all.

She believed she was having one of those epiphany moments often experienced by people at least once in their lives. It was one of those moments that stretched coincidence to its broadest limits and bordered on cliché. She felt fate slapping her around the face once again.

She peered into the car and found Kie sleeping fitfully across the seats, the handbrake digging into his stomach. She shook him gently but he didn't stir. She called his name and shook him again but got no response. Worried that he may be unconscious, she hauled on his arm and yelled at him. He awoke with a cry of pain.

'Ah, Libby,' he let out an agonised breath. 'I must've dozed off.' He clutched at his chest and grimaced. 'Hello Hannah.' He blinked a few times until his focus adjusted to the real world. 'Who the hell are you?'

Father Michael set his jaw.

— — —

'No, really Father, he's a very deep sleeper. He'd sleep through Armageddon if he was tired enough. He's not on drugs, I swear.'

Libby wondered why this night had brought destiny in the form of a meddlesome Catholic priest to her door. Father

Michael had insisted he help Kie to the bedroom and tended to his needs as if he was in his own church. He ran backwards and forwards from the kitchen while Hannah and she looked on helplessly.

'What happened to him?'

'He fell down the stairs.'

The father cast a knowing, suspicious eye over the pair of them.

'You don't have stairs in this house. It's a bungalow.'

'He fell down *his* stairs. He doesn't normally live here.'

'So where does he normally live?' Father Michael accepted the glass of wine that Hannah poured for him and sat down on the sofa.

'He lives near Auchencairn in a house with a lot of stairs.'

'Lovely place with a very spiritual atmosphere. I particularly like Dundrennan Abbey.'

Libby gave him her cheesiest grin. 'Yes, I'm feeling a bit like a crumbling old ruin myself. What brings you across the Irish Sea, Father?' She decided she'd lead the conversation for a change.

'I'm visiting my sister. She lives across the road from you, not that she ever sees you. She says you're a lawyer.'

'That's small communities for you. What they don't know about you, they make up, but yes, for my sins, I'm a lawyer.'

'I was a psychiatrist before I was ordained. There's no reason to be ashamed of the path you choose in life, provided it's for the overall good.'

'Oh, I can do overall good, Father.'

'Are you a Catholic Libby?'

'How could you guess?'

'Non-Catholics don't tend to call me Father.'

'I confess I was baptised but never really did find God.'

'So you've fallen by the wayside?'

'I wouldn't say that. I believe I've been enlightened. I'm afraid to say, I've never found any sign of God along the hedgerows.'

'What makes you afraid to say that?' He glanced at Hannah who sat by the window sipping at her glass of wine.

'Don't look at me. I'm a scientist.'

'So scientists can't believe in the almighty either?'

'If we can't prove it in a formula, then no.'

'What about your patient?'

Libby laughed. 'MacAoidh grew up under the dark, gargantuan shadow of the wee free kirk that didn't quite manage to indoctrinate him into its rigid regime. There's no amount of canonical texts that could persuade Kie God exists. Sorry, Father, you've landed inside a pit of atheist vipers.'

'But your venom is harmless to me.' He raised his glass. 'Tell me about MacAoidh.'

'Why?'

'He's stalked by a demon. I would just like to know why.'

Hannah sprayed the wine from her mouth while Libby stared at the man in awe. His announcement was as casual as a call for the next in line for a benefits interview but he'd obviously seen something tonight that most normal people would've missed.

'Are there such things as coincidence, Father? I mean, is it possible for a group of people to just turn up at a particular moment at a crucial time to set things right?'

'The Lord works in mysterious ways, to coin an old chestnut.'

'Please don't preach that crap to us. The only thing mysterious about the Lord is that he needs blind faith to make him real.' Hannah was not a woman to wrap her views in polite banter. 'That's so last millennium.'

'You have your beliefs and I have mine. Libby was just asking for my opinion and I offered it to her. I, however, see a glint of perplexity in your eyes, Hannah. How can you, as a scientist, explain what you have just witnessed tonight?'

Hannah shook her fiery curls. 'There are many explanations for paranormal phenomena: and I don't deny that what happened tonight with the car cannot be explained through logical reasoning or scientific canons. However, science continues to develop and its rigid doctrines are becoming more flexible. I can't offer an explanation because I haven't investigated it properly. Come back in a few months' time and I may have your answer.'

Libby thought it time to cut through the theology debate. 'MacAoidh unwittingly bought a haunted house a few months ago. A house that has a reputation for being plagued by a poltergeist. He's been bothered by paranormal activity since he moved in and now it's getting violent and personal. It appears, whatever it is that's haunting him, isn't limited to its immediate location. It's followed him here, so there's nowhere he can call safe.'

'Does this not frighten you?'

'I love him, Father, the only thing that frightens me is the thought of losing him. I would go to hell to pull him out.'

To Libby's surprise, Father Michael smiled at her and took her hand. 'You don't have to go that far, my dear. You witnessed yourself how the beast fled at the sniff of God. It didn't flee from me, but from the wrath of the almighty and both of us are going to help you pull him out.'

Chapter 44

THE CATHOLIC PRIEST

'I know you've had something to do with this. I can smell your work all over him.'

Prendergast winced as he walked into the byre where Kie was cleaning an old rotavator which probably hadn't been touched since the nineteen sixties. The farmer's dog was busily digging in the hole at the end of the byre where Kie had taken the wall down. Kie gave it a sharp whistle and threw its ball as far as his broken ribs would allow.

'Should you be lifting that in your condition?'

'I'm not pregnant and it's not heavy.'

Now and again Kie would twitch in pain but he kept quiet about it in his usual no-fuss way.

'All right, MacAoidh, Father Michael is my doing. We had a few beers in the hotel bar the day before yesterday and we got talking about the ever after and then the supernatural. I'll admit I told him about this place and of your plight. He wants to help.'

'You really should stop picking up folk in hotel bars. It'll get you into trouble with the wife.'

Prendy didn't think that little quip deserved a response.

'He'll end up in the same square coffin as the meenister for his troubles. Are you prepared to take on the responsibility of another death? How're you going to explain that one to the Pope?'

'Father Michael's got a strong, stout heart and isn't afraid of violent spirits.'

Kie suddenly stopped what he was doing to look at Prendergast, a shocked expression on his face. 'Please don't tell me he's an exorcist.'

'No, he's not an exorcist. He's a priest who believes in demons and hell and all the other stuff you don't. Don't you want to at least see if his presence here can make a difference or perhaps hear how he intends to help you?'

'I don't believe in the wrath of gods, Prendy.'

'I heard what happened last night in the car.'

'Aye, so did I.'

'Why don't you just come in and speak to him? There's no need for a theology debate. He's an honest and good man who's given up his time today to help you. He also contributed a large part of his evening last night tending to you.'

'He was just making sure I wasn't possessed. I woke up to a vision of a half-naked Jesus hanging from a huge wooden cross in my face.'

'I can think of worse sights to wake up to.'

'I can't.'

'At least come in for lunch and meet him. Hear what he has to say. Stephen's taken him around the house, Hannah's made lunch and everything's nice and quiet.'

'How's Stephen taken to him?'

'He sulked a bit this morning, but he realises this trouble may take more than one set of opinions to solve it. We're going for a concerted effort.'

Kie stood up and stretched his back carefully. 'So we've got God, science and hocus-pocus on the case. All we need now is a voodoo priestess to complete the magic circle.'

'Just leave your doubts in this byre and come and speak to your guests.' Prendergast hoped his words sounded like the appeal he intended.

'I'm tired of all these people who say they know what they're doing but in effect do nothing, Prendy. I'm sick of being treated like a helpless victim of crime one minute and a laboratory specimen the next. I just want one of them to come up with an answer; to tell me how I can get rid of this.'

'They are telling you, lad. You're just not listening.'

Kie wiped his hands on an oily rag and threw it over the machine. 'No talk of God and tell the priest, if he makes any attempt to convert me, he's out on his holy arse.'

'I'll tell him.'

As they walked through the house, they could hear someone shrieking in frustration. Father Michael's gentle voice filled in the lulls in the conversation where Stephen stopped to hyperventilate.

'Ah, MacAoidh, it's yourself.' Father Michael looked relieved to have the company diluted. 'Stephen here and I were just having a little discussion on demonology. Weren't we Stephen?'

The psychic turned to Kie. 'Tell this priest there's no such place as hell, would you?'

'There's no such place as hell,' Kie echoed, his tone flat.

'Well, that's not what I believe. The Catechism tells us of the existence of hell and its eternal fires. It's a punishment for mortal sin.'

Prendergast flinched as Kie hurled himself in to the argument. 'Come on Michael. The concept of hell's simply a deterrent to unacceptable social behaviour. No matter how good we try to be, we're all sinners in the eyes of the bloody church. Who decides who goes to hell and who goes to heaven? The Pope?'

'No, MacAoidh, God does.'

'So God created demons?'

'God created everything, including angels and demons.'

'He should've learned how to keep them on a leash before

he let them loose on his precious world. He's complicit in their behaviour.'

'The devil rules those places where God has been forgotten.' Father Michael crossed his arms and smiled to himself. He was obviously enjoying the banter, even though he was the one deflecting a fair amount of animosity from the two heretics in the room.

'I haven't forgotten God, Michael, I never knew him in the first place.'

'But you believe in the devil?'

'No.'

'What about his minions?'

'There he goes again with his circular arguments,' Stephen sighed and stuffed a sandwich into his mouth.

'No.'

'So what would you call this evil presence lurking in your house and following you down the road?'

'A pain in the ...'

'I see you've already started lunch.' Hannah's timely appearance saved Kie from a few Hail Marys. 'Let's have a look at the damage.' Without asking him, she pulled his shirt from his belt and examined his bruised ribs with the tips of her fingers. 'The swelling's gone down a bit and your breathing's better. Tell me where it hurts the most.' She pushed her fingers into his flanks a few times and he let out a loud yell when she hit the right spot. She tucked his shirt back into his jeans and patted his thigh. 'Don't do any heavy lifting and try to avoid any form of impact. We don't want those brittle rib bones splintering inside you and puncturing a lung. When was the last time you took your pain killers?'

'Last night, I think.'

'Two. Now. Find. Go get.'

Prendergast could hardly believe it when Kie obediently trotted from the kitchen to fetch his tablets, Jim Black's dog at his heel.

'I like your style,' Father Michael said, 'could you get him to find God in the same way?'

Hannah laughed. 'Afraid not, Father. I'm bound to only do what's good for his body. I'm not in charge of his soul.' She turned to Prendergast. 'How are we going to proceed today?'

Before he could answer, Father Michael told her. 'I've had a look around the house already and it's quiet as a church on a Monday morning.'

'Try the loft,' Kie took his tablets with a glass of water.

'I've had a look in the attic. It's full of boxes. I think I'd like to speak with MacAoidh first. Get to know him a bit better.'

'I'll go set a recorder up in the study.' Hannah grabbed a few sandwiches from the table.

'God doesn't need fancy equipment.'

'Maybe not, but science does.'

– – –

'Sit down, my boy.'

Kie sat on the chair by the window of his study. It was the last room he'd renovated and this was the first time he'd been able to use it. He groaned when he saw the camera on a tripod in the corner pointing straight at him. Hannah sat on a chair beside him with a digital voice recorder in her hand. F a t h e r Michael sat at the desk.

'This is a beautiful desk. Is it Irish?' the priest passed his hand over the blind fret carving on the edge of the writing top and smiled.

'I think so. It belonged to my grandfather as did all the furniture in this room.'

'Your grandfather was Irish?'

'No, he was a Scot.' Kie let out a long, exasperated breath. 'Look, Michael, I don't mind you being here and asking questions but please don't try the God thing on me. I'm not a lost lamb and I'm not the right material for a potential convert. I want you to respect my convictions and I'll respect yours.'

'Tell me, MacAoidh, what do you think happens to us when we die?' He tutted only once when Hannah leaped across the room to turn on the camera.

'Sorry.' She sat down again.

Kie shrugged. 'A few weeks ago, I would've said that was the end, but now I'm not so sure.'

'And what do you feel's happened to you to make you unsure?'

Kie didn't like the way this interview was going. The chair was uncomfortable to sit on and his fractured ribs felt as though they were burning. 'The inexplicable events over the past few months have baffled me. Even the scientists can't put a proper explanation to it. I could live with a few stones hurled at folk and objects going missing and reappearing in strange places. I could abide the odd fire starting and even come to terms with the overnight demolition of a thirty-foot barn.'

'Demolition?'

'Aye, something took it down in the night and neatly stacked the pieces up for ease of removal by lorry.'

'Merciful heavens!'

'That's what I said when I saw it.'

He heard Hannah's low laughter and he smiled.

'So what is it you refuse to put up with? What was the last straw for you?'

'It attacked Libby and nearly killed her.'

'Are you very fond of Libby?'

'Aye.'

'Anything else?'

'I saw it. On the stairs, defying me.'

'And what did you do when you saw it?'

'I ran.'

'But you returned to face it yesterday morning?'

'Aye, and I was stupid. I leaped through it and forgot the staircase was on the other side.'

'What did you see MacAoidh?'

Kie suddenly felt he was walking into an ambush with no escape route. He felt his defences rising as the priest leaned forward in his chair, his dark blue eyes burning with intensity.

'Should I not be lying on a couch?'

The spell broken, Father Michael sat back in his chair and hid his disappointment behind a tiny cough. 'You really don't need to be so defensive with me, I'm just trying to determine what's haunting this house.'

'Ask the psychic, he knows.'

'I want to hear it from a man who's not in the business of making money from the dead.'

Kie laughed. If anything, the mild-mannered priest was canny.

'All right, I saw a figure of a cowled man. He had his back to me. His entire form was black and moving like an evening mist rolling in from the sea.'

'How did you know it was a man?'

'I don't know.'

'Did this apparition speak to you?'

'No.'

'How did you feel when you saw it?'

'Tense, astonished, afraid.'

'Why were you afraid?'

He paused to think of an answer but couldn't come up with a plausible one. It was a while before he spoke again. 'I felt it could harm me and there was nothing I could do to prevent it. I felt I was in overwhelming danger that I wouldn't survive if I stayed to fight. I couldn't protect myself, so I ran from it.'

'Yet, knowing that danger, you returned to confront your fears?'

'Aye and look where that got me.'

'It didn't attack you then?'

'No. It disappeared.'

Father Michael paused for a while, tapping his fingers on the desk. 'Take a few minutes to mull over what you've just told me and then let me know your thoughts on your fear.'

That was an odd request. Kie looked to Hannah for elucidation, but she merely shrugged.

He began with caution. 'I think you're trying to tell me that my fear is unfounded.'

'Not unfounded...'

'Let me finish, please. I think you're saying this thing in my house wants me to fear it. It knows how to get to me, through people I care for and through my own weaknesses. I think you're saying that courage and refusal to fear will weaken it. So either the psychic's right: it feeds off fear and negative emotion or it's a physical manifestation of my own fear.'

'What you don't fear can't harm you.'

'Amen to that!' Hannah couldn't hold her tongue.

'That's the nature of demons.' Father Michael began his sermon. 'God does not fear them because He is omnipotent. The demon fears God in the same way as you fear the demon. Evil spirits are feeble and pathetic against the command of the divine and that's why they run from the power of the holy cross. You have a weapon, MacAoidh, and that's the mercy and love of

God. Only in his …'

Father Michael flew from his seat, the wide gash in his head spraying Hannah and Kie with warm blood. He landed on his front at their feet, the blood oozing into the delicate fibres of the Persian rug.

The rock that hit him had come from nowhere and landed beside his body: both were as still as stone.

As Hannah leaped to the victim's aid, Kie staggered out from the study to be greeted by a wild-eyed Prendergast.

'My god! You're covered in blood!'

'Aye, and I think the priest needs an ambulance or a hearse. Hannah's with him, reading him his last rites.'

'I hope you're joking.'

Before Prendergast pushed past him to see for himself, Kie grabbed his arm. He didn't know how to word his request, but he thought he'd say it quickly before he changed his mind.

'I can't fight the devil, Prendy. That's God's work. I'm going to ask you to do one last thing for me.'

'You're in shock, son. Get that blood off you and go and lie down.'

'Prendy, the priest didn't work out. He meant well, but he's not strong enough. I don't have the faith and wouldn't know where to start.' He took a long, painful breath. 'I want you to find me an exorcist.'

THE EXORCIST

'Ouch!'

Libby watched the video tape of Father Michael's psychic braining and shuddered in horror, despite the fact she'd seen it more than ten times over.

'I tell you that stone came from nowhere and deliberately targeted the poor man.' Hannah couldn't hide her excitement at watching the footage again. She'd just returned from the hospital after visiting The Ring's latest victim.

They sat outside on the sun beds in Libby's small garden. There wasn't much sun, but it felt good to be outside and they wore their sunglasses anyway.

'He's lucky it missed the superficial temporal artery and, oddly enough, the blow didn't cause any trauma to the facial nerves nor did it injure his skull. Funny that.'

'Where did all that blood come from then?'

'The gash in his head. The head bleeds like a bitch when it's cut.'

'Will he be all right?'

'He'll make a full recovery physically. Mentally, however, he may have to go for counselling. Apparently he hasn't spoken since he was hospitalised two days ago. He barely acknowledged me. I had to sit around with a bunch of flowers in my hand and read his magazine. The news in the Catholic Universe isn't exactly my favourite choice for catching up on celebrity gossip.'

'His sister gave me a filthy look this morning when I was

hanging out the washing. She probably thought I did it. She speaks very sweetly to Kie, though.'

'You should try and discourage him from going back to The Ring. It's not safe, even in the daytime.'

'Kie does what he wants.'

'Where's Prendy gone this weekend?'

'I don't know. Maybe back to London to see his wife. He didn't really say, which is unusual for him.'

'Is it true he's starting excavations in the grounds on Monday?'

'Yes, the police are going to dig up the steading in an effort to find Peter's body. They're taking a bulldozer to the Ghost Tree. It's really sad.'

'It's dead.'

'It's significant.'

'Not any more. So what's MacAoidh Armstrong going to do with himself now?'

'I don't know. It's stalemate. He can't stay at The Ring and he gets cabin fever here. His ribs still hurt and everything frustrates him. He's putting on a brave face but I can tell he's restless. He just doesn't know what to do.'

'If he remembered to take his pain relief, he wouldn't feel the pain so much.'

They lapsed into silence.

'Maybe you should take him out tonight. It is Saturday, after all. Take him somewhere nice and far away from all this: a change being as good as a rest and all that crap. I've got work to do so I'll stay here with the dog.'

'He doesn't want to go anywhere. He's lost that adventurous spirit: that vibrancy and love of life he had when I first met him. He's becoming more insular and won't let me in.'

'Do you think he's cooling off you?'

'God, I hope not.'

'I think you need to bully him a bit more. You're far too submissive, it's not like you.'

'Not tonight. He says he's got to be at The Ring early tomorrow morning, for some reason. I really wish he'd sell up and find somewhere else to buy that doesn't include demons in the particulars of sale.'

They sighed together and sipped at their cocktails.

'Hello, Libby. I did knock.'

She pulled off her sunglasses and turned her head towards Prendy who stood with a short, middle-aged woman in a dog collar.

'Hi, Prendy, I thought you were in London.'

'No. I've just come back from Glasgow. May I introduce Reverend Anne Jacobson.'

'Oh, Prendy, I really hope you're not thinking …'

Rev Jacobson gave them both a stern nod and stiff sniff at the alcohol in their glasses.

'Reverend Jacobson has accompanied me all the way from Glasgow.' Libby noticed the discomfort in Prendy's countenance. He shuffled his big, flat policeman's feet, which was always a bad sign.

'Prendy, we've just watched the video footage of the felling of the last mighty oak…'

'He was Catholic. I'm Presbyterian,' the minister barked and kept her back straight.

'Does the spirit world recognise denomination?'

'And why shouldn't it?'

Prendergast cut in before there was a fight. 'Reverend Jacobson has agreed to help Kie. She's a well-respected member of the presbytery and has some very special skills that she's going to use to hopefully rid him of his troubles.'

'We've tried everything, Prendy. The Ring has defeated more members of the clergy than the recent investigations into paedophilia in Catholic boys' schools. I really wouldn't want to see Reverend Jacobson carted out in an ambulance too. That attack on Father Michael was particularly vicious.' She wanted to scare the woman away and wondered what had incensed Prendy to bring yet another sacrificial lamb to the slaughter at the steading.

'Reverend Jacobson is an exorcist.'

Libby and Hannah exchanged surprised glances.

'Kie's going to kill you!' She sang her words to him under her breath.

'It was MacAoidh who requested I find him an exorcist and so I have. We're going in tonight at midnight.'

Libby groaned as Hannah squealed with delight.

'Fantastic!' Hannah said.

'This is not a game, girl.' Reverend Jacobson sat down on the end of Libby's sun lounger. 'I'd appreciate some hospitality. I'd like a cup of tea.'

'I'll get it.' Prendy shuffled back through the patio doors.

'Do you do this a lot?' Libby thought she'd begin the serious conversation.

'I've exorcised many demons, both from the bodies of individuals and from homes. The devil keeps me on my toes.'

'And did you get permission from the church to perform an exorcism at The Ring?' She sipped at her cocktail.

'Exorcism has been a liturgical and pastoral practice since the beginning of Christianity. Jesus himself exorcised demons and we have been casting them out ever since by renouncing Satan and giving blessings. Jesus Christ Himself has given me the authority.'

'So baptism is a form of exorcism?'

'In a way, yes. Like the sacrament of communion, we ask the Lord permission to eat and drink at his table. We come to Him with clean hearts and renounce the devil.'

'But doesn't the Kirk teach that God predestines an individual to either eternal beatitude, those who will be saved, or eternal damnation, those who will be lost?'

'Man was born with free will.'

'So it's up to us to make the decision whether to learn to play the harp or stoke fires? I don't get it.'

'Mankind has been called to believe in the divinity of the Lord Jesus Christ, his virgin birth, his atonement for our sins, his death, his resurrection and his ascension into heaven. We are not born evil, but we may choose to seek out evil ways. Only through the repentance and renouncing our sinful ways, may we truly find God's mercy.'

'You may as well call the ambulance now, Prendy.' Libby shouted into the kitchen.

'Amen!' Hannah obviously had enough of theology for one session. 'So what are you going to do with the devil at midnight, Mrs Jacobson? How are you going to cast this manifestation out of MacAoidh's steading?'

'I'm going to banish it. I'm going to convince it that evil will not be tolerated by Christ.'

'You're going to do this through ritual, prayer and symbolism alone?'

'Not alone, girl, for the Lord Jesus Christ will be with us all.'

Hannah and Libby rose their eyes to the skies.

— — —

'No way!'

As Libby approached the drive, she saw the silhouette of Reverend Jacobson staring up at the house, her small form haloed by the bright floodlights. She wore a hat and a black trouser suit and looked every bit like the posters of the eponymous horror novel.

'She certainly looks the part!' Hannah giggled.

'You know, you don't have to do this, Hannah. I've read that exorcisms can be really dangerous affairs. People get killed.'

'That's normally during exorcisms of a person, Libby, and is often associated with defences to murderous intentions.'

'Still. I'm really scared.'

'Then why have you come?'

'I don't know. Curiosity, support, insanity. A number of reasons really.'

'Love?'

'I suppose that too. Hi Kie.' His scowling face shone in the floodlights.

'Get back in the car and go home.'

'It's OK, I know about the exorcist.'

'That's not the point. I don't want you here. It's not safe.'

She puffed out a breath. 'I've been with you since the beginning of all this so that qualifies me to be here at the end of it. I'm staying. Someone's got to look after you.'

'Hannah, please take her home.'

'She's a big girl, Kie. She does what she wants. Do you still have that CCTV set up?'

'Look, Libby,' he pulled her by the arm to the back of the car, 'I can't deal with an exorcism while I'm worrying about your safety and this might not be the end of it. This ritual might just enrage whatever it is that's squatting here and it may end up killing all of us.'

'Then why are you doing this?'

'I have to try.'

She noticed the turbulence sparking in those pale blue eyes

and realised this was his final, desperate hope.

'Do or die?' She breathed out her misery. 'And I can't deal with sitting around at home worrying for your safety. Relationships come with a price, Kie, and my price is you're stuck with me.'

'Then I'm ending our relationship here and now. Go home, Libby, I don't want you here.'

She knew he didn't mean it but his words still stung like a barbed whip.

'Fine. I'll leave after Joan Knox has brought the might of the Reformation down on your demon.'

She pushed past him, knocking his painful ribs with her elbow, and stormed into the house. When she reached the sitting room, she heard a heated conversation.

'You didn't tell me he was an unbeliever. I can't exorcise the secular.' Reverend Jacobson sat amidst a pile of little stones. Another fell on her Bible and she brushed it away with a testy grunt.

'He was baptised into the free kirk and took holy communion as a boy,' Prendy continued his appeal.

'But he's chosen the path of the devil. No wonder he's got a demon burlin' about his house.'

'He's a good man, Anne, a humble, very human man.'

'But not god-fearing.' She crossed her arms.

'I'm a believer.'

'You're not Presbyterian.'

'But the ghost is.' Their attention turned to Libby as she walked into the room. 'If this is the same entity as the Rerrick Parish Poltergeist of antiquity, then it was a Presbyterian exorcism that got rid of it eventually, although it did take two weeks of praying.' She squirmed as she half expected a skip-load of stones to descend on her just for mentioning prayer. 'If we're going to use Christianity as a weapon against evil, then wouldn't any Abrahamic tradition do?'

'You're not Presbyterian either.'

'Actually I am. I was christened into the Presbyterian church when I was six weeks old.'

'You told Father Michael you were Catholic,' Hannah's tone was only slightly chiding.

'I would've told him I was Jedi to shut him up. It worked, didn't it?'

'You lied to God?'

'No, I lied to His blessed priest.'

She felt her heart miss a beat as Kie walked into the room and sat into the sofa, drumming his foot against his knee in the way he did when he was anxious. He looked pale.

'I can't do this with unbelievers in my midst.'

'I'm unbelieving, not unregenerate,' Kie kept his announcement casual.

'Still, you'll have to sit out and I mean outside. Whatever you hear or whatever you see, I don't want you coming back in until I call for you. I'm not going through all this just to have you ruin it. Is that clear?'

'Fine.' Another Kie expression when he was hiding his emotions.

'You,' she directed her attention to Hannah, 'may take a record of the exorcism, but you will not interfere in any way.'

'I'll pretend I'm a fly on the wall,' Hannah said.

'Mr Prendergast will give me a hand. You can come too if you want.'

Libby realised she was directing the words at her.

'No, Libby doesn't believe in God either.'

'She nevertheless has more of an open mind than you do, Mr Armstrong.' Her firm glare quelled any further argument. 'Let's get started then. We'll begin with a prayer.' She closed her eyes and immediately opened one of them. 'Are you still here?'

Kie left the room muttering something under his breath.

'I speak the Gaelic, MacAoidh Armstrong, and I don't take kindly to profanities in the presence of God.'

He shouted something else in Gaelic from the hall and Libby heard the minister's back teeth squealing together.

'Our Father, who art in … Mr Armstrong, do you want me to get rid of this evil presence in your house or not?'

Libby squealed as Kie swept her into his arms and kissed her in front of everyone in the room. She pulled away, breathless.

'Sorry.'

'You will be!' She smiled and watched him leave again.

'Love,' the minister sounded amused as she closed her eyes once more with a small smile on her stern features, 'that's an excellent start.'

Chapter 46

THE EXORCISM

Libby and Prendy followed the minister around the house as she uttered prayers of devotion and sprinkled holy water in each room she entered. Now and again, they were forced to join her in the chorus, which made Libby feel uncomfortable, but she did it anyway hoping her verbal contribution would somehow stand as proxy to her marked lack of meaningful devotion. The lights were so low she could barely see where she was going but she took comfort in the small green glow from Hannah's camera that followed them about like Tinkerbell all the way through the house.

She was grateful there'd been no apparent opposition from the other-worldly members of the household and their sweep of the house and grounds had been hours long but uneventful. Reverend Jacobson finally took them into the dining room where the candlelight flickered and cast dancing shadows across the polished surface of the table.

'We'll make our stand in here,' she shouted as if sounding a horn of battle. 'The beast has gone into hiding. I'm now going to command it to come forward, so hold on to your faith and take a seat.'

A small stone fell onto the table and clattered across its surface, coming to rest at the foot of one of the giant silver candlesticks. She heard another land somewhere close to the fireplace.

'It begins,' the minister whispered, and Libby's eyes widened in panic. 'When it comes, pay it no heed. Do not attempt to speak to it nor look it in the eye.'

'What if I do by mistake?'

'You won't!'

'Aren't you supposed to go through some ritualistic sermon or something?'

'Jesus cast spirits out with just a word. The less said the better.'

Another stone hit the minister on the side of the head as she stood at the end of the table with her arms spread out as if blessing a congregation.

'The Lord Jesus Christ rebuke you; the Lord rebuke you,' she yelled into the heavens.

Libby screamed as what could only be described as a lump of burning peat hit the minister square in the chest. The woman batted it away with her hand and the dark lump lay smoking on the carpet but didn't burn. A tall china lamp she recognised from the study came hurtling through the door, took a turn to the left in mid-air and smashed against the burr-walnut corner cupboard

'The Lord Jesus Christ rebuke you.' The minister bellowed and the candles flickered violently as if a strong gust of wind had just blown across the room.

Libby sat rigid in her seat, ice cold and too afraid to move. She felt her entire body shaking. She looked across the table at Prendergast and noticed he was equally afraid.

'It won't enter this room, I've blessed it. We'll have to go to it. Follow me.'

— — —

MacAoidh sat outside on the patio with his hands in his pockets examining the dark shape of the old plough embedded in his lawn. He whistled loudly to himself so as not to hear the prayers of the minister bellowing from the house. The woman's voice was as unsubtle as her personality. He wondered how on earth he'd found himself in this situation, allowing a Presbyterian exorcist to cast out demons from his house. Had he been the same man he was a few months ago, he would've either laughed at himself or committed himself to a mental institution for a spell of therapy in a padded cell wearing one of those jackets that allowed him to hug himself all night. He looked out into the blackness of the garden beyond the reach of the floodlights and hoped with all his heart that this last ditch effort to rid the steading of its paranormal troubles would pay off. Otherwise, his next step would be to leave.

He hadn't told Libby about the article in the glossy local magazine by Mandy Rutherford because he didn't want to be the cause of the reporter's loss of career and subsequent hospitalisation. If anything, Mandy had done him a favour as he'd been inundated with phone calls from his property manager who'd been fending off a raft of inquiries from potential purchasers, many offering twice what he paid for the place.

He was just grateful that the big black gates blocking the entrance to the driveway came in time. He was expecting a deluge of unwanted visitors in the days to come and decided he'd probably stay away for that time. Whatever happened tonight would decide on whether Auchencairn would remain his home or whether he would take up one of the generous offers of purchase and find somewhere else on the map to live: anywhere without a ghost. The problem was, he was tired of running and longed to put down roots.

Jim Black's dog whined at his feet, staring at him in earnest as dogs did when they wanted something.

'We'll both have to wait for breakfast.' He patted the dog's head and picked up its ball. He hurled it across the garden and it ran off towards the outbuildings. 'Stupid animal.'

He sighed and looked around him, the strong lights cast an eerie glow across the land and outbuildings, falling off sharply into pitch darkness. Prendy's team of grave diggers were coming tomorrow to plough the place up. The wily ex-copper was sure the boy was buried somewhere between here, the Black's property and the burn. That was a very big area to cover and would cost a fortune in manpower and police funds. He snapped his head around to a noise in the byre: it sounded as if something had fallen over. That cold sense of dread returned until he saw the figure of the dog padding in and out of the shadows. He let out a relieved breath.

'Here, girl.' The dog ignored him. He let out a sharp whistle and was surprised the dog didn't respond to it immediately as it always did. Someone whistled back and all the hairs on MacAoidh's body bristled from his skin.

'What now?' He yelled into the shadows.

He stood up, hesitating for long moments, he didn't want to have to deal with any more psychic activity tonight. He was tired of dealing with it. Another whistle and he sighed. He pulled his nerve together and moved towards the barn. The dog sat at the end of the byre where the wall had been pulled down. Its ears stood vertical to its head and it stared at something, wagged its tail and whined as if in anticipation of the next command. MacAoidh squinted into the darkness. 'What do you see?' He remembered the conversation with the psychic who spoke to dogs and how his words intimated that this dog had seen much. 'Go on!'

Jim Black's collie raced towards its favourite hole and began to dig, whining and barking in its enthusiasm. It was then MacAoidh realised every nerve in his body tingled and every neuron in his brain prickled the inside of his skull. He had a

THE EXORCISM

sensation of other-wordliness, a heightened awareness of the environment around him and his own senses sharpening. He was standing by the byre, but he was not. The overwhelming feeling caused his limbs to weaken and he felt he couldn't move; it was as if he stood astride two worlds, one foot planted in each but unable to interact inside either. He knew where Peter Hyslop was buried. He saw him lying twisted and broken under the hard earth. He saw his bones.

A loud crash from the house caused him to snap out of his enchantment and he was caught in another dilemma: whether to run to the house or pick up a spade. Remembering the promise to the minister, he walked to the byre and grabbed a pick and shovel from the wall. Crossing the courtyard to the end of the barn where the dog's front feet moved with frantic urgency, he kicked the animal out of the way and, ignoring the terrible burning from his ribs, heaved the pick over his shoulder and smashed it into the hard earth.

He heard the minister shouting and wondered if Libby was in trouble. The urge to run and save her threatened to take control. That primeval instinct, however, washed over him once more and told him to keep digging.

'Sit doon, son, and stop makin' a dick o' yersel'

He heard Jim Black's voice clearly and his pick became increasingly heavy. Kie gritted his teeth against the pressure and the pain and, locking the voice out of his head, continued to smash up the dirt.

The ground yielded and he threw down the pick to take up the shovel. As he bent down to reach the handle, a heavy pressure landed square on his injured chest, knocking the wind from him and causing him to yell in agony. He lay on the ground, his legs inside the hole he'd dug, his sternum resting on the pile of dirt. He wiped the soil from his eyes and turned himself around, groaning. The cowled figure stood with its back to him just inside the byre. He could see it clearly but couldn't run if he wanted to.

Keeping his eyes on it and fighting against the heavy static bristling the hairs on his head, he picked up the shovel by the handle, spat out the dirt from his mouth, and continued digging. A clod of burning peat hit him on the arm. He scooped it up on the end of his spade and hurled it back with a testy curse before thrusting the tool into the ground once more. It hit something. The figure whistled softly to him, but he ignored it. Instead he made use of his fear and channelled all his energy into the task at hand.

The dog began to bark. The byre walls rumbled and a slate came down, just missing his head. The figure shifted once again into a buffeting cloud and the walls cracked, showering Kie with powdered rock and stone.

Kie threw the spade down and, as he bent over to feel what he'd unearthed, he was hurled across the courtyard to land flat against the stable wall. He yelled as his back bounced off the cold stone and he was thrown onto his front. He felt he'd been stabbed. The pain was so intense he believed he'd never walk again, but that voice inside him told him he was so close.

He picked himself slowly off the ground and limped towards the hole, while the dog barked into the night. Every breath he drew was agonising and he felt his strength failing. The earth shuddered beneath him and the roof began to cave in under the pressure, as if it was being squeezed from either side by a giant hand. The building listed towards him, rocking backwards and forwards, groaning and juddering, and Kie realised he'd have to hurry before it came down. The barn lurched forward and he was showered with flying slates, some smashing into his body, one glancing against the side of his head, tearing the skin. He could feel the hot trickle of blood against his temple and turned his fear into raging anger.

He flew at the figure with his shovel, swiping it like a weapon from side to side in great arcs, but he fought with thin air and the action only served to rip his tendons and cause him further pain. The walls rumbled again, showering him with pieces of splintered timber, dirt and slate.

'Coward!' he roared, his anger consuming him, 'Turn around and fight me.'

Something hit him hard on the back and he spun around to see a flat plank of roof timber hovering in the air. It smashed into the side of his head. He shook the dizziness away and planted both feet on the ground. As it came at him again, he grabbed the plank with both hands, wrestling with it as it tried to tear itself out of his grip. The pressure released and he fell to the dirt. The plank came up and smashed into his body. He felt a sharp pain tearing into his left lung and his breath fled from his mouth in a long, loud exhale.

He lay for a while trying to breathe but he couldn't get his lungs to inflate. He wanted to sleep. Exhausted with life, his ragged breath panting in shallow gasps, he watched the roof shuddering above his head as if it was somewhere else. Fear, anger, energy and emotion spent, he had neither the spirit nor the reserve left to fight. All that was left of him was pain: excruciating, burning pain; draining the life from him.

'That's it. Do your worst. I'm done.' He closed his eyes.

– – –

Libby sat rooted to the chair until Hannah hauled on her arm. 'This is fantastic stuff,' she whispered.

The minister and Prendergast stood in the hallway, their gazes turned upwards to the top of the stairs.

'The Lord Jesus Christ commands you to leave this place.'

Libby now understood why Kie was so loathe to return to the house after dark. She heard Hannah gasp behind her as the camera whirred in her left ear.

A dark mist swirled at the top of the stairs. She heard disjointed voices calling her name from somewhere at the end of a long tunnel.

'The Lord rebuke you, be silent!' the minister roared at it and stepped out the way as another clod of burning peat hurtled towards her.

'Where the hell is that coming from?' She heard Hannah whisper behind her.

Taking the minister's orders as sacrosanct, Libby shrugged in answer.

Armed with her Bible, her cross and a little bottle of holy water, Reverend Jacobson put one foot on the stairs. The next moment she was flying backwards to land by the front door. She picked herself up, brushed herself off and adjusted her bun before marching forwards again with only a small limp.

'*Meddler!*' A voice roared.

'That was clear.'

Libby nudged Hannah to be quiet.

'In the name of Jesus Christ Our Lord, be silent.' Reverend Jacobson charged up the staircase, holding her cross and Bible before her like a sword and shield. Prendergast ran after her, watching her back in case the spirit attacked again. The dark mist roiling on the landing didn't move.

'Get out! In the name of Jesus Christ.'

She threw the contents of her bottle at it and, to Libby's shock, it let out a deafening, unearthly howl that shook her soul.

'Libby, tell her to stop. Libby, please, she's hurting me.'

'Mum?'

'Is that the voice of your mother?' She felt Hannah's breath on her hair.

'Don't speak to it. It's lying to you,' the minister yelled down the stairs. She whirled around to face the apparition again.

Libby and Hannah leaped out the way as the large ceiling chandelier hanging above the staircase crashed to the ground, its precious crystals skidding across the boards.

'Get out of this home. You are not welcome in the house where God abides. Get out!'

'I am sent to warn the land to repent.'

'Silence. You do not have commission to speak or abide here.'

'God gave me commission.'

'Silence! The Lord Jesus Christ commands you to be silent.'

'*Libby! Libby! Speak!*' a thousand voices wailed around her and she pressed her hands to her ears. '*I cannot leave. I am part of the Holy Trinity.*'

'Blasphemer!' The minister yelled.

'Not blasphemy. We are three-in-one.'

The hall table careered across the room and flipped upside down. A hailstorm of tiny stones showered them and the curtain across the window caught fire. Libby rushed to beat it out before another fire started on the staircase. Hannah yelled and was hauled across the floor, kicking and screaming and beating off her unseen assailant.

'By the blood of the Lamb of God who died for our sins, get out of this house!' the minister roared and tumbled backwards into Prendergast as if hit by a great blast.

The glass in the windows exploded and Libby felt the rush of something pass her like a powerful draft before everything went suddenly still.

Prendergast helped the minister to her feet, while Hannah picked herself up off the floor, her hands shaking violently.

'Is it gone?' Hannah whispered, still half expecting to see the shadow on the stairs.

'There's nothing on this earth, whether living or in spirit form, that can withstand the power of God, my lass.' Reverend Jacobson dusted off her shoulder pads and laughed for the first time since Libby had met her.

'Does that mean the house isn't haunted anymore?'

'I would certainly hope not but, to seal the deal, let us thank the Lord in prayer.'

'Before we do that, Reverend Jacobson, can I ask you a question?' Libby looked around at the devastation of Kie's beautiful hallway and wondered if he would be angry. 'What did that thing mean by saying it was the Holy Trinity?'

'It was trying to rile me with its blasphemy.'

'It said it couldn't leave because it was three-in-one. What did it mean?'

'Libby,' Reverend Jacobson turned that impatient glower on and shot it straight at her. 'Evil spirits pit their strengths against the good of God in order to test their own limitations. Jesus is too strong for them. Three-in-One is just another way of expressing that the Father, Son and Holy Spirit is God.'

'What if it meant it can't leave because there are two other spirits holding it here? Two other spirits who can't leave until a certain event takes place?'

Prendergast's shoes crunched against the shattered crystals and stones as he crossed the space between them. She jumped slightly as he put his hand on her shoulder.

'You cast it out the house but not the property.'

Libby felt as if her spine had been stabbed with an ice pick. 'They're outside.'

Prendergast cursed. 'MacAoidh!'

chapter 47

THE BONES

'Ūkīra.'

'No, go away. I'm finished.' He couldn't wake up. He could hear his own voice answer the call but his lips weren't moving.

'Ūkīra, MacAoidh.'

The voice was more persistent this time and he slowly began to waken. He tried to rise but his body felt weak and wasted. The barn quaked again and a hail of splinters and eons of dust rained over the top of him. His senses returning at last, he opened his eyes. He yelled in shock when he saw a white painted face with abstract red markings staring down at him, a breath away from his nose. He recognised those eyes.

'Helen?' The beads, the feathered headdress. His wife knelt by his side in the full traditional dress of a Kikuyu maiden. 'Did I die?'

'Ūkīra.' She stood up and held out her hand for him.

'All right, I'm getting up.' He grasped her wrist, it was warm and vibrant, and the familiar perfume filled his head. He rose to unsteady feet, his body shaking with the effort. The pain was there but he felt it was somewhere else: somewhere high above where it couldn't reach him. He limped from the byre as she led him by the hand and pointed to the hole he'd dug. The white bone of a shattered skull peered from the dirt.

'I found him.'

The spade he'd dropped whizzed through the air and he only just managed to duck before it took his head off. Helen turned to the dark figure in the corner of the groaning building and gently pulled on Kie's hand. The entity began to slowly turn.

'Ūmīrīria.' She told him to be strong.

He staggered backwards. It had no face, just a black emptiness behind the hood. It was then he saw his own body lying on the ground beside the old Fergie tractor and he realised his world was no longer real. Reeling in confusion he tried to wake up, but Helen's smile called him and she squeezed his hand in reassurance. The ceiling looked dangerously near to collapsing as the ground shuddered again and more great cracks appeared along the sides of the walls. Stone and dirt crumbled around him and large chunks of wood and slate fell from the roof, but strangely didn't hit him. The black figure cowered away from her hand as she reached out to touch it, her beads jingling lightly as she moved. It roared as she gently hauled it towards her, as if pulling a veil from a drawer. A piece of wall came down from the side of the barn and landed on the ground in a storm of choking dust.

Kie looked back at his vulnerable body that lay sleeping on the concrete and willed himself to wake up before the barn came down on top of him. Helen held the wailing spirit in her left hand and Kie's hand in the other. She'd come for the spirit, like a vengeful ghost of her ancestors, but she also wanted to take her husband with her.

'Nīngwendete.'

He'd longed to hear her voice again; that soft voice telling him she loved him and the temptation to go with her was strong. Yet, there was another voice echoing in his heart and he recognised the perfume invading all his senses. It wasn't Helen's scent. He could hear her calling him back to her and he didn't want to leave. He snatched his hand away, breaking the contact.

He wanted to tell Helen he loved her but he no longer felt the anguish of her loss. If she'd come back from the grave to take him with her, then he'd resist. If he was lying on the ground dying or dead, he'd fight his way back to life and to Libby.

'I can't go with you, Helen.'

She smiled again and tried to grab his hand. The byre walls rumbled. The dog stood at his physical body and began to bark.

'I want to be with her. She's my life. Please let me go. I love her.'

'*Nĩ ndĩratheka*,' she laughed and grabbed the shrieking spirit with both hands.

Kie awoke with a violent jolt and the long, wet tongue of Jim Black's collie slobbering over his face. Consciousness brought back the burning torture of his pain and he tried to upright himself but didn't have the strength. The shadow had gone, screaming into the night at the end of Helen's grip. He had no idea where she'd taken it, but knew she would make sure it never returned to the land of the living.

A deafening roar caused the roof to explode outwards, sending slates and timber flying into the dark skies. With the last of his failing breath, Kie made a final effort to rise and, with an angry bellow, straightened his back and hobbled across the byre. He made to leap out the way but his weakened state caused him to lose his momentum and his footing. He plunged into the grave while the walls of the byre folded in on top of him, burying its secret once more.

— — —

'Oh my god, Kie!' The floodlights came on in a succession of loud bangs as Libby ran to the barn. She cried out in panic as she watched the clouds of choking dust settling against a heap of debris where the old byre once stood.

Prendergast ran towards the devastation and, covering his nose with his sleeve, leaped on the pile of shattered masonry.

'Call the emergency services,' he yelled, 'get them all here. He's under here somewhere.'

'There!' Libby sprinted towards the dog. It barked and whined and dug its paws into the debris, scratching and pawing at the ground. 'He must be here!' she screamed, 'look at the dog.'

She scrambled over the debris, catching her knees on the sharp stones. Hannah pushed past her in her urgency to help and Libby fell, smashing her shin on a piece of jagged wood. She saw tears in the former detective's eyes as he hauled the large chunks of stonework away and dug at the rubble until his hands bled. The dog continued to bark and wag its tail. Prendy threw himself to the stone and reached his arm into a deep crack, grimacing against the effort.

'I think I've got something,' he pulled his arm out the hole and opened his hand to reveal a spherical object. The dog whined and Prendy hurled the ball into the darkness. Jim Black's collie took after it, barking in delight. 'Stupid animal!'

They ran around the wreckage, stumbling across it, clambering over it and stopping to listen now and again for cries in the dark. Even the minister joined them in the search.

The emergency services turned up eventually and a task force was quickly scrambled. The garden was filled with flashing lights and uniformed bodies. They turned over the rubble and heaved at the heavy blocks of stone.

After an hour or two of searching, Libby noticed the shaking heads.

'Hannah, please take Libby inside.'

'No, we have to find him.'

Prendy moved across to her and cradled her in his arms. 'Libby, I think we may have to brace ourselves for the worst.'

'No!' Libby felt her heart would burst. 'He's under there somewhere, please don't give up. He's alive.'

She pushed him away. Her hands stung from the constant scraping against the sharp stones and she had no skin left on her fingers.

'We're not giving up. We'd never do that. I would never do that, but we may have to come to terms that he's gone.'

As a thin film of dawn light kissed the hills in the horizon, she remembered the shroud she'd seen around his body, the same aura she'd witnessed on two other people who had died soon after her vision. She lost herself in that moment when she saw him standing with the sun in his back, its warm rays dancing across the golden streaks in his hair. His strong silhouette looming over her and those astonishing eyes: vibrant, animated and filled with life.

She wept.

She felt his loss hit her with so much force that her legs gave way beneath her. She sat on the ground and buried her face in her hands, too wrought with misery to feel alive. He'd gone and he'd taken her soul with him. How could she bear such terrible pain?

Reverend Jacobson leaned down to comfort her, the sternness of her eyes had given way to compassion. Libby grabbed her by the lapels of her jacket. 'Don't let Him take him!'

'If it's God's will, there's nothing I can do about it, my dear.'

'Don't let Him take him. I'll do anything. Please!'

'We should pray.'

'No!' Libby pushed the minister's comforting arms away from her. 'What good did prayer do for Kie?'

She heard someone shout and everyone scrambled towards a solitary spot where a uniformed fireman was standing. She rose from the ground slowly, the misery tearing at her heart, and she moved towards the fireman. The spotlights turned towards a section of the rubble where the fireman was heaving back heavy pieces of fallen masonry. He was soon joined by others.

'I think they've found him.' Prendergast ran into the light and scrambled across the debris.

'Libby why don't we go inside? I don't think you should see this.'

'They've found him, Hannah.' She could hear her own voice. It was flat and desolate.

'Yes, that may be so, but it's best you don't see this. Come on.'

'I have to know.'

Hannah grabbed her arms and shook her. 'Look at the size of those stones, Libby. Do you believe anyone could survive being buried under them? Come on, I don't want you to need counselling after this.'

'I want to see him.'

As if in a trance, she walked towards the rescue team as they heaved the rubble away. With every step she took, she felt a tiny weight lifting from her heart. The closer she got, the lighter she felt and Libby realised she was running. She stopped at the edge of the devastated barn and caught her breath as she saw the ground move beneath the rescuers' feet. They took a step back and muttered to each other. A solitary stone rattled across a chunk of boulder and the rubble breathed outwards before it breathed in again. All eyes watched as the debris gently pulsated before it exploded up and out, showering the rescuers in sharp fragments and causing them to yell and scream in panic.

A figure rose from the wreckage. Powdery white with angry eyes, it clambered out into the light and unfolded itself to its full height. Libby staggered forwards.

As dawn broke, MacAoidh Armstrong, covered in blood and rubble, looked like a corpse rising from the grave. He stood tall and strong as he blinked against the glare of the spotlights, his dark shadow spread out behind him. He scanned his eyes over the awed faces of the rescue team and frowned. They took a simultaneous step back.

His gaze then fell on Libby and he smiled, a macabre grin of victory behind a white mask, streaked with blood. He raised his arm and thrust the object he was clutching before him: a shattered skull.

'I found him, Libby,' he rasped and coughed a small stone from his mouth. 'I found his bones. It's over.'

Chapter 48

THE REVELATION

'That was Hannah on the phone,' she wanted to know how the patient was doing.'

'What did you tell her?' Kie stretched his arms and blinked against the sunlight streaming into his bedroom. The rain whispered against the window and a wide rainbow yawned across the horizon. He'd been sleeping for most of the morning.

'I told her you were bad tempered, aching and in pain, despite a week in hospital. You sleep all the time but you're making a good recovery. We were just saying, we can't believe your spleen was lacerated and your lung punctured, yet you refused to get on the stretcher and walked into that hospital by yourself before you collapsed. Bloody hell, you're hardy.'

'It was only a wee cut.'

'You almost died.'

He winced as he sat up in bed. The angry bruises glaring across the muscles were fading to brown.

'I feel better today.'

'That's because you're off the heavy drugs. I think this is the first time in a week you've been awake for more than ten minutes.'

'Sorry, have you missed me?'

'A bit.'

He smiled, that mischievous Kie smile that always carried with it a double meaning.

'It's funny, you know, she sat the tea tray down by the bedside table, 'It's been two weeks since the Final Episode …'

'Don't!'

'It's OK, Kie, I'm sticking to euphemisms just as you've commanded.'

'Good.'

'You were so lucky to have fallen into that grave as the barn came down. It sheltered you from that huge piece of falling masonry.'

'Luck had nothing to do with it.'

'It's strange to think Peter Hyslop probably saved your life.'

'His grave saved my life, Libby, and I dug it.'

'You're not listening to me.' She knew there was a lot more to his story, but she didn't push it. He'd no doubt tell her when he was ready, if ever. She smiled and poured him some tea. 'Hannah and I were just talking about religion and how all this trouble targeted the clergy. It was a lot more unforgiving with them. In turn, it was a member of the faithful who cleared this house. We came to the conclusion that people who have more faith in God must give off a stronger energy than those who don't, thereby attracting a stronger force of negative energy. Opposite poles attracting, and all that.'

'Let's talk about something else.'

Libby laughed at his obstinacy. Since what came to be called 'The Final Episode', Kie had settled into the life he'd always wanted before the paranormal put paid to his good intentions. Unfortunately for him, he was at present too infirm to work at it. He'd made a bad patient and a few times Libby had threatened to tie him to the bed, which only resulted in that wicked smile, then he would fall asleep.

She couldn't get him to talk about the events of the past few months and didn't know whether he believed speaking of it would somehow conjure it back again, or whether he was just enjoying the peace and didn't want to spoil it.

'What do you want to talk about?'

'Hens.'

'As in chickens?'

'Aye, as in chicken and eggs as a food source.'

'Sorry, poultry farming is not one of my fortes. I got chased by a cockerel once. It came at me with its big, sharp spurs when I was a little girl. I told my uncle and he wrung its neck.'

'Good idea.'

'When he told me we'd eaten it for tea, I cried for a week. I never associated real-life animals with food until then.'

'It's called taking responsibility.'

'That may be so, but I couldn't kill an animal and eat it if I've fed it, nurtured it and given it a name.'

'So pigs are out too?'

'Oh God! How do you ring Babe's neck?'

'Come here and I'll show you.'

She saw that glint in his eye and smiled. 'You're all broken into teensy-weensy wee bits. I don't want to hurt you.'

'I've a high pain threshold, come here.'

'You'll fall asleep before I get my clothes off.'

'No I won't,' he held his hand out to her. 'Get over here.'

She scattered her clothes across the room and slipped under the sheets.

'Where can I touch you that won't hurt?' She wished she'd kept her mouth shut when she saw his eyebrows rise. She straddled his lap and gently placed her hands on his shoulders. His eyes drew her towards him and they kissed.

The sound of wheels on gravel caused them to simultaneously groan in disappointment. Libby got out of bed and moved to the window. Her eyes widened and she let out a high-pitched squeal. 'Oh my god, it's your Mercedes!'

'My what?'

She felt panic-stricken. 'The woman, the witch, oh, oh, god, it's your bloody mother!' She ran around the room in a frenzy. 'Where did I put my knickers?'

'Libby calm down. Mother won't bite you.'

She could've slapped the laughter from his face. She heard his mother shrieking from the hallway. 'Her bark's bad enough.' Libby dived into the bedclothes, frantically seeking out her underwear. She popped her head out the bottom of the duvet. 'Help! She's coming up the stairs and there's no door to this room.' She leaped from the bed and threw open the wardrobe door.

'Libby, please tell me you're not hiding in the wardrobe.'

'Shhhh!' She slammed the door shut and cowered into a corner behind the clothes of the huge antique wardrobe.

She heard his mother scream. 'Good lord! What happened to you?'

'I had an accident. I'm fine.'

'You're not fine, you're in bed in the middle of the day. You're wounded, battered and bruised. You look terrible. What on Earth have you been doing to yourself? You've got so thin. I barely recognise my own son. My God, Kie, I turn my back on you for a few weeks and look at the state of you. You're incapable of looking after yourself. What happened to Uncle Robert's chandelier? Whose underwear is that?'

Libby closed her eyes and shuddered.

'Where is she?'

'Give me a break, mother.'

'I'd just like to know where she is and who she is.'

Libby heard the bathroom door open and was glad she hadn't been caught sitting on the loo.

'That's none of your business.'

'When were you going to tell me you had a new girlfriend?'

'Never.'

'Is she nice?'

'Aye.'

'Pretty?'

'Aye.'

'From a good family?'

'An excellent pedigree.'

'Well done, darling. It's about time you found yourself a decent woman. That Catherine was a babbling air-head.'

'I told you so.'

'So where is this lovely girl?'

'In the wardrobe.'

His mother laughed as if he'd just told a hilarious joke while Libby shook with anger, rattling the brass drop handles.

A long silence ensued and Libby listened in the darkness of her ancient mahogany prison, feeling a growing sense of unease. The wardrobe door burst open and Barbara Armstrong's shocked face spilled in with the light. Her gaping mouth was a breath away from hers.

'Hello Mrs Armstrong.'

'Good Lord! It's her.'

She sat naked, hugging her knees, in a corner of a piece of furniture solely intended to hang clothes while a furious Mrs Armstrong screeched into the coved ceiling. Libby pulled one of Kie's dinner jackets from the hanger and put it on, before stepping out onto the carpet as elegantly as she could muster.

Kie sat in his bed with his hands behind his head trying his best not to laugh, while Barbara Armstrong stormed from the room, muttering long sentences in Gaelic.

'You rotten bastard!'

'Aw, come on Libby. That was a ridiculous move. We're adult

lovers in a meaningful relationship that has nothing to do with her. Stand up to her. She'll come around eventually.'

'How would you like it if my father caught you naked in *my* wardrobe?' She felt like crying.

'He wouldn't. There's no way I'd put myself in the position of being caught bare-arsed at the back of your wardrobe.'

He threw off the duvet and got out of bed. She noticed he was a little unsteady on his feet and felt like pushing him over.

'Let's take a shower.'

'After that betrayal. You can take your own shower, Judas. Here's thirty pieces of silver. I'm going home and I hope you slip on the soap and injure yourself.'

'Come on, Libby. Let's get into the shower and make the water hot.'

He didn't appear to understand the subtleties of her outrage. He threw a towel over his shoulder and offered his hand to her.

She slapped it away.

'Maybe you should invite Mother!'

'That's disgusting. His smiling eyes betrayed his feigned reaction. 'Come on.' He gave her an encouraging blink and waggled his fingers. 'We can lather each other up.'

She had to laugh in the end and took his hand. 'All right then but promise me you'll put the door back on this bedroom, I don't feel safe with your mother at large.'

'I'll do it right after our shower.'

— — —

They found Kie's mother sitting at the butcher's block reading a glossy magazine.

'I see you've made the news.' She turned a page over and nibbled on a piece of toast with the tiniest sliver of marmalade. 'MacAoidh returns to Old Haunt', that's very good, but the picture of you looks as though it's been taken with one of those long lenses. Why didn't they take a few of you around this beautiful house?'

Libby felt her anger rising. She'd meant to get onto the Mandygate incident, but Kie's recovery came first, so she'd taken holiday to care for him.

'Well, Miss Butler. I see you're still here. With all that splashing, I thought Kie had drowned you in the bath.'

'We were taking a shower.'

'He's hardly in any shape for physical exertion.'

'On the contrary, he's on excellent form.'

She wanted to make Kie's mother squirm by offering intimate details about the boy she'd given birth to, but the woman was shock-proof when it came to her son. She lit up a cigarette.

'Kindly put that out.' Barbara rudely flicked through the pages of her magazine, obviously more interested in its content than conversing with Libby.

'I have permission from the owner of this property to smoke anywhere I want around the house, provided I don't light up in the bedroom.' She blew out a huge smoke ring.

'You'll give him asthma and probably even lung cancer.'

'I doubt it.'

'You'll render him sterile.'

'Why are you so obsessed with your son's sexual prowess? Isn't that a bit unnatural for a mother?'

'I enjoy embarrassing him. It's not often I get to do that and my simply speaking about sex never fails to make him squirm.'

Kie remained silent as he busied himself with the toaster.

'You could've brushed your hair, dear. You look like a little turnip that's just been pulled from the earth.' Mrs Armstrong turned over another page and hadn't once looked at Libby.

'Thank you. At least I'm fresh. It's better than looking like one that's been boiled in a bag for three weeks and then freeze dried.'

'Kie, are you going to take that from her?' Another page warranted Barbara's casual attention.

'It wasn't me she was insulting, Mother. If you dish out rudeness, you have to be prepared to receive it in return. Do you want a coffee, Libby?'

'Yes please.'

'So,' Barbara slammed the magazine on the butcher's block and peered at Libby over the top of her glasses, 'Liberty Butler.' She smiled, a cold, ingratiating leer that didn't conceal her disapproval. 'Are you here for the whole day?'

'Liberty's here for as long as she likes.'

Libby felt a bit stronger with Kie's support.

'Is she living here with you?'

'She is at the moment.'

'Moved in?'

'Not yet.'

'Intentions?'

He turned around slowly to face her, the milk jug in his hand. 'At present, I don't intend to let her out of my sight. I like her around and she likes being here, I hope.'

'So we'll just have to wait it out.'

'Good, then maybe we can all just try and get on with each other.' Libby knew Kie well enough to realise his casualness hid his deep frustration.

'I don't think so, Kie. I'm not staying here while she's mooching around the house and listening to everything we say; judging me all the time. I want you to myself for the next few days. She'll have to go. You don't mind do you, Libby? I know you don't have children, despite the fact you're probably well over safe childbearing age, but you must understand from a mother's point of view how important it is to have quality time with her only s…'

'Libby's not leaving.' Kie took up the challenge and slammed Libby's coffee down on the marble work surface, spilling it over his hand.

'Why not?'

'Because I want her to stay. Here. With me.'

Libby felt invisible as mother and son faced-off against one another.

'But I'd like some time with you.'

'Then you'll have to share me with her.'

Mother looked astounded, while Kie looked hurt. Libby didn't want to come between them.

'It's OK, Kie, I'll go. I don't want to stay with her around anyway.'

'Thank goodness.' Barbara breathed again.

Libby could bear the stress no longer. She turned on her heels and obeyed her marching orders. To her surprise, Kie hobbled after her.

'Where are you going?'

'Leaving. Out that door, if there was one. I'll see you after she's gone.'

'Why?' He looked genuinely perplexed.

'I don't want to come between you and your family, Kie. A woman has already caused a great rift in your life, pardon the pun, and I don't want to be like her.'

'You're nothing like her.'

'No,' she sighed. 'I'm not.'

'I love my mother.'

'Yes, I know and that's why I'm going. I don't know how you can stomach her interference nor why you allow her to run rings around your life, but that's between you and her.'

'I'll tell you why, Libby.' He grabbed her arm and didn't realise his strong fingers were causing bruises. 'That woman loves me. She loves me with the ferocity of a lioness and she's only ever wanted the best for me. I recognise that fact and it's her pure, unconditional love that's always given me my strength. It's moulded and shaped my life. She's the only person in the world who loves me and I'm hanging on to that. Love, as you know, is very important to me.'

'She's not the only person in the world who loves you, Kie. Open those strange blue eyes of yours and see the world for what it is.'

She hung her head as he stood breathing heavily in front of her.

'You're not going anywhere. Get back in there and sort it out.' His temper rose from nowhere as he hauled her back into the kitchen to face his mother. 'You're staying and you're going to carve a good relationship out between you. The two women who I care about the most in my life are at each other's throats. Deal with it.'

Libby felt a warm feeling of belonging as Kie confessed his feelings towards her to a woman who meant the world to him.

'Why should I?' Barbara appeared the less willing of the two to call a truce. 'She's awful.'

'*Tha gaol agam oirre, Màthair*, and I never want to hear you speaking to her like that ever again. Got it?'

Those were the words Libby had been waiting for. Although they weren't quite the words she'd learned and there were now five of them, she was a linguist and understood perfectly what he wasn't saying to her. The effect of those words on his mother was equally staggering.

'Well done, MacAoidh. You've finally stood up for love.' She turned to Libby. 'Congratulations, Miss Butler, you've won a hard-fought battle and I'd take my hat off to you if it wasn't in a box in the car.' She slipped from her high stool to stand by her son who, by now, was eyeing her suspiciously. 'Had you stood up to your father in the same way five years ago, you would still be living in Assynt.' She passed her smooth palm across his cheek.

'I don't want to talk about him.'

'No, I know you don't, but sometimes life isn't just about you.'

'Arrogance I can stand, but I won't abide racism.'

'Is that why you fell out with him?' Barbara couldn't hide her shock. 'You thought he didn't like the fact Helen was black?' She genuinely looked astounded. 'Good Lord. Is that what all this is about?' She teetered to the centre of the kitchen and sat down again, evidently unsure her legs would hold her. 'Kie, your father didn't give a damn whether your wife was black, green, purple, polka-dot or tartan, he was terrified of losing you. Helen hated Scotland and he thought you'd leave Sutherland to live in Kenya with her. That one thought, that sole reason, made him fearful. Your father has never been the same man since you left. He's lost his wonderful sense of humour, his drive and his energy. It's as if Helen took them to the grave with her. You're not the only one who lost someone, Kie. You may have lost a wife, but I lost a husband; Donald Armstrong lost a son and he's never stopped grieving.'

'I …'

'Those wounds on your body will heal, Kie. Your father's wounds have cut so much deeper and never will.'

'I'll talk to him.'

'He'd like that.'

'In the meantime, I'm going to take that scruffy dog for a walk and the two of you will find a way of getting on without killing each other.'

Chapter 49

THE CALL

'A toast!' Stephen Mitchell banged his fork against his glass for attention. 'Here's to the lovely MacAoidh Armstrong for bringing us all together today as one big happy family.'

'And to absent friends,' Kie's mother returned the sentiment with a toothy grin that reminded Libby of a screaming skull. 'May they stay away forever.'

'I'll drink to that!' Hannah clashed her glass against Libby's and yelled in annoyance as Jim Black's collie shook the muddy water from its drenched body all over the pair of them.

They sat in the front garden, crowded with a large canvas marquis and a number of sizable barbecues that Prendy darted between like an MC at the decks on a Friday night.

The entire community turned out for Kie's celebration barbecue. The event had been Prendy's idea and Libby still pondered on the plausibility of the shy and retiring Highlander allowing such a huge public festivity to plunge him into the spotlight.

'I want to speak to you, Libby.'

She didn't like that look in his eye. 'What about?'

'Let's go into the house.'

Libby shrugged and Hannah winked at her in encouragement.

She followed him into the kitchen and claimed his mother's stool at the butcher's block. Kie was in a good mood, so she knew whatever he wanted to tell her was going to be positive.

'I've just had an offer for The Ring at four times the price I bought it for. It's an English company that's intending to build a holiday centre here. Quite frankly, I don't care what happens to this place. Too many bad memories. I'm going to take it.'

She felt her heart was losing blood in that involuntary way hearts do when they're emptied and the internal heat-source radiated through her body from the outside in, culminating in a deluge of moisture against her cheeks and neck.

'You're selling up?'

'Aye, Libby, *tha mi 'dol dhachaigh.*'

'You're going home?' She didn't need to know the language nor have a sixth sense to understand that sentence, she could see it in the contented resignation in his animated, elated expression. She didn't know how to respond. 'I'm delighted for you. It's the one good move you've made since you got here.' She hated herself for her own ultimate betrayal. He enfolded her in his big arms but she knew he'd already crossed the miles without her.

'Libby, I want to live in a place where seeing the Northern Lights from my window isn't constrained to a bucket list. I want to live in a place where going for a walk out the door often requires a sturdy rope, crampons and an ice hammer. More importantly, I want to live in a place where I belong. I'm going home because I feel its call: in my heart, Libby, in my soul.'

'It must be wonderful to have a place like that. I wish you all the luck in the world.'

'Don't talk about it as if this is the end for us.'

'Isn't it?' She couldn't hide her terrible distress.

He hugged her tightly, rocking her from side to side. 'We'll be six and a half hours away from each other. That's not a long distance between two hearts. We could see each other every weekend and for longer periods over the holidays. We'll take it from there and see where it goes.'

'Would you like that?'

'Of course I would.' He pulled away from her and clutched her shoulders at arms' length, his cool eyes searching out her emotions. 'Would you?'

She knew his intentions were honourable but she also knew long distance affairs rarely worked over time. At least he was still enthusiastic about continuing a relationship with her and she would take what she could get for now.

'Yes, I would.' She flung her arms around him again and called on every ounce of her courage to remain calm. She felt her body shaking with the effort. 'I'm not staying with your mother, though.'

'I've got my own house, Libby. You'd love it there. It's a bit more remote than what you're used to and there's always a lot of snow about.'

'Will you take me to all those places you've talked about?'

'And very many more.'

'Are you going to make an announcement now?'

'Aye. Coming?'

'No, I don't want to be there when you do, if that's OK with you. I couldn't bear the smug expression on your mother's face when she hears it. You go and tell them and I'll come out in a wee while.'

Libby waited for him to leave the house before she burst into tears. She ran to his bedroom, buried herself under the duvet and wailed until she could no longer breathe. It was just her bad fortune to once again meet the man of her dreams only to lose him again. Only this time, she really thought Kie was the one: her soul mate and eternal companion. She couldn't believe he was leaving, but she also would never stop him. Kie belonged to a place that was out of her reach and, regardless of his intentions to see her regularly, she knew she would eventually become another Catherine and time together would become more and more scarce as he immersed himself into the life he was born for. She hugged the pillow that smelled of him and tried to pull herself together but her heart had broken into tiny little pieces and the damage was irreparable.

'Can I come in?'

She rushed into Prendy's arms and howled.

'Now, now, my dear, it's not so bad. It's not as if he's leaving you to go to another world.' He patted her back with his customary awkwardness.

'He may as well be. Sutherland, Prendy. It's so far away.'

'Love will find a way, Libby. You have to believe that.'

She pulled away from him and sat at the end of the bed. She felt as if her entire face had swollen.

He looked at her with those doleful, compassionate eyes which made her want to cry again.

'How did everyone take the news?'

He laughed. 'The local ladies are having apoplexy. I think they realise their handyman's not going to be around to fix things, so they're drawing up a list before he goes.'

'How soon?'

'He intends to vacate the place within the week.'

'A week?' she shrieked and he rushed to her side.

'Come on, Libby, dear. Pull yourself together and see this positively. MacAoidh's suffered nothing but misery since he's been here. He's looking forward to living the life he's always wanted. He'll make peace with his father and he'll spend the remainder of his days in happiness and contentment. There's no one I can think of, apart from you, who deserves that more. He's a fortunate man to have something that most of us can only dream of.'

'Why am I so unlucky in love?'

'I wouldn't say you were unlucky. I think you've been very

fortunate in finding him. It's up to you now to work at it and make sure the relationship continues to flourish.'

She nodded, encouraged by his therapeutic words.

'Maybe I should ask Reverend Jacobson for some spiritual healing. She got rid of his poltergeist, maybe she'll get rid of my bad luck in love.'

Prendergast sighed. 'It wasn't the minister, Libby. In the end it was love that rid MacAoidh of his demon. He told me something the other day.'

She turned her head to face him.

'He told me about a dream he had when he was lying in the byre with a punctured lung and a hole in his spleen while the walls were coming down. He told me he dreamed Helen came and took the spirit away with her.'

'Helen? His dead wife?'

'Yes, he said she tried to take him too but he refused to go with her.'

'Why?'

'Because he realised he wanted to live. He told me you called him back.'

'Me? He said that?'

'Yes. He loves you and love is a most powerful force. That lad was very close to death but he managed to dig himself out of a few tons of fallen masonry and stand up. Once he's made up his mind, he's perverse enough to carry his convictions through'

'I think the word's thrawn.'

'Indeed, but nevertheless, you were the first person he spoke to when he rose out of that grave; the first and only person on his mind. If he says he wants to continue a relationship with you, then there's nothing that'll stop him. Not even you.'

'Thanks, Prendy. You've made me feel a lot better.' She

slipped her arm into his and sniffed. 'What's his mother saying about it?'

'She's elated, of course, and she's already voicing plans for his move. Now, let's get back to the celebrations. I've left my wife downstairs with all those women and Mystic Mitchell.'

'Oh yes, I haven't had a chance to speak to Justine yet. How's she enjoying Scotland?'

Prendy laughed again. 'She hasn't stopped complaining. I think she'd made up her mind that you and I were having some kind of illicit affair when I kept disappearing up here. Now she's met Kie, however, she realises she's been silly. I'm hardly made of his material.'

'You'll always be my hero.' She kissed his cheek and he blushed.

'Peter Hyslop's being buried tomorrow afternoon at two. Are you coming to his funeral?'

'I don't think I can. I've got quite a lot of case work to get through tomorrow and a court appearance in the afternoon that starts at two on the dot. If it's cancelled for some reason, then I'll come.'

'Let's hope he can now rest in peace. It's strange to think the boy was trapped in this steading because the man who killed him wanted to keep his secret, even after he'd died himself.'

'Yes, the poor kid continued to be a victim long after his horrible death. I find it even harder to believe finding his bones was so significant to his eternal peace.'

'I've just been speaking to Stephen about this and he said Peter could have passed over as soon as he died, only the evil entity wanted to keep him grounded to this place. He said it was the entity that manipulated the thoughts and deeds of the others to bind them to it. The numbers gave it strength.'

'Perhaps, like the living, it didn't want to be alone. No one wants to be alone, Prendy, not even an evil spirit.'

They fell into silence with that thought.

'Do you think that spirit was the same one that haunted Rerrick three centuries ago?' She flopped back down on the mattress, staring at the ceiling.

'I don't know and we'll probably never be certain. Perhaps this place is a gateway to hell and maybe the spirit lies dormant until another bad thing happens on its patch to release it.'

'Well, it's not our problem anymore.'

'Indeed not. It's odd to say, but I'm going to miss this place.' He patted her hand and stood up. 'I've learned so much in the past few months; I've have had my beliefs and my nerves rattled about and shaken out; yet, there's a solid, homely atmosphere about The Ring when it's at peace and I'm going to take that memory away with me.'

'It's called MacAoidh Armstrong,' she sighed.

'It certainly is.'

She laughed to herself. 'One thing's for certain, I'm never going to be frightened of anything ever again.'

'Me neither.'

'Spider!'

'Pardon?'

'Spider, spider, spider!' Libby watched in horror as an enormous spider, dangling from a fine filament above her head, landed on the front of her dress and scrambled into her cleavage. She leaped up screaming, her arms flailing as she bounced up and down on the mattress. She flew from the bed and landed on the carpet, running around and beating at her chest like a chimpanzee in a food frenzy.

Prendy tried to calm her down but she tore off her dress and froze.

'Oh god, it's in my bra. Get it out! Get it out! GET IT OUUUUUUUUT!' she screamed into his face, running on the spot as if she was warming up for a marathon.

While he was deliberating whether or not he should go in as ordered, the spider dropped to the carpet. Libby screamed again and with a convulsion of disgust, threw herself onto Prendy's back. Infected with her hysteria, he picked up her discarded dress and beat at the spider until it was nothing more than a tiny, flat hairy mass.

They both breathed a heavy sigh of relief.

'Isn't it bad luck to kill a spider?' She slid off his back, watching for a twitch in its crumpled legs.

'I don't believe in bad luck.'

'Oh no?'

Libby and Prendy both stared in horror at the figure of Justine at the door. Libby stood behind him in her bra and knickers, her arms around his waist, while he held the tattered remains of her dress in his hands.

'I can explain everything, dear.'

– – –

'Mr and Mrs Pullman. I have to admit, I'm surprised to find you back.'

'Oh aye, how's that then?'

'I really hoped you'd be able to reconcile your differences and learn to live together in peace.'

'Well, we cannae.'

'Then, I'm afraid I'm going to have to ask which one of you wants me to act for them and which one wants to seek out another lawyer. The rules are that I can't act for both of you as I have to take a side. One of you is required to seek independent legal advice from another solicitor.'

'But that's gonnae cost a lot mear money. We havnae got cash to chuck awa'.'

'I'm sorry, but that's the rules.' Libby looked around her untidy office and wondered whether she would still be here when she was old and grey, sorting out Mr and Mrs Pullman's anxieties with one another.

She couldn't bear to say goodbye again to Kie this morning, so she'd got up early and left him sleeping. She'd thought about writing him a note telling him how she really felt about his leaving, but she didn't have the heart to divide his loyalties.

He'd been so excited about going home that he had the entire steading emptied within two days of his decision and its contents taken by lorry to his home in Sutherland. It was strange to say goodbye to the place and she'd decided to never set foot in Auchencairn ever again. Without him there, the place would always hurt. She dreaded the thought of going back to her comfortable house in Castle Douglas where he'd been staying for the last two nights. His memory was all over it: the coffee cup he'd last drank out of; the dents in the lawn mower; her sheets he'd slept in. Kie haunted her. She knew she'd be counting the hours until the end of the week when she'd get in her car and take the drive to Sutherland to see for herself what drew him to such a bleak and savage wilderness. All she had to do was get through the week alone and she didn't relish the prospect.

'Are ye listenin'?'

'Sorry, run that past me again?'

'Can we jist no' separate?'

'Why do you want to? This is the third time you've sat here telling me you want a divorce but neither of you have told me why. I think I have a right to know.'

Her forthright attitude had the desired effect as the pair looked to each other for the answer.

'I'll tell you something for free,' Libby started, the emotion welling up inside her chest. 'Very occasionally in someone's life, another person comes along and, without you knowing it, makes such an enormous impression that it changes the way you look at the world forever. Can you remember why you got married to each other in the first place? I mean, what attracted you to Mrs Pullman?' She rounded on him first.

'She had a lovely smile an' wis aye laughin'. That wummin wid laugh at onyhin. She made me smile.'

'Mrs Pullman, can you think of what it was that drew you to Mr Pullman?'

'He wis fit.' Mrs P smiled. 'An' he cud haud his drink.'

'Mr Pullman was good looking and didn't get wasted, despite the amount of drink he consumed, and Mrs Pullman, you were full of laughter and fun. So what happened?'

'We couldnae hae weans.'

'One or both of you was infertile?'

'Aye.' they both looked acutely embarrassed.

'So, instead of coming together and working things through like a couple, you blamed each other and things steadily began to fall apart. Neither of you are thirty yet, have you thought of adoption or fertility treatment?'

'Nah, we dinnae like te talk aboot things like that.'

Libby rose her eyes to the ceiling. 'You are husband and wife, you love each other, why wouldn't you at least want to talk it through? Instead of fighting around the subject, why don't you channel your energies into fighting for it? You're both young enough and I suspect neither of you really want to separate, not just because such would be a costly exercise but possibly, even though neither of you would dare to admit it, you're actually still very fond of each other.' She felt the tears brimming. He would be on his way to Sutherland by now.

'I'll tell you another thing for free, and I'm not going to charge either of you anything for coming here today.' She dabbed at her eyes. 'You should hold on to love. If you're fortunate enough to experience it, you should grab it with both hands, be greedy, and never let it go. Love should never be ruled by condition, tradition nor social acceptability: you can't control it any more than you can ask your own heart to stop beating. It's the power that causes that involuntary muscle to pound inside your chest. Yes, it's painful at times but the joy, the sheer elation, it brings is worth every bit of the agony until it's gone. It's then you'll wish you never loved in the first place. You may not realise it, Mr and Mrs Pullman, but a person invests a huge level of emotion in love: that's a lot of energy that can never be destroyed.'

The traitorous tears fell before she could stop them. 'You'll separate and you'll both go to your empty homes with only your memories of each other to keep you company at nights.' She pulled a paper hankie out of the box on her desk and blew her nose into it. 'Every time you see that beautiful bright moon in a warm evening sky, you'll recall something you did together under that same light and, while you remember the moon rising into the night, your heart will feel like it's made of lead and sink into your stomach. You'll feel sick and there's an emptiness inside you can never fill. The memory of his kiss will become a ravenous craving and you'll stop eating because you feel you're not worthy of the sustenance. You'll drink yourself into a stupor every night, hoping to rid yourself of the agony caused by the mere echo of his smile.' She pressed her face into her hands, her back heaving as she lapsed into a fit of uncontrollable sorrow.

Mrs Pullman rushed across the table to comfort her and Libby threw her arms around her ample waist and bawled into the woman's chest, soaking her T-shirt with relentless tears.

She didn't answer the phone as it rang. She knew Audrey

would be worried about her apparent break-down. Mr Pullman was now standing beside her, patting her back with more discomfiture than Prendergast.

She heard a loud knock on the door but was too miserable to care.

'Piss off, we're busy,' Mrs P sprang immediately to her aid.

The door opened.

'So you're the yin that broke this peer lassie's heyrt?' Mrs P wrestled Libby's arms away from her and marched across the room. 'Ye shid be ashamed o' yersel'. When Libby looked up through her swollen eyes, Kie stood in the doorway. Mrs P balled her large fist and punched him in the jaw. 'Bastart!'

'What …?'

She hit him again with her other fist. 'Sort it or I'll kick the livin' shite oot o' ye!' She signalled with a nod to Mr P who trotted after her. 'We'll be waitin' ootside.' She slammed the door behind her.

He cradled his aching jaw in his hand. 'Why do women always want to hit me?'

'Sorry, Kie. She got me at a bad time. I'm a bit emotional today.'

'Me too.' He sat on the chair opposite her, his foot drumming against his knee.

'Aren't you supposed to have left by now?'

'I couldn't go. I woke up today and you'd gone. The sheets smelled of you; I could smell you all over me; but you weren't there. Just the ghost of you. That wasn't a good feeling.'

'I didn't want to go through another goodbye.' She managed to hold her shattered emotions together. 'I just couldn't cope with it.'

'You understand why I have to go, Libby?'

She nodded. 'It's the right decision for you. We all have to follow our dreams if we can.'

He stood up and walked to the window. She wanted to remember that view of him, his powerful frame gazing into the wheelie bins in the back yard of the offices. 'The car's empty. Everything that belongs to me has gone up to Sutherland apart from the clothes I'm wearing, my wallet, my toothbrush, the dog and you.' He turned around to face her and crossed his arms. 'I want you to come home with me.'

'To Sutherland?'

'Aye, to the savage north-west. You left a dent in the pillow beside me and a larger one in my heart. I've had this gnawing, empty feeling in the pit of my belly that's making me feel sick. You're the only food that'll fill it. I don't want to feel like that for the remainder of my days. I want you to come with me. Be with me. Fill that hole in my heart and in my life.'

'Oh god, you were listening! That's my line.'

'But it's true. Remember that night at the loch?'

'You said love's a positive emotion and we should hang onto it.'

'I meant it. I love you.'

'Say that in Gaelic.'

She rose from her seat and they moved towards each other cautiously.

'*Tha gaol agam ort*, Libby Butler. I'm desperately, hopelessly, insanely and deeply in love with you and I don't have the ability to leave you even if I was foolish enough to try.'

She threw her arms around him and his hug pulled her off her feet.

'Come with me. Now.'

'I've got work. I can't just drop everything.'

'Leave it. It's us, together, that's important. All you have to do is get in the car. We'll drive to your place and pack your things.

We could be on the road within the hour.'

'I can't just leave, Kie. I've got a house, a job…'

'The only thing you should be emotionally attached to is me.'

'The partners will sue me for breaching my contract of employment.'

'We'll run a few rings around them then settle out of court.'

'You're learning fast, I'm impressed.'

'You're my lawyer, I hang onto every word you say.' His smile was filled with earnest and deep affection. 'Come on, Libby, take a chance: a reckless, impulsive chance for once in your life. Come with me and live with me, marry me, whatever you want to do, I'd be happy to do it. I'll never hurt you with harsh words nor test you with unreasonable behaviour. I promise to cherish you, spoil you, love you. You can have an en suite bathroom and I'll even buy you a pony. Just give me the opportunity to wake up every morning to your smile; to sit beside the fireside and grow old with you in my arms.'

Did he just propose to her? She pulled away from him, barely able to believe his words were exclusively meant for her. She didn't deserve the devotion, especially from such a good man. 'Do you mean to tell me there's no en suite?'

'Not at the moment, but there's an outside dunny and a clear, crystal waterfall behind the house.'

'You're joking. Aren't you?'

'Do you really care?'

Her eyes widened a little. 'No. Actually, I don't.'

His kiss sealed her decision.

'Will you come with me then?'

'MacAoidh Armstrong, we've been to hell and back together and a few places in between. I suppose Sutherland will be a breeze by comparison: a draughty, unsheltered, bleak and inhospitable breeze. I'll come with you simply because I can't bear the thought of living a single moment without you.' She kissed him with all the emotion stored in her heart. She only let go of him when she felt he was suffocating. 'Besides, someone needs to watch out for you. You're wonderful at caring for others and your home, but you're terrible at looking after yourself.'

She took his hand, her heart soaring higher with every step she made towards the car. She sat in the passenger seat, the exhilaration threatening to explode in her chest. She patted the head of Jim Black's dog that sat in the back seats whining with excitement at seeing her. She waved to Mr and Mrs P who stood on the pavement holding hands.

As the Discovery pulled off, she decided there and then she'd never look back. Forwards was the only direction from now on. She remembered something important.

'Can we do something before we go? After I've packed, I mean?'

'Only if it involves a hot shower.' He raised his eyebrows and grinned.

'Tempting, but we'll wait until we get to yon waterfall of melted snow. A quick dip in that will put paid to any passion you've built up over the journey. No, it involves returning to Rerrick for a few minutes.'

'What've you got in mind?'

'You know that twig on my window sill? The one you've been watering?'

'Aye, the wee oak shoot.'

'I picked it off the Ghost Tree that day you were speaking to Jim Black. It's part of the original tree, Kie. I put it in my pocket and took it home. It's the only bit I found that was still alive but it could mean the Ghost Tree isn't dead. We should plant it, just in case.'

'The sheep and deer will eat it.'

'Not if it's properly fenced.'

'All right, but I'm not stopping to plant it. We'll give it to Mary Hyslop. She'll make sure it's looked after and, when it's strong enough, she'll return it to the soil.'

'And it'll grow strong and protect the land for another three hundred years.'

'At least,' he laughed.

She let out a heavy, contented sigh, filled with excitement of her new and unexpected life to come. 'Do you have broadband at the butt 'n' ben?'

'Aye, but it's probably quicker to walk.'

'Is it constant?'

'It is when the lightning doesn't burn the router out or the wind take down the line.'

'How often does that happen, then?'

'Oh, about twice a week.'

She watched the road for a while unable to hide her amusement.

'Will you really buy me a pony?'

'Aye but you'll have to look after it yourself and don't give it a name.'

'Why not?'

'We won't be able to wring its neck and eat it when winter comes if you give it a name.'

'Are you trying to put me off?'

'Of course not, I'm just being honest.'

She couldn't read his smile.

THE END

ABOUT THE AUTHOR

Freelance journalist and press officer for a number of arts organisations in south west Scotland, London-born Sara Bain is a former newspaper journalist and editor of professional text books. She writes fantasy and paranormal fiction in a unique and individual style with an emphasis on complex plots and strong characterisation.

SARA BAIN

THE
SLEEPING
WARRIOR

Libby Butler's life is a mess. Her career as a solicitor in a
prestigious London law firm is going nowhere fast, just like
the ill-advised affair with her boss. Then a terrifying, life-
threatening encounter with the notorious Vampire Killer, a
knife-wielding serial murderer, leaves Libby with her courage
and confidence shattered. Desperate to pick up the pieces of
her life, duty calls Libby to the cells of a Metropolitan police
station in the middle of the night. There she meets mysterious
and enigmatic stranger Gabriel Radley, a man on intimate
terms with danger and who has a habit of disappearing from
police custody. Gabriel is searching for a Stone he has lost,
its value beyond human imagination, that will help bring a
monster to justice.

  When Libby agrees to help him find the Stone she senses
a chance at redemption, but unwittingly plunges headfirst
into a series of events that threaten to tear her world apart.
A cult called The Awakened, a gangland thug and his vicious
henchman, a deadly female assassin, a dedicated detective chief
inspector and even the Vampire Killer – all become embroiled

in the chase for the Stone and influenced by the elemental force that is Gabriel.

As the death toll rises, Libby is forced to face her true self, learn the ultimate value of life and discover the potent significance of the Sleeping Warrior within.

'Sara Bain's debut is an action-packed exploration of good versus evil and its blend of realism and fantasy absolutely works. What a debut! One of my favourite reads of the year'
Lucy Literati

'This is an intriguing blend of crime and urban fantasy with a sassy heroine you'd want on your side in a fight. Atmospheric and captivating. Can't wait to see what Sara Bain comes up with next'
Michael Malone

Available from urbanepublications.com, Amazon and all good bookshops

Urbane Publications is dedicated to
developing new author voices, and publishing
fiction and non-fiction that challenges, thrills and
fascinates.
From page-turning novels to innovative
reference books, our goal is to publish what
YOU want to read.

Find out more at
urbanepublications.com